The yellowbacks... classics of popular fiction

The yellowjackets or yellowbacks were a great series of bestselling adventure and crime thrillers that had its origins in the mid to late 19th century following on from the 'penny dreadfuls'. They virtually began the mass market revolution of the early 20th century with a clear standard format and imprint/series livery (what would today be called branding). Hodder & Stoughton published the yellowjackets in two main series with series run dates of: 1923-1939 and later 1949-1957.

As the tagline ('where thrillers really began') on the back cover implies, the imprint and series focused on thrillers that were the bestsellers of their time. This current reissue or retro revival if you will, brings back many of these masterpieces, now classics in their own way and extends it further by including key titles from that period that were either great crime or thriller or even general commercial fiction (including sub-genres of noir, horror, gothic, romance, westerns, etc.) influences of their time. There are some perennial favourites and many rarities either lost or not easily available being revived in the current series. Writers and characters ranged from adventure heroes like Bulldog Drummond, Allan Quatermain, Richard Hannay or the Saint through thriller grandmasters Edgar Wallace and E. Phillips Oppenheim, crime and mystery maestros like Patricia Wentworth, G.K. Chesterton, Agatha Christie and the Detection club, to western and swashbucklers like Zane Grey, Max Brand, Captain Blood and even romance or general fiction classics like Hermina Black, Denise Robins, Marie Corelli or Stella Morton. These were books that had storytelling at their heart and always entertained.

The yellowbacks had both hardback (with varying design elements) and paperback (which built the series look) versions with the latter still carrying the imprint 'yellowjacket'. The current reissues pay tribute to both and use an amalgam of elements from both editions while retaining the complete yellow (or 'mustard-plaster') livery with the author's name in blue beveled type with a 'simulated emboss' effect and a white outer 'outline', and the book title in black. These reissues retain the distinctive size of the original mass market paperback and follow the three main category variations—the thrillers (crime, westerns, mystery, adventure) had blue lettering for the author's name, while Romance and softer general fiction had red; and other categories like humour had green.

For more details and a full list of titles visit https://www.hachetteindia.com/home/yellowbacks

THE COMPLETE THIN MAN

THE COMPLETE THIN MAN

Dashiell Hammett, (1894-1961), was an American writer who created the hard-boiled school of detective fiction. Hammett left school at 13 and worked at a variety of low-paying jobs before working eight years as a detective for the Pinkerton agency. He served in World War I, contracted tuberculosis, and spent the immediate postwar years in army hospitals. He began to publish short stories and novelettes in pulp magazines and wrote two novels—*Red Harvest* and *The Dain Curse* (both published in 1929)—before writing *The Maltese Falcon* (1930), generally considered his finest work. It introduced Sam Spade, Hammett's fictional detective creation, played by Humphrey Bogart in the film version directed by John Huston (1941), which became a classic of its genre. He also wrote *The Glass Key* (1931) and *The Thin Man* (1934), which initiated a motion picture and later a television series built around his detecting couple, Nick and Nora Charles. Nora was based on the playwright Lillian Hellman, with whom he formed a romantic alliance in 1930 that lasted until his death. Her *Pentimento* (1973) has an account of their life together.

After 1934 Hammett devoted his time to left-wing political activities and to the defense of civil liberties. He served in World War II as an enlisted man. In 1951 he went to jail for six months because he refused to reveal the names of the contributors to the bail bond fund of the Civil Rights Congress, of which he was a trustee.

THE COMPLETE THIN MAN

Dashiell Hammett

The Thin Man
After the Thin Man
Another Thin Man
Sequel to the Thin Man
The First Thin Man
(unpublished draft of the book November 4, 1975, *City Magazine*)

HODDER AND STOUGHTON YELLOW JACKET
hachette

The Complete Thin Man by Dashiell Hammett
The Thin Man; *After the Thin Man* (Screen story submitted to MGM September 17, 1935; First published in *Return of the Thin Man*); *Another Thin Man* (Screen story submitted to MGM May 13, 1938; First published in *Return of the Thin Man*); *Sequel to the Thin Man* (Screen story submitted to MGM December 7, 1938; First published in *Return of the Thin Man*); *The First Thin Man* (unpublished draft of the book November 4, 1975, *City Magazine*)

1

The texts in these editions in most cases have been reprinted as is, with minimal editorial changes and by and large no bowdlerizing for political correctness; though in some editions, a few words and phrases considered archaic, or those considered offensive now, along with archaic punctuation may have been modified in places to make the text more accessible to today's readers. The narratives, language, beliefs, social mores and/or cultural depictions, in these volumes are a reflection of their times and must be viewed as such. They may also contain certain cultural, racial and gender prejudices and stereotypes that may be outdated or clearly wrong then and wrong today; but their removal would be tantamount to claiming these prejudices never existed. The Publisher does not endorse or support those depictions or stereotypes; and these books have been made available for a discerning audience that will read it for entertainment value and a chronicle/record of popular fiction of past times.

Cover design by Priya Singh adapted from the original classic yellowjacket by Hodder & Stoughton.

Cover illustration by Ishan Trivedi.

Series note: Some of the books in the series (unless otherwise credited) may have cover or inside illustrations from the original yellowbacks or early editions, and while full restoration has been attempted, some images may be grainy or faded due to the condition of the original material. The end notes or bonus material or blurb details may have been sourced from the public domain or free use publications such as Wikipedia and attribution is hereby made also allowing similar free use reproduction from here. Sources requiring further specific attribution may write in and further detailing and/or corrections shall be made in subsequent printings/editions.

Reprint specifications may be subject to change including but not limited to finishes, paper, colour sections.

ISBN: 978-93-5731-239-4

Hachette Book Publishing India Pvt. Ltd.
4th & 5th Floors, Corporate Centre,
Plot No. 94, Sector 44, Gurugram - 122 003, India

Typeset in Electra LT STD 10/12.5 pt by Manipal Technologies Limited, Manipal

Printed and bound in India by Manipal Technologies Limited, Manipal

FSC www.fsc.org
MIX
Paper from responsible sources
FSC™ C043100

CONTENTS

The Thin Man

1

I was leaning against the bar in a speakeasy on Fifty-second Street, waiting for Nora to finish her Christmas shopping, when a girl got up from the table where she had been sitting with three other people and came over to me. She was small and blonde, and whether you looked at her face or at her body in powder-blue sports clothes the result was satisfactory. 'Aren't you Nick Charles?' she asked.

I said, 'Yes.'

She held out her hand. 'I'm Dorothy Wynant. You don't remember me, but you ought to remember my father, Clyde Wynant. You –'

'Sure,' I said, 'and I remember you now, but you were only a kid of eleven or twelve then, weren't you?'

'Yes, that was eight years ago. Listen: remember those stories you told me? Were they true?'

'Probably not. How is your father?'

She laughed. 'I was going to ask you. Mamma divorced him, you know, and we never hear from him – except when he gets in the newspapers now and then with some of his carryings on. Don't you ever see him?'

My glass was empty. I asked her what she would have to drink, she said Scotch and soda, I ordered two of them and said: 'No, I've been living in San Francisco.'

She said slowly: 'I'd like to see him. Mamma would raise hell if she found it out, but I'd like to see him.'

'Well?'

'He's not where we used to live, on Riverside Drive, and he's not in the phone book or city directory.'

'Try his lawyer,' I suggested.

Her face brightened. 'Who is he?'

'It used to be a fellow named Mac-something-or-other – Macaulay, that's it, Herbert Macaulay. He was in the Singer Building.'

'Lend me a nickel,' she said, and went out to the telephone. She came back smiling. 'I found him. He's just round the corner on Fifth Avenue.'

'Your father?'

'The lawyer. He says my father's out of town. I'm going round to see him,' She raised her glass to me. 'Family reunions. Look, why don't –'

Asta jumped up and punched me in the belly with her front feet. Nora, at the other end of the leash, said: 'She's had a swell afternoon – knocked over a table of toys at Lord & Taylor's, scared a fat woman silly by licking her leg in Saks's, and has been patted by three policemen.'

I made introductions. 'My wife, Dorothy Wynant. Her father was once a client of mine, when she was only so high. A good guy, but screwy.'

'I was fascinated by him,' Dorothy said, meaning me, 'a real live detective, and used to follow him around making him tell me about his experiences. He told me awful lies, but I believed every word.'

I said: 'You look tired, Nora.'

'I am. Let's sit down.'

Dorothy Wynant said she had to go back to her table. She shook hands with Nora; we must drop in for cocktails, they were living at the Gourtland, her mother's name was Jorgensen now. We would be glad to and she must come to see us some time, we were at the Normandie and would be in New York for another week or two. Dorothy patted the dog's head and left us.

We found a table. Nora said: 'She's pretty.'

'If you like them like that.'

She grinned at me. 'You got types?'

'Only you, darling – lanky brunettes with wicked jaws.'

'And how about the red-head you wandered off with at the Quinns' last night?'

'That's silly,' I said. 'She just wanted to show me some French etchings.'

2

The next day Herbert Macaulay telephoned me. 'Hello. I didn't know you were back in town till Dorothy Wynant told me. How about lunch?'

'What time is it?'

'Half past eleven. Did I wake you up?'

'Yes,' I said, 'but that's all right. Suppose you come up here for lunch: I've got a hangover and don't feel like running around much... O.K., say one o'clock.'

I had a drink with Nora, who was going out to have her hair washed, then another after a shower, and was feeling better by the time the telephone rang again.

A female voice asked: 'Is Mr Macaulay there?'

'Not yet.'

'Sorry to trouble you, but would you mind asking him to call his office as soon as he gets there? It's important.'

I promised to do that.

Macaulay arrived about ten minutes later. He was a big, curly-haired, rosy-cheeked, rather good-looking chap of about my age – forty-one – though he looked younger. He was supposed to be a pretty good lawyer. I had worked on several jobs for him when I was living in New York and we had always got along nicely.

Now we shook hands and patted each other's backs, and he asked me how the world was treating me, and I said, 'Fine,' and asked him and he said, 'Fine,' and I told him to call his office.

He came away from the telephone frowning. 'Wynant's back in town,' he said, 'and wants me to meet him.'

I turned around with the drinks I had poured. 'Well, the lunch can –'

'Let him wait,' he said, and took one of the glasses from me.

'Still as screwy as ever?'

'That's no joke,' Macaulay said solemnly. 'You heard they had him in a sanatorium for nearly a year, back in '29?'

'No.'

He nodded. He sat down, put his glass on a table beside his chair, and leaned towards me a little.

'What's Mimi up to, Charles?'

'Mimi? Oh, the wife – the ex-wife. I don't know. Does she have to be up to something?'

'She usually is', he said dryly, and then very slowly, 'and I thought you'd know.'

So that was it. I said: 'Listen, Mac, I haven't been a detective for six years, since 1927.'

He stared at me.

'On the level,' I assured him. 'A year after I got married, my wife's father died and left her a lumber mill and a narrow-gauge railroad and some other things and I quit the Agency to look after them. Anyway I wouldn't be working for Mimi Wynant, or Jorgensen, or whatever her name is – she never liked me and I never liked her.'

'Oh, I didn't think you –' Macaulay broke off with a vague gesture and picked up his glass. When he took it away from his mouth, he said: 'I was just wondering. Here Mimi phones me three days ago – Tuesday – trying to find Wynant; then yesterday Dorothy phones, saying you told her to, and comes around, and – I thought you were still sleuthing, so I was wondering what it was all about.'

'Didn't they tell you?'

'Sure – they wanted to see him for old times' sake. That means a lot.'

'You lawyers are a suspicious crew,' I said. 'Maybe they did – that and money. But what's the fuss about? Is he in hiding?'

Macaulay shrugged. 'You know as much about it as I do. I haven't seen him since October.' He drank again. 'How long are you going to be in town?'

'Till after New Year,' I told him and went to the telephone to ask room service for menus.

3

Nora and I went to the opening of *Honeymoon* at the Little Theatre that night and then to a party given by some people named Freeman or Fielding or something. I felt pretty low when she called me the next morning. She gave me a newspaper and a cup of coffee and said: 'Read that'.

I patiently read a paragraph or two, then put the paper down and took a sip of coffee. 'Fun's fun,' I said, 'but right now I'd swap you all the interviews with Mayor-elect O'Brien ever printed – and throw in the Indian picture – for a slug of whis –'

'Not that, stupid.' She put a finger on the paper. 'That.'

INVENTOR'S SECRETARY
MURDERED IN APARTMENT
JULIA WOLF'S BULLET-RIDDLED BODY FOUND;
POLICE SEEK HER EMPLOYER, CLYDE WYNANT

'The bullet-riddled body of Julia Wolf, thirty-two-year-old confidential secretary to Clyde Miller Wynant, well-known inventor, was discovered late yesterday afternoon in the dead woman's apartment at 411 East Fifty-fourth St by Mrs Christian Jorgensen, divorced wife of the inventor, who had gone there in an attempt to learn her former husband's present address.

'Mrs Jorgensen, who returned Monday after a six-year stay in Europe, told police that she heard feeble groans when she rang the murdered woman's door-bell, whereupon she notified an elevator boy, Mervin Holly, who called Walter Meany, apartment-house superintendent. Miss Wolf was lying on the bedroom floor with four .32-calibre bullet wounds in her chest when they entered the apartment, and died without having recovered consciousness before police and medical aid arrived.

'Herbert Macaulay, Wynant's attorney, told the police that he had not seen the inventor since October. He stated that Wynant called him on the telephone yesterday and made an appointment, but failed to keep it; and disclaimed any knowledge of his client's whereabouts. Miss Wolf, Macaulay stated, had been in the inventor's employ for the past eight years. The attorney said he knew nothing about the dead woman's family or private affairs and could throw no light on her murder.

'The bullet-wounds could not have been self-inflicted, according to...'

The rest of it was the usual police department handout.

'Do you suppose he killed her?' Nora asked when I put the paper down again.

'Wynant? I wouldn't be surprised. He's batty as hell.'

'Did you know her?'

'Yes. How about a drop of something to cut the phlegm?'

'What was she like?'

'Not bad,' I said. 'She wasn't bad-looking and she had a lot of sense and a lot of nerve – and it took both to live with that guy.'

'She lived with him?'

'Yes. I want a drink, please. That is, it was like that when I knew them.'

'Why don't you have some breakfast first? Was she in love with him or was it just business?'

'I don't know. It's too early for breakfast.'

When Nora opened the door to go out, the dog came in and put her front feet on the bed, her face in my face. I rubbed her head and tried to remember something Wynant had once said to me, something about women and dogs. It was not the woman-spaniel-walnut-tree line. I could not remember what it was, but there seemed to be some point in trying to remember.

Nora returned with two drinks and another question: 'What's he like?'

'Tall – over six feet – and one of the thinnest men I've ever seen. He must be about fifty now, and his hair was almost white when I knew him. Usually needs a haircut, ragged brindle mustache, bites his fingernails.' I pushed the dog away to reach for my drink.

'Sounds lovely. What were you doing with him?'

'A fellow who'd worked for him accused him of stealing some kind of idea or invention from him. Rosewater was his name. He tried to shake Wynant down by threatening to shoot him, bomb his house, kidnap his children, cut his wife's throat – I don't know what all – if he didn't come across. We never caught him – must've scared him off. Anyway, the threats stopped and nothing happened.'

Nora stopped drinking to ask: 'Did Wynant really steal it?'

'Tch, tch, tch,' I said. 'This is Christmas Eve: try to think good of your fellow-man.'

4

That afternoon I took Asta for a walk, explained to two people that she was a Schnauzer and not a cross between a Scottie and an Irish terrier, stopped at Jim's for a couple of drinks, ran into Larry Crowley, and brought him back to the Normandie with me. Nora was pouring cocktails for the Quinns, Margot Innes, a man whose name I did not catch, and Dorothy Wynant.

Dorothy said she wanted to talk to me, so we carried our cocktails into the bedroom.

She came to the point right away. 'Do you think my father killed her, Nick?'

'No,' I said. 'Why should I?'

'Well, the police have – Listen, she was his mistress wasn't she?'

I nodded. 'When I knew them.'

She stared at her glass while saying: 'He's my father. I never liked him. I never liked Mamma.' She looked up at me. 'I don't like Gilbert.' Gilbert was her brother.

'Don't let that worry you. Lots of people don't like their relatives.'

'Do you like them?'

'My relatives?'

'Mine.' She scowled at me. 'And stop talking to me as if I was still twelve.'

'It's not that,' I explained. 'I'm getting tight.'

'Well, do you?'

I shook my head. 'You were all right, just a spoiled kid. I could get along without the rest of them.'

'What's the matter with us?' she asked, not argumentatively, but as if she really wanted to know.

'Different things. Your –'

Harrison Quinn opened the door and said: 'Come on over and play some ping-pong, Nick.'

'In a little while.'

'Bring beautiful along.' He leered at Dorothy and went away.

She said: 'I don't suppose you know Jorgensen.'

'I know a Nels Jorgensen.'

'Some people have all the luck. This one's named Christian. He's a honey. That's Mamma – divorces a lunatic and marries a gigolo.' Her eyes became wet. She caught her breath in a sob and asked: 'What am I going to do, Nick?' Her voice was a frightened child's.

I put an arm around her and made what I hoped were comforting sounds. She cried on my lapel. The telephone beside the bed began to ring. In the next room *Rise and Shine* was coming through the radio. My glass was empty. I said: 'Walk out on them.'

She sobbed again. 'You can't walk out on yourself.'

'Maybe I don't know what you're talking about.'

'Please don't tease me,' she said humbly.

Nora, coming in to answer the telephone, looked questioningly at me. I made a face at her over the girl's head.

When Nora said 'Hello' into the telephone, the girl stepped quickly back away from me and blushed. 'I – I'm sorry,' she stammered, 'I didn't –'

Nora smiled sympathetically at her. I said: 'Don't be a dope.'

The girl found her handkerchief and dabbed at her eyes with it.

Nora spoke into the telephone: 'Yes... I'll see if he's in. Who's calling, please?' She put a hand over the mouthpiece and addressed me: 'It's a man named Norman. Do you want to talk to him?'

I said I didn't know and took the telephone. 'Hello.'

A somewhat harsh voice said: 'Mr Charles?... Mr Charles, I understand that you were formerly connected with the Trans-American Detective Agency.'

'Who is this?' I asked.

'My name is Albert Norman, Mr Charles, which probably means nothing to you, but I would like to lay a proposition before you. I am sure you will –'

'What kind of proposition?'

'I can't discuss it over the phone, Mr Charles, but if you will give me half an hour of your time, I can promise –'

'Sorry,' I said. 'I'm pretty busy and –'

'But, Mr Charles, this is –' Then there was a loud noise: it could have been a shot or something falling or anything else that would make a loud noise. I said: 'Hello,' a couple of times, got no answer, and hung up.

Nora had Dorothy over in front of a looking-glass soothing her with powder and rouge. I said: 'A guy selling insurance,' and went into the living-room for a drink.

Some more people had come in. I spoke to them.

Harrison Quinn left the sofa where he had been sitting with Margot Innes and said: 'Now ping-pong.' Asta jumped up and punched me in the belly with her front feet. I shut off the radio and poured myself a cocktail. The man whose name I had not caught was saying: 'Comes the revolution and we'll all be lined up against the wall – first thing.' He seemed to think it was a good idea.

Quinn came over to refill his glass. He looked towards the bedroom door. 'Where'd you find the little blonde?'

'Used to bounce it on my knee.'

'Which knee?' he asked. 'Could I touch it?'

Nora and Dorothy came out of the bedroom. I saw an afternoon paper on the radio and picked it up. Headlines said:

JULIA WOLF ONCE RACKETEER'S GIRL
ARTHUR NUNHEIM IDENTIFIES BODY
WYNANT STILL MISSING

Nora, at my elbow, spoke in a low voice: 'I asked her to have dinner with us. Be nice to the child' – Nora was twenty-six - 'she's all upset.'

'Whatever you say,' I turned around. Dorothy, across the room, was laughing at something Quinn was telling her. 'But if you get mixed up in people's troubles, don't expect me to kiss you where you're hurt.'

'I won't. You're a sweet old fool. Don't read that here now.' She took the newspaper away from me and stuck it out of sight behind the radio.

5

Nora could not sleep that night. She read Chaliapin's memoirs until I began to doze and then woke me up by saying: 'Are you asleep?'

I said I was.

She lit a cigarette for me, one for herself. 'Don't you ever think you'd like to go back to detecting once in a while just for the fun of it? You know, when something special comes up, like the Lindb –'

'Darling,' I said, 'my guess is that Wynant killed her, and the police'll catch him without my help. Anyway, it's nothing in my life.'

'I didn't mean just that, but –'

'But besides I haven't the time: I'm too busy trying to see that you don't lose any of the money I married you for.' I kissed her. 'Don't you think maybe a drink would help you to sleep?'

'No thanks.'

'Maybe it would if I took one.' When I brought my Scotch and soda back to bed, she was frowning into space.

I said: 'She's cute, but she's cuckoo. She wouldn't be his daughter if she wasn't. You can't tell how much of what she says is what she thinks and you can't tell how much of what she thinks ever really happened. I like her, but I think you're letting –'

'I'm not sure I like her,' Nora said thoughtfully, 'she's probably a little brat, but if a quarter of what she told us is true, she's in a tough spot.'

'There's nothing I can do to help her.'

'She thinks you can.'

'And so do you, which shows that no matter what you think, you can always get somebody else to go along with you.'

Nora sighed. 'I wish you were sober enough to talk to.' She leaned over to take a sip of my drink. 'I'll give you your Christmas present now if you'll give me mine.'

I shook my head. 'At breakfast.'

'But it's Christmas now.'

'Breakfast.'

'Whatever you're giving me,' she said, 'I hope I don't like it.'

'You'll have to keep them anyway, because the man at the Aquarium said he positively wouldn't take them back. He said they'd already bitten the tails off the –'

'It wouldn't hurt you any to find out if you can help her, would it? She's got so much confidence in you, Nicky.'

'Everybody trusts Greeks.'

'Please.'

'You just want to poke your nose into things that –'

'I meant to ask you: did his wife know the Wolf girl was his mistress?'

'I don't know. She didn't like her.'

'What's the wife like?'

'I don't know – a woman.'

'Good-looking?'

'Used to be very'

'She old?'

'Forty, forty-two. Cut it out, Nora. You don't want any part of it. Let the Charleses stick to the Charleses' troubles and the Wynants stick to the Wynants'.'

She pouted. 'Maybe that drink would help me.'

I got out of bed and mixed a drink. As I brought it into the bedroom, the telephone began to ring. I looked at my watch on the table. It was nearly five o'clock.

Nora was talking into the telephone: 'Hello... Yes, speaking.' She looked sidewise at me. I shook my head no. 'Yes... Why, certainly... Yes, certainly' She put the telephone down and grinned at me.

'You're wonderful,' I said. 'Now what?'

'Dorothy's coming up. I think she's tight.'

'That's great.' I picked up my bathrobe: 'I was afraid I was going to have to go to sleep.'

She was bending over looking for her slippers. 'Don't be such an old fuff. You can sleep all day.' She found her slippers and stood up in them. 'Is she really as afraid of her mother as she says?'

'If she's got any sense. Mimi's poison.'

Nora screwed up her dark eyes at me and asked slowly: 'What are you holding out on me?'

'Oh dear,' I said, 'I was hoping I wouldn't have to tell you. Dorothy is really my daughter. I didn't know what I was doing, Nora. It was spring in Venice and I was so young and there was a moon over the –'

'Be funny. Don't you want something to eat?'

'If you do. What do you want?'

'Raw chopped beef sandwich with a lot of onion and some coffee.'

Dorothy arrived while I was telephoning an all-night delicatessen. When I went into the living-room, she stood up with some difficulty and said: 'I'm awfully sorry, Nick, to keep bothering you and Nora like this, but I can't go home this way tonight. I can't. I'm afraid to. I don't know what'd happen to me, what I'd do. Please don't make me.' She was very drunk.

Asta sniffed at her ankles.

I said: 'Sh-h-h. You're all right here. Sit down. There'll be some coffee in a little while. Where'd you get the snoutful?'

She sat down and shook her head stupidly. 'I don't know. I've been everywhere since I left you. I've been everywhere except home because I can't go home this way. Look what I got.' She stood up again and took a battered automatic pistol out of her coat pocket. 'Look at that.' She waved it at me while Asta, wagging her tail, jumped happily at it.

Nora made a noise with her breathing. The back of my neck was cold. I pushed the dog aside and took the pistol away from Dorothy. 'What kind of clowning is this? Sit down.' I dropped the pistol into the bathrobe pocket and pushed Dorothy down in her chair.

'Don't be mad at me, Nick,' she whined. 'You can keep it. I don't want to make a nuisance of myself.'

'Where'd you get it?' I asked.

'In a speakeasy on Tenth Avenue. I gave a man my bracelet – the one with the emeralds and diamonds – for it.'

'And then won it back from him in a crap game,' I said. 'You've still got it on.'

She stared at her bracelet. 'I thought I did.'

I looked at Nora and shook my head. Nora said: 'Aw, don't bully her, Nick. She's –'

'He's not bullying me, Nora, he's really not.' Dorothy said quickly. 'He's – he's the only person I got in the world to turn to.'

I remembered Nora had not touched her Scotch and soda, so I went into the bedroom and drank it. When I came back, Nora was sitting on the arm of Dorothy's chair with an arm around the girl. Dorothy was, sniffling; Nora was saying: 'But Nick's not mad, dear. He likes you.' She looked up at me. 'You're not mad, are you, Nicky?'

'No, I'm just hurt.' I sat on the sofa. 'Where'd you get the gun, Dorothy?'

'From a man – I told you.'

'What man?'

'I told you – a man in a speakeasy'

'And you gave him a bracelet for it.'

'I thought I did, but – look – I've still got my bracelet.'

'I noticed that.'

Nora patted the girl's shoulder. 'Of course you've still got your bracelet.'

I said: 'When the boy comes with that coffee and stuff, I'm going to bribe him to stick around. I'm not going to stay alone with a couple of –'

Nora scowled at me, told the girl: 'Don't mind him. He's been like that all night.'

The girl said: 'He thinks I'm a silly little drunken fool.' Nora patted her shoulder some more.

I asked: 'But what'd you want a gun for?'

Dorothy sat up straight and stared at me with wide drunken eyes. 'Him,' she whispered excitedly, 'if he bothered me. I was afraid because I was drunk. That's what it was. And then I was afraid of that, too, so I came here.'

'You mean your father?' Nora asked, trying to keep excitement out of her voice.

The girl shook her head. 'Clyde Wynant's my father. My stepfather.' She leaned against Nora's breast.

Nora said: 'Oh,' in a tone of very complete understanding. Then she said: 'You poor child,' and looked significandy at me.

I said: 'Let's all have a drink.'

'Not me.' Nora was scowling at me again. 'And I don't think Dorothy wants one.'

'Yes, she does. It'll help her sleep.' I poured her a terrific dose of Scotch and saw that she drank it. It worked nicely: she was sound asleep by the time our coffee and sandwiches came.

Nora said: 'Now you're satisfied.'

'Now I'm satisfied. Shall we tuck her in before we eat?'

I carried her into the bedroom and helped Nora undress her. She had a beautiful little body.

We went back to our food. I took the pistol out of my pocket and examined it. It had been kicked around a lot. There were two cartridges in it, one in the chamber, one in the magazine.

'What are you going to do with it?' Nora asked.

'Nothing till I find out if it's the one Julia Wolf was killed with. It's a .32.'

'But she said –'

'She got it in a speakeasy – from a man – for a bracelet. I heard her.'

Nora leaned over her sandwich at me. Her eyes were very shiny and almost black. 'Do you suppose she got it from her stepfather?'

'I do,' I said, but I said it too earnestly.

Nora said: 'You're a Greek louse. But maybe she did; you don't know. And you don't believe her story.'

'Listen, darling, tomorrow I'll buy you a whole lot of detective stories, but don't worry your pretty little head over mysteries tonight. All she was trying to tell you was that she was afraid Jorgensen was waiting to try to make her when she got home and she was afraid she was drunk enough to give in!'

'But her mother!'

'This family's a family. You can –'

Dorothy Wynant, standing unsteadily in the doorway in a nightgown much too long for her, blinked at the light and said: 'Please, can I come in for a little while? I'm afraid in there alone.'

'Sure.'

She came over and curled up beside me on the sofa while Nora went to get something to put around her.

6

The three of us were at breakfast early that afternoon when the Jorgensens arrived. Nora answered the telephone and came away from it trying to pretend she was not tickled. 'It's your mother,' she told Dorothy. 'She's downstairs. I told her to come up.'

Dorothy said: 'Damn it. I wish I hadn't phoned her.'

I said: 'We might just as well be living in the lobby.'

Nora said: 'He doesn't mean that.' She patted Dorothy's shoulder.

The door-bell rang. I went to the door.

Eight years had done no damage to Mimi's looks. She was a little riper, showier, that was all. She was larger than her daughter, and her blondness was more vivid. She laughed and held her hands out to me. 'Merry Christmas. It's awfully good to see you after all these years. This is my husband. Mr Charles, Chris.'

I said: 'I'm glad to see you, Mimi,' and shook hands with Jorgensen. He was probably five years younger than his wife, a tall, thin, erect, dark man, carefully dressed and sleek, with smooth hair and a waxed mustache.

He bowed from the waist. 'How do you do, Mr Charles?' His accent was heavy, Teutonic, his hand was lean and muscular.

We went inside.

Mimi, when the introductions were over, apologized to Nora for popping in on us. 'But I did want to see your husband again, and then I know the only way to get this brat of mine anywhere on time is to carry her off bodily.' She turned her smile on Dorothy. 'Better get dressed, honey.'

Honey grumbled through a mouthful of toast that she didn't see why she had to waste an afternoon at Aunt Alice's even if it was Christmas. 'I bet Gilbert's not going.'

Mimi said Asta was a lovely dog and asked me if I had *any* idea where that ex-husband of hers might be.

'No.'

She went on playing with the dog. 'He's crazy, absolutely crazy, to disappear at a time like this. No wonder the police at first thought he had something to do with it.'

'What do they think now?' I asked.

She looked up at me. 'Haven't you seen the papers?'

'No.'

'It's a man named Morelli – a gangster. He killed her. He was her lover.'

'They caught him?'

'Not yet, but he did it. I wish I could find Clyde. Macaulay won't help me at all. He says he doesn't know where he is, but that's ridiculous. He has powers of attorney from him and everything and I know very well he's in touch with Clyde. Do you think Macaulay's trustworthy?'

'He's Wynant's lawyer,' I said. 'There's no reason why you should trust him.'

'Just what I thought.' She moved over a little on the sofa. 'Sit down. I've got millions of things to ask you.'

'How about a drink first?'

'Anything but egg-nog,' she said. 'It makes me bilious.'

When I came out of the pantry, Nora and Jorgensen were trying their French on each other, Dorothy was still pretending to eat, and Mimi was playing with the dog again. I distributed the drinks and sat down beside Mimi. She said: 'Your wife's lovely.'

'I like her.'

'Tell me the truth, Nick: do you think Clyde's really crazy? I mean crazy enough that something ought to be done about it.'

'How do I know?'

'I'm worried about the children.' she said. 'I've no claim on him any more – the settlement he made when I divorced him took care of all that – but the children have. We're absolutely penniless now and I'm worried about them. If he is crazy he's just as likely as not to throw away everything and leave them without a cent. What do you think I ought to do?'

'Thinking about putting him in the booby-hatch?'

'No – o.' she said slowly, 'but I would like to talk to him.' She put a hand on my arm. 'You could find him.'

I shook my head.

'Won't you help me, Nick? We used to be friends.' Her big blue eyes were soft and appealing.

Dorothy, at the table, was watching us suspiciously.

'For Christ's sake, Mimi,' I said, 'there's a thousand detectives in New York. Hire one of them. I'm not working at it any more.'

'I know, but – Was Dorry very drunk last night?'

'Maybe I was. She seemed all right to me.'

'Don't you think she's got to be a pretty little thing?'

'I always thought she was.'

She thought that over for a moment, then said: 'She's only a child, Nick.'

'What's that got to do with what?' I asked.

She smiled. 'How about getting some clothes on, Dorry?'

Dorothy sulkily repeated that she didn't see why she had to waste an afternoon at Aunt Alice's.

Jorgensen turned to address his wife: 'Mrs Charles has the great kindness to suggest that we do not –'

'Yes,' Nora said, 'why don't you stay a while? There'll be some people coming in. It won't be very exciting, but –' She waved her glass a little to finish the sentence.

'I'd love to,' Mimi replied slowly, 'but I'm afraid Alice –'

'Make our apologies to her by telephone,' Jorgensen suggested.

'I'll do it,' Dorothy said.

Mimi nodded. 'Be nice to her.'

Dorothy went into the bedroom. Everybody seemed much brighter. Nora caught my eye and winked merrily and I had to take it and like it because Mimi was looking at me then.

Mimi asked me: 'You really didn't want us to stay, did you?'

'Of course.'

'Chances are you're lying. Weren't you sort of fond of poor Julia?'

"Poor Julia' sounds swell from you. I liked her all right.'

Mimi put her hand on my arm again. 'She broke up my life with Clyde. Naturally I hated her – then – but that's a long time ago. I had no feeling against her when I went to see her Friday. And, Nick, I saw her die. She didn't deserve to die. It was horrible. No matter what I'd felt there'd be nothing left but pity now. I meant 'poor Julia' when I said it.'

'I don't know what you're up to,' I said. 'I don't know what any of you are up to.'

'Any of us,' she repeated. 'Has Dorry been –'

Dorothy came in from the bedroom. 'I squared it.' She kissed her mother on the mouth and sat down beside her.

Mimi, looking in her compact-mirror to see her mouth had not been smeared, asked: 'She wasn't peevish about it?'

'No, I squared it. What do you have to do to get a drink?'

I said: 'You have to walk over to that table where the ice and bottles are and pour it.'

Mimi said: 'You drink too much.'

'I don't drink as much as Nick.' She went over to the table.

Mimi shook her head. 'These children! I mean you were pretty fond of Julia Wolf, weren't you?'

Dorothy called: 'You want one, Nick?'

'Thanks,' I said; then to Mimi, 'I liked her well enough.'

'You're the damnedest evasive man,' she complained. 'Did you like her as much as you used to like me, for instance?'

'You mean those couple of afternoons we killed?'

Her laugh was genuine. 'That's certainly an answer.'

She turned to Dorothy, carrying glasses towards us. 'You'll have to get a robe that shade of blue, darling. It's very becoming to you.'

I took one of the glasses from Dorothy and said I thought I had better get dressed.

7

When I came out of the bathroom, Nora and Dorothy were in the bedroom, Nora combing her hair, Dorothy sitting on the side of the bed dangling a stocking.

Nora made a kiss at me in the dressing-table mirror. She looked very happy.

'You like Nick, don't you, Nora?' Dorothy asked.

'He's an old Greek fool, but I'm used to him.'

'Charles isn't a Greek name.'

'It's Charalambides,' I explained. 'When the old man came over, the mug that put him through Ellis Island said Charalambides was too long – too much trouble to write – and whittled it down to Charles. It was all right with the old man; they could have called him X so they let him in.'

Dorothy stared at me. 'I never know when you're lying.' She started to put on the stocking, stopped. 'What's Mamma trying to do to you?'

'Nothing. Pump me. She'd like to know what you did and said last night.'

'I thought so. What'd you tell her?'

'What could I tell her? You didn't do or say anything.'

She wrinkled her forehead over that, but when she spoke again it was about something else: 'I never knew there was anything between you and Mamma. Of course I was only a kid then and wouldn't have known what it was all about even if I'd noticed anything, but I didn't even know you called each other by your first names.'

Nora turned from the mirror laughing. 'Now we're getting somewhere.' She waved a comb at Dorothy. 'Go on, dear.'

Dorothy said earnestly: 'Well, I didn't know.'

I was taking laundry pins out of a shirt. 'What do you know now?' I asked.

'Nothing,' she said slowly, and her face began to grow pink, 'but I can guess.' She bent over her stocking.

'Can and do,' I growled. 'You're a dope, but don't look so embarrassed. You can't help it if you've got a dirty mind.'

She raised her head and laughed, but when she asked: 'Do you think I take after Mamma much?' she was serious.

'I wouldn't be surprised.'

'But do you?'

'You want me to say no. No.'

'That's what I have to live with,' Nora said cheerfully. 'You can't do anything with him.'

I finished dressing first and went out to the living-room. Mimi was sitting on Jorgensen's knees. She stood up and asked: 'What'd you get for Christmas?'

'Nora gave me a watch.' I showed it to her.

She said it was lovely, and it was. 'What'd you give her?'

'Necklace.'

Jorgensen said: 'May I?' and rose to mix himself a drink.

The door-bell rang. I let the Quinns and Margot Innes in, introducing them to the Jorgensens. Presently Nora and Dorothy finished dressing and came out of the bedroom and Quinn attached himself to Dorothy. Larry Crowley arrived, with a girl named Denis, and a few minutes later the Edges. I won thirty-two dollars – on the cuff – from Margot at backgammon. The Denis girl had to go into the bedroom and lie down a while. Alice Quinn, with Margot's help, tore her husband away from Dorothy at a little after six and carried him off to keep a date they had. The Edges left. Mimi put on her coat, got her husband and daughter into their coats.

'It's awful short notice,' she said, 'but can't you come to dinner tomorrow night?'

Nora said: 'Certainly'

We shook hands and made polite speeches all around and they went away.

Nora shut the door after them and leaned her back against it. 'God, he's a handsome guy,' she said.

8

So far I had known just where I stood on the Wolf-Wynant-Jorgensen troubles and what I was doing – the answers were, respectively, nowhere and nothing – but when we stopped at Reuben's for coffee on our way home at four the next morning, Nora opened a newspaper and found a line in one of the gossip columns: 'Nick Charles, former Trans-American Detective Agency ace, in from Coast to sift the Julia Wolf murder mystery'; and when I opened my eyes and sat up in bed some six hours later Nora was shaking me and a man with a gun in his hand was standing in the bedroom doorway.

He was a plump, dark, youngish man of medium height, broad through the jaws, narrow between the eyes. He wore a black bowler hat, a black overcoat that fitted him very snugly, a dark suit, and black shoes, all looking as if he had bought them within the past fifteen minutes. The gun, a blunt black .38-calibre automatic, lay comfortably in his hand, not pointing at anything.

Nora was saying: 'He made me let him in, Nick. He said he had to –'

'I got to talk to you,' the man with the gun said. 'That's all, but I got to do that.' His voice was low and rasping.

I had blinked myself awake by then. I looked at Nora. She was excited, but apparently not frightened: she might have been watching a horse she had a bet on coming down the stretch with a nose lead.

I said: 'All right, talk, but do you mind putting the gun away?'

He smiled with his lower lip. 'You don't have to tell me you're tough. I heard about you.' He put the pistol in his overcoat pocket. 'I'm Shep Morelli.'

'I never heard about you,' I said.

He took a step into the room and began to shake his head from side to side. 'I didn't knock Julia off.'

'Maybe you didn't, but you're bringing the news to the wrong place. I got nothing to do with it.'

'I haven't seen her in three months,' he said. 'We were washed up.'

'Tell the police.'

'I wouldn't have any reason to hurt her: she was always on the up and up with me.'

'That's all swell,' I said, 'only you're peddling your fish in the wrong market.'

'Listen.' He took another step towards the bed. 'Studsy Burke tells me you used to be O.K. That's why I'm here. Do the –'

'How is Studsy?' I asked. 'I haven't seen him since the time he went up the river in '23 or '24.'

'He's all right. He'd like to see you. He's got a joint on West Forty-ninth, the Pigiron Club. But listen, what's the law doing to me? Do they think I did it? Or is it just something else to pin on me?'

I shook my head. 'I'd tell you if I knew. Don't let newspapers fool you: I'm not in this. Ask the police.'

'That'd be very smart.' He smiled with his lower lip again. 'That'd be the smartest thing I ever did. Me that a police captain's been in a hospital three weeks on account we had an argument. The boys would like me to come in and ask 'em questions. They'd like it right down to the end of their black-jacks.' He turned a hand over, palm up. 'I come to you on the level. Studsy says you're on the level. Be on the level.'

'I'm being on the level,' I assured him. 'If I knew anything I'd –'

Knuckles drummed on the corridor door, three times, sharply. Morelli's gun was in his hand before the noise stopped. His eyes seemed to move in all directions at once. His voice was a metallic snarl deep in his chest: 'Well?'

'I don't know.' I sat up a little higher in bed and nodded at the gun in his hand. 'That makes it your party.' The gun pointed very accurately at my chest. I could hear the blood in my ears, and my lips felt swollen. I said: 'There's no fire-escape.' I put my left hand out towards Nora, who was sitting on the far side of the bed.

The knuckles hit the door again, and a deep voice called: 'Open up. Police.'

Morelli's lower lip crawled up to lap the upper, and the whites of his eyes began to show under the irises. 'You rat,' he said slowly, almost as if he were sorry for me. He moved his feet the least bit, flattening them against the floor.

A key touched the outer lock.

I hit Nora with my left hand, knocking her down across the room. The pillow I chucked with my right hand at Morelli's gun seemed to have no weight; it drifted slow as a piece of tissue paper. No noise in the world, before or after, was ever so loud as Morelli's gun going off. Something pushed my left side as I sprawled across the floor. I caught one of his ankles and rolled over with it, bringing him down on me, and he clubbed my back with the gun until I got a hand free and began to hit him as low in the body as I could.

Men came in and dragged us apart.

It took us five minutes to bring Nora to.

She sat up holding her cheek and looked around the room until she saw Morelli, nippers on one wrist, standing between two detectives. Morelli's face was a mess; the coppers had worked him over a little just for the fun of it. Nora glared at me: 'You damned fool,' she said, 'you didn't have to knock me cold. I knew you'd take him, but I wanted to see it.'

One of the coppers laughed. 'God,' he said admiringly, 'there's a woman with grit.'

She smiled at him and stood up. When she looked at me she stopped smiling. 'Nick, you're –'

I said I didn't think it was much and opened what was left of my pyjama-coat. Morelli's bullet had scooped out a gutter perhaps four inches long under my left nipple. A lot of blood was running out of it, but it was not very deep.

Morelli said: 'Tough luck. A couple of inches over would make a lot of difference the right way.'

The copper who had admired Nora – he was a big, sandy man of forty-eight or fifty in a gray suit that did not fit him very well – slapped Morelli's mouth.

Keyser, the Normandie's manager, said he would get a doctor and went to the telephone. Nora ran to the bathroom for towels.

I put a towel over the wound and lay down on the bed. 'I'm all right. Don't let's fuss over it till the doctor comes. How'd you people happen to pop in?'

The copper who had slapped Morelli said: 'We happen to hear this is getting to be kind of a meeting-place for Wynant's family and his lawyer and everybody, so we think we'll kind of keep an eye on it in case he happens to show up, and this morning when Mac here, who was the eye we were kind of keeping on it at the time, sees this bird duck in, he gives us a ring and we get hold of Mr Keyser and come on up, and pretty lucky for you.'

'Yes, pretty lucky for me, or maybe I wouldn't've got shot.'

He eyed me suspiciously. His eyes were pale gray and watery. 'This bird a friend of yours?'

'I never saw him before.'

'What'd he want of you?'

'Wanted to tell me he didn't kill the Wolf girl.'

'What's that to you?'

'Nothing.'

'What'd he think it was to you?'

'Ask him. I don't know.'

'I'm asking you.'

'Keep on asking.'

'I'll ask you another one: you're going to swear to the complaint on him shooting you?'

'That's another one I can't answer right now. Maybe it was an accident.'

'Ok. There's plenty of time. I guess we got to ask you a lot more things than we'd figured on.' He turned to one of his companions: there were four of them. 'We'll frisk this joint.'

'Not without a warrant,' I told him.

'So you say. Come on, Andy.' They began to search the place.

The doctor – a colorless wisp of a man with the snuffles – came in, clucked and sniffed over my side, got the bleeding stopped and bandage on, and told me I would have nothing to worry about if I lay still for a couple of days. Nobody would tell the doctor anything. The police would not let him touch Morelli. He went away looking even more colorless and vague.

The big, sandy man had returned from the living-room holding one hand behind him. He waited until the doctor had gone, then asked: 'Have you got a pistol permit?'

'No.'

'Then what are you doing with this?' He brought from behind him the gun I had taken from Dorothy Wynant.

There was nothing I could say.

'You've heard about the Sullivan Act?' he asked.

'Yes.'

'Then you know where you stand. This gun yours?'

'No.'

'Whose is it?'

'I'll have to try to remember.'

He put the pistol in his pocket and sat down on a chair beside the bed. 'Listen, Mr Charles,' he said. 'I guess we're both of us doing this wrong. I don't want to get tough with you and I don't guess you really want to get tough with me. That hole in your side can't be making you feel any too good, so I ain't going to bother you any more till you've had a little rest. Then maybe we can get together the way we ought to.'

'Thanks,' I said and meant it. 'We'll buy a drink.'

Nora said: 'Sure,' and got up from the edge of the bed.

The big, sandy man watched her go out of the room. He shook his head solemnly. His voice was solemn: 'By God, sir, you're a lucky man.' He suddenly held out his hand. 'My name's Guild, John Guild.'

'You know mine.' We shook hands.

Nora came back with a siphon, a bottle of Scotch, and some glasses on a tray. She tried to give Morelli a drink, but Guild stopped her. 'It's mighty kind of you, Mrs Charles, but it's against the law to give a prisoner drinks or drugs except on a doctor's say-so.' He looked at me. 'Ain't that right?'

I said it was. The rest of us drank.

Presently Guild set down his empty glass and stood up. 'I got to take this gun along with me, but don't you worry about that. We got plenty of time to talk when you're feeling better.' He took Nora's hand and made an awkward bow over it. 'I hope you didn't mind what I said back there a while ago, but I mean it in a –'

Nora can smile very nicely. She gave him one of her nicest smiles. 'Mind? I liked it.'

She let the policemen and their prisoner out. Keyser had gone a few minutes before.

'He's sweet,' she said when she came back from the door. 'Hurt much?'

'No.'

'It's pretty much my fault, isn't it?'

'Nonsense. How about another drink?'

She poured me one. 'I wouldn't take too many of these today.'

'I won't,' I promised. 'I could do with some kippers for breakfast. And, now our troubles seem to be over for a while, you might have them send up our absentee watch-dog. And tell the operator not to give us any calls; there'll probably be reporters.'

'What are you going to tell the police about Dorothy's pistol? You'll have to tell them something, won't you?'

'I don't know yet.'

'Tell me the truth, Nick: have I been too silly?'

I shook my head. 'Just silly enough.'

She laughed, said: 'You're a Greek louse,' and went around to the telephone.

9

Nora said: 'You're just showing off, that's all it is. And what for? I know bullets bounce off you. You don't have to prove it to me.'

'It's not going to hurt me to get up.'

And it's not going to hurt you to stay in bed at least one day. The doctor said –'

'If he knew anything he'd cure his own snuffles.' I sat up and put my feet on the floor. Asta tickled them with her tongue.

Nora brought me slippers and robe. 'All right, hard guy, get up and bleed on the rugs.'

I stood up cautiously and seemed to be all right as long as I went easy with my left arm and kept out of the way of Asta's front feet.

'Be reasonable,' I said. 'I didn't want to get mixed up with these people – still don't – but a fat lot of good that's doing me. Well, I can't just blunder out of it. I've got to see.'

'Let's go away' she suggested. 'Let's go to Bermuda or Havana for a week or two, or back to the Coast.'

'I'd still have to tell the police some kind of story about that gun. And suppose it turns out to be the gun she was killed with? If they don't know already they're finding out.'

'Do you really think it is?'

'That's guessing. We'll go there for dinner tonight and –'

'We'll do nothing of the kind. Have you gone completely nuts? If you want to see anybody, have them come here.'

'It's not the same thing.' I put my arms around her. 'Stop worrying about this scratch. I'm all right.'

'You're showing off,' she said. 'You want to let people see you're a hero who can't be stopped by bullets.'

'Don't be nasty.'

'I will be nasty. I'm not going to have you –'

I shut her mouth with a hand over it. 'I want to see the Jorgensens together at home, I want to see Macaulay, and I want to see Studsy Burke. I've been pushed around too much. I've got to see about things.'

'You're so damned pig-headed,' she complained. 'Well, it's only five o'clock. Lie down till it's time to dress.'

I made myself comfortable on the living-room sofa. We had the afternoon papers sent up. Morelli, it seemed, had shot me – twice for one of the papers and three times for another – when I tried to arrest him for Julia Wolf's murder, and I was too near death to see anybody or to be moved to hospital. There were pictures of Morelli and a thirteen-year-old one of me in a pretty funny-looking hat, taken, I remembered, when I was working on the Wall Street explosion. Most of the follow-up stories on the murder of Julia Wolf were rather vague. We were reading them when our little constant visitor, Dorothy Wynant, arrived.

I could hear her at the door when Nora opened it: 'They wouldn't send my name up, so I sneaked up. Please don't send me away. I can help you nurse Nick. I'll do anything. Please, Nora.'

Nora had a chance then to say: 'Come on in.'

Dorothy came in. She goggled at me. 'B-but the papers said you –'

'Do I look like I'm dying? What's happened to you?' Her lower lip was swollen and cut near one corner, there was a bruise on one cheek-bone and two fingernail scratches down the other cheek, and her eyes were red and swollen.

'Mamma beat me,' she said. 'Look.' She dropped her coat on the floor, tore off a button unbuttoning her dress, took an arm out of its sleeve, and pushed the dress down to show her back. There were dark bruises on her arm, and her back was criss-crossed by long red welts. She was crying now. 'See?'

Nora put an arm around her. 'You poor kid.'

'What'd she beat you for?' I asked.

She turned from Nora and knelt on the floor beside my sofa. Asta came over and nuzzled her. 'She thought I came – came to see you about father and Julia Wolf.' Sobs broke up her sentences. 'That's why she came over here – to find out – and you made her think I didn't. You – you made her think you didn't care anything about what happened – just like you made me – and she was all right till she saw the papers this afternoon. Then she knew you'd been lying about not having anything to do with it. She beat me to try to make me tell her what I'd told you.'

'What'd you tell her?'

'I couldn't tell her anything. I – I couldn't tell her about Chris. I couldn't tell her anything.'

'Was he there?'

'Yes.'

'And he let her beat you like this?'

'But he – he never makes her stop.'

I said to Nora: 'For God's sake, let's have a drink.'

Nora said: 'Sure,' picked up Dorothy's coat, laid it across the back of a chair, and went into the pantry.

Dorothy said: 'Please let me stay here, Nick. I won't be any trouble, honestly, and you told me yourself I ought to walk out on them. You know you did, and I've got nowhere else to go. Please.'

'Take it easy. This thing needs a little figuring out. I'm as much afraid of Mimi as you are, you know. What did she think you'd told me?'

'She must know something – something about the murder that she thinks I know – but I don't, Nick. Honest to God, I don't.'

'That helps a lot,' I complained. 'But listen, sister: there are things you know and we're going to start with those. You come clean at and from the beginning – or we don't play.'

She made a movement as if she were about to cross her heart. 'I swear I will,' she said.

'That'll be swell. Now let's drink.' We took a glass apiece from Nora. 'Tell her you were leaving for good?'

'No, I didn't say anything. Maybe she doesn't know yet I'm not in my room.'

'That helps some.'

'You're not going to make me go back?' she cried.

Nora said over her glass: 'The child can't stay and be beaten like that, Nick.'

I said: 'Sh-h-h. I don't know. I was just thinking that if we're going there for dinner maybe it's better for Mimi not to know –'

Dorothy stared at me with horrified eyes while Nora said: 'Don't think you're going to take me there now.'

Then Dorothy spoke rapidly: 'But Mamma doesn't expect you. I don't even know whether she'll be there. The papers said you were dying. She doesn't think you're coming.'

'So much the better,' I said. 'We'll surprise them.'

She put her face, white now, close to mine, spilling some of her drink on my sleeve in her excitement. 'Don't go. You can't go there now. Listen to me. Listen to Nora. You can't go.' She turned her white face around to look up at Nora. 'Can he? Tell him he can't.'

Nora, not shifting the focus of her dark eyes from my face, said: 'Wait, Dorothy. He ought to know what's best. What is it, Nick?'

I made a face at her. 'I'm just fumbling around. If you say Dorothy stays here, she stays. I guess she can sleep with Asta.

But you've got to leave me alone on the rest of it. I don't know what I'm going to do because I don't know what's being done to me. I've got to find out. I've got to find out in my own way.'

'We won't interfere,' Dorothy said. 'Will we, Nora?'

Nora continued to look at me, saying nothing.

I asked Dorothy: 'Where'd you get that gun? And nothing out of books this time.'

She moistened her lower lip and her face became pinker. She cleared her throat.

'Careful,' I said. 'If it's another piece of chewing-gum, I'll phone Mimi to come and get you.'

'Give her a chance,' Nora said.

Dorothy cleared her throat again. 'Can – can I tell you something that happened to me when I was a little child?'

'Has it got anything to do with the gun?'

'Not exactly, but it'll help you understand why I –'

'Not now. Some other time. Where'd you get the gun?'

'I wish you'd let me.' She hung her head.

'Where'd you get the gun?'

Her voice was barely audible. 'From a man in a speakeasy.'

I said: 'I knew we'd get the truth at last.' Nora frowned and shook her head at me. 'All right, say you did. What speakeasy?'

Dorothy raised her head. 'I don't know. It was on Tenth Avenue, I think. Your friend Mr Quinn would know. He took me there.'

'You met him after you left us that night?'

'Yes.'

'By accident, I suppose.'

She looked reproachfully at me. 'I'm trying to tell you the truth, Nick. I'd promised to meet him at a place called the Palma Club. He wrote the address down for me. So after I said good night to you and Nora, I met him there and we went to a lot of places, winding up in this place where I got the gun.

It was an awful tough place. You can ask him if I'm not telling the truth.'

'Quinn get the gun for you?'

'No. He'd passed out then. He was sleeping with his head on the table. I left him there. They said they'd get him home all right.'

'And the gun?'

'I'm coming to it.' She began to blush. 'He told me it was a gunman's hang-out. That's why I'd said let's go there. And after he went to sleep I got to talking to a man there, an awful tough-looking man. I was fascinated. And all the time I didn't want to go home, I wanted to come back here, but I didn't know if you'd let me.' Her face was quite red now and in her embarrassment she blurred her words. 'So I thought perhaps if I – if you thought I was in a terrible fix – and besides, that way I wouldn't feel so silly. Anyhow, I asked this awful tough-looking gangster, or whatever he was, if he would sell me a pistol or tell me where I could buy one. He thought I was kidding and laughed at first, but I told him I wasn't, and then he kept on grinning, but he said he'd see, and when he came back he said yes, he could get me one and asked how much I would pay for it. I didn't have much money, but I offered him my bracelet, but I guess he didn't think it was any good, because he said no, he'd have to have cash, so finally I gave him twelve dollars – all I had but a dollar for the taxi – and he gave me the pistol and I came over here and made up that about being afraid to go home because of Chris.' She finished so rapidly her words ran together, and she sighed as if very glad to have finished.

'Then Chris hasn't been making passes at you?'

She bit her lip. 'Yes, but not – not that bad.' She put both hands on my arms, and her face almost touched mine. 'You've got to believe me. I couldn't tell you all that, couldn't make myself out such a cheap little lying fool, if it wasn't the truth.'

'It makes more sense if I don't believe you,' I said. 'Twelve bucks isn't enough money. We'll let that rest for a minute, though. Did you know Mimi was going to see Julia Wolf that afternoon?'

'No. I didn't even know she was trying to find my father then. They didn't say where they were going that afternoon.'

'They?'

'Yes, Chris left the apartment with her.'

'What time was that?'

She wrinkled her forehead. 'It must've been pretty close to three o'clock – after two-thirty, anyway – because I remember I was late for a date to go shopping with Elsie Hamilton and was hurrying into my clothes.'

'They come back together?'

'I don't know. They were both home before I came.'

'What time was that?'

'Some time after six. Nick, you don't think they – Oh, I remember something she said while she was dressing. I don't know what Chris said, but she said: 'When I ask her she'll tell me,' in that Queen-of-France way she talks sometimes. You know. I didn't hear anything else. Does that mean anything?'

'What'd she tell you about the murder when you came home?'

'Oh, just about finding her and how upset she was and about the police and everything.'

'She seemed very shocked?'

Dorothy shook her head. 'No, just excited. You know Mamma.' She stared at me for a moment, asked slowly: 'You don't think she had anything to do with it?'

'What do you think?'

'I hadn't thought. I just thought about my father.' A little later she said gravely: 'If he did it, it's because he's crazy, but she'd kill somebody if she wanted to.'

'It doesn't have to be either of them,' I reminded her. 'The police seem to have picked Morelli. What'd she want to find your father for?'

'For money. We're broke: Chris spent it all.' She pulled down the corners of her mouth. 'I suppose we all helped, but he spent most of it. Mamma's afraid he'll leave her if she hasn't any money.'

'How do you know that?'

'I've heard them talk.'

'Do you think he will?'

She nodded with certainty. 'Unless she has money.'

I looked at my watch and said: 'The rest of it'll have to wait till we get back. You can stay here tonight, anyhow. Make yourself comfortable and have the restaurant send up your dinner. It's probably better if you don't go out.'

She stared miserably at me and said nothing.

Nora patted her shoulder. 'I don't know what he's doing, Dorothy, but if he says we ought to go there for dinner he probably knows what he's talking about. He wouldn't –'

Dorothy smiled and jumped up from the floor. 'I believe you. I won't be silly any more.'

I called the desk on the telephone and asked them to send up our mail. There were a couple of letters for Nora, one for me, some belated Christmas cards, a number of telephone-call memoranda slips, and a telegram from Philadelphia:

NICK CHARLES
THE NORMANDIE NEW YORK NY
WILL YOU COMMUNICATE WITH HERBERT MACAULAY
TO DISCUSS TAKING CHARGE OF INVESTIGATIONS
OF WOLF MURDER STOP AM GIVING HIM FULL
INSTRUCTIONS STOP BEST REGARDS
CLYDE MILLER WYNANT

I put the telegram in an envelope with a note saying it had just reached me and sent it by messenger to the Police Department Homicide Bureau.

10

In the taxicab Nora asked: 'You're sure you feel all right?'

'Sure.'

'And this isn't going to be too much for you?'

'I'm all right. What'd you think of the girl's story?'

She hesitated. 'You don't believe her, do you?'

'God forbid - at least till I've checked it up.'

'You know more about this kind of thing than I do,' she said, 'but I think she was at least trying to tell the truth.'

'A lot of the fancier yarns come from people who are trying to do that. It's not easy once you're out of the habit.'

She said: 'I bet you know a lot about human nature, Mr Charles. Now don't you? Sometimes you must tell me about your experiences as a detective.'

I said: 'Buying a gun for twelve bucks in a speakeasy. Well, maybe, but...'

We rode a couple of blocks in silence. Then Nora asked: 'What's really the matter with her?'

'Her old man's crazy: she thinks she is.'

'How do you know?'

'You asked me. I'm telling you.'

'You mean you're guessing?'

'I mean that's what's wrong with her; I don't know whether Wynant's actually nuts and I don't know whether she inherited any of it if he is, but she thinks both answers are yes, and it's got her doing figure eights.'

When we stopped in front of the Courtland she said: 'That's horrible, Nick. Somebody ought to –'

I said I didn't know: maybe Dorothy was right. 'Likely as not she's making doll clothes for Asta right now.'

We sent our names up to the Jorgensens and, after some delay, were told to go up. Mimi met us in the corridor when we stepped out of the elevator, met us with open arms and many words. 'Those wretched newspapers. They had me frantic with their nonsense about your being at death's door. I phoned twice, but they wouldn't give me your apartment, wouldn't tell me how you were.' She had both of my hands. 'I'm so glad, Nick, that it was just a pack of lies, even if you will have to take pot luck with us tonight. Naturally I didn't expect you and – But you're pale. You really have been hurt.'

'Not much,' I said. 'A bullet scraped my side, but it doesn't amount to anything.'

'And you came to dinner in spite of that! That is flattering, but I'm afraid it's foolish, too.' She turned to Nora. 'Are you sure it was wise to let him –'

'I'm not sure,' Nora said, 'but he wanted to come.'

'Men are such idiots,' Mimi said. She put an arm around me. 'They either make mountains out of nothing or utterly neglect things that may – But come in. Here, let me help you.'

'It's not that bad,' I assured her, but she insisted on leading me to a chair and packing me in with half a dozen cushions.

Jorgensen came in, shook hands with me, and said he was glad to find me more alive than the newspapers had said. He bowed over Nora's hand. 'If I may be excused one little minute more I will finish the cocktails.' He went out.

Mimi said: 'I don't know where Dorry is. Off sulking somewhere, I suppose. You haven't any children, have you?'

Nora said: 'No.'

'You're missing a lot, though they can be a great trial sometimes.' Mimi sighed. 'I suppose I'm not strict enough.

When I do have to scold Dorry she seems to think I'm a complete monster.' Her face brightened. 'Here's my other tot. You remember Mr Charles, Gilbert. And this is Mrs Charles.'

Gilbert Wynant was two years younger than his sister, a gangling, pale, blond boy of eighteen with not too much chin under a somewhat slack mouth. The size of his remarkably clear blue eyes, and the length of the lashes, gave him a slightly effeminate look. I hoped he had stopped being the whining little nuisance he was as a kid.

Jorgensen brought in his cocktails, and Mimi insisted on being told about the shooting. I told her, making it even more meaningless than it had been.

'But why should he have come to you?' she asked.

'God knows. I'd like to know. The police'd like to know.'

Gilbert said: 'I read somewhere that when habitual criminals are accused of things they didn't do – even little things – they're much more upset by it than other people would be. Do you think that's so, Mr Charles?'

'It's likely.'

'Except,' Gilbert added, 'when it's something big, you know, something they would like to've done.'

I said again it was likely.

Mimi said: 'Don't be polite to Gil if he starts talking nonsense, Nick. His head's so cluttered up with reading. Get us another cocktail, darling.'

He went over to get the shaker. Nora and Jorgensen were in a corner sorting gramophone records.

I said: 'I had a wire from Wynant today.'

Mimi looked warily around the room, then leaned forward, and her voice was almost a whisper: 'What did he say?'

'Wanted me to find out who killed her. It was sent from Philadelphia this afternoon.'

She was breathing heavily. 'Are you going to do it?'

I shrugged. 'I turned it over to the police.'

Gilbert came back with the shaker. Jorgensen and Nora had put Bach's *Little Fugue* on the gramophone. Mimi quickly drank her cocktail and had Gilbert pour her another.

He sat down and said: 'I want to ask you: can you tell dope-addicts by looking at them?' He was trembling.

'Very seldom. Why?'

'I was wondering. Even if they're confirmed addicts?'

'The further along they are, the better the chances of noticing that something's wrong, but you can't often be sure it's dope.'

'Another thing,' he said. 'Gross says when you're stabbed you only feel a sort of push at the time and it's not until afterwards that it begins to hurt. Is that so?'

'Yes, if you're stabbed reasonably hard with a reasonably sharp knife. A bullet's the same way: you only feel the blow – and with a small-calibre, steel-jacketed bullet not much of that – at first. The rest comes when the air gets to it.'

Mimi drank her third cocktail and said: 'I think you're both being indecently gruesome, especially after what happened to Nick today. Do try to find Dorry, Gil. You must know some of her friends. Phone them. I suppose she'll be along presently, but I worry about her.'

'She's over at our place,' I said.

'At your place?' Her surprise may have been genuine.

'She came over this afternoon and asked if she could stay with us a while.'

She smiled tolerantly and shook her head. 'These youngsters!' She stopped smiling. 'A while?'

I nodded.

Gilbert, apparently waiting to ask me another question, showed no interest in this conversation between his mother and me.

Mimi smiled again and said: 'I'm sorry she's bothering you and your wife, but it's a relief to know she's there instead of off the Lord only knows where. She'll have finished her pouting by the time you get back. Send her along home, will you?' She poured me a cocktail. 'You've been awfully nice to her.'

I did not say anything.

Gilbert began: 'Mr Charles, do criminals – I mean professional criminals – usually –'

'Don't interrupt, Gil,' Mimi said. 'You will send her along home, won't you?' She was pleasant, but she was Dorothy's Queen-of-France.

'She can stay if she wants. Nora likes her.'

She shook a crooked finger at me. 'But I won't have you spoiling her like that. I suppose she told you all sorts of nonsense about me.'

'She did say something about a beating.'

'There you are,' Mimi said complacently, as if that proved her point. 'No, you'll have to send her home, Nick.'

I finished my cocktail.

'Well?' she asked.

'She can stay with us if she wants, Mimi. We like having her.'

'That's ridiculous. Her place is at home. I want her here.' Her voice was a little sharp. 'She's only a baby. You shouldn't encourage her foolish notions.'

'I'm not doing anything. If she wants to stay, she stays.'

Anger was a very pretty thing in Mimi's blue eyes. 'She's my child and she's a minor. You've been very kind to her, but this isn't being kind to her or to me, and I won't have it. If you won't send her home, I'll take steps to bring her home. I'd rather not be disagreeable about it, but' – she leaned forward and deliberately spaced her words – 'she's coming home.'

I said: 'You don't want to pick a fight with me, Mimi.'

She looked at me as if she were going to say I love you, and asked: 'Is that a threat?'

'All right,' I said, 'have me arrested for kidnapping, contributing to the delinquency of a minor, and mopery.'

She said suddenly in a harsh enraged voice: 'And tell your wife to stop pawing my husband.'

Nora, looking for another gramophone record with Jorgensen, had a hand on his sleeve. They turned to look at Mimi in surprise.

I said: 'Nora, Mrs Jorgensen wants you to keep your hands off Mr Jorgensen.'

'I'm awfully sorry.' Nora smiled at Mimi, then looked at me, put a very artificial expression of concern on her face, and in a somewhat sing-song voice, as if she were a school child reciting a piece, said: 'Oh, Nick, you're pale. I'm sure you have exceeded your strength and will have a relapse. I'm sorry, Mrs Jorgensen, but I think I should get him home and to bed right away. You will forgive us, won't you?'

Mimi said, she would. Everybody was the soul of politeness to everybody else. We went downstairs and got a taxi-cab.

'Well,' Nora said, 'so you talked yourself out of a dinner. What do you want to do now? Go home and eat with Dorothy?'

I shook my head. 'I can do without Wynants for a little while. Let's go to Max's: I'd like some snails.'

'Right. Did you find out anything?'

'Nothing.'

She said meditatively: 'It's a shame that guy's so handsome.'

'What's he like?'

'Just a big doll. It's a shame.'

We had dinner and went back to the Normandie. Dorothy was not there. I felt as if I had expected that.

Nora went through the rooms, called up the desk. No note, no message had been left for us.

'So what?' she asked.

It was not quite ten o'clock. 'Maybe nothing,' I said. 'Maybe anything. My guess is she'll show up about three in the morning, tight, with a machine-gun she bought in Child's.'

Nora said: 'To hell with her. Get into pyjamas and lie down.'

11

My side felt a lot better when Nora called me at noon the next day. 'My nice policeman wants to see you,' she said. 'How do you feel?'

'Terrible. I must've gone to bed sober.' I pushed Asta out of the way and got up.

Guild rose with a drink in his hand when I entered the living-room, and smiled all across his broad, sandy face. 'Well, well, Mr Charles, you look spry enough this morning.'

I shook hands with him and said yes I felt pretty good, and we sat down.

He frowned good-naturedly. 'Just the same, you oughtn't've played that trick on me.'

'Trick?'

'Sure, running off to see people when I'd put off asking you questions to give you a chance to rest up. I kind of figured that ought to give me first call on you, as you might say.'

'I didn't think,' I said. 'I'm sorry. See that wire I got from Wynant?'

'Uh-huh. We're running it out in Philly.'

'Now about that gun,' I began, 'I –'

He stopped me. 'What gun? That ain't a gun any more. The firing pin's busted off, the guts are rusted and jammed. If anybody's fired it in six months – or could – I'm the Pope of Rome. Don't let's waste any time talking about that piece of junk.'

I laughed. 'That explains a lot. I took it away from a drunk who said he'd bought it in a speakeasy for twelve bucks. I believe him now.'

'Somebody'll sell him the City Hall one of these days. Man to man, Mr Charles, are you working on the Wolf job or ain't you?'

'You saw the wire from Wynant.'

'I did. Then you ain't working for him. I'm still asking you.'

'I'm not a private detective any more. I'm not any kind of a detective.'

'I heard that. I'm still asking you.'

'All right. No.'

He thought for a moment, said: 'Then let me put it another way: are you interested in the job?'

'I know the people, naturally I'm interested.'

'And that's all?'

'Yes.'

'And you don't expect to be working on it?'

The telephone rang and Nora went to answer it.

'To be honest with you, I don't know. If people keep on pushing me into it, I don't know how far they'll carry me.'

Guild wagged his head up and down. 'I can see that. I don't mind telling you I'd like to have you in on it – on the right side.'

'You mean not on Wynant's side. Did he do it?'

'That I couldn't say, Mr Charles, but I don't have to tell you he ain't helping us to find out who did it.'

Nora appeared in the doorway. 'Telephone, Nick.'

Herbert Macaulay was on the wire. 'Hello, Charles. How's the wounded?'

'I'm all right, thanks.'

'Did you hear from Wynant?'

'Yes.'

'I got a letter from him saying he had wired you. Are you too sick to –'

'No, I'm up and around. If you'll be in your office late this afternoon I'll drop in.'

'Swell,' he said. 'I'll be here till six.'

I returned to the living-room. Nora was inviting Guild to have lunch while we had breakfast. He said it was mighty kind of her. I said I ought to have a drink before breakfast. Nora went to order meals and pour drinks.

Guild shook his head and said: 'She's a mighty fine woman, Mr Charles.'

I nodded solemnly.

He said: 'Suppose you should get pushed into this thing, as you say, I'd like it a lot more to feel you were working with us than against us.'

'So would I.'

'That's a bargain then,' he said. He hunched his chair around a little. 'I don't guess you remember me, but back when you were working this town I was walking beat on Forty-third Street.'

'Of course,' I said, lying politely. 'I knew there was something familiar about – Being out of uniform makes a difference.'

'I guess it does. I'd like to be able to take it as a fact that you're not holding out anything we don't already know.'

'I don't mean to. I don't know what you know. I don't know very much. I haven't seen Macaulay since the murder and I haven't even been following it in the newspapers.'

The telephone was ringing again. Nora gave us our drinks and went to answer it.

'What we know ain't much of a secret,' Guild said, 'and if you want to take the time to listen I don't mind giving it to you.' He tasted his drink and nodded approvingly. 'Only there's a thing I'd like to ask first. When you went to Mrs Jorgensen's last night, did you tell her about getting the telegram from him?'

'Yes, and I told her I'd turned it over to you.'

'What'd she say?'

'Nothing. She asked questions. She's trying to find him.'

He put his head a little to one side and partly closed one eye. 'You don't think there's any chance of them being in cahoots, do you?' He held up a hand. 'Understand, I don't know why they would be or what it'd be all about if they were, but I'm just asking.'

'Anything's possible,' I said, 'but I'd say it was pretty safe they aren't working together. Why?'

'I guess you're right.' Then he added vaguely: 'But there's a couple of points.' He sighed. 'There always is. Well, Mr Charles, here's just about all we know for certain and if you can give us a little something more here and there as we go along I'll be mighty thankful to you.'

I said something about doing my best.

'Well, along about the 3rd of last October Wynant tells Macaulay he's got to leave town for a while. He don't tell Macaulay where he's going or what for, but Macaulay gets the idea that he's off to work on some invention or other that he wants to keep quiet – and he gets it out of Julia Wolf later that he's right – and he guesses Wynant's gone off to hide somewhere in the Adirondacks, but when he asks her about that later she says she don't know any more about it than he does.'

'She know what the invention was?'

Guild shook his head. 'Not according to Macaulay, only that it was probably something that he needed room for and machinery or things that cost money, because that's what he was fixing up with Macaulay. He was fixing it so Macaulay could get hold of his stocks and bonds and other things he owned and turn 'em into money when he wanted it and take care of his banking and everything just like Wynant himself.'

'Power of attorney covering everything, huh?'

'Exactly. And listen, when he wanted money, he wanted it in cash.'

'He was always full of screwy notions,' I said.

'That's what everybody says. The idea seems to be he don't want to take any chances on anybody tracing him through checks, or anybody up there knowing he's Wynant. That's why he didn't take the girl along with him – didn't even let her know where he was, if she was telling the truth – and let his whiskers grow.' With his left hand he stroked an imaginary beard.

"Up there",' I quoted. 'So he was in the Adirondacks?'

Guild moved one shoulder. 'I just said that because that and Philadelphia are the only ideas anybody's given us. We're trying the mountains, but we don't know. Maybe Australia.'

'And how much of this money in cash did Wynant want?'

'I can tell you that exactly.' He took a wad of soiled, bent and dog-eared papers out of his pocket, selected an envelope that was a shade dirtier than most of the others, and stuffed the others back in his pocket. 'The day after he talked to Macaulay he drew five thousand out of the bank himself, in cash. On the 28th – this is October, you understand – he had Macaulay get another five for him, and twenty-five hundred on the 6th of November, and a thousand on the 15th, and seventy-five hundred on the 30th, and fifteen hundred on the 6th – that would be December – and a thousand on the 18th, and five thousand on the 22nd, which was the day before she was killed.'

'Nearly thirty thou,' I said. 'A nice bank balance he had.'

'Twenty-eight thousand five hundred, to be exact.' Guild returned the envelope to his pocket. 'But, you understand, it wasn't all in there. After the first call Macaulay would sell something every time to raise the dough.' He felt in his pocket again. 'I got a list of the stuff he sold, if you want to see it.'

I said I didn't. 'How'd he turn the money over to Wynant?'

'Wynant would write the girl when he wanted it, and she'd get it from Macaulay. He's got her receipts.'

'And how'd she get it to Wynant?'

Guild shook his head. 'She told Macaulay she used to meet him places he told her, but he thinks she knew where he was, though she always said she didn't.'

'And maybe she still had that last five thousand on her when she was killed, huh?'

'Which might make it robbery, unless'– Guild's watery, gray eyes were almost shut – 'he killed her when he came there to get it.'

'Or unless,' I suggested, 'somebody else who killed her for some other reason, found the money there, and thought they might as well take it along.'

'Sure,' he agreed. 'Things like that happen all the time. It even happens sometimes that the first people that find a body like that pick up a little something before they turn in the alarm.' He held up a big hand. 'Of course, with Mrs Jorgensen – a lady like that – I hope you don't think I'm –'

'Besides,' I said, 'she wasn't alone, was she?'

'For a little while. The phone in the apartment was out of whack, and the elevator boy rode the superintendent down to phone from the office. But get me right on this, I'm not saying Mrs Jorgensen did anything funny. A lady like that wouldn't be likely –'

'What was the matter with the phone?' I asked.

The door-bell rang.

'Well,' Guild said, 'I don't know just what to make of it. The phone had –'

He broke off as a waiter came in and began to set a table.

'About the phone,' Guild said when we were sitting at the table, 'I don't know just what to make of it, as I said. It had a bullet right smack through the mouthpiece of it.'

'Accidental or –?'

'I'd just as lief ask you. It was from the same gun as the four that hit her, of course, but whether he missed her with that one or did it on purpose I don't know. It seems like a kind of noisy way to put a phone on the bum.'

'That reminds me,' I said, 'didn't anybody hear all this shooting? A .32's not a shotgun, but somebody ought to've heard it.'

'Sure,' he said disgustedly. 'The place is lousy with people that think they hear things now, but nobody did anything about it then, and God knows they don't get together much on what they think they heard.'

'It's always like that,' I said sympathetically.

'Don't I know it.' He put a forkful of food in his mouth. 'Where was I? Oh, yes, about Wynant. He gave up his apartment when he went away, and put his stuff in storage. We been looking through it – the stuff – but ain't found anything yet to show where he went or even what he was working on, which we thought maybe might help. We didn't have any better luck in his shop on First Avenue. It's been locked up too since he went away, except that she used to go down there for an hour or two twice a week to take care of his mail and things. There's nothing to tell us anything in the mail that's come since she got knocked off. We didn't find anything in her place to help.' He smiled at Nora. 'I guess this must be pretty dull to you, Mrs Charles.'

'Dull?' She was surprised. 'I'm sitting on the edge of my chair.'

'Ladies usually like more color,' he said, and coughed. 'Kind of glamour. Anyways, we got nothing to show where he's been, only he phones Macaulay last Friday and says to meet him at two o'clock in the Plaza lobby. Macaulay wasn't in, so he just left the message.'

'Macaulay was here,' I said, 'for lunch.'

'He told me. Well, Macaulay don't get to the Plaza till nearly three and he don't find any Wynant there and Wynant ain't registered there. He tried describing him, with and without a beard, but nobody at the Plaza remembers seeing him. He phones his office, but Wynant ain't called up again. And then he phones Julia Wolf and she tells him she don't even know Wynant's in town, which he figures is a lie, because he had just given her five thousand dollars for Wynant yesterday and figures Wynant's come for it, but he just says all right and hangs up and goes on about his business.'

'His business such as what?' I asked.

Guild stopped chewing the piece of roll he had just bitten off. 'I guess it wouldn't hurt to know, at that. I'll find out. There didn't seem to be anything pointing at him, so we didn't bother with that, but it don't ever hurt any to know who's got an alibi and who ain't.'

I shook my head no at the question he had decided not to ask. 'I don't see anything pointing at him, except that he's Wynant's lawyer and probably knows more than he's telling.'

'Sure. I understand. Well, that's what people have lawyers for, I guess. Now about the girl: maybe Julia Wolf wasn't her real name at all. We ain't been able to find out for sure yet, but we have found out she wasn't the kind of dame you'd expect him to be trusting to handle all that dough – I mean if he knew about her.'

'Had a record?'

He wagged a head up and down. 'This is elegant stew. A couple of years before she went to work for him she did six months on a badger-game charge out West, in Cleveland, under the name of Rhoda Stewart.'

'You suppose Wynant knew that?'

'Search me. Don't look like he'd've turned her loose with that dough if he did, but you can't tell. They tell me he was kind of nuts about her, and you know how guys can go. She was running around off and on with this Shep Morelli and his boys too.'

'Have you really got anything on him?' I asked.

'Not on this,' he said regretfully, 'but we wanted him for a couple of other things.' He drew his sandy brows together a little. 'I wish I knew what sent him here to see you. Of course these junkies are likely to do anything, but I wish I knew.'

'I told you all I knew.'

'I'm not doubting that,' he assured me. He turned to Nora. 'I hope you don't think we were too rough with him, but you see you got to –'

Nora smiled and said she understood perfectly and filled his cup with coffee.

'Thank you, ma'am.'

'What's a junkie?' she asked.

'Hop-head.'

She looked at me. 'Was Morelli – ?'

'Primed to the ears,' I said.

'Why didn't you tell me?' she complained. 'I miss everything.'

She left the table to answer the telephone.

Guild asked: 'You going to prosecute him for shooting you?'

'Not unless you need it.'

He shook his head. His voice was casual, though there was some curiosity in his eyes. 'I guess we got enough on him for a while.'

'You were telling me about the girl.'

'Yes,' he said. 'Well, we found out she's been spending a lot of nights away from her apartment – two or three days at a stretch sometimes. Maybe that's when she was meeting Wynant. I don't know. We ain't been able to knock any holes in Morelli's story of not seeing her for three months. What do you make of that?'

'The same thing you do,' I replied. 'It's just about three months since Wynant went off. Maybe it means something, maybe not.'

Nora came in and said Harrison Quinn was on the telephone. He told me he had sold some bonds I was writing off losses on and gave me the prices.

'Have you seen Dorothy Wynant?' I asked.

'Not since I left her in your place, but I'm meeting her at the Palma for cocktails this afternoon. Come to think of it, she told me not to tell you. How about that gold, Nick? You're missing something if you don't get in on it. Those wild men from the West are going to give us some kind of inflation as soon as Congress meets, that's certain, and even if they don't, everybody expects them to. As I told you last week, there's already talk of a pool being –'

'All right,' I said, and gave him an order to buy some Dome Mines at 12.

He remembered then that he had seen something in the newspapers about my having been shot. He was pretty vague about it and paid very little attention to my assurances that I was all right. 'I suppose that means no ping-pong for a couple of days,' he said with what seemed genuine regret. 'Listen: you've got tickets for the opening tonight. If you can't use them I'll be –'

'We're going to use them. Thanks just the same.'

He laughed and said good-bye.

A waiter was carrying away the table when I returned to the living-room. Guild had made himself comfortable on the sofa. Nora was telling him:- '... have to go away over the Christmas holidays every year because what's left of my family make a fuss over them and if we're home they come to visit us or we have to visit them, and Nick doesn't like it.' Asta was licking her paws in a corner.

Guild looked at his watch. 'I'm taking up a lot of you folks' time. I didn't mean to impose –'

I sat down and said: 'We were just about up to the murder, weren't we?'

'Just about.' He relaxed on the sofa again. 'That was on Friday the 23rd at some time before twenty minutes after three in the afternoon, which was the time Mrs Jorgensen got there and found her. It's kind of hard to say how long she'd been laying there dying before she was found. The only thing we know is that she was all right and answered the phone – and the phone was all right – at about half past two, when

Mrs Jorgensen called her up, and was still all right around three, when Macaulay phoned.'

'I didn't know Mrs Jorgensen phoned.'

'It's a fact.' Guild cleared his throat. 'We didn't suspect anything there, you understand, but we checked it up just as a matter of course and found out from the girl at the switchboard at the Courtland that she put the call through for Mrs J. about two-thirty.'

'What did Mrs J. say?'

'She said she called up to ask where she could find Wynant, but this Julia Wolf said she didn't know, so Mrs J., thinking she's lying and maybe she can get her to tell the truth if she sees her, asked if she can drop in for a minute, and she says sure.' He frowned at my right knee. 'Well, she went there and found her. The apartment-house people don't remember seeing anybody going in or out of the Wolf apartment, but that's easy. A dozen people could do it without being seen. The gun wasn't there. There wasn't any signs of anybody busting in, and things in the place hadn't been disturbed any more than I've told you. I mean the place didn't look like it had been frisked. She had on a diamond ring that must've been worth a few hundred and there was thirty-some bucks in her bag. The people there know Wynant and Morelli – both of 'em have been in and out enough – but claim they ain't seen either for some time. The fire-escape window was locked and the fire-escape didn't look like it had been walked on recently' He turned his hands over, palms up. 'I guess that's the crop.'

'No fingerprints?'

'Hers, some belonging to the people that clean up the place, near as we can figure. Nothing any good to us.'

'Nothing out of her friends?'

'She didn't seem to have any – not any close ones.'

'How about the – what was his name? – Nunheim who identified her as a friend of Morelli's?'

'He just knew her by sight through seeing her around with Morelli and recognized her picture when he saw it in the paper.'

'Who is he?'

'He's all right. We know all about him.'

'You wouldn't hold out on me, would you,' I asked, 'after getting me to promise not to hold out on you?'

Guild said: 'Well, if it don't go any further, he's a fellow that does some work for the department now and then.'

'Oh.'

He stood up. 'I hate to say it, but that's just about as far as we've got. You got anything you can help with?'

'No.'

He looked at me steadily for a moment. 'What do you think of it?'

'That diamond ring, was it an engagement ring?'

'She had it on that finger.' After a pause he asked: 'Why?'

'It might help to know who bought it for her. I'm going to see Macaulay this afternoon. If anything turns up I'll give you a ring. It looks like Wynant, all right, but –'

He growled good-naturedly: 'Uh-huh, but,' shook hands with Nora and me, thanked us for our whisky, our lunch, our hospitality, and our kindness in general, and went away.

I told Nora: 'I'm not one to suggest that your charm wouldn't make any man turn himself inside out for you, but don't be too sure that guy isn't kidding us.'

'So it's come to that,' she said. 'You're jealous of policemen.'

12

Macaulay's letter from Clyde Wynant was quite a document. It was very badly typewritten on plain, white paper and dated Philadelphia, Pa., December 26, 1932. It read:

Dear Herbert:

I am telegraphing Nick Charles who worked for me you will remember some years ago and who is in New York to get in touch with you about the terrible death of poor Julia. I want you to do everything in your power to [a line had been x'd and m'd out here so that it was impossible to make anything at all of it] persuade him to find her murderer. I don't care what it costs – pay him!

Here are some facts I want you to give him outside of all you know about it yourself. I don't think he should tell these facts to the police, but he will know what is best and I want him to have a completely free hand as I have got the utmost confidence in him. Perhaps you had better just show him this letter, after which I must ask you to carefully destroy it.

Here are the facts.

When I met Julia Thursday night to get that $1,000 from her she told me she wanted to quit her job. She said she hadn't been at all well for some time and her doctor had told her she ought to go away and rest and now that her uncle's estate had been settled she could afford to and wanted to do it. She had never said anything about bad health before and I thought she was hiding her real reason and tried to get it out of her, but she stuck to what she had said. I didn't know anything about her uncle dying either. She said it was her Uncle John in Chicago. I suppose that could be looked up if it's important. I couldn't persuade her to change her mind, so she was to leave the last day of the month. She seemed worried or frightened, but she said she wasn't. I was sorry at first that she was going, but then I wasn't, because I had always been able to trust her and now I wouldn't be if she was lying, as I thought she was.

The next fact I want Charles to know is that whatever anybody may think of whatever was true some time ago Julia and I ['are now' was x'd out lightly] were at the time of her murder *and had been for more than a year* not anything more to each other than employee and employer. This relationship was the result of mutual agreement.

Next, I believe some attempt should be made to learn the present whereabouts of the Victor Rosewater with whom we had trouble some years ago inasmuch as the experiments I am now engaged in are in line with those he claimed I cheated him out of and I consider him quite insane enough to have killed Julia in a rage at her refusal to tell him where I could be found.

Fourth, *and most important*, has my divorced wife been in communication with Rosewater? How did she learn I was carrying out experiments with which he once assisted me?

Fifth, the police must be convinced at once that I can tell them nothing about the murder so that they will take no steps to find me – steps that might lead to a discovery of and a premature exposure of my experiments, which I would consider *very dangerous* at this time. This can best be avoided by clearing up the mystery of her murder immediately, and that is what I wish to have done.

I will communicate with you from time to time and if in the meantime anything should arise to make communication with me *imperative* insert the following advertisement in the *Times*:

Abner. Yes. Bunny.

I will thereupon arrange to get in touch with you. I hope you sufficiently understand the necessity of persuading Charles to act for me, since he is already acquainted with the Rosewater trouble and knows most of the people concerned.

Yours truly,
CLYDE MILLER WYNANT

I put the letter down on Macaulay's desk and said: 'It makes a lot of sense. Do you remember what his row with Rosewater was about?'

'Something about changes in the structure of crystals. I can look it up.' Macaulay picked up the first sheet of the letter and frowned at it. 'He says he got a thousand dollars from her that night, I gave her five thousand for him; she told me that's what he wanted.'

'Four thousand from Uncle John's estate?' I suggested.

'Looks like it. That's funny: I never thought she'd gyp him. I'll have to find out about the other money I turned over to her.'

'Did you know she'd done a jail sentence in Cleveland on a badger-game charge?'

'No. Had she really?'

'According to the police – under the name of Rhoda Stewart. Where'd Wynant find her?'

He shook his head. 'I've no idea.'

'Know anything about where she came from originally, relatives, things like that?'

He shook his head again.

'Who was she engaged to?' I asked.

'I didn't know she was engaged.'

'She was wearing a diamond ring on that finger.'

'That's news to me,' he said. He shut his eyes and thought. 'No, I can't remember ever noticing an engagement ring.' He put his forearms on his desk and grinned over them at me. 'Well, what are the chances of getting you to do what he wants?'

'Slim.'

'I thought so.' He moved a hand to touch the letter. 'You know as much about how he feels as I do. What would make you change your mind?'

'I don't –'

'Would it help any if I could persuade him to meet you? Maybe if I told him that was the only way you'd take it –'

'I'm willing to talk to him,' I said, 'but he'd have to talk a lot straighter than he's writing.'

Macaulay asked slowly: 'You mean you think he may have killed her?'

'I don't know anything about that,' I said. 'I don't know as much as the police do, and it's a cinch they haven't got enough on him to make the pinch even if they could find him.'

Macaulay sighed. 'Being a goof's lawyer is not much fun. I'll try to make him listen to reason, but I know he won't.'

'I meant to ask, how are his finances these days? Is he as well fixed as he used to be?'

'Almost. The depression's hurt him some, along with the rest of us, and the royalties from his smelting process have gone pretty much to hell now that the metals are dead, but he can still count on fifty or sixty thousand a year from his glassine and sound-proofing patents, with a little more coming in from odds and ends like –' He broke off to ask: 'You're not worrying about his ability to pay whatever you ask?'

'No, I was just wondering.' I thought of something else: 'Has he any relatives outside of his ex-wife and children?'

'A sister, Alice Wynant, that hasn't been on speaking terms with him for – it must be four or five years now.'

'I supposed that was the Aunt Alice the Jorgensens had not gone to see Christmas afternoon. 'What'd they fall out about?' I asked.

'He gave an interview to one of the papers saying he didn't think the Russian Five-Year Plan was necessarily doomed to failure. Actually he didn't make it much stronger than that.'

I laughed. 'They're a –'

'She's even better than he is. She can't remember things. The time her brother had his appendix out, she and Mimi were in a taxi going to see him the first afternoon and they passed a hearse coming from the direction of the hospital. Miss Alice turned pale and grabbed Mimi by the arm and said: 'Oh dear! If that should be what's-his-name!'"

'Where does she live?'

'On Madison Avenue. It's in the phone book.' He hesitated. 'I don't think –'

'I'm not going to bother her.' Before I could say anything else his telephone began to ring.

He put the receiver to his ear and said: 'Hello... Yes, speaking... Who?... Oh, yes...' Muscles tightened around his mouth, and his eyes opened a little wider. 'Where?' He listened some more. 'Yes, surely. Can I make it?' He looked at his watch on his left wrist. 'Right. See you on the train.' He put the telephone down. 'That was Lieutenant Guild,' he told me. 'Wynant's tried to commit suicide in Allentown, Pennsylvania.'

13

Dorothy and Quinn were at the bar when I went into the Palma Club. They did not see me until I came up beside Dorothy and said: 'Hello, folks.' Dorothy had on the same clothes I had last seen her in. She looked at me and at Quinn and her face flushed. 'You had to tell him.'

'The girl's in a pet,' Quinn said cheerfully. 'I got that stock for you. You ought to pick up some more and what are you drinking?'

'Old-fashioned. You're a swell guest – ducking out without leaving a word behind you.'

Dorothy looked at me again. The scratches on her face were pale, the bruise barely showed, and her mouth was no longer swollen. 'I trusted you,' she said. She seemed about to cry.

'What do you mean by that?'

'You know what I mean. Even when you went to dinner at Mamma's I trusted you.'

'And why not?'

Quinn said: 'She's been in a pet all afternoon. Don't bait her.' He put a hand on one of hers. 'There, there, darling, don't you –'

'Please shut up.' She took her hand away from him. 'You know very well what I mean,' she told me. 'You and Nora both made fun of me to Mamma and –'

I began to see what had happened. 'She told you that and you believed it?' I laughed. 'After twenty years you're still a sucker for her lies? I suppose she phoned you after we left: we had a row and didn't stay long.'

She hung her head and said: 'Oh, I am a fool,' in a low miserable voice: 'Listen, let's go over and see Nora now. I've got to square myself with her. I'm such an ass. It'd serve me right if she never –'

'Sure. There's plenty of time. Let's have this drink first.'

Quinn said: 'Brother Charles, I'd like to shake your hand. You've brought sunshine back into the life of our little tot and joy to –' He emptied his glass. 'Let's go over and see Nora. The booze there is just as good and costs us less.'

'Why don't you stay here?' she asked him.

He laughed and shook his head. 'Not me. Maybe you can get Nick to stay here, but I'm going with you. I've put up with your snottiness all afternoon: now I'm going to bask in the sunshine.'

Gilbert Wynant was with Nora when we reached the Normandie. He kissed his sister and shook hands with me and, when he had been introduced, Harrison Quinn.

Dorothy immediately began to make long and earnest and none too coherent apologies to Nora.

Nora said: 'Stop it. There's nothing to forgive. If Nick's told you I was sore or hurt or anything of the sort he's just a Greek liar. Let me take your coat.'

Quinn turned on the radio. At the stroke of the gong it was five thirty-one and one quarter, Eastern Standard Time.

Nora told Quinn: 'Play bartender: you know where the stuff is,' and followed me into the bathroom. 'Where'd you find her?'

'In a speak. What's Gilbert doing here?'

'He came over to see her, so he said. She didn't go home last night and he thought she was still here.' She laughed. 'He wasn't surprised at not finding her, though. He said she was always wandering off somewhere, she has dromomania, which comes from a mother-fixation, and is very interesting. He said Stekel claims people who have it usually show kleptomaniac impulses, too, and he's left things around to see if she'd steal them, but she never has yet that he knows of.'

'He's quite a lad. Did he say anything about his father?'

'No.'

'Maybe he hadn't heard. Wynant tried to commit suicide down in Allentown. Guild and Macaulay have gone down to see him. I don't know whether to tell the youngsters or not. I wonder if Mimi had a hand in his coming over here.'

'I wouldn't think so, but if you do –'

'I'm just wondering,' I said. 'Has he been here long?'

'About an hour. He's a funny kid. He's studying Chinese and writing a book on Knowledge and Belief – not in Chinese – and thinks Jack Oakie's very good.'

'So do I. Are you tight?'

'Not very.'

When we returned to the living-room, Dorothy and Quinn were dancing to *Eadie was a Lady*.

Gilbert put down the magazine he was looking at and politely said he hoped I was recovering from my injury.

I said I was.

'I've never been hurt, really hurt,' he went on, 'that I can remember. I've tried hurting myself, of course, but that's not the same thing. It just made me uncomfortable and irritable and sweat a lot.'

'That's pretty much the same thing,' I said.

'Really? I thought there'd be more – well, more to it.' He moved a little closer to me. 'It's things like that I don't know. I'm so horribly young I haven't had a chance to – Mr Charles, if you're too busy or don't want to, I hope you'll say so, but I'd appreciate it very much if you'd let me talk to you some time when there aren't a lot of people around to interrupt us. There are so many things I'd like to ask you, things I don't know anybody else could tell me and –'

'I'm not so sure about that,' I said, 'but I'll be glad to try any time you want.'

'You really don't mind? You're not just being polite?'

'No, I mean it, only I'm not sure you'll get as much help as you expect. It depends on what you want to know.'

'Well, things like cannibalism,' he said. 'I don't mean in places like Africa and New Guinea – in the United States, say. Is there much of it?'

'Not nowadays. Not that I know of.'

'Then there was once?'

'I don't know how much, but it happened now and then before the country was completely settled. Wait a minute: I'll give you a sample.' I went over to the bookcase and got the copy of Duke's *Celebrated Criminal Cases of America* that Nora had picked up in a second-hand book store, found the place I wanted, and gave it to him. 'It's only three or four pages.'

ALFRED G. PACKER. THE 'MANEATER', WHO MURDERED HIS FIVE COMPANIONS IN THE MOUNTAINS OF COLORADO, ATE THEIR BODIES AND STOLE THEIR MONEY.

'In the fall of 1873 a party of twenty daring men left Salt Lake City, Utah, to prospect in the San Juan country. Having heard glowing accounts of the fortunes to be made, they were light-hearted and full of hope as they started on their journey, but as the weeks rolled by and they beheld nothing but barren wastes and snowy mountains, they grew despondent. The farther they proceeded, the less inviting appeared the country, and they finally became desperate when it appeared that their only reward would be starvation and death.

'Just as the prospectors were about to give up in despair, they saw an Indian camp in the distance, and while they had no assurance as to what treatment they would receive at the hands of the 'Reds", they decided that any death was preferable to starvation, so they agreed to take a chance.

'When they approached the camp they were met by an Indian who appeared to be friendly and escorted them to Chief Ouray. To their great surprise, the Indians treated them with every consideration and insisted upon their remaining in the camp until they had fully recuperated from their hardships.

'Finally the party decided to make another start, with the Los Pinos Agency as their goal. Ouray attempted to dissuade them from continuing the journey, and did succeed in influencing ten of the party to abandon the trip and return to Salt Lake. The other ten determined to continue, so Ouray supplied them with provisions and admonished them to follow the Gunnison River, which was named after Lieutenant Gunnison, who was murdered in 1852. (See life of Joe Smith, the Mormon.)

'Alfred G. Packer, who appeared as the leader of the party which continued the journey, boasted of his knowledge of the topography of the country and expressed confidence in his ability to find his way without difficulty. When his party had traveled a short distance, Packer told them that rich mines had recently been discovered near the headquarters of the Rio Grande River, and he offered to guide the party to the mines.

'Four of the party insisted that they follow Ouray's instructions, but Packer persuaded five men, named Swan, Miller, Noon, Bell and Humphrey, to accompany him to the mines, while the other four proceeded along the river.

'Of the party of four, two died from starvation and exposure, but the other two finally reached the Los Pinos Agency in February, 1874, after enduring indescribable hardships. General Adams was in command of this agency, and the unfortunate men were treated with every consideration. When they regained their strength they started back to civilization.

'In March, 1874, General Adams was called to Denver on business, and one cold, blizzardy morning, while he was still away, the employees of the agency, who were seated at the breakfast table, were startled by the appearance at the door of a wild-looking man who begged piteously for food and shelter. His face was frightfully bloated but otherwise he appeared to be in fairly good condition, although his stomach would not retain the food given him. He stated that his name was Packer and claimed that his five companions had deserted him while he was ill, but had left a rifle with him which he brought into the Agency.

After partaking of the hospitality of the employees at the Agency for ten days, Packer proceeded to a place called Saquache, claiming that he intended to work his way to Pennsylvania, where he had a brother. At Saquache, Packer drank heavily and appeared to be well supplied with money. While intoxicated, he told many conflicting stories regarding the fate of his companions, and it was suspected that he had disposed of his erstwhile associates by foul means.

'At this time General Adams stopped at Saquache on his return from Denver to the Agency, and while at the home of Otto Mears he was advised to arrest Packer and investigate his movements. The General decided to take him back to the Agency, and while *en route* they stopped at the cabin of Major Downey, where they met the ten men who listened to the Indian chief and abandoned the trip. It was then proven that a great part of Packer's statement was false, so the General decided that the matter required a complete investigation, and Packer was bound and taken to the Agency, where he was held in close confinement.

'On April 2, 1874, two wildly excited Indians ran into the Agency, holding strips of flesh in their hands which they called 'white man's meat", and which they stated they found just outside the Agency. As it had been lying on the snow and the weather had been extremely cold, it was still in good condition.

'When Packer caught sight of the exhibits, his face became livid, and with a low moan he sank to the floor. Restoratives were administered and after pleading for mercy, he made a statement substantially as follows:

"When I and five others left Ouray's camp, we estimated that we had sufficient provisions for the long and arduous journey before us, but our food rapidly disappeared and we were soon on the verge of starvation. We dug roots from the ground upon which we subsisted for some days, but as they were not nutritious and as the extreme cold had driven all animals and birds to shelter, the situation became desperate. Strange looks came into the eyes of each of the party and they all became suspicious of each other. One day I went out to gather wood for the fire and when I returned I found that Mr Swan, the oldest man in the party, had been struck on the head and killed, and the remainder of the party were in the act of cutting up the body preparatory to eating it. His money, amounting to $2,000, was divided among the remainder of the party.

"This food only lasted a few days, and I suggested that Miller be the next victim because of the large amount of flesh he carried. His skull was split open with a hatchet as he was in the act of picking up a piece of wood. Humphrey and Noon were the next victims. Bell and I then entered into a solemn compact that as we were the only ones left we would stand by each other whatever befell, and rather than harm each other we would die of starvation. One day Bell said: 'I can't stand it no longer,' and he rushed at me like a famished tiger, at the same time attempting to strike me with his gun. I parried the blow and killed him with a hatchet. I then cut his flesh into strips which I carried with me as I pursued my journey. When I espied the Agency from the top of the hill, I threw away the strips I had left, and I confess I did so reluctantly as I had grown fond of human flesh, especially that portion around the breast."

'After relating this gruesome story, Packer agreed to guide a party in charge of H. Lauter to the remains of the murdered men. He led them to some high, inaccessible mountains, and as he claimed to be bewildered, it was decided to abandon the search and start back the next day.

'That night Packer and Lauter slept side by side, and during the night Packer assaulted him with the intent to commit murder and escape, but he was overpowered, bound, and after the party reached the Agency, he was turned over to the Sheriff.

'Early in June of that year, an artist named Reynolds, from Peoria, while sketching along the shores of Lake Christoval, discovered the remains of the five men lying in a grove of hemlocks. Four of the bodies were lying in a row, and the fifth, minus the head, was found a short distance away. The bodies of Bell, Swan, Humphreys and Noon had rifle bullet wounds in the back of the head, and when Miller's body was found it was crushed in, evidently by a blow from a rifle which was lying near by, the stock being broken from the barrel.

'The appearance of the bodies clearly indicated that Packer had been guilty of cannibalism as well as murder. He probably spoke the truth when he stated his preference for the breast of man, as in each instance the entire breast was cut away to the ribs.

'A beaten path was found leading from the bodies to a near-by cabin, where blankets and other articles belonging to the murdered men were discovered, and everything indicated that Packer lived in this cabin for many days after the murders, and that he made frequent trips to the bodies for his supply of human meat.

'After these discoveries the Sheriff procured warrants charging Packer with five murders, but during his absence the prisoner escaped.

'Nothing was heard of him again until January 29, 1883, nine years later, when General Adams received a letter from

Cheyenne, Wyoming, in which a Salt Lake prospector stated that he had met Packer face to face in that locality. The informant stated that the fugitive was known as John Schwartze, and was suspected of being engaged in operations with a gang of outlaws.

'Detectives began an investigation, and on March 12, 1883, Sheriff Sharpless of Laramie County arrested Packer, and on the 17th inst. Sheriff Smith of Hindale County brought the prisoner back to Lake City, Col.

'His trial on the charge of murdering Israel Swan in Hinsdale County on March 1, 1874, was begun on April 3, 1883. It was proven that each member of the party except Packer possessed considerable money. The defendant repeated his former statement, wherein he claimed that he had only killed Bell, and had done so in self-defence.

'On April 13, the jury found the defendant guilty with the death penalty attached. A stay of execution was granted to Packer, who immediately appealed to the Supreme Court. In the meantime he was transferred to the Gunnison jail to save him from mob violence.

'In October, 1885, the Supreme Court granted a new trial and it was then decided to bring him to trial on five charges of manslaughter. He was found guilty on each charge and was sentenced to serve eight years for each offence, making a total of forty years.

'He was pardoned on January 1, 1901, and died on a ranch near Denver on April 24, 1907.'

While Gilbert was reading this, I got myself a drink. Dorothy stopped dancing to join me. 'Do you like him?' she asked, jerking her head to indicate Quinn.

'He's all right.'

'Maybe, but he can be terribly silly. You didn't ask me where I stayed last night. Don't you care?'

'It's none of my business.'

'But I found out something for you.'

'What?'

'I stayed at Aunt Alice's. She's not exactly right in the head, but she's awfully sweet. She told me she had a letter from my father today warning her against Mamma.'

'Warning her now? Just what did he say?'

'I didn't see it. Aunt Alice has been mad with him for several years and she tore it up. She says he's become a Communist and she's sure the Communists killed Julia Wolf and will kill him in the end. She thinks it's all over some secret betrayed.'

I said: 'Oh my God!'

'Well, don't blame me. I'm just telling you what she told me. I told you she wasn't exactly right in the head.'

'Did she tell you that junk was in the letter?'

Dorothy shook her head. 'No. She only said the warning was. As near as I remember she said he wrote her not to trust Mamma under any circumstances and not to trust anybody connected with her, which I suppose means all of us.'

'Try to remember more.'

'But there wasn't any more. That's all she told me.'

'Where was the letter from?' I asked.

'She didn't know – except that it had come airmail. She said she wasn't interested.'

'What did she think of it? I mean, did she take the warning seriously?'

'She said he was a dangerous radical – they're her very words – and she wasn't interested in anything he had to say.'

'How seriously do you take it?'

She stared at me for a long moment and she moistened her lips before she spoke. 'I think he –'

Gilbert, book in hand, came over to us. He seemed disappointed in the story I had given him. 'It's very interesting,' he said, 'but if you know what I mean, it's not a pathological case.' He put an arm around his sister's waist. 'It was more a matter of that or starving.'

'Not unless you want to believe him,' I said.

Dorothy asked: 'What is it?'

'A thing in the book,' Gilbert replied.

'Tell him about the letter your aunt got,' I said to Dorothy.

She told him.

When she had finished, he grimaced impatiently. 'That's silly. Mamma's not really dangerous. She's just a case of arrested development. Most of us have outgrown ethics and morals and so on. Mamma's just not grown up to them yet.' He frowned and corrected himself thoughtfully: 'She might be dangerous, but it would be like a child playing with matches.'

Nora and Quinn were dancing.

'And what do you think of your father?' I asked.

Gilbert shrugged. 'I haven't seen him since I was a child. I've got a theory about him, but a lot of it's guesswork. I'd like – the chief thing I'd like to know is if he's impotent.'

I said: 'He tried to kill himself today, down in Allentown.'

Dorothy cried: 'He didn't,' so sharply that Quinn and Nora stopped dancing, and she turned and thrust her face up at her brother's. 'Where's Chris?' she demanded.

Gilbert looked from her face to mine and quickly back to hers. 'Don't be an ass,' he said coldly. 'He's off with that girl of his, that Fenton girl.'

Dorothy did not look as if she believed him.

'She's jealous of him,' he explained to me. 'It's that mother-fixation.'

I asked: 'Did either of you ever see the Victor Rosewater your father had trouble with back when I first knew you?'

Dorothy shook her head. Gilbert said: 'No. Why?'

'Just an idea I had. I never saw him either, but the description they gave me, with some easy changes, could be made to fit your Chris Jorgensen.'

14

That night Nora and I went to the opening of the Radio City Music Hall, decided we had had enough of the performance after an hour, and left. 'Where to?' Nora asked.

'I don't care. Want to hunt up that Pigiron Club that Morelli told us about? You'll like Studsy Burke. He used to be a safe-burglar. He claims to've cracked the safe in the Hagerstown jail while he was doing thirty days there for disorderly conduct.'

'Let's,' she said.

We went down to Forty-ninth Street and, after asking two taxi-drivers, two newsboys, and a policeman, found the place. The doorman said he didn't know about any Burkes, but he'd see. Studsy came to the door. 'How are you, Nick?' he said. 'Come on in.'

He was a powerfully built man of medium height, a little fat now, but not soft. He must have been at least fifty, but looked ten years younger than that. He had a broad, pleasantly ugly, pock-marked face under not much hair of no particular color, and even his baldness could not make his forehead seem large. His voice was a deep bass growl.

I shook hands with him and introduced him to Nora.

'A wife,' he said. 'Think of that. By God, you'll drink champagne or you'll fight me.'

I said we wouldn't fight and we went inside. His place had a comfortably shabby look. It was between hours: there were only three customers in the place. We sat at a table in a corner and Studsy told the waiter exactly which bottle of wine to bring. Then he examined me carefully and nodded. 'Marriage done you good.' He scratched his chin. 'It's a long time I don't see you.'

'A long time,' I agreed.

'He sent me up the river,' he told Nora.

She clucked sympathetically. 'Was he a good detective?' Studsy wrinkled what forehead he had. 'Folks say, but I don't know. The once he caught me was an accident: I led with my right.'

'How come you sicked this wild man Morelli on me?' I asked.

'You know how foreigners are,' he said; 'they're hysterical. I don't know he's going to do nothing like that. He's worrying about the coppers trying to hang that Wolf dame's killing on him and we see in the paper you got something to do with it and I say to him: 'Nick might not maybe sell his own mother out and you feel like you got to talk to somebody," so he says he will. What'd you do, make faces at him?'

'He let himself be spotted sneaking in and then blamed me for it. How'd he find me?'

'He's got friends and you wasn't hiding, was you?'

'I'd only been in town a week and there was nothing in the paper saying where I was staying.'

'Is that so?' Studsy asked with interest. 'Where you been?'

'I live in San Francisco now. How'd he find me?'

'That's a swell town. I ain't been there in years, but it's one swell town. I oughtn't to tell you, Nick. Ask him. It's his business.'

'Except that you sent him to me.'

'Well, yes,' he said, 'except that, of course; but then, see, I was putting in a boost for you.' He said it seriously.

I said: 'My pal.'

'How did I know he was going to blow his top? Anyways, he didn't hurt you much, did he?'

'Maybe not, but it didn't do me any good and I –' I stopped as the waiter arrived with the champagne. We tasted it and said it was swell. It was pretty bad. 'Think he killed the girl?' I asked.

Studsy shook his head sidewise with certainty. 'No chance.'

'He's a fellow you can persuade to shoot,' I said.

'I know – these foreigners are hysterical – but he was around here all that afternoon.'

'All?'

'All. I'll take my oath to it. Some of the boys and girls were celebrating upstairs and I know for a fact he wasn't off his hip, let alone out of here, all afternoon. No kidding, that's a thing he can prove.'

'Then what was he worried about?'

'Do I know? Ain't that what I been asking him myself? But you know how these foreigners are.'

I said: 'Uh-huh. They're hysterical. He wouldn't've sent a friend around to see her, would he?'

'I think you got the boy wrong,' Studsy said. 'I knew the dame. She used to come in here with him sometimes. They was just playing. He wasn't nuts enough about her that he'd have any reason for weighting her down like that. On the level.'

'Was she on the stuff, too?'

'I don't know. I seen her take it sometimes, but maybe she was just being sociable, taking a shot because he did.'

'Who else did she play around with?'

'Nobody I know,' Studsy replied indifferently. 'There was a rat named Nunheim used to come in here that was on the make for her, but he didn't get nowhere that I could see.'

'So that's where Morelli got my address.'

'Don't be silly. All Morelli'd want of him would be a crack at him. What's it to him telling the police Morelli knew the dame? A friend of yours?'

I thought it over and said: 'I don't know him. I hear he does chores for the police now and then.'

'M-m-m. Thanks.'

'Thanks for what? I haven't said anything.'

'Fair enough. Now you tell me something: what's all this fiddlededee about, huh? That guy Wynant killed her, didn't he?'

'A lot of people think so,' I said, 'but fifty bucks'll get you a hundred he didn't.'

He shook his head. 'I don't bet with you in your own racket' – his face brightened – 'but I tell you what I will do and we can put some dough on it if you want. You know that time you copped me, I did lead with my right like I said, and I always wondered if you could do it again. Some time when you're feeling well I'd like –'

I laughed and said: 'No, I'm all out of condition.'

'I'm hog-fat myself,' he insisted.

'Besides that was a fluke: you were off balance and I was set.'

'You're just trying to let me down easy,' he said, and then more thoughtfully, 'though, I guess you did get the breaks at that. Well, if you won't – Here, let me fill your glasses.'

Nora decided that she wanted to go home early and sober, so we left Studsy and his Pigiron Club at a little after eleven o'clock. He escorted us to a taxicab and shook our hands vigorously. 'This has been a fine pleasure,' he told us.

We said equally polite things and rode away.

Nora thought Studsy was marvelous. 'Half his sentences I can't understand at all.'

'He's all right.'

'You didn't tell him you'd quit gumshoeing.'

'He'd've thought I was trying to put something over on him,' I explained. 'To a mug like him, once a sleuth always a sleuth, and I'd rather lie to him than have him think I'm lying. Have you got a cigarette? He really trusts me, in a way.'

'Were you telling the truth when you said Wynant didn't kill her?'

'I don't know. My guess is I was.'

At the Normandie there was a telegram for me from Macaulay in Allentown:

> MAN HERE IS NOT WYNANT AND DID NOT TRY TO COMMIT SUICIDE.

15

I had a stenographer in the next morning and got rid of most of the mail that had been accumulating; had a telephone conversation with our lawyer in San Francisco – we were trying to keep one of the mill's customers from being thrown into bankruptcy; spent an hour going over a plan we had for lowering our state taxes; was altogether the busy business man, and felt pretty virtuous by two o'clock, when I knocked off work for the day and went out to lunch with Nora.

She had a date to play bridge after lunch. I went down to see Guild: I had talked to him on the telephone earlier in the day.

'So it was a false alarm?' I said after we had shaken hands and made ourselves comfortable in chairs.

'That's what it was. He wasn't any more Wynant than I am. You know how it is: we told the Philly police he'd sent a wire from there and broadcasted his description, and for the next week anybody that's skinny and maybe got whiskers is Wynant to half of the State of Pennsylvania. This was a fellow named Barlow, a carpenter out of work as near as we can figure out, that got shot by a nigger trying to stick him up. He can't talk much yet.'

'He couldn't've been shot by somebody who made the same mistake the Allentown police did?' I asked.

'You mean thought he was Wynant? I guess that could be – if it helps any. Does it?'

I said I didn't know. 'Did Macaulay tell you about the letter he got from Wynant?'

'He didn't tell me what was in it.'

I told him. I told him what I knew about Rosewater.

He said: 'Now, that's interesting.'

I told him about the letter Wynant had sent his sister.

He said: 'He writes a lot of people, don't he?'

'I thought of that.' I told him Victor Rosewater's description with a few easy changes would fit Christian Jorgensen.

He said: 'It don't hurt any to listen to a man like you. Don't let me stop you.'

I told him that was the crop.

He rocked back in his chair and screwed his pale gray eyes up at the ceiling. 'There's some work to be done there,' he said presently.

'Was this fellow in Allentown shot with a .32?' I asked.

Guild stared curiously at me for a moment, then shook his head. 'A .44. You got something on your mind?'

'No. Just chasing the set-up around in my head.'

He said: 'I know what that is,' and leaned back to look at the ceiling some more. When he spoke again it was as if he was thinking of something else. 'That alibi of Macaulay's you was asking about is all right. He was late for a date then and we know for a fact he was in a fellow's office named Hermann on Fifty-seventh Street from five minutes after three till twenty after, the time that counts.'

'What's the five minutes after three?'

'That's right, you don't know about that. Well, we found a fellow named Caress with a cleaning and dyeing place on First Avenue that called her up at five minutes after three to ask her if she had any work for him, and she said no and told him she was liable to go away. So that narrows the time down to from three-five to three-twenty. You ain't really suspicious of Macaulay?'

'I'm suspicious of everybody,' I said. 'Where were you between three-five and three-twenty?'

He laughed. 'As a matter of fact,' he said, 'I'm just about the only one of the lot that ain't got an alibi. I was at the moving pictures.'

'The rest of them have?'

He wagged his head up and down. 'Jorgensen left his place with Mrs Jorgensen – that was about five minutes to three – and sneaked over on West Seventy-third Street to see a girl named Olga Fenton – we promised not to tell his wife – and stayed there till about five. We know what Mrs Jorgensen did. The daughter was dressing when they left and she took a taxi at a quarter past and went straight to Bergdorf-Goodman's. The son was in the Public Library all afternoon – God, he reads funny books. Morelli was in a joint over in the Forties.' He laughed. 'And where was you?'

'I'm saving mine till I really need it. None of those look too air-tight, but legitimate alibis seldom do. How about Nunheim?'

Guild seemed surprised. 'What makes you think of him?'

'I hear he had a yen for the girl.'

'And where'd you hear it?'

'I heard it.'

He scowled. 'Would you say it was reliable?'

'Yes.'

'Well,' he said slowly, 'he's one guy we can check up on. But look here, what do you care about these people? Don't you think Wynant done it?'

I gave him the same odds I had given Studsy: 'Twenty-five'll get you fifty he didn't.'

He scowled at me over that for a long silent moment, then said: 'That's an idea, anyways. Who's your candidate?'

'I haven't got that far yet. Understand, I don't know anything. I'm not saying Wynant didn't do it. I'm just saying everything doesn't point at him.'

'And saying it two to one. What don't point at him?'

'Call it a hunch, if you want,' I said, 'but –'

'I don't want to call it anything,' he said. 'I think you're a smart detective. I want to listen to what you got to say.'

'Mostly I've got questions to say. For instance, how long was it from the time the elevator boy let Mrs Jorgensen off at the Wolf girl's floor until she rang for him and said she heard groans?'

Guild pursed his lips, opened them to ask: 'You think she might've –?' and left the rest of the question hanging in the air.

'I think she might've. I'd like to know where Nunheim was. I'd like to know the answers to the questions in Wynant's letter. I'd like to know where the four-thousand-dollar difference between what Macaulay gave the girl and what she seems to have given Wynant went. I'd like to know where her engagement ring came from.'

'We're doing the best we can,' Guild said. 'Me – just now I'd like to know why, if he didn't do it, Wynant don't come in and answer questions for us.'

'One reason might be that Mrs Jorgensen'd like to slam him in the squirrel cage again.' I thought of something. 'Herbert Macaulay's working for Wynant: you didn't just take Macaulay's word for it that the man in Allentown wasn't him?'

'No. He was a younger man than Wynant, with damned little gray in his hair and no dye, and he didn't look like the pictures we got.' He seemed positive. 'You got anything to do the next hour or so?'

'No.'

'That's fine.' He stood up. 'I'll get some of the boys working on these things we been discussing and then maybe me and you will pay some visits.'

'Swell,' I said, and he went out of the office.

There was a copy of the *Times* in his waste-basket. I fished it out and turned to the Public Notices columns. Macaulay's advertisement was there:

'Abner. Yes. Bunny.'

When Guild returned I asked: 'How about Wynant's help, whoever he had working in the shop? Have they been looked up?'

'Uh-huh, but they don't know anything. They was laid off at the end of the week that he went away – there's two of them – and haven't seen him since.'

'What were they working on when the shop was closed?'

'Some kind of paint or something – something about a permanent green. I don't know. I'll find out if you want.'

'I don't suppose it matters. Is it much of a shop?'

'Looks like a pretty good lay-out, far as I can tell. You think the shop might have something to do with it?'

'Anything might.'

'Uh-huh. Well, let's run along.'

16

'First thing,' Guild said as we left his office, 'we'll go see Mr Nunheim. He ought to be home: I told him to stick around till I phoned him.'

Mr Nunheim's home was on the fourth floor of a dark, damp, and smelly building made noisy by the Sixth Avenue elevated. Guild knocked on the door.

There were sounds of hurried movements inside, then a voice asked: 'Who is it?' The voice was a man's, nasal, somewhat irritable.

Guild said, 'John.'

The door was hastily opened by a small, sallow man of thirty-five or -six whose visible clothes were an undershirt, blue pants, and black silk stockings. 'I wasn't expecting you, Lieutenant,' he whined. 'You said you'd phone.' He seemed frightened. His dark eyes were small and set close together; his mouth was wide, thin, and loose; and his nose was peculiarly limber, a long, drooping nose, apparently boneless.

Guild touched my elbow with his hand and we went in. Through an open door to the left an unmade bed could be seen. The room we entered was a living-room, shabby and dirty, with clothing, newspapers, and dirty dishes sitting around. In an alcove to the right there was a sink and a stove. A woman stood between them holding a sizzling skillet in her hand. She was a big-boned, full-fleshed, red-haired woman of perhaps twenty-eight, handsome in a rather brutal, sloppy way.

She wore a rumpled pink kimono and frayed pink mules with lopsided bows on them. She stared sullenly at us.

Guild did not introduce me to Nunheim and he paid no attention to the woman. 'Sit down,' he said, and pushed some clothing out of the way to make a place for himself on an end of the sofa.

I removed part of a newspaper from a rocking-chair and sat down. Since Guild kept his hat on I did the same with mine.

Nunheim went over to the table, where there was about two inches of whisky in a pint bottle and a couple of tumblers, and said: 'Have a shot?'

Guild made a face. 'Not that vomit. What's the idea of telling me you just knew the Wolf girl by sight?'

'That's all I did, Lieutenant, that's the truth.' Twice his eyes slid sidewise towards me and he jerked them back. 'Maybe I said hello to her, or how are you or something like that when I saw her, but that's all I knew her. That's the truth.'

The woman in the alcove laughed, once, derisively, and there was no merriment in her face.

Nunheim twisted himself around to face her. 'All right,' he told her, his voice shrill with rage, 'put your mouth in and I'll pop a tooth out of it.'

She swung her arm and let the skillet go at his head. It missed, crashing into the wall. Grease and egg-yolks made fresher stains on wall, floor, and furniture.

He started for her. I did not have to rise to put out a foot and trip him. He tumbled down on the floor. The woman had picked up a paring knife.

'Cut it out,' Guild growled. He had not stood up either. 'We come here to talk to you, not to watch this rough-house comedy. Get up and behave yourself.'

Nunheim got slowly to his feet. 'She drives me nuts when she's drinking,' he said. 'She's been nagging me all day.' He moved his right hand back and forth. 'I think I sprained my wrist.'

The woman walked past us without looking at any of us, went into the bedroom, and shut the door.

Guild said: 'Maybe if you'd quit sucking around after other women you wouldn't have so much trouble with this one.'

'What do you mean, Lieutenant?' Nunheim was surprised and innocent and perhaps pained.

'Julia Wolf.'

The little sallow man was indignant now. 'That's a lie, Lieutenant. Anybody that says I ever –'

Guild interrupted him by addressing me: 'If you want to take a poke at him, I wouldn't stop on account of his bum wrist: he couldn't even hit hard anyhow.'

Nunheim turned to me with both hands out. 'I didn't mean you were a liar. I meant maybe somebody made a mistake if they –'

Guild interrupted him again: 'You wouldn't've taken her if you could've got her?'

Nunheim moistened his lower lip and looked warily at the bedroom door. 'Well,' he said slowly in a cautiously low voice, 'of course she was a classy number. I guess I wouldn't've turned it down.'

'But you never tried to make her?'

Nunheim hesitated; then moved his shoulders and said: 'You know how it is. A fellow knocking around tries most everything he runs into.'

Guild looked sourly at him. 'You'd done better to tell me that in the beginning. Where were you the afternoon she was knocked off?'

The little man jumped as if he had been stuck with a pin. 'For Christ's sake, Lieutenant, you don't think I had anything to do with that. What would I want to hurt her for?'

'Where were you?'

Nunheim's loose lips twitched nervously. 'What day was she –' He broke off as the bedroom door opened.

The big woman came out carrying a suitcase. She had put on street clothes.

'Miriam,' Nunheim said.

She stared at him dully and said: 'I don't like crooks, and even if I did, I wouldn't like crooks that are stool-pigeons, and if I liked crooks that are stool-pigeons, I still wouldn't like you.' She turned to the outer door.

Guild, catching Nunheim's arms to keep him from following the woman, repeated: 'Where were you?'

Nunheim called: 'Miriam. Don't go. I'll behave, I'll do anything. Don't go, Miriam.'

She went out and shut the door.

'Let me go,' he begged Guild. 'Let me bring her back. I can't get along without her. I'll bring her right back and tell you anything you want to know. Let me go. I've got to have her.'

Guild said: 'Nuts. Sit down.' He pushed the little man down in a chair. 'We didn't come here to watch you and that broad dance around a maypole. Where were you the afternoon the girl was killed?'

Nunheim put his hands over his face and began to cry.

'Keep on stalling,' Guild said, 'and I'm going to slap you silly.'

I poured some whisky in a tumbler and gave it to Nunheim.

'Thank you, sir, thank you.' He drank it, coughed, and brought out a dirty handkerchief to wipe his face with. 'I can't remember off-hand, Lieutenant,' he whined. 'Maybe I was over at Charlie's shooting pool, maybe I was here. Miriam would remember if you'll let me go bring her back.'

Guild said: 'The hell with Miriam. How'd you like to be thrown in the can on account of not remembering?'

'Just give me a minute. I'll remember. I'm not stalling, Lieutenant. You know I always come clean with you. I'm just upset now. Look at my wrist.' He held up his right wrist to let us see it was swelling. 'Just one minute.' He put his hands over his face again.

Guild winked at me and we waited for the little man's memory to work.

Suddenly he took his hands down from his face and laughed. 'Holy hell! It would serve me right if you had pinched me. That's the afternoon I was – Wait, I'll show you.' He went into the bedroom.

After a few minutes Guild called: 'Hey, we haven't got all night. Shake it up.'

There was no answer.

The bedroom was empty when we went into it, and when we opened the bathroom door the bathroom was empty. There was an open window and a fire-escape.

I said nothing, tried to look nothing.

Guild pushed his hat back a little from his forehead and said: 'I wish he hadn't done that.' He went to the telephone in the living-room.

Whilst he was telephoning, I poked around in drawers and closets, but found nothing. My search was not very thorough and I gave it up as soon as he finished putting the police machinery in action.

'I guess we'll find him all right,' he said. 'I got some news. We've identified Jorgensen as Rosewater.'

'Who made the identification?'

'I sent a man over to talk to the girl that gave him his alibi, this Olga Fenton, and he finally got it out of her. He says he couldn't shake her on the alibi, though. I'm going over and have a try at her. Want to come along?'

I looked at my watch and said: 'I'd like to, but it's too late. Picked him up yet?'

'The order's out.' He looked thoughtfully at me. 'And will that baby have to do some talking!'

I grinned at him. 'Now who do you think killed her?'

'I'm not worrying,' he said. 'Just let me have things to squeeze enough people with and I'll turn up the right one before the whistle blows.'

In the street he promised to let me know what happened, and we shook hands and separated. He ran after me a couple of seconds later to send his very best regards to Nora.

17

Home, I delivered Guild's message to Nora and told her the day's news.

'I've got a message for you, too,' she said. 'Gilbert Wynant dropped in and was quite disappointed at missing you. He asked me to tell you he has something of the 'utmost importance' to tell you.'

'He's probably discovered that Jorgensen has a mother-fixation.'

'Do you think Jorgensen killed her?' she asked.

'I thought I knew who did it,' I said, 'but it's too mixed up right now for anything but guesses.'

'And what's your guess?'

'Mimi, Jorgensen, Wynant, Nunheim, Gilbert, Dorothy, Aunt Alice, Morelli, you, me, or Guild. Maybe Studsy did it. How about shaking up a drink?'

She mixed some cocktails. I was on my second or third when she came back from answering the telephone and said: 'Your friend Mimi wants to talk to you.'

I went to the telephone. 'Hello, Mimi.'

'I'm awfully sorry I was so rude the other night, Nick, but I was so upset and I just simply lost my temper and made a show of myself. Please forgive me.' She ran through this very rapidly, as if anxious to get it over with.

'That's all right,' I said.

She hardly let me get three words out before she was speaking again, but slower and more earnestly now: 'Can I see you, Nick? Something horrible has happened, something – I don't know what to do, which way to turn.'

'What is it?'

'I can't tell you over the phone, but you've got to tell me what to do. I've got to have somebody's advice. Can't you come over?'

'You mean now?'

'Yes. Please.'

I said: 'All right,' and went back to the living-room. 'I'm going to run over and see Mimi. She says she's in a jam and needs help.'

Nora laughed. 'Keep your legs crossed. She apologize to you? She did to me.'

'Yes, all in one breath. Is Dorothy home or still at Aunt Alice's?'

'Still at Auntie's, according to Gilbert. How long will you be?'

'No longer than I have to. The chances are they've copped Jorgensen and she wants to know if it can be fixed.'

'Can they do anything to him? I mean if he didn't kill the Wolf girl.'

'I suppose the old charges against him – threats by mail, attempted extortion – could be raked up.' I stopped drinking to ask Nora and myself a question: 'I wonder if he and Nunheim know each other.' I thought that over, but could make nothing more than a possibility of it. 'Well, I'm on my way.'

18

Mimi received me with both hands. 'It's awfully, awfully nice of you to forgive me, Nick, but then you've always been awfully nice. I don't know what got into me Monday night.'

I said: 'Forget it.'

Her face was somewhat pinker than usual and the firmness of its muscles made it seem younger. Her blue eyes were very bright. Her hands had been cold on mine. She was tense with excitement, but I could not figure out what kind of excitement it was.

She said: 'It was awfully sweet of your wife, too, to –'

'Forget it.'

'Nick, what can they do to you for concealing evidence that somebody's guilty of a murder?'

'Make you an accomplice – accomplice after the fact is the technical term – if they want.'

'Even if you voluntarily change your mind and give them the evidence?'

'They can. Usually they don't.'

She looked around the room as if to make sure there was nobody else there and said: 'Clyde killed Julia. I found the proof and hid it. What'll they do to me?'

'Probably nothing except give you hell – if you turn it in. He was once your husband: you and he are close enough together that no jury'd be likely to blame you for trying to cover him up – unless, of course, they had reason to think you had some other motive.'

She asked coolly, deliberately: 'Do you?'

'I don't know,' I said. 'My guess would be that you had intended to use this proof of his guilt to shake him down for some dough as soon as you could get in touch with him, and that now something else has come up to make you change your mind.'

She made a claw of her right hand and struck at my face with her pointed nails. Her teeth were together, her lips drawn far back over them.

I caught her wrist. 'Women are getting tough,' I said, trying to sound wistful. 'I just left one that heaved a skillet at a guy.'

She laughed, though her eyes did not change. 'You always think the worst of me, don't you?'

I took my hand away from her wrist and she rubbed the marks my fingers had left on it.

'Who was the woman who threw the skillet?' she asked. 'Anyone I know?'

'It wasn't Nora, if that's what you mean. Have they arrested Victor-Christian Rosewater-Jorgensen yet?'

'What?'

I believed in her bewilderment, though both it and my belief in it surprised me. 'Jorgensen is Rosewater,' I said. 'You remember him. I thought you knew.'

'You mean that horrible man who – ?'

'Yes.'

'I won't believe it.' She stood up working her fingers together. 'I won't. I won't.' Her face was sick with fear, her voice strained, unreal as a ventriloquist's. 'I won't believe it.'

'That'll help a lot,' I said.

She was not listening to me. She turned her back to me and went to a window, where she stood with her back to me.

I said: 'There's a couple of men in a car out front who look like they might be coppers waiting to pick him up when he –'

She turned around and asked sharply: 'Are you sure he's Rosewater?' Most of the fear had already gone out of her face and her voice was at least human again.

'The police are.'

We stared at each other, both of us busy thinking. I was thinking she had not been afraid that Jorgensen killed Julia Wolf, or even that he might be arrested: she was afraid his only reason for marrying her had been as a move in some plot against Wynant.

When I laughed – not because the idea was funny, but because it had come to me so suddenly – she started and smiled uncertainly. 'I won't believe it,' she said, and her voice was very soft now, 'until he tells me himself.'

'And when he does – then what?'

She moved her shoulders a little, and her lower lip quivered. 'He is my husband.'

That should have been funny, but it annoyed me. I said: 'Mimi, this is Nick. You remember me, N-i-c-k.'

'I know you never think any good of me,' she said gravely. 'You think I'm –'

'All right. All right. Let it pass. Let's get back to the dope on Wynant you found.'

'Yes, that,' she said, and turned away from me. When she turned back her lip was quivering again. 'That was a lie, Nick, I didn't find anything.' She came close to me. 'Clyde had no right to send those letters to Alice and Macaulay trying to make everybody suspicious of me and I thought it would serve him right if I made up something against him, because I really did think – I mean, I do think – he killed her and it was only –'

'What'd you make up?' I asked.

'I – I hadn't made it up yet. I wanted to find out about what they could do – you know, the things I asked you – first.

I might've pretended she came to a little when I was alone with her, while the others were phoning, and told me he did it.'

'You didn't say you heard something and kept quiet, you said you found something and hid it.'

'But I hadn't really made up my mind what I –'

'When'd you hear about Wynant's letter to Macaulay?'

'This afternoon,' she said; 'there was a man here from the police.'

'Didn't he ask you anything about Rosewater?'

'He asked me if I knew him or had ever known him, and I thought I was telling the truth when I said no.'

'Maybe you did,' I said, 'and for the first time I now believe you were telling the truth when you said you found some sort of evidence against Wynant.'

She opened her eyes wider. 'I don't understand.'

'Neither do I, but it could be like this: you could've found something and decided to hold it out, probably with the idea of selling it to Wynant; then when his letters started people looking you over, you decided to give up the money idea and both pay him back and protect yourself by turning it over to the police; and, finally, when you learn that Jorgensen is Rosewater, you make another about-face and hold it out, not for money this time, but to leave Jorgensen in as bad a spot as possible as punishment for having married you as a trick in his game against Wynant and not for love.'

She smiled calmly and asked: 'You really think me to be capable of anything, don't you?'

'That doesn't matter,' I said. 'What ought to matter to you is that you'll probably wind up your life in prison somewhere.'

Her scream was not loud, but it was horrible, and the fear that had been in her face before was as nothing to that there now. She caught my lapels and clung to them, babbling:

'Don't say that, please don't. Say you don't think it.' She was trembling so I put an arm around her to keep her from falling.

We did not hear Gilbert until he coughed and asked:

'Aren't you well? Mamma?'

She slowly took her hands down from my lapels and moved back a step and said: 'Your mother's a silly woman.' She was still trembling, but she smiled at me and she made her voice playful: 'You're a brute to frighten me like that.'

I said I was sorry.

Gilbert put his coat and hat on a chair and looked from one to the other of us with polite interest. When it became obvious that neither of us was going to tell him anything he coughed again, said: 'I'm awfully glad to see you,' and came over to shake hands with me.

I said I was glad to see him.

Mimi said: 'Your eyes look tired. I bet you've been reading all afternoon without your glasses again.' She shook her head and told me: 'He's as unreasonable as his father.'

'Is there any news of Father?' he asked.

'Not since that false alarm about his suicide,' I said. 'I suppose you heard it was a false alarm.'

'Yes.' He hesitated. 'I'd like to see you for a few minutes before you go.'

'Sure.'

'But you're seeing him now, darling,' Mimi said. 'Are there secrets between you that I'm not supposed to know about?' Her tone was light enough. She had stopped trembling.

'It would bore you.' He picked up his hat and coat, nodded at me, and left the room.

Mimi shook her head again and said: 'I don't understand that child at all. I wonder what he made of our tableau.' She did not seem especially worried. Then, more seriously. 'What made you say that, Nick?'

'About you winding up in – ?'

'No, never mind.' She shuddered. 'I don't want to hear it. Can't you stay for dinner? I'll probably be all alone.'

'I'm sorry I can't. Now how about this evidence you found.'

'I didn't really find anything. That was a lie.' She frowned earnestly. 'Don't look at me like that. It really was a lie.'

'So you sent for me just to lie to me?' I asked. 'Then why'd you change your mind?'

She chuckled. 'You must really like me, Nick, or you wouldn't always be so disagreeable.'

I could not follow that line of reasoning. I said: 'Well, I'll see what Gilbert wants and run along.'

'I wish you could stay.'

'I'm sorry I can't,' I said again. 'Where'll I find him?'

'The second door to the – Will they really arrest Chris?'

'That depends,' I told her, 'on what kind of answers he gives them. He'll have to talk pretty straight to stay out.'

'Oh, he'll –' she broke off, looked sharply at me, asked: 'You're not playing a trick on me? He's really that Rosewater?'

'The police are sure enough of it.'

'But the man who was here this afternoon didn't ask a single question about Chris,' she objected. 'He only asked me if I knew –'

'They weren't sure then,' I explained. 'It was just a half-idea.'

'But they're sure now?'

I nodded.

'How'd they find out?'

'From a girl he knows,' I said.

'Who?' Her eyes darkened a little, but her voice was under control.

'I can't remember her name.' Then I went back to the truth: 'The one that gave him his alibi for the afternoon of the murder.'

'Alibi?' she asked indignantly. 'Do you mean to tell me the police would take the word of a girl like that?'

'Like what?'

'You know what I mean.'

'I don't. Do you know the girl?'

'No,' she said as if I had insulted her. She narrowed her eyes and lowered her voice until it was not much more than a whisper: 'Nick, do you suppose he killed Julia?'

'What would he do that for?'

'Suppose he married me to get revenge on Clyde,' she said, 'and – You know he did urge me to come over here and try to get some money from Clyde. Maybe I suggested it – I don't know – but he did urge me. And then suppose he happened to run into Julia. She knew him, of course, because they worked for Clyde at the same time. And he knew I was going over to see her that afternoon and was afraid if I made her mad she might expose him to me and so – Couldn't that be?'

'That doesn't make any sense at all. Besides, you and he left here together that afternoon. He wouldn't've had time to –'

'But my taxicab was awfully slow,' she said, 'and then I may have stopped somewhere on – I think I did. I think I stopped at a drug store to get some aspirin.' She nodded energetically. 'I remember I did.'

'And he knew you were going to stop, because you had told him,' I suggested. 'You can't go on like this, Mimi. Murder's serious. It's nothing to frame people for just because they played tricks on you.'

'Tricks?' she asked, glaring at me. 'Why, that...' She called Jorgensen all the usual profane, obscene, and otherwise insulting names, her voice gradually rising until towards the end she was screaming into my face.

When she stopped for breath I said: 'That's pretty cursing, but it –'

'He even had the nerve to hint that I might've killed her,' she told me. 'He didn't have nerve enough to ask me, but he kept leading up to it until I told him positively that – well, that I didn't do it.'

'That's not what you started to say. You told him positively what?'

She stamped her foot. 'Stop heckling me.'

'All right and to hell with you,' I said. 'Coming here wasn't my idea.' I started towards my hat and coat.

She ran after me, caught my arm. 'Please, Nick, I'm sorry. It's this rotten temper of mine. I don't know what I –'

Gilbert came in and said: 'I'll go along part of the way with you.'

Mimi scowled at him. 'You were listening.'

'How can I help it, the way you screamed?' he asked. 'Can I have some money?'

'And we haven't finished talking,' she said.

I looked at my watch. 'I've got to run, Mimi. It's late.'

'Will you come back after you get through with your date?'

'If it's not too late. Don't wait for me.'

'I'll be here,' she said. 'It doesn't matter how late it is.'

I said I would try to make it. She gave Gilbert his money. He and I went downstairs.

19

'I was listening,' Gilbert told me as we left the building. 'I think it's silly not to listen whenever you get a chance if you're interested in studying people, because they're never exactly the same as when you're with them. People don't like it when they know about it, of course, but' – he smiled – 'I don't suppose birds and animals like having naturalists spying on them either.'

'Hear much of it?' I asked.

'Oh, enough to know I didn't miss any of the important part.'

'And what'd you think of it?'

He pursed his lips, wrinkled his forehead, said judicially: 'It's hard to say exactly. Mamma's good at hiding things sometimes, but she's never much good at making them up. It's a funny thing – I suppose you've noticed it – the people who lie the most are nearly always the clumsiest at it, and they're easier to fool with lies than most people, too. You'd think they'd be on the look-out for lies, but they seem to be the very ones that will believe almost anything at all. I suppose you've noticed that, haven't you?'

'Yes.'

He said: 'What I wanted to tell you: Chris didn't come home last night. That's why Mamma's more upset than usual, and when I got the mail this morning there was a letter for him that I thought might have something in it, so I steamed it open.' He took a letter from his pocket and held it out to me. 'You'd better read it and then I'll seal it again and put it with tomorrow's mail in case he comes back, though I don't think he will.'

'Why don't you?' I asked as I took the letter.

'Well, he's really Rosewater...'

'You say anything to him about it?'

'I didn't have a chance. I haven't seen him since you told me.'

I looked at the letter in my hand. The envelope was postmarked Boston, Massachusetts, December 27, 1932, and addressed in a slightly childish feminine hand to Mr Christian Jorgensen, Courtland Apts, New York, N.Y. 'How'd you happen to open it?' I asked, taking the letter out of the envelope.

'I don't believe in intuition,' he said, 'but there are probably odours, sounds, maybe something about the handwriting, that you can't analyse, maybe aren't even conscious of, that influence you sometimes. I don't know what it was: I just felt there might be something important in it.'

'You often feel that way about the family mail?'

He glanced quickly at me as if to see whether I was spoofing, then said: 'Not often, but I have opened their mail before. I told you I was interested in studying people.'

I read the letter:

DEAR VIC –

Olga wrote me about you being back in the US married to another woman and using the name of Christian Jorgensen. That is not right Vic as you very well know the same as leaving without word of any kind all these years. And no money. I know that you had to go away on account of that trouble you had with Mr Wynant but am sure he has long since forgot all about that and I do think you might have written to me as you know very well I have always been your friend and am willing to do anything within my power for you at any time. I do not want to scold you Vic but I have to see you. I will be off from the store Sunday and Monday on account of New Year and will come down to NY Saturday night and must have a talk with you. Write me where you will meet me and what time as I do not want to make any trouble for you. Be sure and write me right away so I will get it in time.

Your true wife,
GEORGIA.

There was a street address.

I said: 'Well, well, well,' and put the letter back in its envelope. 'And you resisted the temptation to tell your mother about this?'

'Oh, I knew what her reaction would be. You saw how she carried on with just what you told her. What do you think I ought to do about it?'

'You ought to let me tell the police.'

He nodded immediately. 'If you think that's the best thing. You can show it to them if you want.'

I said: 'Thanks,' and put the letter in my pocket.

He said: 'Now there's another thing: I had some morphine I was experimenting with and somebody stole it, about twenty grains.'

'Experimenting how?'

'Taking it. I wanted to study the effects.'

'And how'd you like them?' I asked.

'Oh, I didn't expect to like it. I just wanted to know about it. I don't like things that dull my mind. That's why I don't often drink, or even smoke. I want to try cocaine, though, because that's supposed to sharpen the brain, isn't it?'

'It's supposed to. Who do you think copped the stuff?'

'I suspect Dorothy, because I have a theory about her. That's why I'm going over to Aunt Alice's for dinner: Dorry's still there and I want to find out. I can make her tell me anything.'

'Well, if she's been over there,' I asked, 'how could she –'

'She was home for a little while last night,' he said, 'and, besides, I don't know exactly when it was taken. Today was the first time I opened the box it was in for three or four days.'

'Did she know you had it?'

'Yes. That's one of the reasons I suspect her. I don't think anybody else did. I experimented on her too.'

'How'd she like it?'

'Oh, she liked it all right, but she'd have taken it anyhow. But what I want to ask you is could she have become an addict in a little time like that?'

'Like what?'

'A week – no – ten days.'

'Hardly, unless she thought herself into it. Did you give her much?'

'No.'

'Let me know if you find out,' I said. 'I'm going to grab a taxi here. Be seeing you.'

'You're coming over later tonight, aren't you?'

'If I can make it. Maybe I'll see you then.'

'Yes,' he said, 'and thanks awfully.'

At the first drug store I stopped to telephone Guild, not expecting to catch him in his office, but hoping to learn how to reach him at his home. He was still there, though.

'Working late,' I said.

His 'That's what' sounded very cheerful.

I read Georgia's letter to him, gave him her address.

'Good pickings,' he said.

I told him Jorgensen had not been home since the day before.

'Think we'll find him in Boston?' he asked.

'Either there,' I guessed, 'or as far south as he could manage to get by this time.'

'We'll try 'em both,' he said, still cheerful. 'Now I got a bit of news for you. Our friend Nunheim was filled full of .32s just about an hour after he copped the sneak on us – deader'n hell. The pills look like they come from the same gun that cut down the Wolf dame. The experts are matching 'em up now. I guess he wishes he'd stayed and talked to us.'

20

Nora was eating a piece of cold duck with one hand and working on a jigsaw puzzle with the other when I got home.

'I thought you'd gone to live with her,' she said. 'You used to be a detective: find me a brownish piece shaped something like a snail with a long neck.'

'Piece of duck or puzzle? Don't let's go to the Edges' tonight: they're dull folk.'

'All right, but they'll be sore.'

'We wouldn't be that lucky,' I complained. 'They'd get sore at the Quinns and –'

'Harrison called you up. He told me to tell you now's the time to buy some McIntyre Porcupine – I think that's right – to go with your Dome stock. He said it closed at twenty and a quarter.' She put a finger on her puzzle. 'The piece I want goes in there.'

I found the piece she wanted and told her, almost word for word, what had been done and said at Mimi's.

'I don't believe it,' she said. 'You made it up. There aren't any people like that. What's the matter with them? Are they the first of a new race of monsters?'

'I just tell you what happens; I don't explain it.'

'How would you explain it? There doesn't seem to be a single one in the family – now that Mimi's turned against her Chris – who has even the slightest reasonably friendly feeling for any of the others, and yet there's something very alike in all of them.'

'Maybe that explains it,' I suggested.

'I'd like to see Aunt Alice,' she said. 'Are you going to turn that letter over to the police?'

'I've already phoned Guild,' I replied, and told her about Nunheim.

'What does that mean?' she asked.

'For one thing, if Jorgensen's out of town, as I think he is, and the bullets are from the same gun that was used on Julia Wolf, and they probably are, then the police'll have to find his accomplice if they want to hang anything on him.'

'I'm sure if you were a good detective you'd be able to make it much clearer to me than it is.' She went to work on her puzzle again. 'Are you going back to see Mimi?'

'I doubt it. How about letting that dido rest while we get some dinner?'

The telephone rang and I said I would answer it. It was Dorothy Wynant. 'Hello. Nick?'

'The same. How are you, Dorothy?'

'Gil just got here and asked me about that you-know, and I wanted to tell you I did take it, but I only took it to try to keep him from becoming a dope-fiend.'

'What'd you do with it?' I asked.

'He made me give it back to him and he doesn't believe me, but, honestly, that's the only reason I took it.'

'I believe you.'

'Will you tell Gil, then? If you believe me, he will, because he thinks you know all about things like that.'

'I'll tell him as soon as I see him,' I promised.

There was a pause, then she asked: 'How's Nora?'

'Looks all right to me. Want to talk to her?'

'Well, yes, but there's something I want to ask you. Did – did Mamma say anything about me when you were over there today?'

'Not that I remember. Why?'

'And did Gil?'

'Only about the morphine.'

'Are you sure?'

'Pretty sure,' I said. 'Why?'

'It's nothing, really – if you're sure. It's just silly'

'Right. I'll call Nora.' I went into the living-room. 'Dorothy wants to talk to you. Don't ask her to eat with us.'

When Nora returned from the telephone she had a look in her eye.

'Now what's up?' I asked.

'Nothing. Just 'How are you' and all that.'

I said: 'If you're lying to the old man, God'll punish you.'

We went over to a Japanese place on Fifty-eighth Street for dinner and then I let Nora talk me into going to the Edges' after all.

Halsey Edge was a tall, scrawny man of fifty-something, with a pinched, yellow face and no hair at all. He called himself 'a ghoul by profession and inclination' – his only joke, if that is what it was – by which he meant he was an archaeologist, and he was very proud of his collection of battle-axes. He was not so bad once you had resigned yourself to the fact that you were in for occasional cataloguings of his armoury – stone axes, copper axes, bronze axes, double-bladed axes, faceted axes, polygonal axes, scalloped axes, hammer axes, adze axes, Mesopotamian axes, Hungarian axes, Nordic axes, and all of them looking pretty moth-eaten. It was his wife we objected to. Her name was Leda, but he called her Tip. She was very small and her hair, eyes, and skin, though naturally of different shades, were all muddy. She seldom sat – she perched on things – and liked to cock her head a little to one side. Nora had a theory that once when Edge opened an antique grave, Tip ran out of it, and Margot Innes always spoke of her as the gnome, pronouncing all the letters. She once told me that she did not think any literature of twenty years ago would live, because it had no psychiatry in it. They lived in a pleasant old three-storey house on the edge of Greenwich Village and their liquor was excellent.

A dozen or more people were there when we arrived. Tip introduced us to the ones we did not know and then backed me into a corner. 'Why didn't you tell me that those people I met at your place Christmas were mixed up in a murder mystery?' she asked, tilting her head to the left until her ear was practically resting on her shoulder.

'I don't know that they are. Besides, what's one murder mystery nowadays?'

She tilted her head to the right. 'You didn't even tell me you had taken the case.'

'I had done what? Oh, I see what you mean. Well, I hadn't and haven't. My getting shot ought to prove I was an innocent bystander.'

'Does it hurt much?'

'It itches. I forgot to have the dressing changed this afternoon.'

'Wasn't Nora utterly terrified?'

'So was I and so was the guy that shot me. There's Halsey. I haven't spoken to him yet.'

As I slid around her to escape she said: 'Harrison promised to bring the daughter tonight.'

I talked to Edge for a few minutes – chiefly about a place in Pennsylvania he was buying – then found myself a drink and listened to Larry Crowley and Phil Thames swap dirty stories until some woman came over and asked Phil – he taught at Columbia – one of the questions about technocracy that people were asking that week. Larry and I moved away.

We went over to where Nora was sitting. 'Watch yourself', she told me. 'The gnome's hell-bent on getting the inside story of Julia Wolf's murder out of you.'

'Let her get it out of Dorothy,' I said. 'She's coming with Quinn.'

'I know.'

Larry said: 'He's nuts over that girl, isn't he? He told me he was going to divorce Alice and marry her.'

Nora said: 'Poor Alice,' sympathetically. She did not like Alice.

Larry said: 'That's according to how you look at it.' He liked Alice. 'I saw that fellow who's married to the girl's mother yesterday. You know, the tall fellow I met at your house.'

'Jorgensen.'

'That's it. He was coming out of a pawnshop on Sixth Avenue near Forty-sixth.'

'Talk to him?'

'I was in a taxi. It's probably polite to pretend you don't see people coming out of pawnshops, anyhow.'

Tip said: 'Sh-h-h,' in all directions, and Levi Oscant began to play the piano. Quinn and Dorothy arrived while he was playing. Quinn was drunk as a lord and Dorothy seemed to have something better than a glow.

She came over to me and whispered: 'I want to leave when you and Nora do.'

I said: 'You won't be here for breakfast.'

Tip said: 'Sh-h-h,' in my direction.

We listened to some more music.

Dorothy fidgeted beside me for a minute and whispered again: 'Gil says you're going over to see Mamma later. Are you?'

'I doubt it.'

Quinn came unsteadily around to us. 'How're you, boy? How's you, Nora? Give him my message?' (Tip said: 'Sh-h-h,' at him. He paid no attention to her. Other people looked relieved and began to talk.) 'Listen, boy, you bank at the Golden Gate Trust in San Francisco, don't you?'

'Got a little money there.'

'Get it out, boy. I heard tonight they're plenty shaky.'

'All right. I haven't got much there, though.'

'No? What do you do with all your money?'

'Me and the French hoard gold.'

He shook his head solemnly. 'It's fellows like you that put the country on the bum.'

'And it's fellows like me that don't go on the bum with it,' I said. 'Where'd you get the skinful?'

'It's Alice. She's been sulking for a week. If I didn't drink I'd go crazy.'

'What's she sulking about?'

'About my drinking. She thinks –' He leaned forward and lowered his voice confidentially. 'Listen. You're all my friends and I'm going to tell you what I'm going to do. I'm going to get a divorce and marry –'

He had tried to put an arm around Dorothy. She pushed it away and said: 'You're silly and you're tiresome. I wish you'd leave me alone.'

'She thinks I'm silly and tiresome,' he told me. 'You know why she don't want to marry me? I bet you don't. It's because she's in –'

'Shut up! Shut up, you drunken fool!' Dorothy began to beat his face with both hands. Her face was red, her voice shrill. 'If you say that again I'll kill you!'

I pulled Dorothy away from Quinn; Larry caught him, kept him from falling. He whimpered: 'She hit me, Nick.' Tears ran down his cheeks.

Dorothy had her face against my coat and seemed to be crying.

We had what audience there was. Tip came ninning, her face bright with curiosity. 'What is it, Nick?'

I said: 'Just a couple of playful drunks. They're all right. I'll see that they get home all right.'

Tip was not for that: she wanted them to stay at least until she had a chance to discover what had happened. She urged Dorothy to lie down a while, offered to get something – whatever she meant by that – for Quinn, who was having trouble standing up now.

Nora and I took them out. Larry offered to go along, but we decided that was not necessary. Quinn slept in a corner of the taxicab during the ride to his apartment, and Dorothy sat stiff and silent in the other corner, with Nora between them. I clung to a folding seat and thought that anyway we had not stayed long at the Edges'.

Nora and Dorothy remained in the taxicab while I took Quinn upstairs. He was pretty limp.

Alice opened the door when I rang. She had on green pyjamas and held a hairbrush in one hand. She looked wearily at Quinn and spoke wearily: 'Bring it in.'

I took it in and spread it on a bed. It mumbled something I could not make out and moved one hand feebly back and forth, but its eyes stayed shut.

'I'll tuck him in,' I said, and loosened his tie.

Alice leaned on the foot of the bed. 'If you want to. I've given up doing it.'

I took off his coat, vest, and shirt.

'Where'd he pass out this time?' she asked with not much interest. She was still standing at the foot of the bed, brushing her hair now.

'The Edges'.' I unbuttoned his pants.

'With that little Wynant bitch?' The question was casual.

'There were a lot of people there.'

'Yes,' she said. 'He wouldn't pick a secluded spot.' She brushed her hair a couple of times. 'So you don't think it's clubby to tell me anything.'

Her husband stirred a little and mumbled: 'Dorry.'

I took off his shoes.

Alice sighed. 'I can remember when he had muscles'. She stared at her husband until I took off the last of his clothes and rolled him under the covers. Then she sighed again and said: 'I'll get you a drink.'

'You'll have to make it short: Nora's waiting in the cab.'

She opened her mouth as if to speak, shut it, opened it again to say: 'Righto.'

I went into the kitchen with her.

Presently she said: 'It's none of my business, Nick, but what do people think of me?'

'You're like everybody else: some people like you, some people don't, and some have no feeling about it one way or the other.'

She frowned. 'That's not exactly what I meant. What do people think about my staying with Harrison with him chasing everything that's hot and hollow?'

'I don't know, Alice.'

'What do you think?'

'I think you probably know what you're doing and whatever you do is your own business.'

She looked at me with dissatisfaction. 'You'll never talk yourself into any trouble, will you?' She smiled bitterly. 'You know I'm only staying with him for his money, don't you? It may not be a lot to you, but it is to me – the way I was raised.'

'There's always divorce and alimony. You ought to have –'

'Drink your drink and get the hell out of here,' she said wearily.

21

Nora made a place for me between her and Dorothy in the taxicab. 'I want some coffee,' she said. 'Reuben's?'

I said: 'All right,' and gave the driver the address.

Dorothy asked timidly: 'Did his wife say anything?'

'She sent her love to you.'

Nora said: 'Stop being nasty.'

Dorothy said: 'I don't really like him, Nick. I won't ever see him again – honestly.' She seemed pretty sober now. 'It was – well, I was lonesome and he was somebody to run around with.'

I started to say something, but stopped when Nora poked me in the side.

Nora said: 'Don't worry about it. Harrison's always been a simpleton.'

'I don't want to stir things up,' I said, 'but I think he's really in love with the girl.'

Nora poked me in the side again.

Dorothy peered at my face in the dim light. 'You're – you're not – you're not making fun of me, Nick?'

'I ought to be.'

'I heard a new story about the gnome tonight,' Nora said in the manner of one who did not mean to be interrupted, and explained to Dorothy: 'That's Mrs Edge. Levi says...' The story was funny enough if you knew Tip. Nora went on talking about her until we got out of the taxicab at Reuben's.

Herbert Macaulay was in the restaurant, sitting at a table with a plump, dark-haired girl in red. I waved at him and, after we had ordered some food, went over to speak to him.

'Nick Charles, Louise Jacobs,' he said. 'Sit down. What's news?'

'Jorgensen's Rosewater,' I told him.

'The hell he is!'

I nodded. 'And he seems to have a wife in Boston.'

'I'd like to see him,' he said slowly. 'I knew Rosewater. I'd like to make sure.'

'The police seem sure enough. I don't know whether they've found him yet. Think he killed Julia?'

Macaulay shook his head with emphasis. 'I can't see Rosewater killing anybody – not as I knew him – in spite of those threats he made. You remember I didn't – take them very seriously at the time. What else has happened?' When I hesitated, he said: 'Louise is all right. You can talk.'

'It's not that. I've got to go back to my folks and food. I came over to ask if you'd got an answer to your ad. in this morning's *Times.*'

'Not yet. Sit down, Nick, there's a lot I want to ask you. You told the police about Wynant's letter, didn't –'

'Come up to lunch tomorrow and we'll bat it around. I've got to get back to my folks.'

'Who is the little blonde girl?' Louise Jacobs asked. 'I've seen her places with Harrison Quinn.'

'Dorothy Wynant.'

'You know Quinn?' Macaulay asked me.

'Ten minutes ago I was putting him to bed.'

Macaulay grinned. 'I hope you keep his acquaintance like that – social.'

'Meaning what?'

Macaulay's grin became rueful. 'He used to be my broker, and his advice led me right up to the poorhouse steps.'

'That's sweet,' I said. 'He's my broker now and I'm following his advice.'

Macaulay and the girl laughed. I pretended I was laughing and returned to my table.

Dorothy said: 'It's not midnight yet and Mamma said she'd be expecting you. Why don't we all go to see her?'

Nora was very carefully pouring coffee into her cup.

'What for?' I asked. 'What are you two up to now?'

It would have been hard to find two more innocent faces than theirs.

'Nothing, Nick,' Dorothy said. 'We thought it would be nice. It's early and –'

'And we all love Mimi.'

'No – o, but –'

'It's too early to go home,' Nora said.

'There are speakeasies,' I suggested, 'and night clubs and Harlem.'

Nora made a face. 'All your ideas are alike.'

'Want to go over to Barry's and try our luck at faro?'

Dorothy started to say yes, but stopped when Nora made another face.

'That's the way I feel about seeing Mimi again,' I said. 'I've had enough of her for one day.'

Nora sighed to show she was being patient. 'Well, if we're going to wind up in a speakeasy as usual, I'd rather go to your friend Studsy's, if you won't let him give us any more of that awful champagne. He's cute.'

'I'll do my best,' I promised and asked Dorothy: 'Did Gilbert tell you he caught Mimi and me in a compromising position?'

She tried to exchange glances with Nora, but Nora's glance was occupied with her plate. 'He – he didn't exactly say that.'

'Did he tell you about the letter?'

'From Chris's wife? Yes.' Her blue eyes glittered. 'Won't Mamma be furious!'

'You like it, though.'

'Suppose I do? What did she ever do to make me –'

Nora said: 'Nick, stop bullying the child.'

I stopped.

22

Business was good at the Pigiron Club. The place was full of people, noise, and smoke. Studsy came from behind the cash register to greet us. 'I was hoping you'd come in.' He shook my hand and Nora's and grinned broadly at Dorothy.

'Anything special?' I asked.

He made a bow. 'Everything's special with ladies like these.'

I introduced him to Dorothy.

He bowed to her and said something elaborate about any friend of Nick's and stopped a waiter. 'Pete, put a table up here for Mr Charles.'

'Pack them in like this every night?' I asked.

'I got no kick,' he said. 'They come once, they come back again. Maybe I ain't got no black marble cuspidors, but you don't have to spit out what you buy here. Want to lean against the bar whilst they're putting up the table?'

We said we did and ordered drinks.

'Hear about Nunheim?' I asked.

He looked at me for a moment before making up his mind to say: 'Uh-huh, I heard. His girl's down there' – he moved his head to indicate the other end of the room – 'celebrating, I guess.'

I looked past Studsy down the room and presently picked out big red-haired Miriam sitting at a table with half a dozen men and women. 'Hear who did it?' I asked.

'She says the police done it – he knew too much.'

'That's a laugh,' I said.

'That's a laugh,' he agreed. 'There's your table. Sit right down. I'll be back in a minute.'

We carried our glasses over to a table that had been squeezed in between two tables which had occupied a space large enough for one and made ourselves as nearly comfortable as we could.

Nora tasted her drink and shuddered. 'Do you suppose this could be the 'bitter vetch' they used to put in crossword puzzles?'

Dorothy said: 'Oh, look.'

We looked and saw Shep Morelli coming towards us. His face had attracted Dorothy's attention. Where it was not dented it was swollen and its coloring ranged from deep purple around one eye to the pale pink of a piece of court-plaster on his chin.

He came to our table and leaned over a little to put both fists on it. 'Listen,' he said, 'Studsy says I ought to apologize.'

Nora mumured: 'Old Emily Post Studsy,' while I asked: 'Well?'

Morelli shook his battered head. 'I don't apologize for what I do – people've got to take it or leave it – but I don't mind telling you I'm sorry I lost my noddle and cracked down on you and I hope it ain't bothering you much and if there's anything I can do to square it I –'

'Forget it. Sit down and have a drink. This is Mr Morelli, Miss Wynant.'

Dorothy's eyes became wide and interested.

Morelli found a chair and sat down. 'I hope you won't hold it against me, neither,' he told Nora.

She said: 'It was fun.'

He looked at her suspiciously.

'Out on bail?' I asked.

'Uh-huh, this afternoon.' He felt his face gingerly with one hand. 'That's where the new ones come from. They had me resisting some more arrest just for good measure before they turned me loose.'

Nora said indignantly: 'That's horrible. You mean they really –'

I patted her hand.

Morelli said: 'You got to expect it.' His swollen lower lip moved in what was meant for a scornful smile. 'It's all right as long as it takes two or three of 'em to do it.'

Nora turned to me. 'Did you do things like that?'

'Who? Me?'

Studsy came over to us carrying a chair. 'They lifted his face, huh?' he said, nodding at Morelli. We made room for him and he sat down. He grinned complacently at Nora's drink and at Nora. 'I guess you don't get no better than that in your fancy Park Avenue joints – and you pay four bits a slug for it here.'

Nora's smile was weak, but it was a smile. She put her foot on mine under the table.

I asked Morelli: 'Did you know Julia Wolf in Cleveland?'

He looked sidewise at Studsy, who was leaning back in his chair, gazing around the room, watching his profits mount.

'When she was Rhoda Stewart,' I added.

He looked at Dorothy.

I said: 'You don't have to be cagey. She's Clyde Wynant's daughter.'

Studsy stopped gazing around the room and beamed on Dorothy. 'So you are? And how is your pappy?'

'But I haven't seen him since I was a little girl,' she said.

Morelli wet the end of a cigarette and put it between his swollen lips. 'I come from Cleveland.' He struck a match. His eyes were dull – he was trying to keep them dull. 'She wasn't Rhoda Stewart except once – Nancy Kane.' He looked at Dorothy again. 'Your father knows it.'

'Do you know my father?'

'We had some words once.'

'What about?' I said.

'Her.' The match in his hand had burned down to his fingers. He dropped it, struck another, and lit his cigarette. He raised his eyebrows at me, wrinkling his forehead. 'Is this O.K.?'

'Sure. There's nobody here you can't talk in front of.'

'O.K. He was jealous as hell. I wanted to take a poke at him, but she wouldn't let me. That was all right: he was her bank-roll.'

'How long ago was this?'

'Six months, eight months.'

'Have you seen him since she got knocked off?'

He shook his head. 'I never seen him but a couple of times, and this time I'm telling you about is the last.'

'Was she gypping him?'

'She don't say she is. I figure she is.'

'Why?'

'She's a wise head – plenty smart. She was getting dough somewheres. Once I wanted five grand.' He snapped his fingers. 'Cash.'

I decided against asking if he had paid her back. 'Maybe he gave it to her.'

'Sure – maybe.'

'Did you tell any of this to the police?' I asked.

He laughed once, contemptuously. 'They thought they could smack it out of me. Ask 'em what they think now. You're a right guy, I don't –' He broke off, took the cigarette from between his lips. 'The erysipelas kid,' he said, and put out a hand to touch the ear of a man who, sitting at one of the tables we had squeezed in between, had been leaning further and further back towards us.

The man jumped and turned a startled, pale, pinched face around over his shoulder at Morelli.

Morelli said: 'Pull in that lug – it's getting in our drinks.'

The man stammered: 'I d-didn't mean nothing, Shep,' and rammed his belly into his table trying to get as far as possible from us, which still did not take him out of earshot.

Morelli said: 'You won't ever mean nothing, but that don't keep you from trying,' and returned his attention to me. 'I'm willing to go all the way with you – the kid's dead, it's not going to hurt her any – but Mulrooney ain't got a wrecking crew that can get it out of me.'

'Swell,' I said. 'Tell me about her, where you first ran into her, what she did before she tied up with Wynant, where he found her.'

'I ought to have a drink.' He twisted himself around in his chair and called: 'Hey, garsong – you with the boy on your back!'

The somewhat hunch-backed waiter Studsy had called Pete pushed through people to our table and grinned affectionately down at Morelli. 'What'll it be?' He sucked a tooth noisily.

We gave our orders and the waiter went away.

Morelli said: 'Me and Nancy lived in the same block. Old man Kane had a candy store on the corner. She used to pinch cigarettes for me.' He laughed. 'Her old man kicked hell out of me once for showing her how to get nickels out of the telephone with a piece of wire. You know, the old-style ones. We couldn't've been more than in the third grade.' He laughed again, low in his throat. 'I wanted to glaum some fixtures from a row of houses they were building around the corner and plant 'em in his cellar and tell Schultz, the cop on the beat, to pay him back, but she wouldn't let me.'

Nora said: 'You must've been a little darling.'

'I was that,' he said fondly. 'Listen. Once when I was no more'n five or –'

A feminine voice said: 'I thought that was you.'

I looked up and saw it was red-haired Miriam speaking to me. I said: 'Hello.'

She put her hands on her hips and stared somberly at me. 'So he knew too much for you.'

'Maybe, but he took it on the lam down the fire-escape with his shoes in his hand before he told us any of it.'

'Boloney!'

'All right. What do you think he knew that was too much for us?'

'Where Wynant is,' she said.

'So? Where is he?'

'I don't know. Art knew.'

'I wish he'd told us. We –'

'Boloney!' she said again. 'You know and the police know. Who do you think you're kidding?'

'I'm not kidding. I don't know where Wynant is.'

'You're working for him and the police are working with you. Don't kid me. Art thought knowing was going to get him a lot of money, poor sap. He didn't know what it was going to get him.'

'Did he tell you he knew?' I asked.

'I'm not as dumb as you think. He told me he knew something that was going to get him big dough and I've seen how it worked out. I guess I can put two and two together.'

'Sometimes the answer's four,' I said, 'and sometimes it's twenty-two. I'm not working for Wynant. Now don't say 'Boloney' again. Do you want to help –'

'No. He was a rat and he held out on the people he was ratting for. He asked for what he got, only don't expect me to forget that I left him with you and Guild, and the next time anybody saw him he was dead.'

'I don't want you to forget anything. I'd like you to remember whether –'

'I've got to go,' she said, and walked away. Her carriage was remarkably graceful.

'I don't know as I'd want to be mixed up with that dame,' Studsy said thoughtfully. 'She's mean medicine.'

Morelli winked at me.

Dorothy touched my arm. 'I don't understand, Nick.'

I told her that was all right and addressed Morelli: 'You were telling us about Julia Wolf.

'Uh-huh. Well, old man Kane booted her out when she was fifteen or sixteen and got in some kind of jam with a high-school teacher and she took up with a guy called Face Peppler, a smart kid if he didn't talk too much. I remember once me and Face were –' He broke off and cleared his throat. 'Anyways, Face and her stuck together – what the hell – it must be five, six years, throwing out the time he was in the army and she was living with some guy that I can't remember his name – a cousin of Dick O'Brien's, a skinny, dark-headed guy that liked his liquor. But she went back to Face when he come out of the army, and they stuck together till they got nailed trying to shake down some bird from Toronto. Face took it and got her off with six months – they gave him the business. Last I heard he was still in. I saw her when she came out – she touched me for a couple hundred to blow town. I hear from her once, when she sends it back to me and tells me Julia Wolf's her name now and she likes the big city fine, but I know Face is hearing from her right along. So when I move here in '28, I look her up. She's –'

Miriam came back and stood with her hands on her hips as before. 'I've been thinking over what you said. You must think I'm pretty dumb.'

'No,' I said, not very truthfully.

'It's a cinch I'm not dumb enough to fall for that song and dance you tried to give me. I can see things when they're right in front of me.'

'All right.'

'It's not all right. You killed Art and –'

'Not so loud, girlie.' Studsy rose and took her arm. His voice was soothing. 'Come along. I want to talk to you.' He led her towards the bar.

Morelli winked again. 'He likes that. Well, I was saying I looked her up when I moved here, and she told me she had this job with Wynant and he was nuts about her and she was sitting pretty. It seems they learned her shorthand in Ohio when she was doing her six months and she figures maybe it'll be an in to something – you know, maybe she can get a job somewheres where they'll go out and leave the safe open. An agency had sent her over to do a couple days' work for Wynant and she figured maybe he'd be worth more for a long pull than for a quick tap and a getaway, so she give him the business and wound up with a steady connexion. She was smart enough to tell him she had a record and was trying to go straight now and all that, so's not to have the racket spoiled if he found out anyhow, because she said his lawyer was a little leery of her and might have her looked up. I don't know just what she was doing, you understand, because it's her game and she don't need my help, and even if we are pals in a way there's no sense in telling me anything I might want to go to her boss with. Understand, she wasn't my girl or anything – we was just a couple of old friends, been kids playing together. Well, I used to sec her every once in a while – we used to come here a lot – till he kicked up too much of a fuss and then she said she was going to cut it out, she wasn't going to lose a soft bed over a few drinks with me. So that was that. That was October, I guess, and she stuck to it. I haven't seen her since.'

'Who else did she run around with?' I asked.

Morelli shook his head. 'I don't know. She don't do much talking about people.'

'She was wearing a diamond engagement ring. Know anything about it?'

'Nothing except she didn't get it from me. She wasn't wearing it when I see her.'

'Do you think she meant to throw in with Peppler again when he got out?'

'Maybe. She didn't seem to worry much about him being in, but she liked to work with him all right and I guess they'd've teamed up again.'

'And how about the cousin of Dick O'Brien, the skinny, dark-headed lush? What became of him?'

Morelli looked at me in surprise. 'Search me.'

Studsy returned alone. 'Maybe I'm wrong,' he said as he sat down, 'but I think somebody could do something with that cluck if they took hold of her right.'

Morelli said: 'By the throat.'

Studsy grinned good-naturedly. 'No. She's trying to get somewhere. She works hard at her singing lessons and –'

Morelli looked at his empty glass and said: 'This tiger milk of yours must be doing her pipes a lot of good.' He turned his head to yell at Pete: 'Hey, you with the knapsack, some more of the same. We got to sing in the choir tomorrow.'

Pete said: 'Coming up, Sheppy.' His lined, gray face lost its dull apathy when Morelli spoke to him.

An immensely fat blond man – so blond he was nearly albino – who had been sitting at Miriam's table came over and said to me in a thin, tremulous, effeminate voice: 'So you're the party who put it to little Art Nunhei –'

Morelli hit the fat man in his fat belly, as hard as he could without getting up. Studsy, suddenly on his feet, leaned over Morelli and smashed a big fist into the fat man's face. I noticed, foolishly, that he still led with his right. Hunch-backed Pete came up behind the fat man and banged his empty tray down with full force on the fat man's head. The fat man fell back, upsetting three people and a table. Both bartenders were with us by then. One of them hit the fat man with a blackjack as he tried to get up, knocking him forward on hands and knees, the other put a hand down inside the fat man's collar in back, twisting the collar to choke him. With Morelli's help they got the fat man to his feet and hustled him out.

Pete looked after them and sucked a tooth. 'That god-damned Sparrow,' he exclaimed to me, 'you can't take no chances on him when he's drinking.'

Studsy was at the next table, the one that had been upset, helping people pick up themselves and their possessions. 'That's bad,' he was saying, 'bad for business, but where are you going to draw the line? I ain't running a dive, but I ain't trying to run a young ladies' seminary neither.'

Dorothy was pale, frightened; Nora wide-eyed and amazed. 'It's a madhouse,' she said. 'What'd they do that for?'

'You know as much about it as I do,' I told her.

Morelli and the bartenders came in again, looking pretty pleased with themselves. Morelli and Studsy returned to their seats at our table.

'You boys are impulsive,' I said.

Studsy repeated: 'Impulsive,' and laughed: 'Ha-ha-ha.'

Morelli was serious. 'Any time that guy starts anything, you got to start it first. It's too late when he gets going. We seen him like that before, ain't we, Studsy?'

'Like what?' I asked. 'He hadn't done anything.'

'He hadn't, all right,' Morelli said slowly, 'but it's a kind of feeling you get about him sometimes. Ain't that right, Studsy?'

Studsy said: 'Uh-huh, he's hysterical.'

23

It was about two o'clock when we said good night to Studsy and Morelli and left the Pigiron Club.

Dorothy slumped down in her corner of the taxicab and said: 'I'm going to be sick. I know I am.' She sounded as if she was telling the truth.

Nora said: 'That booze.' She put her head on my shoulder. 'Your wife is drunk, Nicky. Listen, you've got to tell me what happened – everything. Not now, tomorrow. I don't understand a thing that was said or a thing that was done. They're marvelous.'

Dorothy said: 'Listen, I can't go to Aunt Alice's like this. She'd have a fit.'

Nora said: 'They oughtn't've hit that fat man like that, though it must've been funny in a cruel way.'

Dorothy said: 'I suppose I'd better go to Mamma's.'

Nora said: 'Erysipelas hasn't got anything to do with ears. What's a lug, Nicky?'

'An ear.'

Dorothy said: 'Aunt Alice would have to see me because I forgot the key and I'd have to wake her up.'

Nora said: 'I love you, Nicky, because you smell nice and know such fascinating people.'

Dorothy said: 'It's not much out of your way to drop me at Mamma's, is it?'

I said: 'No,' and gave the driver Mimi's address.

Nora said: 'Come home with us.'

Dorothy said: 'No – o, I'd better not.'

Nora asked: 'Why not?' and Dorothy said: 'Well, I don't think I ought to,' and that kind of thing went on until the taxicab stopped at the Courtland.

I got out and helped Dorothy out. She leaned heavily on my arm. 'Please come up, just for a minute.'

Nora said: 'Just for a minute,' and got out of the taxicab.

I told the driver to wait. We went upstairs. Dorothy rang the bell, Gilbert, in pyjamas and bathrobe, opened the door. He raised one hand in a warning gesture and said in a low voice: 'The police are here.'

Mimi's voice came from the living-room: 'Who is it, Gil?'

'Mr and Mrs Charles and Dorothy.'

Mimi came to meet us as we went in. 'I never was so glad to see anybody I just didn't know which way to turn.' She had on a pinkish satin robe over a pinkish silk nightgown, and her face was pink and by no means unhappy. She ignored Dorothy, squeezed one of Nora's hands, one of mine. 'Now I'm going to stop worrying and leave it all up to you, Nick. You'll have to tell the foolish little woman what to do.'

Dorothy, behind me, said: 'Boloney!' under her breath, but with a lot of feeling.

Mimi did not show that she had heard her daughter. Still holding our hands, she drew us back towards the living-room, chattering: 'You know Lieutenant Guild. He's been very nice, but I'm sure I must have tried his patience. I've been so – well – I mean I've been so bewildered. But now you're here and –'

We went into the living-room.

Guild said, 'Hello,' to me and, 'Good evening, ma'am,' to Nora. The man with him, the one he had called Andy and who had helped him search our rooms the morning of Morelli's visit, nodded and grunted at us.

'What's up?' I asked.

Guild looked at Mimi out of the corners of his eyes, then at me, and said: 'The Boston police found Jorgensen or Rosewater or whatever you want to call him at his first wife's place and asked him some questions for us. The chief answer seems to be he don't have anything to do with Julia Wolf getting killed or not getting killed and Mrs Jorgensen can prove it because she's been holding out what amounts to the goods on Wynant.' His eyes slid sidewise in their sockets to focus on Mimi again. 'The lady kind of don't want to say yes and kind of don't want to say no. To tell you the truth, Mr Charles, I don't know what to make of her in a lot of ways.'

I could understand that. I said: 'She's probably frightened,' and Mimi tried to look frightened. 'Has he been divorced from the first wife?'

'Not according to the first wife.'

Mimi said: 'She's lying, I bet.'

I said: 'Sh-h-h. Is he coming back to New York?'

'It looks like he's going to make us extradite him if we want him. Boston says he's squawking his head off for a lawyer.'

'Do you want him that bad?'

Guild moved his big shoulders. 'If bringing him back'll help us on this murder. I don't care much about any of the old charges of the bigamy. I never believe in hounding a man over things that are none of my business.'

I asked Mimi: 'Well?'

'Can I talk to you alone?'

I looked at Guild, who said: 'Anything that'll help.'

Dorothy touched my arm. 'Nick, listen to me first. I –' She broke off. Everybody was staring at her.

'What?' I asked.

'I – I want talk to you first.'

'Go ahead.'

'I mean alone,' she said.

I patted her hand. 'Afterwards.'

Mimi led me into her bedroom and carefully shut the door. I sat on the bed and lit a cigarette. Mimi leaned back against the door and smiled at me very gently and trustingly. Half a minute passed that way.

Then she said, 'You do like me, Nick,' and when I said nothing she asked: 'Don't you?'

'No.'

She laughed and came away from the door. 'You mean you don't approve of me.' She sat on the bed beside me. 'But you do like me well enough to help me?'

'That depends.'

'Depends on wha –'

The door opened and Dorothy came in. 'Nick, I've got to –'

Mimi jumped up and confronted her daughter. 'Get out of here,' she said through her teeth.

Dorothy flinched, but she said: 'I won't. You're not going to make a –'

Mimi slashed Dorothy across the mouth with the back of her right hand. 'Get out of here.'

Dorothy screamed and put a hand to her mouth. Holding it there, holding her wide frightened eyes on Mimi's face, she backed out of the room.

Mimi shut the door again.

I said: 'You must come over to our place some time and bring your little white whips.'

She did not seem to hear me. Her eyes were heavy, brooding, and her lips were thrust out a little in a half-smile, and when she spoke, her voice seemed heavier, throatier, than usual. 'My daughter's in love with you.'

'Nonsense.'

'She is and she's jealous of me. She has absolute spasms whenever I get within ten feet of you.' She spoke as if thinking of something else.

'Nonsense. Maybe she's got a little hangover from that crush she had on me when she was twelve, but that's all it is.'

Mimi shook her head. 'You're wrong, but never mind.' She sat down on the bed beside me again. 'You've got to help me out of this. I –'

'Sure,' I said. 'You're a delicate *fleur* that needs a great big man's protection.'

'Oh, that?' She waved a hand at the door through which Dorothy had gone. 'You're surely not getting – Why, it's nothing you haven't heard about before – and seen and done, for that matter. It's nothing to worry you.' She smiled as before, with heavy, brooding eyes, and lips thrust out a little. 'If you want Dorry, take her, but don't get sentimental about it. But never mind that. Of course I'm not a delicate *fleur*. You never thought I was.'

'No,' I agreed.

'Well, then,' she said with an air of finality.

'Well then what?'

'Stop being so damned coquettish,' she said. 'You know what I mean. You understand me as well as I understand you.'

'Just about, but you've been doing the coquetting ever since –'

'I know. That was a game. I'm not playing now. That guy made a fool of me, Nick, an out and out fool, and now he's in trouble and expects me to help him. I'll help him.' She put a hand on my knee and her pointed nails dug into my flesh. 'The police, they don't believe me. How can I make them believe that he's lying, that I know nothing more than I've told them about the murder?'

'You probably can't,' I said slowly, 'especially since Jorgensen's only repeating what you told me a few hours ago.'

She caught her breath, and her nails dug into me again. 'Did you tell them that?'

'Not yet.' I took her hand off my knee.

She sighed with relief. 'And of course you won't tell them now, will you?'

'Why not?'

'Because it's a lie. He lied and I lied. I didn't find anything, anything at all.'

I said: 'We're back where we were earlier, and I believe you just as much now as I did then. What happened to those new terms we were on? You understanding me, me understanding you, no coquetting, no games, no playing.'

She slapped my hand lightly. 'All right. I did find something – not much, but something – and I'm not going to give it up to help that guy. You can understand how I feel about it, Nick. You'd feel the same –'

'Maybe,' I said, 'but the way it stands, I've got no reason for putting in with you. Your Chris is no enemy of mine. I've got nothing to gain by helping you frame him.'

She sighed. 'I've been thinking about that a lot. I don't suppose what money I could give you would mean much to you now' – she smiled crookedly – 'nor my beautiful white body. But aren't you interested in saving Clyde?'

'Not necessarily.'

She laughed at that. 'I don't know what that means.'

'It might mean I don't think he needs saving. The police haven't got much on him. He's screwy, he was in town the day Julia was killed, and she had been gypping him. That's not enough to arrest him on.'

She laughed again. 'But with my contribution?'

'I don't know. What is it?' I asked, and went on without waiting for the answer I did not expect. 'Whatever it is, you're being a sap, Mimi. You've got Chris cold on bigamy. Sock that to him. There's no –'

She smiled sweetly and said: 'But I am holding that in reserve to use after this if he –'

'If he gets past the murder charge, huh? Well, it won't work out that way, lady. You can get him about three days in jail. By that time the District Attorney will have questioned him and checked up on him enough to know that he didn't kill Julia and that you've been making a chump of the D.A., and when you spring your little bigamy charge the D.A. will tell you to go jump in the lake, and he'll refuse to prosecute.'

'But he can't do that, Nick.'

'Can and will,' I assured her, 'and if he can dig up proof that you're holding out something he'll make it as tough for you as he can.'

She chewed her lower lip, asked: 'You're being honest with me?'

'I'm telling you exactly what'll happen, unless district attorneys have changed a lot since my day.'

She chewed her lip some more. 'I don't want him to get off,' she said presently, 'and I don't want to get into any trouble myself.' She looked up at me. 'If you're lying to me, Nick...'

'There's nothing you can do about it except believe me or disbelieve me.'

She smiled and put a hand on my cheek and kissed me on the mouth and stood up. 'Well, I'm going to believe you.' She walked down to the other end of the room and back again. Her eyes were shiny, her face pleasantly excited.

'I'll call Guild,' I said.

'No, wait. I'd rather see what you think of it first.'

'All right, but no clowning.'

'You're certainly afraid of your shadow,' she said, 'but don't worry, I'm not going to play any tricks on you.'

I said that would be swell and how about showing me whatever she had to show me. 'The others will be getting restless.'

She went around the bed to a closet, opened the door, pushed some clothes aside, and put a hand among other clothes behind them. 'That's funny,' she said.

'Funny?' I stood up. 'It's a panic. It'll have Guild rolling on the floor.' I started towards the door.

'Don't be so bad-tempered,' she said. 'I've got it.' She turned to me holding a wadded handkerchief in her hand. As I approached, she opened the handkerchief to show me a three-inch length of watch-chain, broken at one end, attached at the other to a small gold knife. The handkerchief was a woman's and there were brown stains on it.

'Well?' I asked.

'It was in her hand and I saw it when they left me with her and I knew it was Clyde's, so I took it.'

'You're sure it's his?'

'Yes,' she said impatiently. 'See, they're gold, silver, and copper links. He had it made out of the first batches of metal that came through that smelting process he invented. Anybody who knows him at all well can identify it – there can't be another like it.' She turned the knife over to let me see the C M W engraved in it. 'They're his initials. I never saw the knife before, but I'd know the chain anywhere. Clyde's worn it for years.'

'Did you remember it well enough that you could've described it without seeing it again?'

'Of course.'

'Is that your handkerchief?'

'Yes.'

'And the stain on it's blood?'

'Yes. The chain was in her hand – I told you – and there was some blood on them.' She frowned at me. 'Don't you – You act as if you don't believe me.'

'Not exactly,' I said, 'but I think you ought to be sure you're telling your story straight this time.'

She stamped her foot. 'You're –' She laughed and anger went out of her face. 'You can be the most annoying man. I'm telling the truth now, Nick. I've told you everything that happened exactly as it happened.'

'I hope so. It's about time. You're sure Julia didn't come to enough to say anything while you were alone with her?'

'You're trying to make me mad again. Of course I'm sure.'

'All right,' I said. 'Wait here. I'll get Guild, but if you tell him the chain was in Julia's hand and she wasn't dead yet, he's going to wonder whether you didn't have to rough her up a little to get it away from her.'

She opened her eyes wide. 'What should I tell him?'

I went out and shut the door.

24

Nora, looking a little sleepy, was entertaining Guild and Andy in the living-room. The Wynant offspring were not in sight.

'Go ahead,' I told Guild. 'First door to the left. I think she's readied up for you.'

'Crack her?' he asked.

I nodded.

'What'd you get?'

'See what you get and we'll put them together and see how they add up,' I suggested.

'O.K. Come on, Andy.' They went out.

'Where's Dorothy?' I asked.

Nora yawned. 'I thought she was with you and her mother. Gilbert's around somewhere. He was here till a few minutes ago. Do we have to hang around long?'

'Not long.' I went back down the passageway past Mimi's door to another bedroom door, which was open, and looked in. Nobody was there. A door facing it was shut. I knocked on it.

Dorothy's voice: 'What is it?'

'Nick,' I said and went in.

She was lying on her side on a bed, dressed except for her slippers. Gilbert was sitting on the bed beside her. Her mouth seemed a little puffy, but it may have been from crying: her eyes were red. She raised her head to stare sullenly at me.

'Still want to talk to me?' I asked.

Gilbert got up from the bed. 'Where's Mamma?'

'Talking to the police.'

He said something I did not catch and left the room.

Dorothy shuddered. 'He gives me the creeps,' she said, and then remembered to stare sullenly at me again.

'Still want to talk to me?'

'What made you turn against me like that?'

'You're being silly' I sat down where Gilbert had been sitting. 'Do you know anything about this knife and chain your mother's supposed to have found?'

'No. Where?'

'What'd you want to tell me?'

'Nothing – now,' she said disagreeably, 'except you might at least wipe her lipstick off your mouth.'

I wiped it off. She snatched the handkerchief from my hand and rolled over to pick up a package of matches from the table on that side of the bed. She struck a match.

'That's going to stink like hell,' I said.

She said: 'I don't care,' but she blew out the match. I took the handkerchief, went to the window, opened it, dropped the handkerchief out, shut the window, and went back to my seat on the bed. 'If that makes you feel any better.'

'What did Mamma say – about me?'

'She said you're in love with me.'

She sat up abruptly. 'What did you say?'

'I said you just liked me from when you were a kid.'

Her lower lip twitched. 'Do – do you think that's what it is?'

'What else could it be?'

'I don't know.' She began to cry. 'Everybody's made so much fun of me about it – Mamma and Gilbert and Harrison – I –'

I put my arms around her. 'To hell with them.'

After a while she asked: 'Is Mamma in love with you?'

'Good God, no! She hates men more than any woman I've ever known.'

'But she's always having some sort of –'

'That's the body. Don't let it fool you. Mimi hates men – all of us – bitterly.'

She had stopped crying. She wrinkled her forehead and said: 'I don't understand. Do you hate her?'

'Not as a rule.'

'Now?'

'I don't think so. She's being stupid and she's sure she's being very clever, and that's a nuisance, but I don't think I hate her.'

'I do,' Dorothy said.

'So you told me last week. Something I meant to ask you: did you know or did you ever see the Arthur Nunheim we were talking about in the speakeasy tonight?'

She looked sharply at me. 'You're just trying to change the subject.'

'I want to know. Did you?'

'No.'

'He was mentioned in the newspapers,' I reminded her. 'He was the one who told the police about Morelli knowing Julia Wolf.'

'I didn't remember his name,' she said. 'I don't remember ever having heard it until tonight.'

I described him. 'Ever seen him?'

'No.'

'He may have been known as Albert Norman sometimes. Does that sound familiar?'

'No.'

'Know any of the people we saw at Studsy's tonight? Or anything about them?'

'No. Honestly, Nick, I'd tell you if I knew anything at all that might help you.'

'No matter who it hurt?'

'Yes,' she said immediately, then: 'What do you mean?'

'You know damned well what I mean.'

She put her hands over her face, and her words were barely audible: 'I'm afraid, Nick. I –' She jerked her hands down as someone knocked on the door.

'All right,' I called.

Andy opened the door far enough to stick his head in. He tried to keep curiosity from showing in his face while saying: 'The Lieutenant wants to see you.'

'Be right out,' I promised.

He opened the door wider. 'He's waiting.' He gave me what was probably meant to be a significant wink, but a corner of his mouth moved more than his eye did and the result was a fairly startling face.

'I'll be back,' I told Dorothy, and followed him out.

He shut the door behind me and put his mouth close to my ear. 'The kid was at the keyhole,' he muttered.

'Gilbert?'

'Yep. He had time to get away from it when he heard me coming, but he was there, right enough.'

'That's mild for him,' I said. 'How'd you all make out with Mrs J.?'

He pucked his thick lips up in an *o* and blew breath out noisily. 'What a dame!'

25

We went into Mimi's bedroom. She was sitting in a deep chair by a window looking very pleased with herself. She smiled gaily at me and said: 'My soul is spotless now. I've confessed everything.'

Guild stood by a table wiping his face with a handkerchief. There were still some drops of sweat on his temples, and his face seemed old and tired. The knife and chain, and the handkerchief they had been wrapped in, were on the table.

'Finished?' I asked.

'I don't know, and that's a fact,' he said. He turned his head to address Mimi: 'Would you say we were finished?'

Mimi laughed. 'I can't imagine what more there would be.'

'Well,' Guild said slowly, somewhat reluctantly, 'in that case I guess I'd like to talk to Mr Charles, if you'll excuse us for a couple of minutes.' He folded his handkerchief carefully and put it in his pocket.

'You can talk here.' She got up from the chair. 'I'll go out and talk to Mrs Charles till you're through.' She tapped my cheek playfully with the tip of a forefinger as she passed me. 'Don't let them say too horrid things about me, Nicky.'

Andy opened the door for her, shut it behind her, and made the *o* and the blowing noise again.

I lay down on the bed. 'Well,' I asked, 'what's what?'

Guild cleared his throat. 'She told us about finding this here chain and knife on the floor where the Wolf dame had most likely broke it off fighting with Wynant, and she told us the reasons why she's hid it till now. Between me and you, that don't make any too much sense, looking at it reasonably, but maybe that ain't the way to look at it in this case. To tell you the plain truth, I don't know what to make of her in a lot of ways, I don't for a fact.'

'The chief thing,' I advised them, 'is not to let her tire you out. When you catch her in a lie, she admits it and gives you another lie to take its place and, when you catch her in that one, admits it and gives you still another, and so on. Most people – even women – get discouraged after you've caught them in the third or fourth straight lie and fall back on either the truth or silence, but not Mimi. She keeps trying and you've got to be careful or you'll find yourself believing her, not because she seems to be telling the truth, but simply because you're tired of disbelieving her.'

Guild said: 'Hm–m–m. Maybe.' He put a finger inside his collar. He seemed very uncomfortable. 'Look here, do you think she killed that dame?'

I discovered that Andy was staring at me so intently that his eyes bulged. I sat up and put my feet on the floor. 'I wish I knew. That chain business looks like a plant all right, but... We can find out whether he had a chain like that, maybe whether he still has it. If she remembered the chain as well as she said she did, there's no reason why she couldn't have told a jeweler how to make one, and anybody can buy a knife and have any initials they want engraved on it. There's plenty to be said against the probability of her having gone that far. If she did plant it, it's more likely she had the original chain – maybe she's had it for years – but all that's something for you folks to check up.'

'We're doing the best we can,' Guild said patiently. 'So you do think she did it?'

'The murder?' I shook my head. 'I haven't got that far yet. How about Nunheim? Did the bullets match up?'

'They did – from the same gun as was used on the dame – all five of them.'

'He was shot five times?'

'He was, and close enough to burn his clothes.'

'I saw his girl, the big red-head, tonight in a speak,' I told him. 'She's saying you and I killed him because he knew too much.'

He said: 'Hm-m-m. What speak was that? I might want to talk to her.'

'Studsy Burke's Pigiron Club,' I said, and gave him the address. 'Morelli hangs out there, too. He tells me Julia Wolf's real name is Nancy Kane and she has a boyfriend doing time in Ohio – Face Peppler.'

From the tone of Guild's 'Yes?' I imagined he had already found out about Peppler and about Julia's past. 'And what else did you pick up in your travels?'

'A friend of mine – Larry Crowley, a press agent – saw Jorgensen coming out of a hock-shop on Sixth near Forty–sixth yesterday afternoon.'

'Yes?'

'You don't seem to get excited about my news. I'm –'

Mimi opened the door and came in with glasses, whisky, and mineral water on a tray. 'I thought you'd like a drink,' she said cheerfully.

We thanked her.

She put the tray on the table, said: 'I don't mean to interrupt,' smiled at us with that air of amused tolerance which women like to affect towards male gatherings, and went out.

'You were saying something,' Guild reminded me.

'Just that if you people think I'm not coming clean with you, you ought to say so. We've been playing along together so far and I wouldn't want –'

'No, no,' Guild said hastily, 'it's nothing like that, Mr Charles.' His face had reddened a little. 'I been – The fact is the Commissioner's been riding us for action and I guess I been kind of passing it on. This second murder's made things tough.' He turned to the tray on the table. 'How'll you have yours?'

'Straight, thanks. No leads on it?'

'Well, the same gun and a lot of bullets, same as with her, but that's about all. It was a rooming-house hallway in between a couple stores. Nobody there claims they know Nunheim or Wynant or anybody else we can connect. The door's left unlocked, anybody could walk in, but that don't make too much sense when you come to think of it.'

'Nobody saw or heard anything?'

'Sure, they heard the shooting, but they didn't see anybody doing it.' He gave me a glass of whisky.

'Find any empty shells?' I asked.

He shook his head. 'Neither time. Probably a revolver.'

'And he emptied it both times – counting the shot that hit her telephone – if, like a lot of people, he carried an empty chamber under the hammer.'

Guild lowered the glass he was raising towards his mouth. 'You're not trying to find a Chinese angle on it, are you?' he complained. 'Just because they shoot like that.'

'No, but any kind of angle would help some. Find out where Nunheim was the afternoon the girl was killed?'

'Uh-huh. Hanging around the girl's building – part of the time anyhow. He was seen in front and he was seen in back, if you're going to believe people that didn't think much of it at the time and haven't got any reason for lying about it. And the day before the killing he had been up to her apartment, according to an elevator boy. The boy says he came down right away and he don't know whether he got in or not.'

I said: 'So. Maybe Miriam's right, maybe he did know too much. Find out anything about the four thousand difference between what Macaulay gave her and what Clyde Wynant says he got from her?'

'No.'

'Morelli says she always had plenty of money. He says she once lent him five thousand in cash.'

Guild raised his eyebrows. 'Yes?'

'Yes. He also says Wynant knew about her record.'

'Seems to me,' Guild said slowly, 'Morelli did a lot of talking to you.'

'He likes to talk. Find out anything more about what Wynant was working on when he left, or what he was going away to work on?'

'No. You're kind of interested in that shop of his.'

'Why not? He's an inventor, the shop's his place. I'd like to have a look at it some time.'

'Help yourself. Tell me some more about Morelli, and how you go about getting him to open up.'

'He likes to talk. Do you know a fellow called Sparrow? A big, fat, pale fellow with a pansy voice?'

Guild frowned. 'No. Why?'

'He was there – with Miriam – and wanted to take a crack at me, but they wouldn't let him.'

'And what'd he want to do that for?'

'I don't know. Maybe because she told him I helped knock Nunheim off – helped you.'

Guild said: 'Oh.' He scratched his chin with a thumbnail, looked at his watch. 'It's getting kind of late. Suppose you drop in and see me some time tomorrow – today.'

I said: 'Sure,' instead of the things I was thinking, nodded at him and Andy, and went out to the living-room.

Nora was sleeping on the sofa. Mimi put down the book she was reading and asked: 'Is the secret session over?'

'Yes.' I moved towards the sofa.

Mimi said: 'Let her sleep a while, Nick. You're going to stay till after your police friends have gone, aren't you?'

'All right. I want to see Dorothy again.'

'But she's asleep.'

'That's all right. I'll wake her up.'

'But –'

Guild and Andy came in, said their good nights, Guild looked regretfully at the sleeping Nora, and they left.

Mimi sighed. 'I'm tired of policemen,' she said. 'You remember that story?'

'Yes.'

Gilbert came in. 'Do they really think Chris did it?'

'No,' I said.

'Who do they think?'

'I could've told you yesterday. I can't today.'

'That's ridiculous,' Mimi protested. 'They know very well and you know very well that Clyde did it.' When I said nothing she repeated, more sharply: 'You know very well that Clyde did it.'

'He didn't,' I said.

An expression of triumph brightened Mimi's face. 'You *are* working for him, now aren't you?'

My 'No' bounced off her with no effect whatever.

Gilbert asked, not argumentatively, but as if he wanted to know: 'Why couldn't he?'

'He could've, but he didn't. Would he have written those letters throwing suspicion on Mimi, the one person who's helping him by hiding the chief evidence against him?'

'But maybe he didn't know that. Maybe he thought the police were simply not telling all they knew. They often do that, don't they? Or maybe he thought he could discredit her, so they wouldn't believe her if –'

'That's it,' Mimi said. 'That's exactly what he did, Nick.'

I said to Gilbert: 'You don't think he killed her.'

'No, I don't think he did, but I'd like to know why you don't think so – you know – your method.'

'And I'd like to know yours.'

His face flushed a little and there was some embarrassment in his smile. 'Oh, but I – it's different.'

'He *knows* who killed her,' Dorothy said from the doorway. She was still dressed. She stared at me fixedly, as if afraid to look at anybody else. Her face was pale and she held her small body stiffly erect.

Nora opened her eyes, pushed herself up on an elbow, and asked: 'What?' sleepily. Nobody answered her.

Mimi said: 'Now, Dorry, don't let's have one of those idiotic dramatic performances.'

Dorothy said: 'You can beat me after they've gone. You will.' She said it without taking her eyes off mine.

Mimi tried to look as if she did not know what her daughter was talking about.

'Who does he know killed her?' I asked.

Gilbert said: 'You're making an ass of yourself, Dorry, you're –'

I interrupted him: 'Let her. Let her say what she's got to say. Who killed her, Dorothy?'

She looked at her brother and lowered her eyes and no longer held herself erect. Looking at the floor, she said indistinctly: 'I don't know. He knows.' She raised her eyes to mine and began to tremble. 'Can't you see I'm afraid?' she cried. 'I'm afraid of them. Take me away and I'll tell you, but I'm afraid of them.'

Mimi laughed at me. 'You asked for it. It serves you right.'

Gilbert was blushing. 'It's so silly,' he mumbled.

I said: 'Sure, I'll take you away, but I'd like to have it out now while we're all together.'

Dorothy shook her head. 'I'm afraid.'

Mimi said: 'I wish you wouldn't baby her so, Nick. It only makes her worse. She –'

I asked Nora: 'What do you say?'

She stood up and stretched without lifting her arms. Her face was pink and lovely as it always is when she has been sleeping.

She smiled drowsily at me and said: 'Let's go home. I don't like these people. Come on, get your hat and coat, Dorothy.'

Mimi said to Dorothy: 'Go to bed.'

Dorothy put the tips of the fingers of her left hand to her mouth and whimpered through them: 'Don't let her beat me, Nick.'

I was watching Mimi, whose face wore a placid half-smile, but her nostrils moved with her breathing and I could hear her breathing.

Nora went around to Dorothy. 'Come on, we'll wash your face and –'

Mimi made an animal noise in her throat, muscles thickened on the back of her neck, and she put her weight on the balls of her feet.

Nora stepped between Mimi and Dorothy. I caught Mimi by a shoulder as she started forward, put my other arm round her waist from behind, and lifted her off her feet. She screamed and hit back at me with her fists and her hard sharp high heels made dents in my shins.

Nora pushed Dorothy out of the room and stood in the doorway watching us. Her face was very live. I saw it clearly, sharply: everything else was blurred. When clumsy ineffectual blows on my back and shoulder brought me around to find Gilbert pommelling me, I could see him but dimly and I hardly felt the contact when I shoved him aside. 'Cut it out. I don't want to hurt you, Gilbert.' I carried Mimi over to the sofa and dumped her on her back on it, sat on her knees, got a wrist in each hand.

Gilbert was at me again. I tried to pop his knee-cap, but kicked him too low, kicked his leg from under him. He went down on the floor in a tangle. I kicked at him again, missed, and said: 'We can fight afterwards. Get some water.'

Mimi's face was becoming purple. Her eyes protruded, glassy, senseless, enormous. Saliva bubbled and hissed between clenched teeth with her breathing, and her red throat – her whole body – was a squirming mass of veins and muscles swollen until it seemed they must burst. Her wrists were hot in my hands and sweat made them hard to hold.

Nora beside me with a glass of water was a welcome sight. 'Chuck it in her face,' I said.

Nora chucked it. Mimi separated her teeth to gasp and she shut her eyes. She moved her head violently from side to side, but there was less violence in the squirming of her body.

'Do it again,' I said.

The second glass of water brought a spluttering protest from Mimi and the fight went out of her body. She lay still limp, panting.

I took my hands away from her wrists and stood up. Gilbert, standing on one foot, was leaning against a table nursing the leg I had kicked. Dorothy, big-eyed and pale, was in the doorway, undecided whether to come in or run off and hide. Nora, beside me, holding the empty glass in her hand, asked: 'Think she's all right?'

'Sure.'

Presently Mimi opened her eyes, tried to blink the water out of them. I put a handkerchief in her hand. She wiped her face, gave a long shivering sigh, and sat up on the sofa. She looked around the room, still blinking a little. When she saw me she smiled feebly. There was guilt in her smile, but nothing you could call remorse. She touched her hair with an unsteady hand and said: 'I've certainly been drowned.'

I said: 'Some day you're going into one of those things and not come out of it.'

She looked past me at her son. 'Gil. What's happened to you?' she asked.

He hastily took his hand off his leg and put his foot down on the floor. 'I – uh – nothing,' he stammered. 'I'm perfectly all right.' He smoothed his hair, straightened his necktie.

She began to laugh. 'Oh, Gil, did you really try to protect me? And from Nick?' Her laughter increased. 'It was awfully sweet of you, but awfully silly. Why, he's a monster, Gil. Nobody could –' She put my handkerchief over her mouth and rocked back and forth.

I looked sidewise at Nora. Her mouth was set and her eyes were almost black with anger. I touched her arm. 'Let's blow. Give your mother a drink, Gilbert. She'll be all right in a minute or two.'

Dorothy, hat and coat in her hands, tiptoed to the outer door. Nora and I found our hats and coats and followed her out, leaving Mimi laughing into my handkerchief on the sofa.

None of the three of us had much to say in the taxicab that carried us over to the Normandie. Nora was brooding, Dorothy seemed still pretty frightened, and I was tired – it had been a full day.

It was nearly five o'clock when we got home. Asta greeted us boisterously. I lay down on the floor to play with her while Nora went into the pantry to make coffee. Dorothy wanted to tell me something that happened to her when she was a little child.

I said: 'No. You tried that Monday. What is it? A gag? It's late. What was it you were afraid to tell me over there?'

'But you'd understand better if you'd let me –'

'You said *that* Monday. I'm not a psycho-analyst. I don't know anything about early influences. I don't give a damn about them. And I'm tired – I've been ironing all day.'

She pouted at me. 'You seem to be trying to make it as hard for me as you can.'

'Listen, Dorothy,' I said, 'you either know something you were afraid to say in front of Mimi and Gilbert or you don't. If you do, spit it out. I'll ask you about any of it I find myself not understanding.'

She twisted a fold of her skirt and looked sulkily at it, but when she raised her eyes they became bright and excited. She spoke in a whisper loud enough for anybody in the room to hear: 'Gil's been seeing my father and he saw him today and my father told him who killed Miss Wolf.'

'Who?'

She shook her head. 'He wouldn't tell me. He'd just tell me that.'

'And that's what you were afraid to say in front of Gil and Mimi?'

'Yes. You'd understand that if you'd let me tell you –'

'Something that happened when you were a little child. Well, I won't. Stop it. What else did he tell you?'

'Nothing.'

'Nothing about Nunheim?'

'No, nothing.'

'Where is your father?'

'Gil didn't tell me.'

'When did he meet him?'

'He didn't tell me. Please don't be mad, Nick. I've told you everything he told me.'

'And a fat lot it is,' I growled. 'When'd he tell you this?'

'Tonight. He was telling me when you came in my room, and honest, that's all he told me.'

I said: 'It'd be swell if just once one of you people would make a clear and complete statement about something – it wouldn't matter what.'

Nora came in with the coffee. 'What's worrying you now, son?' she asked.

'Things,' I said, 'riddles, lies, and I'm too old and too tired for them to be any fun. Let's go back to San Francisco.'

'Before New Year's?'

'Tomorrow, today.'

'I'm willing.' She gave me a cup. 'We can fly back, if you want, and be there for New Year's Eve.'

Dorothy said tremulously: 'I didn't lie to you, Nick. I told you everything I – Please, please don't be mad with me. I'm so –' She stopped talking to sob.

I rubbed Asta's head and groaned.

Nora said: 'We're all worn out and jumpy. Let's send the pup downstairs for the night and turn in and do our talking after we've had some rest. Come on, Dorothy, I'll bring your coffee into the bedroom and give you some night-clothes.'

Dorothy got up, said: 'Good night,' to me. 'I'm sorry I'm so silly,' and followed Nora out.

When Nora returned she sat down on the floor beside me. 'Our Dorry does her share of weeping and whining,' she said. 'Admitting life's not too pleasant for her just now, still...' She yawned. 'What was her fearsome secret?'

I told her what Dorothy had told me. 'It sounds like a lot of hooey.'

'Why?'

'Why not? Everything else we've got from them has been hooey.'

Nora yawned again. 'That may be good enough for a detective, but it's not convincing enough for me. Listen, why don't we make a list of all the suspects and all the motives and clues, and check them off against –'

'You do it. I'm going to bed. What's a clue, Mamma?'

'It's like when Gilbert tiptoed over to the phone tonight when I was alone in the living-room, and he thought I was asleep, and told the operator not to put through any incoming calls until morning.'

'Well, well.'

And,' she said, 'it's like Dorothy discovering that she had Aunt Alice's key all the time.'

'Well, well.'

'And it's like Studsy nudging Morelli under the table when he started to tell you about the drunken cousin of – what was it? – Dick O'Brien's that Julia Wolf knew.'

I got up and put our cups on a table. 'I don't see how any detective can hope to get along without being married to you, but, just the same, you're overdoing it. Studsy nudging Morelli is my idea of something to spend a lot of time not worrying about. I'd rather worry about whether they pushed Sparrow around to keep me from being hurt or to keep me from being told something. I'm sleepy.'

26

Nora shook me awake at a quarter past ten. 'The telephone,' she said. 'It's Herbert Macaulay and he says it's important.'

I went into the bedroom – I had slept in the living-room – to the telephone. Dorothy was sleeping soundly. I mumbled: 'Hello,' into the telephone.

Macaulay said: 'It's too early for that lunch, but I've got to see you right away. Can I come up now?'

'Sure. Come up for breakfast.'

'I've had it. Get yours and I'll be up in fifteen minutes.'

'Right.'

Dorothy opened her eyes less than half-way, said: 'It must be late,' sleepily, turned over, and returned to unconsciousness.

I put cold water on my face and hands, brushed my teeth and hair, and went back to the living-room. 'He's coming up,' I told Nora. 'He's had breakfast, but you'd better order some coffee for him. I want chicken livers.'

'Am I invited to your party or do I –'

'Sure. You've never met Macaulay, have you? He's a pretty good guy. I was attached to his outfit for a few days once, up around Vaux, and we looked each other up after the war. He threw a couple of jobs my way, including the Wynant one. How about a drop of something to cut the phlegm?'

'Why don't you stay sober today?'

'We didn't come to New York to stay sober. Want to see a hockey game tonight?'

'I'd like to.' She poured me a drink and went to order breakfast.

I looked through the morning papers. They had the news of Jorgensen's being picked up by the Boston police and of Nunheim's murder, but further developments of what the tabloids called 'The Hell's Kitchen Gang War', the arrest of 'Prince Mike' Ferguson, and an interview with the 'Jafsie' of the Lindbergh kidnapping negotiations got more space.

Macaulay and the bellboy who brought Asta up arrived together. Asta liked Macaulay because when he patted her he gave her something to set her weight against: she was never very fond of gentleness.

He had lines around his mouth this morning and some of the rosiness was gone from his cheeks. 'Where'd the police get this new line?' he asked. 'Do they think –' He broke off as Nora came in. She had dressed.

'Nora, this is Herbert Macaulay,' I said. 'My wife.'

They shook hands and Nora said: 'Nick would only let me order some coffee for you. Can I –'

'No thanks, I've just finished breakfast.'

I said: 'Now what's this about the police?'

He hesitated.

'Nora knows practically everything I know,' I assured him, 'so unless it's something you'd rather not –'

'No, no, nothing like that,' he said. 'It's – well – for Mrs Charles's sake. I don't want to cause her anxiety.'

'Then out with it. She only worries about things she doesn't know. What's the new police line?'

'Lieutenant Guild came to see me this morning,' he said. 'First he showed me a piece of watch-chain with a knife attached to it and asked me if I'd ever seen them before. I had: they were Wynant's. I told him I thought I had: I thought they looked like Wynant's. Then he asked me if I knew of any way in which they could have come into anybody else's possession and, after some beating about the bush, I discovered that by anybody else he meant you or Mimi. I told him certainly – Wynant could have given them to either of you, you could have stolen them or found them on the street or have been given them by somebody who stole them or found them on the street, or you could have got them from somebody Wynant gave them to. There were other ways, too, for you to have got them, I told him, but he knew I was kidding him, so he wouldn't let me tell him about them.'

There were spots of color in Nora's cheeks and her eyes were dark. 'The idiot!'

'Now, now,' I said. 'Maybe I should have warned you – he was heading in that direction last night. I think it's likely my old pal Mimi gave him a prod or two. What else did he turn the searchlight on?'

'He wanted to know about – what he asked was: 'Do you figure Charles and the Wolf dame was still playing around together? Or was that all washed up?"

'That's the Mimi touch, all right,' I said. 'What'd you tell him?'

'I told him I didn't know whether you were 'still' playing around together because I didn't know that you had ever played around together, and reminded him that you hadn't been living in New York for a long time anyway.'

Nora asked him: 'Did you?'

I said: 'Don't try to make a liar out of Mac. What'd he say to that?'

'Nothing. He asked me if I thought Jorgensen knew about you and Mimi and, when I asked him what about you and Mimi, he accused me of acting the innocent – they were his words – so we didn't get very far. He was interested in the times I had seen you, also, where and when to the exact inch and second.'

'That's nice,' I said. 'I've got lousy alibis.'

A waiter came in with our breakfast. We talked about this and that until he had set the table and gone away.

Then Macaulay said: 'You've nothing to be afraid of. I'm going to turn Wynant over to the police.' His voice was unsteady and a little choked.

'Are you sure he did it?' I asked. 'I'm not.'

He said simply: 'I know.' He cleared his throat. 'Even if there was a chance in a thousand of my being wrong – and there isn't – he's a madman, Charles. He shouldn't be loose.'

'That's probably right enough,' I began, 'and if you know –'

'I know,' he repeated. 'I saw him the afternoon he killed her; it couldn't've been half an hour after he'd killed her, though I didn't know that, didn't even know she'd been killed. I – well – I know it now.'

'You met him in Hermann's office?'

'What?'

'You were supposed to have been in the office of a man named Hermann, on Fifty-seventh Street, from around three o'clock till around four that afternoon. At least, that's what the police told me.'

'That's right,' he said. 'I mean that's the story they got. What really happened: after I failed to find Wynant or any news of him at the Plaza and phoned my office and Julia with no better results, I gave him up and started walking down to Hermann's. He's a mining engineer, a client of mine; I had just finished drawing up some articles of incorporation for him, and there were some minor changes to be made in them. When I got to Fifty-seventh Street I suddenly got a feeling that I was being followed – you know the feeling. I couldn't think of any reason for anybody shadowing me, but still, I'm a lawyer, and there might be. Anyhow, I wanted to find out, so I turned east on Fifty-seventh and walked over to Madison and still wasn't sure. There was a small sallow man I thought I'd seen around the Plaza, but – The quickest way to find out seemed to be by taking a taxi, so I did that and told the driver to drive east. There was too much traffic there for me to see whether this small man or anybody else took a taxi after me, so I had my driver turn south at Third, east again on Fifty-sixth and south again on Second Avenue, and by that time I was pretty sure a yellow taxi was following me. I couldn't see whether my small man was in it, of course; it wasn't close enough for that. And at the next corner, when a red light stopped us, I saw Wynant. He was in a taxicab going west on Fifty-fifth Street. Naturally, that didn't surprise me very much: we were only two blocks from Julia's and I took it for granted she hadn't wanted me to know he was there when I phoned and that he was now on his way over to meet me at the Plaza. He was never very punctual. So I told my driver to turn west, but at Lexington Avenue – we were half a block behind him – Wynant's taxicab turned south. That wasn't the way to the Plaza and wasn't even the way to my office, so I said to hell with him and turned my attention back to the taxi following me – and it wasn't there any more. I kept a look-out behind all the way over to Hermann's and saw no sign at all of anybody following me.'

'What time was it when you saw Wynant?' I asked.

'It must've been fifteen or twenty minutes past three. It was twenty minutes to four when I got to Hermann's and I imagine that was twenty or twenty-five minutes later. Well, Hermann's secretary – Louise Jacobs, the girl I was with when I saw you last night – told me he had been locked up in a conference all afternoon, but would probably be through in a few minutes, and he was, and I got through with him in ten or fifteen minutes and went back to my office.'

'I take it you weren't close enough to Wynant to see whether he looked excited, was wearing his watch-chain, smelled of gunpowder – things like that.'

'That's right. All I saw was his profile going past, but don't think I'm not sure it was Wynant.'

'I won't. Go ahead,' I said.

'He didn't phone again. I'd been back about an hour when the police phoned – Julia was dead. Now you must understand that I didn't think Wynant had killed her – not for a minute. You can understand that – you still don't think he did. So when I went over there and the police began to ask me questions about him and I could see they suspected him, I did what ninety-nine out of a hundred lawyers would've done for their clients – I said nothing about having seen him in that neighbourhood at about the time that the murder must have been committed. I told them what I told you – about having the date with him and him not showing up – and let them understand that I had gone over to Hermann's straight from the Plaza.'

'That's understandable enough,' I agreed. 'There was no sense in your saying anything until you had heard his side of the story.'

'Exactly, and, well, the catch is I never heard his side of the story. I'd expected him to show up, phone me, something, but he didn't – until Tuesday, when I got that letter from him from Philadelphia, and there was not a word in it about his failure to meet me Friday, nothing about – but you saw the letter. What'd you think of it?'

'You mean did it sound guilty?'

'Yes.'

'Not particularly,' I said. 'It's about what could be expected from him if he didn't kill her – no great alarm over the police suspecting him except as it might interfere with his work, a desire to have it all cleaned up with no inconvenience to him – not too bright a letter to have come from anybody else, but in line with his particular form of goofiness. I can see him sending it off without the faintest notion that the best thing he could do would be to account for his own actions on the day of the murder. How sure are you he was coming from Julia's when you saw him?'

'I'm sure now. I thought it likely at first. Then I thought he may have been to his shop. It's on First Avenue, just a few blocks from where I saw him, and though it's been closed since he went away, we renewed the lease last month and everything's there waiting for him to come back to it, and he could have been there that afternoon. The police couldn't find anything there to show whether he had or hadn't.'

'I meant to ask you: there was some talk about his having grown whiskers. Was he –'

'No – the same long bony face with the same ragged near-white mustache.'

'Another thing: there was a fellow named Nunheim killed yesterday, a small –'

'I'm coming to that,' he said.

'I was thinking about the little fellow you thought might be shadowing you.'

Macaulay stared at me. 'You mean that might've been Nunheim?'

'I don't know. I was wondering.'

'And I don't know,' he said. 'I never saw Nunheim, far as I –'

'He was a little fellow, not more than five feet three, and would weigh maybe a hundred and twenty. I'd say he was thirty-five or -six. Sallow, dark hair and eyes, with the eyes set pretty close together, big mouth, long limp nose, batwing ears – shifty looking.'

'That could easily be him,' he said, 'though I didn't get too close a view of my man. I suppose the police would let me see him' – he shrugged – 'not that it matters now. Where was I? Oh, yes, about not being able to get in touch with Wynant. That put me in an uncomfortable position, since the police clearly thought I was in touch with him and lying about it. So did you, didn't you?'

'Yes,' I admitted.

'And you *also*, like the police, probably suspected that I *had* met him, either at the Plaza or later, on the day of the murder.'

'It seemed possible.'

'Yes. And of course you were partly right. I had at least seen him, and seen him at a place and time that would've spelled Guilty with a capital G to the police, so, having lied instinctively and by inference, I now lied directly and deliberately. Hermann had been tied up in a conference all that afternoon and didn't know how long I had been waiting to see him. Louise Jacobs is a good friend of mine. Without going into details, I told her she could help me help a client by saying I had arrived there at a minute or two after three o'clock and she agreed readily enough. To protect her in case of trouble, I told her that if anything went wrong she could always say that she hadn't remembered what time I arrived, but that I, the next day, had casually mentioned my arrival at that time and she had no reason for doubting me – throwing the whole thing on me.' Macaulay took a deep breath. 'None of that's important now. What's important is that I heard from Wynant this morning.'

'Another one of those screwy letters?' I asked.

'No, he phoned. I made a date with him for tonight – for you and me. I told him you wouldn't do anything for him unless you could see him, so he promised to meet us tonight. I'm going to take the police, of course; I can't go on justifying my shielding him like this. I can get him an acquittal on grounds of insanity and have him put away. That's all I can do, all I want to do.'

'Have you told the police yet?'

'No. He didn't phone till just after they'd left. Anyway, I wanted to see you first. I wanted to tell you I hadn't forgotten what I owed you and –'

'Nonsense,' I said.

'It's not.' He turned to Nora. 'I don't suppose he ever told you he saved my life once in a shell-hole in –'

'He's nuts,' I told her. 'He fired at a fellow and missed and I fired at him and didn't and that's all there was to it.' I addressed him again: 'Why don't you let the police wait a while? Suppose you and I keep this date tonight and hear what he's got to say. We can sit on him and blow whistles when the meeting's about to break up if we're convinced he's the murderer.'

Macaulay smiled wearily. 'You're still doubtful, aren't you? Well, I'm willing to do it that way if you want, though it seems like a – But perhaps you'll change your mind when I tell you about our telephone conversation.'

Dorothy, wearing a nightgown and a robe of Nora's, both much too long for her, came in yawning. 'Oh!' she exclaimed when she saw Macaulay, and then, when she had recognized him: 'Oh, hello, Mr Macaulay. I didn't know you were here. Is there any news of my father?'

He looked at me. I shook my head. He told her: 'Not yet, but perhaps we'll have some today.'

I said: 'Dorothy's had some, indirectly. Tell Macaulay about Gilbert.'

'You mean about – about my father?' she asked hesitantly, staring at the floor.

'Oh, dear me, no,' I said.

Her face flushed and she glanced reproachfully at me; then, hastily, she told Macaulay: 'Gil saw my father yesterday and he told Gil who killed Miss Wolf.'

'What?'

She nodded four or five times, earnestly.

Macaulay looked at me with puzzled eyes.

'This doesn't have to've happened,' I reminded him. 'It's what Gil says happened.'

'I see. Then you think he might be –?'

'You haven't done much talking to that family since hell broke loose, have you?' I asked.

'No.'

'It's an experience. They're all sex-crazy, I think, and it backs up into their heads. They start off –'

Dorothy said angrily: 'I think you're horrid. I've done my best to –'

'What are you kicking about?' I demanded. 'I'm giving you the break this time: I'm willing to believe Gil did tell you that. Don't expect too much of me.'

Macaulay asked: 'And who killed her?'

'I don't know. Gil wouldn't tell me.'

'Had your brother seen him often?'

'I don't know how often. He said he had been seeing him.'

'And was anything said – well – about the man Nunheim?'

'No. Nick asked me that. He didn't tell me anything else at all.'

I caught Nora's eye and made signals. She stood up saying: 'Let's go in the other room, Dorothy, and give these lads a chance to do whatever it is they think they're doing.'

Dorothy went reluctantly, but she went out with Nora.

Macaulay said: 'She's grown up to be something to look at.' He cleared his throat. 'I hope your wife won't –'

'Forget it. Nora's all right. You started to tell me about your conversation with Wynant.'

'He phoned right after the police left and said he'd seen the ad. in the *Times* and wanted to know what I wanted. I told him you weren't anxious to get yourself mixed up in his troubles and had said you wouldn't touch it at all without talking it over with him first, and we made the date for tonight. Then he asked if I'd seen Mimi and I told him I'd seen her once or twice since her return from Europe and had also seen his daughter. And then he said this: 'If my wife should ask for money, give her any sum in reason."

'I'll be damned,' I said.

Macaulay nodded. 'That's the way I felt about it. I asked him why and he said what he'd read in the morning papers had convinced him that she was Rosewater's dupe, not his confederate, and he had reason to believe she was 'kindly disposed' towards him, Wynant. I began to see what he was up to, then, and I told him she had already turned the knife and chain over to the police. And try to guess what he said to that.'

'I give up.'

'He hemmed and hawed a bit – not much, mind you – and then as smooth as you like asked: 'You mean the chain and knife on the watch I left with Julia to be repaired?"

I laughed. 'What'd you say?'

'That stumped me. Before I could think up an answer he was saying: 'However, we can discuss that more fully when we meet tonight.' I asked him where and when we'd meet him and he said he'd have to phone me, he didn't know where he'd be. He's to phone me at my house at ten o'clock. He was in a hurry now, though he had seemed leisurely enough before, and hadn't time to answer any of the things I wanted to ask, so he hung up and I phoned you. What do you think of his innocence now?'

'Not so much as I did,' I replied slowly. 'How sure are you of hearing from him at ten tonight?'

Macaulay shrugged. 'You know as much about that as I do.'

'Then if I were you I wouldn't bother the police till we've grabbed our wild man and can turn him over to them. This story of yours isn't going to make them exactly love you and, even if they don't throw you in the can right away, they'll make things pretty disagreeable for you if Wynant gives us a run-around tonight.'

'I know, but I'd like to get the load off my shoulders.'

'A few hours more oughtn't to matter much,' I said. 'Did either of you say anything about his not keeping the date at the Plaza?'

'No. I didn't get a chance to ask him. Well, if you say wait, I'll wait, but –'

'Let's wait till tonight, anyhow, till he phones you – if he does – and then we can make up our minds whether to take the police along.'

'You don't think he'll phone?'

'I'm not too sure,' I said. 'He didn't keep his last date with you, and he seems to have gone pretty vague on you as soon as he learned that Mimi had turned in the watch-chain and knife. I wouldn't be too optimistic about it. We'll see, though. I'd better get out to your house at about nine o'clock, hadn't I?'

'Come for dinner.'

'I can't, but I'll make it as early as I can, in case he's ahead of time. We'll want to move fast. Where do you live?'

Macaulay gave me his address, in Scarsdale, and stood up. 'Will you say goodbye to Mrs Charles for me and thank – Oh, by the way, I hope you didn't misunderstand me about Harrison Quinn last night. I meant only just what I said, that I'd had bad luck taking his advice on the market. I didn't mean to insinuate that there was anything – you know – or that he might not've made money for his other customers.'

'I understand,' I said, and called Nora.

She and Macaulay shook hands and made polite speeches to each other and he pushed Asta around a little and said: 'Make it as early as you can,' to me and went away.

'There goes the hockey game,' I said, 'unless you find somebody else to go with.'

'Did I miss anything?' Nora asked.

'Not much.' I told her what Macaulay had told me. 'And don't ask me what I think of it. I don't know. I know Wynant's crazy, but he's not acting like a crazy man and he's not acting like a murderer. He's acting like a man playing some kind of game. God only knows what the game is.'

'I think,' she said, 'that he's shielding somebody else.'

'Why don't you think he did it?'

She looked surprised. 'Because you don't.'

I said that was a swell reason. 'Who is the somebody else?'

'I don't know yet. Now don't make fun of me: I've thought about it a lot. It wouldn't be Macaulay, because he's using him to help shield whoever it is and –'

'And it wouldn't be me,' I suggested, 'because he wants to use me.'

'That's right,' she said, 'and you're going to feel very silly if you make fun of me and then I guess who it is before you do. And it wouldn't be either Mimi or Jorgensen, because he tried to throw suspicion on them. And it wouldn't be Nunheim, because he was most likely killed by the same person and, furthermore, wouldn't have to be shielded now. And it wouldn't be Morelli, because Wynant was jealous of him and they'd had a row.' She frowned at me. 'I wish you'd found out more about that big fat man they called Sparrow and that big red-haired woman.'

'But how about Dorothy and Gilbert?'

'I wanted to ask you about them. Do you think he's got any very strong paternal feeling for them?'

'No.'

'You're probably just trying to discourage me,' she said. 'Well, knowing them, it's hard to think either of them might've been guilty, but I tried to throw out my personal feelings and stick to logic. Before I went to sleep last night I made a list of all the –'

'There's nothing like a little logic-sticking to ward off insomnia. It's like –'

'Don't be so damned patronizing. Your performance so far has been a little less than dazzling.'

'I didn't mean no harm,' I said and kissed her. 'That a new dress?'

'Ah! Changing the subject, you coward.'

27

I went to see Guild early in the afternoon and went to work on him as soon as we had shaken hands. 'I didn't bring my lawyer along. I thought it looked better if I came by myself.'

He wrinkled his forehead and shook his head as if I had hurt him. 'Now it was nothing like that,' he said patiently.

'It was too much like that.'

He sighed. 'I wouldn't've thought you'd make the mistake that a lot of people make thinking just because we – You know we got to look at every angle, Mr Charles.'

'That sounds familiar. Well, what do you want to know?'

'All I want to know is who killed her – and him.'

'Try asking Gilbert,' I suggested.

Guild pursed his lips. 'Why him exactly?'

'He told his sister he knew who did it, told her he got it from Wynant.'

'You mean he's been seeing the old man?'

'So she says he said. I haven't had a chance to ask him about it.'

He squinted his watery eyes at me. 'Just what is that lay-out over there, Mr Charles?'

'The Jorgensen family? You probably know as much about it as I do'.

'I don't,' he said, 'and that's a fact. I just can't size them up at all. This Mrs Jorgensen, now, what is she?'

'A blonde.'

He nodded gloomily. 'Uh-huh, and that's all I know. But look, you've known them a long time and from what she says you and her –'

'And me and her daughter,' I said, 'and me and Julia Wolf and me and Mrs Astor. I'm hell with the women.'

He held up a hand. 'I'm not saying I believe everything she says, and there's nothing to get sore about. You're taking the wrong attitude, if you don't mind me saying it. You're acting like you thought we were out to get you, and that's all wrong, absolutely all wrong.'

'Maybe, but you've been talking double to me ever since last –'

He looked at me with steady pale eyes and said calmly: 'I'm a copper and I got my work to do.'

'That's reasonable enough. You told me to come in today. What do you want?'

'I didn't tell you to come in, I asked you.'

'All right. What do you want?'

'I don't want this,' he said. 'I don't want anything like this. We've been talking man to man up to this time and I'd kind of like to go on that way.'

'You made the change.'

'I don't think that's a fact. Look here, Mr Charles, would you take your oath, or even just tell me straight out, that you've been emptying your pockets to me right along?'

There was no use saying yes – he would not have believed me. I said: 'Practically.'

'Practically yes,' he grumbled. 'Everybody's been telling me practically the whole truth. What I want's some impractical son of a gun that'll shoot the works.'

I could sympathize with him: I knew how he felt. I said: 'Maybe nobody you've found knows the whole truth.'

He made an unpleasant face. 'That's very likely, ain't it? Listen, Mr Charles. I've talked to everybody I could find.

If you can find any more for me, I'll talk to them too. You mean Wynant? Don't you suppose we got every facility the department's got working night and day trying to turn him up?'

'There's his son,' I suggested.

'There's his son,' he agreed. He called in Andy and a swarthy bow-legged man named Kline. 'Get me that Wynant kid – the punk – I want to talk to him.' They went out. He said: 'See, I want people to talk to.'

I said: 'Your nerves are in pretty bad shape this afternoon, aren't they? Are you bringing Jorgensen down from Boston?'

He shrugged his big shoulders. 'History listens all right to me. I don't know. Want to tell me what you think of it?'

'Sure.'

'I'm kind of jumpy this afternoon, for a fact,' he said. 'I didn't get a single solitary wink of sleep last night. It's a hell of a life. I don't know why I stick at it. A fellow can get a piece of land and some wire fencing and a few head of silver fox and – Well, anyways, when you people scared Jorgensen off back in '25, he says he lit out for Germany, leaving his wife in the lurch – though he don't say much about that – and changing his name to give you more trouble finding him, and on the same account he's afraid to work at his regular job – he calls himself some kind of a technician or something – so pickings are kind of slim. He says he worked at one thing and another, whatever he could get, but near as I can figure out he was mostly gigoloing, if you know what I mean, and not finding too many heavy money dames. Well, along about '27 or '28 he's in Milan – that's a city in Italy – and he sees in the Paris *Herald* where this Mimi, recently divorced wife of Clyde Miller Wynant, has arrived in Paris. He don't know her personally and she don't know him, but he knows she's a dizzy blonde that likes men and fun and hasn't got much sense. He figures a bunch of Wynant's dough must've come to her with the divorce and, the way he looks at it, any of it he could take away from her wouldn't be any more than what Wynant had gypped him out of – he'd only be getting some of what belonged to him. So he scrapes up the fare to Paris and goes up there. All right so far?'

'Sounds all right.'

'That's what I thought. Well, he don't have any trouble getting to know her in Paris – either picking her up or getting somebody to introduce him or whatever happened – and the rest of it's just as easy. She goes for him in a big way – bing, according to him – right off the bat, and the first thing you know she's one jump ahead of him, she's thinking about marrying him. Naturally he don't try to talk her out of that. She'd gotten a lump sum – two hundred thousand berries, by God! – out of Wynant instead of alimony so her marrying again wasn't stopping any payments, and it'll put him right in the middle of the cash-drawer. So they do it. According to him, it was a trick marriage up in some mountains he says are between Spain and France and was done by a Spanish priest on what was really French soil, which don't make it legal, but I figure he's just trying to discourage a bigamy rap. Personally, I don't care one way or the other. The point is he got his hands on the dough and kept them on it till there wasn't any more dough. And all this time, understand, he says she didn't know he was anybody but Christian Jorgensen, a fellow she met in Paris, and still didn't know it up to the time we grabbed him in Boston. Still sound all right?'

'Still sounds all right,' I said, 'except, as you say, about the marriage, and even that could be all right.'

'Uh-huh, and what difference does it make anyways? So comes the winter and the bank-roll's getting skinny and he's getting ready to take a run-out on her with the last of it, and then she says maybe they could come back to America and tap Wynant for some more. He thinks that's fair enough if it can be done, and she thinks it can be done, so they get on a boat and –'

'The story cracks a little there,' I said.

'What makes you think so? He's not figuring on going to Boston, where he knows his first wife is, and he's figuring on keeping out of the way of the few people that know him, including especially Wynant, and somebody's told him there's a statute of limitation making everything just lovely after seven years. He don't figure he's running much risk. They ain't going to stay here long.'

'I still don't like that part of his story,' I insisted, 'but go ahead.'

'Well, the second day he's here – while they're still trying to find Wynant – he gets a bad break. He runs into a friend of his first wife's – this Olga Fenton – on the street and she recognizes him. He tries to talk her out of tipping off the first wife and does manage to stall her along a couple days with a moving-picture story he makes up – what an imagination that guy's got! – but he don't fool her long, and she goes to her parson and tells him about it and asks him what she ought to do and he says she ought to tell the first wife, and so she does, and the next time she sees Jorgensen she tells him what she's done, and he lights out for Boston to try to keep his wife from kicking up trouble and we pick him up there.'

'How about his visit to the hock-shop?' I asked.

'That was part of it. He says there was a train for Boston leaving in a few minutes and he didn't have any dough with him and didn't have time to go home for some – besides not being anxious to face the second wife till he had the first one quieted down – and the banks were closed, so he soaked his watch. It checks up.'

'Did you see the watch?'

'I can. Why?'

'I was wondering. You don't think it was once on the other end of that piece of chain Mimi turned over to you?'

He sat up straight. 'By God!' Then he squinted at me suspiciously and asked: 'Do you know anything about it or are you –'

'No. I was just wondering. What does he say about the murders now? Who does he think did them?'

'Wynant. He admits for a while he thought Mimi might've, but he says she convinced him different. He claims she wouldn't tell him what she had on Wynant. He might be just trying to cover himself up on that. I don't guess there's any doubt about them meaning to use it to shake him down for that money they wanted.'

'Then you don't think she planted the knife and chain?'

Guild pulled down the ends of his mouth. 'She could've planted them to shake him down with. What's wrong with that?'

'It's a little complicated for a fellow like me,' I said. 'Find out if Face Peppler's still in the Ohio pen?'

'Uh-huh. He gets out next week. That accounts for the diamond ring. He had a pal of his on the outside send it to her for him. Seems they were planning to get married and go straight together after he got out, or some such. Anyways, the warden says he saw letters passing between them reading like that. This Peppler won't tell the warden that he knows anything that'll help us, and the warden don't call to mind anything that was in their letters that's any good to us. Of course, even this much helps some, with the motive. Say Wynant's jealous and she's wearing this other guy's ring and getting ready to go away with him. That'll –' He broke off to answer his telephone. 'Yes,' he said into it. 'Yes... what?... Sure... Sure, but leave somebody there... That's right.' He pushed the telephone aside. 'Another bum steer on that west Twenty-ninth Street killing yesterday.'

'Oh,' I said. 'I thought I heard Wynant's name. You know how some telephone voices carry.'

He blushed, cleared his throat. 'Maybe something sounded like it – why not. I guess. Uh-huh, that could sound like it – *why not*. I almost forgot: we looked up that fellow Sparrow for you.'

'What'd you find out?'

'It looks like there's nothing there for us. His name's Jim Brophy. It figures out that he was making a play for that girl at Nunheim's and she was sore at you and he was just drunk enough to think he could put himself in solid with her by taking a poke at you.'

'A nice idea,' I said. 'I hope you didn't make any trouble for Studsy.'

'A friend of yours? He's an ex-con, you know, with a record as long as your arm.'

'Sure. I sent him over once.' I started to gather up my hat and overcoat. 'You're busy I'll run along and –'

'No, no,' he said. 'Stick around if you got the time. I got a couple of things coming in that'll maybe interest you, and you can give me a hand with that Wynant kid, too, maybe.' I sat down again.

'Maybe you'd like a drink,' he suggested, opening a drawer of his desk, but I had never had much luck with policemen's liquor, so I said: 'No thanks.'

His telephone rang again and he said into it: 'Yes... Yes... That's all right. Come on in.' This time no words leaked out to me.

He rocked back in his chair and put his feet on his desk. 'Listen, I'm on the level about that silver fox farming and I want to ask you what you think of California for a place.'

I was trying to decide whether to tell him about the lion and ostrich farms in the lower part of the state when the door opened and a fat, red-haired man brought Gilbert Wynant in. One of Gilbert's eyes was completely shut by swollen flesh around it and his left knee showed through a tear in his pants-leg.

28

I said to Guild: 'When you say bring 'em in, they bring 'em in, don't they?'

'Wait,' he told me. 'This is more'n you think.' He addressed the fat, red-haired man: 'Go ahead, Flint, let's have it.'

Flint wiped his mouth with the back of a hand. 'He's, a wildcat for fair, the young fellow. He don't look tough, but, man, he didn't want to come along, I can tell you that. And can he run!'

Guild growled: 'You're a hero and I'll see the Commissioner about your medal right away, but never mind that now. Talk turkey.'

'I wasn't saying I did anything great,' Flint protested. 'I was just –'

'I don't give a damn what you did,' Guild said. 'I want to know what he did.'

'Yes, sir, I was getting to that. I relieved Morgan at eight o'clock this morning and everything went along smooth and quiet as per usual, with not a creature stirring, as the fellow says, till along about ten minutes after two, and then what do I hear but a key in the lock.' He sucked in his lips and gave us a chance to express our amazement.

'The Wolf dame's apartment,' Guild explained to me. 'I had a hunch.'

'And what a hunch!' Flint exclaimed, practically top-heavy with admiration. 'Man, what a hunch!' Guild glared at him and he went on hastily: 'Yes, sir, a key, and then the door opens and this young fellow comes in.' He grinned proudly, affectionately, at Gilbert. 'Scared stiff, he looked, and when I went for him he was out and away like a streak and it wasn't till the first floor that I caught him, and then, by golly, he put up a tussle and I had to bat him in the eye to tone him down. He don't look tough, but –'

'What'd he do in the apartment?' Guild asked.

'He didn't have a chance to do nothing. I –'

'You mean you jumped him without waiting to see what he was up to?' Guild's neck bulged over the edge of his collar, and his face was as red as Flint's hair.

'I thought it was best not to take no chances.'

Guild stared at me with angry incredulous eyes. I did my best to keep my face blank. He said in a choking voice: 'That'll do, Flint. Wait outside.'

The red-haired man seemed puzzled. He said: 'Yes, sir,' slowly. 'Here's his key' He put the key on Guild's desk and went to the door. There he twisted his head over a shoulder to say: 'He claims he's Clyde Wynant's son.' He laughed merrily.

Guild, still having trouble with his voice, said: 'Oh, he does, does he?'

'Yeah. I seen him somewhere before. I got an idea he used to belong to Big Shorty Dolan's mob. Seems to me I used to see him around –'

'Get out!' Guild snarled, and Flint got out. Guild groaned from deep down in his big body. 'That mug gets me. Big Shorty Dolan's mob!' He shook his head hopelessly and addressed Gilbert: 'Well, son?'

Gilbert said: 'I know I shouldn't've done it.'

'That's a fair start,' Guild said genially. His face was becoming normal again. 'We all make mistakes. Pull yourself up a chair and let's see what we can do about getting you out of the soup. Want anything for that eye?'

'No, thank you, it's quite all right.' Gilbert moved a chair two or three inches towards Guild and sat down.

'Did that bum smack you just to be doing something?'

'No, no, it was my fault. I – I did resist.'

'Oh, well,' Guild said, 'nobody likes to be arrested, I guess. Now what's the trouble?'

Gilbert looked at me with his one good eye.

'You're in as bad a hole as Lieutenant Guild wants to put you,' I told him. 'You'll make it easy for yourself by making it easy for him.'

Guild nodded earnestly. 'And that's a fact.' He settled himself comfortably in his chair and asked, in a friendly tone: 'Where'd you get the key?'

'My father sent it to me in his letter.' He took a white envelope from his pocket and gave it to Guild.

I went around behind Guild and looked at the envelope over his shoulder. The address was typewritten, *Mr Gilbert Wynant. The Courtland*, and there was no postage stamp stuck on it.

'When'd you get it?' I asked.

'It was at the desk when I got in last night, around ten o'clock. I didn't ask the clerk how long it had been there, but I don't suppose it was there when I went out with you, or they'd have given it to me.'

Inside the envelope were two sheets of paper covered with the familiar unskilful typewriting. Guild and I read together:

> DEAR GILBERT:
>
> If all these years have gone by without my having communicated with you, it is only because your mother wished it so and if now I break this silence with a request for your assistance it is because only great need could make me go against your mother's wishes. Also you are a man now and I feel that you yourself are the one to decide whether or not we should go on being strangers or whether we should act in accordance with our ties of blood. That I am in an

embarrassing situation now in connexion with Julia Wolf's so-called murder I think you know and I trust that you still have remaining enough affection for me to at least hope that I am in all ways guiltless of any complicity therein, which is indeed the case. I turn to you now for help in demonstrating my innocence once and for all to the police and to the world with every confidence that even could I not count on your affection for me I nevertheless could count on your natural desire to do anything within your power to keep unblemished the name that is yours and your sister's as well as your Father's. I turn to you also because while I have a lawyer who is able and who believes in my innocence and who is leaving no stone unturned to prove it and have hopes of engaging Mr Nick Charles to assist him I cannot ask either of them to undertake what is after all a patently illegal act nor do I know anybody else except you that I dare confide in. What I wish you to do is this, tomorrow go to Julia Wolf's apartment at 411 East 54th St to which the enclosed key will admit you and between the pages of a book called *The Grand Manner* you will find a certain paper or statement which you are to read and destroy immediately. You are to be sure you destroy it completely leaving not so much as an ash and when you have read it you will know why this must be done and will understand why I have entrusted this task to you. In the event that something should develop to make a change in our plans advisable I will call you on the telephone late tonight. If you do not hear from me I will telephone you tomorrow evening to learn if you have carried out my instructions and to make arrangements for a meeting. I have every confidence that you will realize the tremendous responsibility I am placing on your shoulders and that my confidence is not misplaced.

Affectionately,
YOUR FATHER

Wynant's sprawling signature was written in ink beneath 'Your Father'.

Guild waited for me to say something. I waited for him. After a little of that he asked Gilbert: 'And did he phone?'

'No, sir.'

'How do you know?' I asked. 'Didn't you tell the operator not to put any calls through?'

'I – yes, I did. I was afraid you'd find out who it was if he called up while you were there, but he'd've left some kind of message with the operator, I think, and he didn't.'

'Then you haven't been seeing him?'

'No.'

'And he didn't tell you who killed Julia Wolf?'

'No.'

'You were lying to Dorothy?'

He lowered his head and nodded at the floor. 'I was – it was – I suppose it was jealousy really' He looked up at me now and his face was pink. 'You see, Dorry used to look up to me and think I knew more than anybody else about almost everything and – you know – she'd come to me if there was anything she wanted to know and she always did what I told her, and then, when she got seeing you, it was different. She looked up to you and respected you more – she naturally would, I mean, she'd've been silly if she hadn't, because there's no comparison, of course, but I – I suppose I was jealous and resented – well, not exactly resented it, because I looked up to you too – but I wanted to do something to impress her again – show off, I guess you'd call it – and when I got that letter I pretended I'd been seeing my father and he'd told me who committed those murders, so she'd think I knew things even you didn't.' He stopped, out of breath, and wiped his face with a handkerchief.

I outwaited Guild again until presently he said: 'Well, I guess there ain't been a great deal of harm done, sonny, if you're sure you ain't doing harm by holding back some other things we ought to know.'

The boy shook his head. 'No, sir, I'm not holding back anything.'

'You don't know anything about that knife and chain your mother give us?'

'No, sir, and I didn't know a thing about it till after she had given it to you.'

'How is she?' I asked.

'Oh, she's all right, I think, though she said she was going to stay in bed today.'

Guild narrowed his eyes. 'What's the matter with her?'

'Hysteria,' I told him. 'She and the daughter had a row last night and she blew up.'

'A row about what?'

'God knows – one of those feminine brainstorms.'

Guild said: 'Hm–m–m,' and scratched his chin.

'Was Flint right in saying you didn't get a chance to hunt for your paper?' I asked the boy.

'Yes. I hadn't even had time to shut the door when he ran at me.'

'They're grand detectives I got working for me,' Guild growled. 'Didn't he yell, 'Boo!' when he jumped out at you? Never mind. Well, son, I can do one of two things, and the which depends on you. I can hold you for a while or I can let you go in exchange for a promise that you'll let me know as soon as your father gets in touch with you and let me know what he tells you and where he wants you to meet him, if any.'

I spoke before Gilbert could speak: 'You can't ask that of him, Guild. It's his own father.'

'I can't, huh?' He scowled at me. 'Ain't it for his father's good if he's innocent?'

I said nothing.

Guild's face cleared slowly. 'All right, then, son, suppose I put you on a kind of parole. If your father or anybody else asks you to do anything, will you promise to tell them you can't because you give me your word of honor you wouldn't?'

I said: 'That sounds reasonable.'

Gilbert said: 'Yes, sir, I'll give you my word.'

Guild made a large gesture with one hand. 'Ok. Run along.'

The boy stood up saying: 'Thank you very much, sir.' He turned to me. 'Are you going to be –'

'Wait for me outside,' I told him, 'if you're not in a hurry.'

'I will. Goodbye, Lieutenant Guild, and thank you.' He went out.

Guild grabbed his telephone and ordered *The Grand Manner* and its contents found and brought to him. That done, he clasped his hands behind his head and rocked back in his chair. 'So what?'

'It's anybody's guess,' I said.

'Look here, you don't still think Wynant didn't do it?'

'What difference does it make what I think? You've got plenty on him now with what Mimi gave you.'

'It makes a lot of difference,' he assured me. 'I'd like a lot to know what you think and why.'

'My wife thinks he's trying to cover up somebody else.'

'Is that so? Hm-m-m. I was never one to belittle women's intuition and, if you don't mind me saying so, Mrs Charles is a mighty smart woman. Who does she think it is?'

'She hadn't decided, the last I heard.'

He sighed. 'Well, maybe that paper he sent the kid for will tell us something.'

But the paper told us nothing that afternoon: Guild's men could not find it, could not find a copy of *The Grand Manner* in the dead woman's room.

29

Guild had red–haired Flint in again and put the thumbscrews on him. The red-haired man sweated away ten pounds, but he stuck to it that Gilbert had had no opportunity to disturb anything in the apartment and throughout Flint's guardianship nobody hadn't touched nothing. He did not remember having seen a book called *The Grand Manner*, but he was not a man you would expect to memorize book tides. He tried to be helpful and made idiotic suggestions until Guild chased him out.

'The kid's probably waiting for me outside,' I said, 'if you think talking to him again will do any good.'

'Do you?'

'No.'

'Well, then. But, by God, somebody took that book and I'm going to –'

'Why?' I asked.

'Why what?'

'Why'd it have to be there for somebody to take?'

Guild scratched his chin. 'Just what do you mean by that?'

'He didn't meet Macaulay at the Plaza the day of the murder, he didn't commit suicide in Allentown, he says he only got a thousand from Julia Wolf when we thought he was getting five thousand, he says they were just friends when we think they were lovers, he disappoints us too much for me to have much confidence in what he says.'

'It's a fact,' Guild said, 'that I'd understand it better if he'd either come in or run away. Him hanging around like this, just messing things up, don't fit in anywheres that I can see.'

'Are you watching his shop?'

'We're kind of keeping an eye on it. Why?'

'I don't know,' I said truthfully, 'except that he's pointed his finger at a lot of things that got us nowhere. Maybe we ought to pay some attention to the things he hasn't pointed at, and the shop's one of them.'

Guild said: 'Hm-m-m.'

I said: 'I'll leave you with that bright thought,' and put on my hat and coat. 'Suppose I wanted to get hold of you late at night, how would I reach you?'

He gave me his telephone number, we shook hands, and I left.

Gilbert Wynant was waiting for me in the corridor. Neither of us said anything until we were in a taxicab. Then he asked: 'He thinks I was telling the truth, doesn't he?'

'Sure. Weren't you?'

'Oh, yes, but people don't always believe you. You won't say anything to Mamma about this, will you?'

'Not if you don't want me to.'

'Thank you,' he said. 'In your opinion, is there more opportunity for a young man out West than here in the East?'

I thought of him working on Guild's fox farm while I replied: 'Not now. Thinking of going west?'

'I don't know. I want to do something.' He fidgeted with his necktie.

We had a couple of blocks of silence after that. Then he said: 'There's another funny question I'd like to ask you: what do you think of me?' He was more self-conscious about it than Alice Quinn had been.

'You're all right,' I told him, 'and you're all wrong.'

He looked away, out the window. 'I'm so awfully young.'

We had some more silence. Then he coughed and a little blood trickled from one corner of his mouth.

'That guy did hurt you,' I said.

He nodded shamefacedly and put his handkerchief to his mouth. 'I'm not very strong.'

At the Courtland he would not let me help him out of the taxicab and he insisted he could manage alone, but I went upstairs with him, suspecting that otherwise he would say nothing to anybody about his condition.

I rang the apartment bell before he could get his key out, and Mimi opened the door. She goggled at his black eye.

I said: 'He's hurt. Get him to bed and get him a doctor.'

'What happened?'

'Wynant sent him into something.'

'Into what?'

'Never mind that until we get him fixed up.'

'But Clyde was here,' she said. 'That's why I phoned you.'

'What?'

'He was.' She nodded vigorously. 'And he asked where Gil was. He was here for an hour or more. He hasn't been gone ten minutes.'

'All right, let's get him to bed.'

Gilbert stubbornly insisted that he needed no help, so I left him in the bedroom with his mother and went out to the telephone.

'Any calls?' I asked Nora when I had her on the line.

'Yes, sir. Messrs Macaulay and Guild want you to phone them, and Mesdames Jorgensen and Quinn want you to phone them. No children so far.'

'When did Guild call?'

About five minutes ago. Mind eating alone? Larry asked me to go to see the new Osgood Perkins show with him.'

'Go ahead. See you later.'

I called up Herbert Macaulay.

'The date's off,' he told me. 'I heard from our friend and he's up to God knows what. Listen, Charles, I'm going to the police. I've had enough of it.'

'I guess there's nothing else to do now,' I said. 'I was thinking about telephoning some policemen myself. I'm at Mimi's. He was here a few minutes ago. I just missed him.'

'What was he doing there?'

'I'm going to try and find out now.'

'Were you serious about phoning the police?'

'Sure.'

'Then suppose you do that and I'll come on over.'

'Right. Be seeing you.'

I called up Guild.

'A little news came in right after you left,' he said.

'Are you where I can give it to you?'

'I'm at Mrs Jorgensen's. I had to bring the kid home. That red–head lad of yours has got him bleeding somewhere inside.'

'I'll kill that mug,' he snarled. 'Then I better not talk.'

'I've got some news, too. Wynant was here for about an hour this afternoon, according to Mrs Jorgensen, and left only a few minutes before I got here.'

There was a moment of silence, then he said: 'Hold everything. I'll be right up.'

Mimi came into the living-room while I was looking up the Quinns' telephone number. 'Do you think he's seriously hurt?' she asked.

'I don't know, but you ought to get your doctor right away.' I pushed the telephone towards her. When she was through with it, I said: 'I told the police Wynant had been here.'

She nodded. 'That's what I telephoned you for, to ask if I ought to tell them.'

'I phoned Macaulay, too. He's coming over.'

'He can't do anything,' she said indignantly. 'Clyde gave them to me of his own free will – they're mine.'

'What's yours?'

'Those bonds; the money.'

'What bonds? What money?'

She went to the table and pulled the drawer out. 'See?'

Inside were three packages of bonds held together by thick rubber bands. Across the top of them lay a pink check on the Park Avenue Trust Company to the order of Mimi Jorgensen for ten thousand dollars, signed Clyde Miller Wynant, and dated January 3, 1933.

'Dated five days ahead,' I said. 'What kind of nonsense is that?'

'He said he hadn't that much in his account and might not be able to make a deposit for a couple of days.'

'There's going to be hell about this,' I warned her. 'I hope you're ready for it.'

'I don't see why,' she protested. 'I don't see why my husband – my former husband – can't provide for me and his children if he wants to.'

'Cut it out. What'd you sell him?'

'Sell him?'

'Uh-huh. What'd you promise to do in the next few days or he fixes it so the check's no good?'

She made an impatient face. 'Really, Nick, I think you're a half-wit sometimes with your silly suspicions.'

'I'm studying to be one. Three more lessons and I get my diploma. But remember I warned you yesterday that you'll probably wind up in –'

'Stop it,' she cried. She put a hand over my mouth. 'Do you have to keep saying that? You know it terrifies me and –' Her voice became soft and wheedling. 'You must know what I'm going through these days, Nick. Can't you be a little kinder?'

'Don't worry about me,' I said. 'Worry about the police.' I went back to the telephone and called up Alice Quinn. 'This is Nick. Nora said you –'

'Yes. Have you seen Harrison?'

'Not since I left him with you.'

'Well, if you do, you won't say anything about what I said last night, will you? I didn't mean it, really I didn't mean a word of it.'

'I didn't think you did,' I assured her, 'and I wouldn't say anything about it anyway. How's he feeling today?'

'He's gone,' she said.

'What?'

'He's gone. He's left me.'

'He's done that before. He'll be back.'

'I know, but I'm afraid this time. He didn't go to his office. I hope he's just drunk somewhere and – but this time I'm afraid. Nick, do you think he's really in love with that girl?'

'He seems to think he is.'

'Did he tell you he was?'

'That wouldn't mean anything.'

'Do you think it would do any good to have a talk with her?'

'No.'

'Why don't you? Do you think she's in love with him?'

'No.'

'What's the matter with you?' she asked irritably.

'No. I'm not at home.'

'What? Oh, you mean you're some place where you can't talk?'

'That's it.'

'Are you – are you at her house?'

'Yes.'

'Is she there?'

'No.'

'Do you think she's with him?'

'I don't know. I don't think so.'

'Will you call me when you can talk, or, better still, will you come up to see me?'

'Sure,' I promised, and hung up.

Mimi was looking at me with amusement in her blue eyes. 'Somebody's taking my brat's affairs seriously?' When I did not answer her, she laughed and asked: 'Is Dorry still being the maiden in distress?'

'I suppose so.'

'She will be, too, as long as she can get anybody to believe in it. And you, of all people, to be fooled, you who are afraid to believe that – well – that I, for instance, am ever telling the truth.'

'That's a thought,' I said. The door-bell rang before I could go on.

Mimi let the doctor in – he was a roly-poly elderly man with a stoop and a waddle – and took him in to Gilbert.

I opened the table-drawer again and looked at the bonds, Postal Telegraph & Cable 5s, Sao Paulo City 6½s, American Type Founders 6s, Certain-teed Products 5½s, Upper Austria 6½s, United Drugs 5s, Philippine Railway 4s, Tokio Electric Lighting 6s, about sixty thousand dollars at face value, I judged, and – guessing – between a quarter and a third of that at the market.

When the door-bell rang I shut the drawer and let Macaulay in. He looked tired. He sat down without taking off his overcoat and said: 'Well, tell me the worst. What was he up to here?'

'I don't know yet, except that he gave Mimi some bonds and a check.'

'I know that.' He fumbled in his pocket and gave me a letter:

> DEAR HERBERT:
>
> I am today giving Mrs Mimi Jorgensen the securities listed below and a ten thousand dollar check on the Park Ave Trust dated Jan. 3. Please arrange to have sufficient money there on that date to cover it. I would suggest that you sell some more of the utility bonds, but use your own

> judgement. I find that I cannot spend any more time in New York at present and probably will not be able to get back here for several months, but will communicate with you from time to time. I am sorry I will not be able to wait over to see you and Charles tonight.
>
> Yours truly,
> CLYDE MILLER WYNANT

Under the sprawling signature was a list of the bonds. 'How'd it come to you?' I asked.

'By messenger. What do you suppose he was paying her for?'

I shook my head. 'I tried to find out. She said he was 'providing for her and his children".'

'That's likely, as likely as that she'd tell the truth.'

'About these bonds,' I asked, 'I thought you had all his property in your hands?'

'I thought so too, but I didn't have these, didn't know he had them.' He put his elbows on his knees, his head in his hands. 'If all the things I don't know were laid end to end...'

30

Mimi came in with the doctor, said, 'Oh, how do you do,' a little stiffly to Macaulay, and shook hands with him. 'This is Doctor Grant, Mr Macaulay, Mr Charles.'

'How's the patient?' I asked.

Doctor Grant cleared his throat and said he didn't think there was anything seriously the matter with Gilbert, effects of a beating, slight haemorrhage of course, should rest, though. He cleared his throat again and said he was happy to have met us, and Mimi showed him out.

'What happened to the boy?' Macaulay asked me.

'Wynant sent him on a wild-goose chase over to Julia's apartment and he ran into a tough copper.'

Mimi returned from the door. 'Has Mr Charles told you about the bonds and the check?' she asked.

'I had a note from Mr Wynant saying he was giving them to you,' Macaulay said.

'Then there will be no –'

'Difficulty? Not that I know of.'

She relaxed a little and her eyes lost some of their coldness. 'I didn't see why there should be, but he' – pointing at me – 'likes to frighten me.'

Macaulay smiled politely. 'May I ask whether Mr Wynant said anything about his plans?'

'He said something about going away, but I don't suppose I was listening very attentively. I don't remember whether he told me when he was going or where.'

I grunted to show scepticism; Macaulay pretended he believed her. 'Did he say anything that you could repeat to me about Julia Wolf, or about his difficulties, or about anything connected with the murder at all?' he asked.

She shook her head emphatically. 'Not a word I could either repeat or couldn't, not a word at all. I asked him about it, but you know how unsatisfactory he can be when he wants. I couldn't get as much as a grunt out of him about it.'

I asked the question Macaulay seemed too polite to ask: 'What did he talk about?'

'Nothing really, except ourselves and the children, particularly Gil. He was very anxious to see him and waited nearly an hour, hoping he'd come home. He asked about Dorry, but didn't seem very interested.'

'Did he say anything about having written Gilbert?'

'Not a word. I can repeat our whole conversation, if you want me to. I didn't know he was coming, he didn't even phone from downstairs. The door–bell just rang and when I went to the door there he was, looking a lot older than when I'd seen him last and even thinner, and I said: 'Why, Clyde' or something like that, and he said: 'Are you alone?' I told him I was and he came in. Then he –'

The door-bell rang and she went to answer it.

'What do you think of it?' Macaulay asked in a low voice.

'When I start believing Mimi,' I said, 'I hope I have sense enough not to admit it.'

She returned from the door with Guild and Andy. Guild nodded to me and shook hands with Macaulay, then turned to Mimi and said: 'Well, ma'am, I'll have to ask you to tell –'

Macaulay interrupted him: 'Suppose you let me tell what I have to tell first, Lieutenant. It belongs ahead of Mrs Jorgensen's story and –'

Guild waved a big hand at the lawyer. 'Go ahead.' He sat down on an end of the sofa.

Macaulay told him what he had told me that morning. When he mentioned having told it to me that morning Guild glanced bitterly at me, once, and thereafter ignored me completely. Guild did not interrupt Macaulay, who told his story clearly and concisely. Twice Mimi started to say something, but each time broke off to listen. When Macaulay had finished, he handed Guild the note about the bonds and check. 'That came by messenger this afternoon.'

Guild read the note very carefully and addressed Mimi: 'Now then, Mrs Jorgensen.'

She told him what she had told us about Wynant's visit, elaborating the details as he patiently questioned her, but sticking to her story that he had refused to say a word about anything connected with Julia Wolf or her murder, that in giving her the bonds and check he had simply said that he wished to provide for her and the children, and that though he had said he was going away she did not know where or when. She seemed not at all disturbed by everybody's obvious disbelief. She wound up smiling, saying: 'He's a sweet man in a lot of ways, but quite mad.'

'You mean he's really insane, do you?' Guild asked; 'Not just nutty?'

'Yes.'

'What makes you think that?'

'Oh, you'd have to live with him really to know how mad he is,' she replied airily.

Guild seemed dissatisfied. 'What kind of clothes was he wearing?'

'A brown suit and brown overcoat and hat and I think brown shoes and a white shirt and a greyish necktie with either red or reddish-brown figures in it.'

Guild jerked his head at Andy. 'Tell 'em.'

Andy went out.

Guild scratched his jaw and frowned moughtfully. The rest of us watched him. When he stopped scratching, he looked at Mimi and Macaulay, but not at me, and asked: 'Any of you know anybody that's got the initials of D. W. Q.?'

Macaulay shook his head from side to side slowly.

Mimi said: 'No. Why?'

Guild looked at me now. 'Well?'

'I don't know them.'

'Why?' Mimi repeated.

Guild said, 'Try to remember back. He'd most likely've had dealings with Wynant.'

'How far back?' Macaulay asked.

'That's hard to say right now. Maybe a few months, maybe a few years. He'd be a pretty large man, big bones, big belly, and maybe lame.'

Macaulay shook his head again. 'I don't remember anybody like that.'

'Neither do I,' Mimi said, 'but I'm bursting with curiosity. I wish you'd tell us what it's all about.'

'Sure, I'll tell you.' Guild took a cigar from his vest pocket, looked at it, returned it to the pocket. 'A dead man like that's buried under the floor of Wynant's shop.'

I said: 'Ah.'

Mimi put both hands to her mouth and said nothing. Her eyes were round and glassy.

Macaulay, frowning, asked: 'Are you sure?'

Guild sighed. 'Now you know that ain't something anybody would guess at,' he said wearily.

Macaulay's face flushed and he smiled sheepishly. 'That was a silly question. How did you happen to find him – it?'

'Well, Mr Charles here kept hinting that we ought to pay more attention to that shop, so, figuring that Mr Charles here is a man that's liable to know a lot more things than he tells anybody right out, I sent some men around this morning to see what they could find. We'd give it the once-over before and hadn't turned up nothing, but this time I told 'em to take the dump apart, because Mr Charles here had said we ought to pay more attention to it. And Mr Charles here was right.' He looked at me with cool unfriendliness. 'By and by they found a corner of the cement floor looking a little newer maybe than the rest and they cracked it and there was the mortal remains of Mr D. W. Q. What do you think of that?'

Macaulay said: 'I think it was a damned good guess of Charles's.' He turned to me. 'How did you –'

Guild interrupted him. 'I don't think you ought to say that. When you call it just a guess, you ain't giving Mr Charles here the proper credit for being as smart as he is.'

Macaulay was puzzled by Guild's tone. He looked questioningly at me.

'I'm being stood in the corner for not telling Lieutenant Guild about our conversation this morning,' I explained.

'There's that,' Guild agreed calmly, 'among other things.'

Mimi laughed, and smiled apologetically at Guild when he stared at her.

'How was Mr D. W. Q. killed?' I asked.

Guild hesitated, as if making up his mind whether to reply, then moved his big shoulders slightly and said: 'I don't know yet, or how long ago. I haven't seen the remains yet, what there is of them, and the Medical Examiner wasn't through the last I heard.'

'What there is of them?' Macaulay repeated.

'Uh–huh. He'd been sawed up in pieces and buried in lime or something so there wasn't much flesh left on him, according to the report I got, but his clothes had been stuck in with him rolled up in a bundle, and enough was left of the inside ones to tell us something. There was part of a cane, too, with a rubber tip. That's why we thought he might be lame, and we –' He broke off as Andy came in. 'Well?'

Andy shook his head gloomily. 'Nobody sees him come, nobody sees him go. What was that joke about a guy being so thin he had to stand in the same place twice to throw a shadow?'

I laughed – not at the joke – and said: 'Wynant's not that thin, but he's thin enough, say as thin as the paper in that check and in those letters people have been getting.'

'What's that?' Guild demanded, his face reddening, his eyes angry and suspicious.

'He's dead. He's been dead a long time except on paper. I'll give you even money they're his bones in the grave with the fat, lame man's clothes.'

Macaulay leaned towards me. 'Are you sure of that, Charles?'

Guild snarled at me: 'What are you trying to pull?'

'There's the bet if you want it. Who'd go to all that trouble with a corpse and then leave the easiest thing of all to get rid of – the clothes – untouched unless they –'

'But they weren't untouched. They –'

'Of course not. That wouldn't look right. They'd have to be partly destroyed, only enough left to tell you what they were supposed to tell. I bet the initials were plenty conspicuous.'

'I don't know,' Guild said with less heat. 'They were on a belt buckle.'

I laughed.

Mimi said angrily: 'That's ridiculous, Nick. How could that be Clyde? You know he was here this afternoon. You know he –'

'Sh-h-h. It's very silly of you to play along with him,' I told her. 'Wynant's dead, your children are probably his heirs, that's more money than you've got over there in the drawer. What do you want to take part of the loot for when you can get it all?'

'I don't know what you mean,' she said. She was very pale.

Macaulay said: 'Charles thinks Wynant wasn't here this afternoon and that you were given those securities and the check by somebody else, or perhaps stole them yourself. Is that it?' he asked me.

'Practically.'

'But that's ridiculous,' she insisted.

'Be sensible, Mimi,' I said. 'Suppose Wynant was killed three months ago and his corpse disguised as somebody else. He's supposed to have gone away leaving powers of attorney with Macaulay. All right, then, the estate's completely in Macaulay's hands for ever and ever, or at least until he finishes plundering it, because you can't even –'

Macaulay stood up saying: 'I don't know what you're getting at, Charles, but I'm –'

'Take it easy,' Guild told him. 'Let him have his say out.'

'He killed Wynant and he killed Julia and he killed Nunheim,' I assured Mimi. 'What do you want to do? Be next on the list? You ought to know damned well that once you've come to his aid by saying you've seen Wynant alive – because that's his weak spot, being the only person up to now who claims to have seen Wynant since October – he's not going to take any chances on having you change your mind – not when it's only a matter of knocking you off with the same gun and putting the blame on Wynant. And what are you doing it for? For those few crummy bonds in the drawer, a fraction of what you get your hands on through your children if we prove Wynant's dead.'

Mimi turned to Macaulay and said: 'You rat!'

Guild gaped at her, more surprised by that than by anything else that had been said.

Macaulay started to move. I did not wait to see what he meant to do, but slammed his chin with my left fist. The punch was all right, it landed solidly and dropped him, but I felt a burning sensation on my left side and knew I had torn the bullet-wound open.

'What do you want me to do?' I growled at Guild. 'Put him in cellophane for you?'

31

It was nearly three in the morning when I let myself into our apartment at the Normandie. Nora, Dorothy, and Larry Crowley were in the living-room, Nora and Larry playing backgammon, Dorothy reading a newspaper.

'Did Macaulay really kill them?' Nora asked immediately.

'Yes. Did the morning papers have anything about Wynant?'

Dorothy said: 'No, just about Macaulay being arrested. Why?'

'Macaulay killed him too.'

Nora said: 'Really?' Larry said: 'I'll be damned.' Dorothy began to cry. Nora looked at Dorothy in surprise. Dorothy sobbed: 'I want to go home to Mamma.'

Larry said not very eagerly: 'I'll be glad to take you home if...'

Dorothy said she wanted to go. Nora fussed over her but did not try to talk her out of going. Larry, trying not to look too unwilling, found his hat and coat. He and Dorothy left.

Nora shut the door behind them and leaned against it. 'Explain that to me, Mr Charalambides,' she said.

I shook my head.

She sat on the sofa beside me. 'Now out with it. If you skip a single word, I'll –'

'I'd have to have a drink before I could do any talking.'

She cursed me and brought me a drink. 'Has he confessed?'

'Why should he? You can't plead guilty of murder in the first degree. There were too many murders – and at least two of them were too obviously done in cold blood – for the District Attorney to let him plead guilty of second-degree murder. There's nothing for him to do but fight it out.'

'But he did commit them?'

'Sure.'

She pushed my glass down from my mouth. 'Stop stalling and tell me about it.'

'Well, it figures out that he and Julia had been gypping Wynant for some time. He'd dropped a lot of money in the market and he'd found out about her past – as Morelli hinted – and the pair of them teamed up on the old man. We're sticking accountants on Macaulay's books and Wynant's and shouldn't have much trouble tracing some of the loot from one to the other.'

'Then you don't know positively that he was robbing Wynant?'

'Sure we know. It doesn't click any other way. The chances are Wynant was going away on a trip the 3rd of October, because he did draw five thousand dollars out of the bank in cash, but didn't close up his shop and give up his apartment. That was done by Macaulay a few days later. Wynant was killed at Macaulay's in Scarsdale on the night of the 3rd. We know that because on the morning of the 4th, when Macaulay's cook, who slept at home, came to work, Macaulay met her at the door with some kind of trumped-up complaint and two weeks' wages and fired her on the spot, not letting her in the house to find any corpses or blood-stains.'

'How did you find that out? Don't skip details.'

'Ordinary routine. Naturally after we grabbed him we went to his office and house to see what we could find out – you know, where-were-you-on-the-night-of-June-6, – 1894 stuff – and the present cook said she'd only been working for him since the 8th of October, and that led to that. We also found a table with a very faint trace of what we hope is human blood not quite scrubbed out. The scientific boys are making shavings of it now to see if they can soak out any results for us.' (It turned out to be beef-blood.)

'Then you're not sure he –'

'Stop saying that. Of course we're sure. That's the only way it clicks. Wynant had found out that Julia and Macaulay were gypping him and also thought, rightly or wrongly, that Julia and Macaulay were cheating on him – and we know he was jealous – so he went up there to confront him with whatever proof he had, and Macaulay, with prison looking him in the face, killed the old man. Now don't say we're not sure. It doesn't make any sense otherwise. Well, there he is with a corpse, one of the harder things to get rid of. Can I stop to take a swallow of whisky?'

'Just one,' Nora said. 'But this is just a theory, isn't it?'

'Call it any name you like. It's good enough for me.'

'But I thought everybody was supposed to be considered innocent until they were proved guilty and if there was any reasonable doubt, they –'

'That's for juries, not detectives. You find the guy you think did the murder and you slam him in the can and let everybody know you think he's guilty and put his picture all over the newspapers, and the District Attorney builds up the best theory he can on what information you've got and meanwhile you pick up additional details here and there and people who recognize his picture in the paper – as well as people who'd think he was innocent if you hadn't arrested him – come in and tell you things about him and presently you've got him sitting on the electric chair.' (Two days later a woman in Brooklyn identified Macaulay as a George Foley who for the past three months had been renting an apartment from her.)

'But that seems so loose.'

'When murders are committed by mathematics,' I said, 'you can solve them by mathematics. Most of them aren't and this one wasn't. I don't want to go against your idea of what's right and wrong, but when I say he probably dissected the body so he could carry it into town in bags I'm only saying what seems most probable. That would be on the 6th of October or later, because it wasn't until then that he laid off the two mechanics Wynant had working in the shop – Prentice and McNaughton – and shut it up. So he buried Wynant under the floor, buried him with a fat man's clothes and a lame man's stick and a belt marked D. W Q., all arranged so they wouldn't get too much of the lime – or whatever he used to eat off the dead man's features and flesh – on them, and he re-cemented the floor over the grave. Between police routine and publicity we've got more than a fair chance of finding out where he bought or otherwise got the clothes and stick and the cement.' (We traced the cement to him later – he had bought it from a coal and wood dealer uptown – but had no luck with the other things.)

'I hope so,' she said, not too hopefully.

'So now that's taken care of. By renewing the lease on the shop and keeping it vacant – supposedly waiting for Wynant to return – he can make sure – reasonably sure – that nobody will discover the grave, and if it is accidentally discovered, then fat Mr D. W. Q. – by that time Wynant's bones would be pretty bare and you can't tell whether a man was thin or fat by his skeleton – was murdered by Wynant, which explains why Wynant has made himself scarce. That taken care of, Macaulay forges the power of attorney and, with Julia's help, settles down to the business of gradually transferring the late Clyde's money to themselves. Now I'm going theoretical again. Julia doesn't like murder, and she's frightened, and he's not too sure she won't weaken on him. That's why he makes her break with Morelli – giving Wynant's jealousy as an excuse. He's afraid she might confide to Morelli in a weak moment and, as the time draws near for her still closer friend, Face Peppler, to get out of prison, he gets more and more worried. He's been safe there as long as Face stayed in, because she's not likely to put anything dangerous in a letter that has to pass through the warden's hands, but now... Well, he starts to plan, and then all hell breaks loose. Mimi and her children arrive and start hunting for Wynant and I come to town and am in touch with them and he thinks I'm helping them. He decides to play safe on Julia by putting her out of the way. Like it so far?'

'Yes, but...'

'It gets worse as it goes along,' I assured her. 'On his way here for lunch that day he stops and phones his office, pretending he's Wynant, and making that appointment at the Plaza, the idea being to establish Wynant's presence in town. When he leaves here he goes to the Plaza and asks people if they've seen Wynant, to make that plausible, and for the same reason phones his office to ask if any further word has come in from Wynant, and phones Julia. She tells him she's expecting Mimi and she tells him Mimi thought she was lying when she said she didn't know where Wynant was, and Julia probably sounds pretty frightened. So he decides he's got to beat Mimi to the interview and he does. He beats it over there and kills her. He's a terrible shot. I saw him shoot during the war. It's likely he missed her with the first shot, the one that hit the telephone, and didn't succeed in killing her right away with the other four, but he probably thought she was dead, and, anyhow, he had to get out before Mimi arrived, so he dropped the piece of Wynant's chain that he had brought along as a clincher – and his having saved that for three months makes it look as if he'd intended killing her from the beginning – and scoots over to the engineer Hermann's office, where he takes advantage of the breaks and fixes himself up with an alibi. The two things he doesn't expect – couldn't very well have foreseen – are that Nunheim, hanging around trying to get at the girl, had seen him leave her apartment – may even have heard the shot – and that Mimi, with blackmail in her heart, was going to conceal the chain for use in shaking down her ex-husband. That's why he had to go down to Philadelphia and send me that wire and the letter to himself and one to Aunt Alice later – if Mimi thinks Wynant's throwing suspicion on her she'll get mad enough to give the police the evidence she's got against him. Her desire to hurt Jorgensen nearly gummed that up, though. Macaulay, by the way, knew Jorgensen was Rosewater. Right after he killed Wynant he had detectives look Mimi and her family up in Europe – their interest in the estate made them potentially dangerous – and the detectives found out who Jorgensen was. We found the reports in Macaulay's file. He pretended he was getting the information for Wynant, of course. Then he started worrying about me, about my not thinking Wynant guilty and –'

'And why didn't you?'

'Why should he write letters antagonizing Mimi, the one who was helping him by holding back incriminating evidence? That's why I thought the chain had been planted when she did turn it in, only I was a little bit too willing to believe she had done the planting. Morelli worried Macaulay, too, because he didn't want suspicion thrown on anybody who might, in clearing themselves, throw it in the wrong direction. Mimi was all right, because she'd throw it back on Wynant, but everybody else was out. Suspicion thrown on Wynant was the one thing that was guaranteed to keep anybody from suspecting that Wynant was dead, and if Macaulay hadn't killed Wynant, then there was no reason for his having killed either of the others. The most obvious thing in the whole layout and the key to the whole layout was that Wynant had to be dead.'

'You mean you thought that from the beginning?' Nora demanded, fixing me with a stern eye.

'No, darling, though I ought to be ashamed of myself for not seeing it, but once I heard there was a corpse under the floor, I wouldn't have cared if doctors swore it was a woman's. I'd have insisted it was Wynant's. It had to be. It was the one right thing.'

'I guess you're awfully tired. That must be what makes you talk like this.'

'Then he had Nunheim to worry about too. After pointing the finger at Morelli, just to show the police he was being useful, he went to see Macaulay. I'm guessing again, sweetheart. I had a phone-call from a man who called himself Albert Norman, and the conversation ended with a noise on his end of the wire. My guess is that Nunheim went to see Macaulay and demanded some dough to keep quiet and, when Macaulay tried to bluff him, Nunheim said he'd show him and called me up to make a date with me to see if I'd buy his information – and Macaulay grabbed the phone and gave Nunheim something, if only a promise, but when Guild and I had our little talk with Nunheim, and he ran out on us, then he phoned Macaulay and demanded real action, probably a lump sum, with a promise to beat it out of town, away from us meddling sleuths. We do know he called up that afternoon – Macaulay's telephone-operator remembers a Mr Albert Norman calling up, and she remembers that Macaulay went out right after talking to him, so don't get snooty about this – uh – reconstruction of mine. Macaulay wasn't silly enough to think Nunheim was to be trusted even if he paid him, so he lured him down to this spot he had probably picked out ahead of time and let him have it – and that took care of that.'

'Probably,' Nora said.

'It's a word you've got to use a lot in this business. The letter to Gilbert was only for the purpose of showing that Wynant had a key to the girl's apartment, and sending Gilbert there was only a way of making sure that he'd fall into the hands of the police, who'd squeeze him and not let him keep the information about the letter and the key to himself. Then Mimi finally comes through with the watch-chain, but meanwhile another worry comes up. She's persuaded Guild to suspect me a little. I've an idea that when Macaulay came to me this morning with that hooey he intended to get me up to Scarsdale and knock me off, making me number three on the list of Wynant's victims. Maybe he just changed his mind, maybe he thought I was suspicious, too willing to go up there without policemen. Anyhow, Gilbert's lie about having seen Wynant gave him another idea. If he could get somebody to say they had seen Wynant and stick to it... Now this part we know definitely.'

'Thank God.'

'He went to see Mimi this afternoon – riding up two floors above hers and walking down so the elevator boys wouldn't remember having carried him to her door – and made her a proposition. He told her there was no question about Wynant's guilt, but that it was doubtful if the police would ever catch him. Meanwhile he, Macaulay, had the whole estate in his hands. He couldn't take a chance on appropriating any of it, but he'd fix it so she could – if she would split with him. He'd give her these bonds he had in his pocket and this check, but she'd have to say that Wynant had given them to her and she'd have to send this note, which he also had, over to Macaulay as if from Wynant. He assured her that Wynant, a fugitive, could not show up to deny his gift, and, except for herself and her children, there was no one else who had any interest in the estate, any reason for questioning the deal. Mimi's not very sensible where she sees a chance to make a profit, so it was all O.K. with her, and he had what he wanted – somebody who'd seen Wynant alive. He warned her that everybody would think Wynant was paying her for some service, but if she simply denied it there would be nothing anybody could prove.'

'Then what he told you this morning about Wynant instructing him to give her any amount she asked for was simply in preparation?'

'Maybe; maybe it was an earlier fumbling towards that idea. Now are you satisfied with what we've got on him?'

'Yes, in a way. There seems to be enough of it, but it's not very neat.'

'It's neat enough to send him to the chair,' I said, 'and that's all that counts. It takes care of all the angles and I can't think of any other theory that would. Naturally it wouldn't hurt to find the pistol, and the typewriter he used for the Wynant letters, and they must be somewhere around where he can get at them when he needs them.' (We found them in the Brooklyn apartment he had rented as George Foley.)

'Have it your own way,' she said, 'but I always thought detectives waited until they had every little detail fixed in –'

'And then wonder why the suspects had time to get to the farthest country that has no extradition treaty.'

She laughed. 'All right, all right. Still want to leave for San Francisco tomorrow?'

'Not unless you're in a hurry. Let's stick around a while. This excitement has put us behind in our drink.'

'It's all right by me. What do you think will happen to Mimi and Dorothy and Gilbert now?'

'Nothing new. They'll go on being Mimi and Dorothy and Gilbert just as you and I will go on being us and the Quinns will go on being the Quinns. Murder doesn't round out anybody's life except the murdered's and sometimes the murderer's.'

'That may be,' Nora said, 'but it's all pretty unsatisfactory.'

After the Thin Man

AFTER THE THIN MAN

September 17, 1935

A train whistle sounds as the Chief arrives slowly in the Santa Fe Station in San Francisco. A stateroom on the train is stacked high with hatboxes, and suitcases, books, flowers, magazines, half-empty baskets of fruit. Although it is afternoon the stateroom is not yet made up. The top berth is down, piled high with bed-covers and sheets. On the lower berth is an array of White Rock bottles, glasses, bowls of ice, and a glass cocktail shaker propped against a pillow, almost full. There is also a half-packed bag open. Nick Charles standing before a mirror in the lavatory trying to shave. He is dressed except for his collar and coat. He has an old-fashioned open razor in his hand. He is swaying with the motion of the car, trying to balance himself on his widespread feet. Suddenly the car lurches, and he is thrown forward against the mirror, just missing by a fraction cutting off an ear. He looks reproachfully at the mirror, and then decides to go out into the stateroom to shave. Precariously he makes his way to the mirror behind the outer door, leading to the corridor. As he has the razor poised at his throat, the door is thrown open from the outside, pushing him back behind it, out of sight. Nora Charles, his wife, bursts in. She is in a negligee and slippers, fresh from her shower, with her toilet things in her hand. She is excited. She looks for Nick in the stateroom as she comes in.

Nora: 'Nickie! Nickie! Where are you?'

She shuts the door after her and sees Nick behind the door, jammed up against the wall, his razor still at his throat, his eyes fixed in a glassy stare.

Nick, with the sickly sweet grin of a man who has just escaped death: 'Hello, darling.'

Nora, amazed at his position: 'What are you trying to do?'

Nick: 'Just having a little fun, darling.'

Nora goes quickly to the lower berth, putting her toilet things in an open bag.

Nora: 'You'd better hurry. We're getting into San Francisco in five minutes.'

She takes a dress down from a hook. There is another hanging underneath it. Then she opens up a big hatbox, starting to pull a hat from it. She looks down, amazed and indignant.

Nora: 'Asta!'

He is comfortably curled up in the hatbox on a large hat. He looks up and wiggles with delight.

Nora: 'My best Sunday-go-to-meeting hat.'

Asta jumps quickly out of the hatbox. Nora pulls out the hat and puts it on her head, making a very ridiculous appearance with her negligee, talking to Nick as she does so. Nick is leaning under the berth, pouring a drink from the cocktail shaker.

Nora: 'I thought you were going to pack.'

Nick: 'I am. I've been putting away this likker.'

As he throws his head back to drink the cocktail his skull cracks against the upper berth.

Nora: 'You know, if you break that, they can sue you.'

She goes quickly into the lavatory.

Nick: 'I'm going to miss this little room of ours. It's left some lasting impressions on me.'

He feels his head ruefully, then pours himself another drink.

Nora: 'Pack these, will you, Nickie?'

Her filmy nightgown and negligee come flying at him from the bathroom. He extricates himself from them.

Nick: 'Delighted.'

He rolls them casually into a ball and stuffs them into the open bag. He picks up the cocktail shaker, still three-quarters full, and looks at it lovingly.

Nick: 'I hate to leave this.'

Nora, anxiously, from the lavatory: 'Oh, don't leave anything.'

Nick puts the top of the cocktail shaker on, and looks around for something to wrap it in. He catches sight of Nora's dress hanging on the wall. He puts his hand out toward it.

Nick: 'Going to wear this dress?'

Nora's voice: 'No. You can put that in.'

Nick: 'Fine.'

He takes down the dress, wraps the cocktail shaker lovingly in it, and stuffs it into the bag, enthusiastically viewing the result.

The photographers and reporters are standing on the station platform looking into the distance, watching for the train. One of the men, looking off-scene, calls:

'Here she comes!'

In a body they all start to run toward the train.

Porters are hurrying out. Baggage men stand waiting. The train pulls in. The reporters and photographers who ran to meet it are now running back beside the train, trying to catch up with the Pullmans. The train comes to a stop, and a porter jumps off. The reporters rush up to him.

One of the reporters: 'Nick Charles on this car?'

Porter: 'Two cars back.' The reporters and cameramen start to run back.

The porter puts down his little stepping block as Nick and Nora appear at the top of the steps. The reporters and photographers come running up. Asta is straining on the leash in Nick's hand.

1st Photographer: 'Hold it there, Mr Charles.'

He snaps his picture and prepares to take another. Meanwhile the reporters are all talking at once, and the other photographers are taking pictures.

Reporters: 'Hello, Nick.' 'How does it feel to be home?'

'How are you, Mrs Charles? I'm from the *Chronicle*'

'Going to stay with us for a while?'

'Got a story for the *Examiner*, Nick?'

Nick, as Asta pulls him in a frenzy of excitement: 'Gangway, boys! Gangway!'

Asta pulls Nick down the stairs. Nora follows, clinging to her purse and a little jewel case.

1st Reporter: 'Going to keep on with the detective work, Nick?'

Nick: 'No. I've retired. Just going to take care of my wife's money so I'll have something in my old age.'

2nd Reporter: 'You took that Wynant case in New York.'

Nick: 'I just did that for my wife. She wanted some excitement.'

1st Reporter, turning to Nora: 'I guess you had some excitement all right.'

Nora: 'It was wonderful. Two men tried to kill him.'

Nick gives Nora a look. A big ex-prize-fighter pushes his way through the crowd. He is Harold, the Charleses' chauffeur. He is very correctly dressed in uniform, and chewing gum as fast as his jaws will let him.

Nora: 'Oh, Harold!'

Harold, grinning: 'How are you, Mrs Charles?'

Then with a change to a tone of utter familiarity: 'Hi'yer, Nick.'

He grasps Nick's hand and almost crushes it. Nick pulls it away, shaking it to get the circulation going.

Nick: 'A little out of condition.'

Harold starts to collect the bags belonging to Nick and Nora. The reporters are still hanging around, hoping for a story.

1st Reporter: 'Come on, Nick. Give us a break. What are your plans?'

Nick: 'My immediate plans?'

1st Reporter, eagerly: 'Yes.'

Nick: 'Just a hot bath.'

He looks at Asta, and speaks reproachfully: 'Asta!'

The reporter looks down, and shakes his trouser leg.

Nick: 'You'll have to forgive us. We've been cooped up for four days.'

As Harold is picking up the bag that we saw Nick pack, Nora is horrified to see a stream of liquid pouring out.

Nora: 'Oh, Nick, look! Something's leaked.'

Nick sniffs at it, apprehensive, and then turns with relief.

Nick: 'Thank Heaven. I thought it was the cocktails!'

Nora: 'Cocktails! Oh, Nick!'

1st Photographer: 'Just one more picture, Mr Charles. Would you mind getting up on the steps again?'

Nick, pleasantly: 'Certainly not.'

He takes Nora's arm as they go up on the steps again.

2nd Photographer: 'I'd like that, too.'

All of the photographers look down into their cameras, ready to snap Nick and Nora. Then look up puzzled.

Nick and Nora are just disappearing out of sight, down the steps on the other side of the train. As they come through the crowd at the station, followed by porters and Harold, a little inconspicuous man bumps against Nora, who is trying to manage Asta on his leash. Nora stops, and pleasantly acknowledges the man's mumbled words of apology. The man is about to go on, when Nick sees him and recognizes him.

Nick, cordially: 'Hello, Fingers.'

Fingers turns, startled at the sound of Nick's voice. Then he sees who it is. He doesn't realize that Nick is with Nora.

Fingers: 'Well, Nick! How are you?'

Nick: 'How's business?'

Fingers: 'Oh, I quit that racket.'

Suddenly Nora, standing at one side, looks down and sees that her purse is gone... she is grasping only the strap of it in her hand. She turns excitedly to Nick.

Nora: 'Nick... my purse. It's gone!'

But Nick takes it very easily.

Nick: 'Oh, that's a shame.'

He turns to Fingers: 'Nora, I want you to meet Fingers.'

Then, to Fingers: 'This is the wife.'

Fingers looks abashed and embarrassed. Nora, her mind on her lost purse, acknowledges the introduction a little distractedly.

Fingers: 'Your wife. Well, gee! I'm sorry about your purse, Mrs Charles.'

Nora: 'What'll I do, Nick? I know I had it with me.'

Nick: 'It'll turn up... won't it, Fingers?'

Fingers: 'I certainly hope so.'

He shakes hands with Nick, patting him affectionately with the other hand. Fingers: 'Well, so long, Nick. Glad I bumped into you. Goodbye, Mrs Charles. Happy New Year to you.'

He goes off. Nick starts to walk Nora toward their car.

Nick, to Nora: 'Come on.'

But she is pulling back, wanting to go look for her purse.

Nora: 'I can't just go off and...'

Nick, soothingly: 'Come on. Come on. You don't want to embarrass him.

Nora: 'What do you mean?'

Nick: 'He's a purse snatcher. Think of his feelings.'

He begins to feel in his pocket, on the side where Fingers gave him an affectionate pat.

Nora: 'A purse snatcher! He must have taken it!'

She tries to turn back, but Nick holds her firmly. Nick's fingers have found something in his pocket. He turns and waves a genial goodbye and 'all's well' to Fingers.

Nick: 'So long, Fingers.'

He pulls the purse out of his pocket and hands it to Nora: 'He said it would turn up.'

Nora: 'You do know the nicest people!'

The car comes to a stop in front of the Charleses' house. Nick gets out of the car, pulled by Asta. The dog is straining at his leash, frantically excited at being home again. Nick bends down, trying to undo the leash.

Nick: 'Just a minute, Asta. There you are.'

He lets Asta loose and the dog starts to tear in and out around the trees, rushing back and forth... rolling on the ground, delighted to be home again. Suddenly he stops and looks off toward the backyard, then goes scurrying around the corner of the house.

There is a dog run and a little kennel in it, in the foreground. Asta comes tearing around the corner of the house, and pulls up short in front of the dog run.

A wirehaired female, just like Asta, is lying surrounded by about five puppies, all like her. She is looking up at Asta, and gently wagging her tail.

He barks delightedly at his wife. His tail seems to be wagging his whole body.

As Asta's excited bark continues, a little black Scottie puppy, of the same age as the others, comes waddling out of the kennel and makes his way to Mrs Asta. Asta's bark suddenly stops.

As he looks at this black intruder, his high spirits suddenly evaporate. Asta turns toward the sound of a short bark.

The black Scottie is halfway through a hole he has dug under the fence separating the next-door yard from the Charleses'.

He is very evidently the father of the little black puppy with Mrs Asta. He is looking belligerently over at Asta. Asta bounds into the yard. The Scottie immediately drops his belligerent attitude, and backs hurriedly through the hole into his own backyard, and flees ignominiously. Asta bristles for a second, then turns his back and starts to dig furiously, filling up the tunnel underneath the fence.

Nick and Nora are standing at the front door of their house. Nick has his hand on the doorbell.

Nora: 'All I want is a hot bath.'

Nick: 'I'll take a hot bath and a cold drink.'

The door is flung open, letting out a blare of sound.

A man in the doorway is slightly drunk and very good-naturedly hospitable. He evidently has not the slightest idea of who Nick and Nora are. He is acting the part of the genial host. From behind him comes a din... a piano playing, voices shrieking with laughter, a girl's voice singing, a trap drum being played with more enthusiasm than skill.

The Man: 'Come in! Come in! Make yourself at home!'

He steps back into the house, holding the door open.

Nick and Nora are looking amazed at the man. Nick steps back and looks at the number of the house.

Nick: 'It's our house all right!'

Nora: 'Let's go in. He says it's all right.'

They start into the house.

The din is worse inside. Nick and Nora come slowly in. They look around them. Through different doorways we see crowds of people at the bar... and in the living room, surrounding the piano. A crap game is going on in another room.

The Man: 'There's the bar right in there. Help yourself.'

Nick: 'Thanks.'

The Man: 'Okay.'

Nora: 'What's the celebration?'

The Man: 'We're giving a surprise party to Nick and Nora.'

Nick: 'Nick and Nora?'

The Man: 'Don't you know Nick and Nora?'

Nora: 'No.'

The Man: 'Neither do I. But that's not going to spoil my fun. It's New Year's... so what's the odds? Go on in. Fake it. It's a cinch.'

Nick: 'Thanks for the tip.'

The Man: 'Get in there... and get some of that Napoleon brandy before it's all gone. See you later.'

Nick, turning formally to Nora: 'May I have this dance?'

Nora goes into his arms, smiling, and starts dancing toward the living room. A nice group of young people are crowded around the piano, most of them Nora's age, friends of hers when she was a debutante, men with whom she played around, before she married Nick. Some of them are in evening clothes, ready to go on to other parties; the rest are in street clothes. A man is sitting playing the piano, and beside him, a girl is trying to play a trap drum. Several couples are dancing. Nick and Nora dance in from the hallway. The guests are so absorbed that they don't pay any attention to them. There is a hum of conversation. The inevitable girl who knows all the words of the songs wants to sing, and couples call to the girl at the trap drum to keep better time. One couple is doing very complicated steps, and the rest are watching them, cheering them on.

About six men and girls are clustered around one man in a corner. He is talking earnestly, if a little drunkenly, to them.

The Man: 'Listen, boys and girls. This is supposed to be a surprise party. So when they come in the door, we want to hide. Don't let them know there's a soul here.'

One Girl: 'That's a great idea!'

Another Girl: 'You'd better tell the rest of them, Jerry.'

Jerry: 'You're right.'

He steps out of the huddled group.

Nick and Nora are looking around, amused at their not being recognized.

Jerry: 'Listen, everybody. This is supposed to be a surprise party. Let's get together on this.'

A Girl: 'Well, I'm acting surprised.'

Nick gently steers Nora into the dining room.

A couple is dancing in the dining room.

The man is the one who greeted Nick and Nora at the door. He is dancing with a very lovely girl. Nick and Nora come in, still dancing. For a minute, the man and girl sway in position, as the man speaks to Nick. The girl's back is toward Nick and Nora.

The Man, indicating the girl with him: 'Not bad, eh?'

Nick: 'Not a-tall bad.'

The Man: 'How are you doing? Anyone wise to you yet?'

Nora, amused: 'No.'

The Man: 'What'd I tell you?'

He dances away with his girl. Nick and Nora laugh, and make a sudden dash for the pantry door.

There is bedlam in the kitchen behind the scenes. The fat cook, Rose, is trying to make sandwiches and hors d'oeuvres for the unexpected guests. She is, at any other time, a good-natured individual... a heritage from Nora's mother. She is being helped by a pretty young maid, Ethel. The butler is getting in the way, trying to get some ice cubes out of a tray. They are all absorbed in their various occupations. Nick and Nora come in through the pantry, but the three servants are too busy to notice them.

Nick, softly, so that he will not be heard by the party inside: 'Hey, there!'

Rose, thinking it is some hungry guest: 'Coming! Coming!'

She turns with a plate of hors d'oeuvres in her hand, and suddenly sees that it is Nick and Nora. Her attitude changes immediately. She is delighted to see them: 'Miss Nora! And Mr Charles!'

The other two servants turn and eagerly smile at them.

Ethel: 'Happy New Year, ma'am.'

Nick, in a whisper: 'Shush! Don't spoil their fun. They haven't surprised us yet.'

Nora, in a whisper: 'How are you, Rose?'

Then to the maid and butler: 'Hello, Ethel... Peters.'

The maid and the butler smile at them and whisper.

Ethel: 'Nice to see you, ma'am.'

Rose, also in a whisper: 'We missed you something fierce.'

From this time on they all speak in whispers.

Nora: 'We missed *you* something fierce.'

Nora sees the sandwiches and picks up one of them. She is about to eat it, when Nick takes it from her.

Nick: 'You can't have that. It's for the guests.'

He puts the whole sandwich into his mouth. Nora gives him a look, and then goes snooping over toward the stove. The butler starts into the dining room with a bucket of ice cubes.

Nora: 'What're we going to have for dinner, Rose? I'm hungry.'

Rose: 'Your aunt telephoned, Miss Nora. She expects you there.'

Nora looks at Nick, appalled. This is evidently the last place she wants to go.

Nora: 'My aunt!'

But she gets no help from Nick. He leans over and kisses her.

Nick: 'Goodbye, darling. See you next year.'

Rose: 'She expects you, too, Mr Charles.'

Nick looks around at Rose, unable to believe his ears.

Nick: 'Me?'

Rose: 'Yes, sir.'

Nick, turning back to Nora: 'What have your family got against me?'

Nora: 'It's that annual family dinner.'

Nick, picking up another sandwich: 'Remind me not to go.'

There is the sound of a doorbell. Nora: 'What excuse'll I make?'

Nick: 'Tell her I left a collar button in New York, and we have to go back for it.'

Three pistol reports from the front door are followed by the sound of a door crashing back against a wall, and a man's hoarse exclamation.

Nick, followed by Nora, goes to the front door. The man who admitted them to the house—sober now—is standing at the door staring down with horrified face at a dead man huddled on the vestibule floor at his feet. The man at the door turns his frightened face to Nick and gasps: 'I opened the door—bang, bang—he said, 'Mees Selma Young,' and fell down like that.'

Nick corrects him mechanically—'Bang, bang, bang'—while kneeling to examine the man on the floor. He rises again almost immediately, saying: 'Dead.' By now guests and servants are crowding around them. Nora, craning her neck to look past Nick at the dead man's face, exclaims: 'Nick, it's Pedro!'

Nick: 'Who is Pedro?'

Nora: 'You remember. Pedro Dominges—used to be Papa's gardener.'

Nick says: 'Oh, yes,' doubtfully, looking at Pedro again. Pedro is a lanky Portuguese of fifty-five, with a pleasant, swarthy face and gray handlebar mustache. Nick addresses the butler: 'Phone the police, Peters.' Then he turns to discover that the man who opened the door has tiptoed past the corpse and is now going down the steps to the street. 'Wait a minute,' Nick calls. The man turns around on the bottom step and says very earnestly:

'Listen, I—I—this kind of thing upsets me. I got to go home and lay down.'

Nick looks at the man without saying anything and the man reluctantly comes back up the steps, complaining: 'All right, brother, but you're going to have a sick man on your hands.'

A little man, obviously a crook of some sort, plucks at Nick's elbow and whines: 'You got to let *me* out, Nick. You know I'm in no spot to be messing with coppers right now.'

Nick says: 'You should have thought of that before you shot him.'

The little man jumps as if he had been kicked.

During this scene a crowd has been gradually assembling in the street around the door: first a grocer's delivery boy, then a taxi driver, pedestrians, etc. Now a policeman pushes his way through the crowd, saying: 'What's going on here?' and comes up the steps. He salutes Nick respectfully, says: 'How do you do, Mr Charles? Glad to see you back,' then sees the dead man and goggles at him.

Nick says: 'We called in.'

The policeman goes down the steps and begins to push the crowd around, growling: 'Get back there! Get back there!' In the distance a police siren can be heard.

Indoors, a few minutes later, Lieutenant Abrams of the Police Homicide Detail—who looks somewhat like an older version of Arthur Caesar—is saying to Nora: 'You're sure of the identification, Mrs Charles? He's the Pedro Dominges that used to be your gardener?'

Nora: 'Absolutely sure.'

Abrams: 'How long ago was that?'

Nora: 'Six years at least. He left a little before my father died.'

Abrams: 'Why'd he leave?'

Nora: 'I don't know.'

Abrams: 'Ever see him since?'

Nora: 'No.'

Abrams: 'What did he want here?'

Nora: 'I don't know. I—'

Abrams: 'All right. Thanks.' He speaks to one of his men: 'See what you can get.' The man goes to a phone in another room. (In this scene, the impression to be conveyed is that Abrams has already asked his preliminary questions and is now patiently going over the same ground again, checking up, filling in details.)

Abrams turns to the guests: 'And none of you admit you know him, huh?' Several of them shake their heads, the others remain quiet.

Abrams: 'And none of you know a Miss Selma Young?'

There is the same response.

Abrams: 'All right.' Then, more sharply: 'Mullen, have you remembered anything else?'

The man who had opened the door runs his tongue over his lips and says: 'No, sir. It's just like I told you. I went to the door when it rang, thinking it was maybe some more guests, or maybe them'—nodding at Nick and Nora—'and then there was the shots and he kind of gasped what sounded to me like 'Mees Selma Young' and fell down dead like that. I guess there was an automobile passing maybe—I don't know.'

Abrams, aside to Nick: 'Who is he?'

Nick: 'Search me.'

Abrams to Mullen: 'Who are you? What were you doing here?'

Mullen, hesitantly: 'I come to see about buying a puppy and somebody give me a drink and—' His face lights up and he says with enthusiasm: 'It was a *swell* party. I never—'

Abrams interrupts him: 'What are you doing answering the doorbell if you just chiseled in?'

Mullen, sheepishly: 'Well, I guess I had a few drinks and was kind of entering in the spirit of the thing.'

Abrams addresses one of his men: 'Take good-time Charlie out to where he says he lives and works and find out about him.' The man takes Mullen and goes out.

In another room, the detective at the phone is saying: 'Right, Mack. I got it.' He hangs up. As he reaches the door, the phone rings. He glances around, goes softly back to it.

In the hallway, the butler answers the phone: 'Mr Charles's residence ... Yes, Mrs Landis ... Yes, ma'am.' He goes into the room where the others are and speaks aside to Nora: 'Mrs Landis is on the telephone, ma'am.'

Nora goes to the phone, says: 'Hello, Selma. How are you, dear?'

Selma, in hat and street clothes, her face wild, cries hysterically: 'Nora, you and Nick have simply got to come tonight! Something terrible has happened! I don't know what to—I'll kill myself if—you've got to! If you don't, I'll—' She breaks off as she sees Aunt Katherine standing in the doorway looking sternly at her. Aunt Katherine is very old, but still big-boned and powerful, with a grim, iron-jawed face. She, too, is in hat and street clothes and leans on a thick cane. Selma catches her breath in a sob, and says weakly: 'Please come.'

Nora, alarmed: 'Certainly we'll come, dear. We'll do—'

Selma says hastily: 'Thanks,' and hangs up, avoiding Aunt Katherine's eyes. Aunt Katherine, not taking her eyes from Selma, puts out a hand and rings a bell, saying, when a servant comes in: 'A glass of water.' Both women remain as they are in silence until the servant returns with the water. Then Aunt Katherine takes the water from the servant, takes a tablet from a small bottle in her own handbag, and with water in one hand, tablet in the other, goes to Selma and says: 'Take this and lie down until time for dinner.'

Selma objects timidly: 'No, Aunt Katherine, please. I'm all right. I'll be quite all right.'

Aunt Katherine: 'Do as I say—or I shall call Dr Kammer.'

Selma slowly takes the tablet and water.

The detective at Nick's who has been listening on the extension quickly puts down the phone and, returning to the room where the others are, calls Abrams aside and whispers into his ear, telling him what he overheard. While this is going on, Nora returns and tells Nick: 'You're in for it, my boy. I promised Selma we'd come to Aunt Katherine's for dinner tonight. I had to. She's so upset she—'

Nick says: 'That means outside of putting up with the rest of your family, we'll have to listen to her troubles with Robert. I won't—'

Nora says coaxingly: 'But you like Selma.'

Nick: 'Not that much.'

Nora: 'Please, Nickie.'

Nick: 'I won't go sober.'

Nora pats his cheek, saying: 'You're a darling.'

Abrams comes back from his whispered conference with the other detective and says: 'Mrs Charles, I'll have to ask you who you were talking to on the phone.'

Nora, puzzled: 'My cousin, Selma Landis.'

Abrams: 'She married?'

Nora: 'Yes.'

Abrams: 'What was her last name before she was married?'

Nora: 'Forrest, the same as mine.'

Abrams: 'She ever go by the name of Young?'

Nora: 'Why no! Surely you don't think—' She looks at Nick.

Abrams: What was she so excited about?'

Nora, indignantly: 'You listened?'

Abrams, patiently: 'We're policemen, Mrs Charles, and a man's been killed here. We got to try to find out what goes on the best way we can. Now is there any connection between what she was saying and what happened here?'

Nora: 'Of course not. It's probably her husband.'

Abrams: 'You mean this fellow that was killed?'

Nick: 'That's a thought!' He asks Nora solemnly: 'Do you suppose Selma was ever married to Pedro?'

Nora: 'Stop it, Nick.' Then, to Abrams: 'No, no—it's her husband she was talking about.'

Abrams nods, says: 'Maybe that's right. I can see that. I'm a married man myself.' After a moment's thought he asks: 'Did she know this fellow that was killed?'

Nora: 'I suppose so. She and my husband and her husband were all friends and used to come there before any of us were married.'

Abrams: 'Then her husband might know him, too, huh?'

Nora: 'He might.'

Abrams turns to Nick: 'How come you didn't recognize him before Mrs Charles told you?'

Nick: 'Who notices a gardener unless he squirts a hose on you?'

Abrams: 'There's something in that. I remember once when—well, never mind.' He addresses the detective who phoned: 'Find out anything about Dominges?'

The Detective: 'Did a little bootlegging before repeal—bought hisself a apartment house at 346 White Street—lives there and runs it hisself. Not married. No record on him.'

Abrams asks the assembled company: '346 White Street mean anything to anybody?' Nobody says it does. He asks his men: 'Got all their names and addresses?'

'Yes.'

Abrams: 'All right. You people can clear out. We'll let you know when we want to see you again.'

The guests start to leave as if glad to go, especially a little group of men who have been herded into a corner by a couple of policemen, but this group is halted by one of the policemen, who says: 'Take it easy, boys. We've got a special wagon outside for you. We been hunting for some of you for months.' They are led out between policemen.

Abrams, alone in the room with Nick and Nora, looks at Nick and says: 'Well?'

Nick says: 'Oh, sure,' and begins to mix drinks.

Abrams: 'I didn't mean that exactly. I mean what do you make all this add up to? He's killed coming to see you. He knows you two, and Mrs Charles's relations, and that's all we know he does know. What do you make of it?'

Nick, handing him a drink: 'Maybe he was a fellow who didn't get around much.'

At the Landis home:

Aunt Katherine, in the doorway of the drawing room, is surveying the occupants of the room grimly.

Aunt Katherine: 'Good evening all.'

The men of the family all rise to their feet, some of them with difficulty, to greet Aunt Katherine. The next to Katherine in point of age is Aunt Lucy, Katherine's cousin, a tottering old lady whose only interest is her accumulating years. Next, there is the General, Katherine's brother. He is a tall, solidly fat man of eighty, with a bald head, bushy white brows and whiskers, and the shiny appearance of just having been scrubbed. Although Katherine calls him Thomas, the rest speak of him as the General.

The others, in order of their ages, are:

Burton Forrest, a gaunt man of seventy-two, who has a tic, which makes him crinkle his nose as if he had suddenly smelled a bad smell.

Charlotte, Burton's wife, a short, roly-poly woman of seventy, who is more interested in her dinner than anything else.

Hattie, a spinster of sixty-something. She is very deaf, and wears an audio phone, with its sounding box conspicuously pinned on the front of her chest, and cords going from it to her ears.

William, a few years younger than Hattie. A plump man whose clothes are too tight. He has a great deal of difficulty in understanding things, and, even in this family, is considered not quite bright.

Lucius, a tired man in his late fifties.

Helen and Emily, colorless women of fifty-three or fifty-four... married to William and Lucius. They stick together as if not sure of their places in this family that they have married into.

As Katherine makes her entrance, they all greet her with deferential murmurs, addressing her as 'Katherine' or 'Cousin Katherine' or 'Aunt Katherine,' according to their ages.

The women sit stiffly erect; the men stand stiffly erect. The men wear white ties and tails. The women's gowns range in style from the Victorianism of Katherine's to the comparatively modern, but none of them is gay. Aunt Lucy, the very old lady, comes tottering up to Katherine.

Aunt Lucy: 'I had a birthday last week, Katherine. I'm eighty-three years old. Eighty-three years old. What do you think of that?'

Aunt Katherine: 'That's fine, Lucy.'

Aunt Lucy: 'Eighty-three! Next year I'll be eighty-four.'

Aunt Katherine dismisses Aunt Lucy with a brief word: 'That's splendid.'

She turns to the rest. 'While we're alone, I have something important to tell all of you.'

Aunt Hattie leans forward in her chair, holding her audio phone toward Katherine.

Aunt Hattie: 'What'd she say?'

Lucius: 'Shush!'

Aunt Katherine, looking at Hattie, irritated: 'Isn't that thing working, Hattie?'

Aunt Hattie: 'This works perfectly. It's you! You mumble!'

Lucius, stepping into the breach: 'What is it, Katherine?'

Aunt Katherine: 'Nora and her husband are coming tonight.'

They all look at Katherine, appalled.

Family: 'Her husband!'

'After the last time...'

'But Katherine...'

'Really, Katherine...'

This news has brought on Burton's tic worse than ever. The General is regarding Katherine with offended dignity.

The General: 'But you said yourself that you wouldn't have him again.'

Aunt Katherine: 'I know I did. And my opinion of him and what he represents hasn't changed a particle.'

Burton: 'Then I can't understand why you asked him.'

His face twitches violently.

Aunt Katherine: 'I have a very good reason for asking him, which you will know in time.' There is a muffled sound of a bell. 'That's probably they now.'

She turns to include the others: 'Understand now, I want you all to be pleasant to him.'

She walks toward Hattie and Lucius, near the door. The rest of the family look after her. There are murmurs from them.

The Family: 'Of course, if you say so.... It's going to be difficult... Poor Nora. My heart bleeds for that child.'

Hattie is still looking from face to face bewildered. Katherine passes the old butler as he goes slowly through the hall: 'If that is Mr and Mrs Charles, show them right in.'

Butler: 'Yes, madam.'

Aunt Hattie: 'What is it? What's happened?'

Lucius, bending down and talking right into her audio phone: 'You're to be pleasant to Nora's husband.'

Aunt Hattie: 'Who said so?'

Aunt Katherine: 'I did!'

Aunt Hattie: 'I'll be just as pleasant as you are... no more!'

Nick and Nora, in evening clothes, are waiting for the butler to open the door. Nick is muttering to himself. Nora looks at him, puzzled.

Nora: 'What are you muttering to yourself?'

Nick: 'I'm getting all the bad words out of my system.'

Nora: 'You'd better pull yourself together.'

Nick: 'Don't worry. One squint at Aunt Katherine would sober anyone!'

The door is opened by Henry, the butler.

Nora: 'Good evening, Henry.'

There is a chill in the massive hallway, with its dim lights. Nick and Nora come in as Henry holds the door open.

Henry, in a hushed whisper: 'Good evening, madam—sir.'

Nick: 'Is this the wax-works?'

Henry: 'I beg pardon, sir?'

Nora, smiling at Henry: 'Nothing, Henry. Nothing.'

She gives Nick a warning look. Starting for the library: 'I'll just leave my things down here.'

She goes down the hall, taking off her evening coat as she goes. The butler turns to Nick and helps him off with his coat. He touches Nick's things as if the mere contact with them might contaminate him.

Nick: 'It's all right—it's not catching.'

The butler puts them down and starts toward the drawing-room door.

Butler: 'Will you walk this way, sir.'

The butler hobbles away ahead of Nick, hardly able to move on his rheumatic legs. Nick looks after him.

Nick: 'I'll *try*.'

He starts to follow the butler, giving a grotesque imitation of his walk. As he passes the library door, Nora comes out, catches up with him, and grabs his arm, laughing at him.

Butler, announcing them at the door of the drawing room: 'Mr and Mrs Charles.'

As they hear the announcement, they straighten up.

Nick: 'Here goes!'

They start to walk in, sedately.

As Nick and Nora come in the door, Aunt Katherine comes forward to greet them.

Aunt Katherine, to Nora: 'How do you do, my dear?'

Nora kisses Aunt Katherine and then turns to include Nick.

Nora: 'You remember Nick?'

Although she is doing her best to be gracious, Aunt Katherine finds it impossible to look at him.

Aunt Katherine: 'How are you, Nicholas?'

As Nick hears his name, he starts. Katherine turns back toward the roomful of people: 'Come right in.'

Helen comes up to Nora, who turns to greet her.

Nora: 'Hello, Cousin Helen.'

Helen, giving her a peck: 'How are you, you poor child?'

Nick gives Cousin Helen a swift look as he hears the commiserating tone of her voice. But Aunt Katherine has him in tow, and he follows her.

Aunt Katherine, speaking to the whole family: 'This is Nora's husband.'

Nick looks from one to the other of the people. They are doing their best to appear pleasant, but the result is not very cordial. Aunt Katherine turns back to him: 'I think you know everyone.'

Nick: 'I seem to remember the old faces.'

Nora quickly takes Nick's arm and pilots him toward another group.

Nick, under his breath to her as they go: 'What's up? They're all so polite.'

Nora smiles and takes him to Charlotte and William.

Nora: 'This is Aunt Charlotte, and Uncle Willie.'

Nick acknowledges the introduction with the same sickly sweet smile that they give him.

Nora: 'And now for Aunt Hattie.'

From behind them, Charlotte's voice is heard: 'Poor Nora is so brave.'

Again Nick hears the commiserating 'poor' Nora. He whispers to Nora: 'What's this 'poor Nora' business?'

Nora: 'That's because I'm married to you.'

Then, as they reach Aunt Hattie: 'Aunt Hattie, you remember my husband?'

Nick: 'How are you?'

Aunt Hattie: 'Don't mumble, young man. Don't mumble.'

Nick, a little louder: 'How are you?'

Still Aunt Hattie doesn't hear.

Nora: 'She's deaf as a post.'

Nick: 'You're telling me!'

Aunt Hattie, holding out her receiving box of the audio phone: 'What did he say?'

Nick, taking the box, and speaking into it as if it were a microphone: 'When you hear the chime, it will be exactly...'

But Nora gives him a slight boot from behind. Nick turns sharply toward her. Nora catches sight of Selma in the doorway.

Nora, with a note of relief at seeing a friend: 'Selma!'

Selma has managed to regain some of her composure. Nora comes quickly to her, kissing her warmly.

Selma, on the point of breaking again: 'Oh Nora... Nora. It's so good to see you.'

Nora, affectionately: 'How are you, Selma?'

Nick approaches, and Selma turns to him.

Selma: 'Hello, Nick.'

Nick: 'Hello.'

Selma: 'It's sweet of you to come.'

Nick, who's really enjoying himself by now: 'I wouldn't have missed it for a million dollars.'

Nora: 'What's the trouble, Selma? Tell me.'

But Aunt Katherine comes up quickly, putting a firm hand on Selma's arm: 'We'll postpone any discussion until after dinner.'

She turns to speak to the rest: 'Shall we go in now?'

She holds out her hand to the General: 'Thomas?'

The General comes quickly to her side, and gives her his arm.

Nick, to Selma: 'Where's Robert?'

Selma is about to speak, but Aunt Katherine hastily intervenes.

Aunt Katherine: 'Robert telephoned that he was unavoidably detained. So we'll start without him.'

Selma gives her a bitter look and turns away. Nick notices the look between the two.

'We haven't quite enough men to go around, so, Lucius, will you take Hattie and Charlotte? Willie, you take Helen and Ethel? Burton, will you take Nora? And Nicholas, will you take Aunt Lucy?'

Aunt Katherine walks toward the hallway, on the General's arm. Nick goes toward Aunt Lucy, as Burton comes up to Nora. He offers his arm to her.

Nora: 'How are you, Cousin Burton?'

Burton: 'I'm very well, thank you.'

He makes a sudden violent face, as his tic starts in.

Nora: 'That's fine.'

Unconsciously, she imitates his tic. She realizes with horror what she has done, and turns and starts off quickly without him.

Nick offers his arm to Aunt Lucy. She looks up at him as she takes it, resenting having him as a partner.

Aunt Lucy: 'Maybe you didn't know it, but I'm eighty-three years old.'

Nick: 'Eighty-three?'

Aunt Lucy: 'Yes.'

Nick: 'Well, well. You don't look a *day* over a hundred.'

Aunt Lucy: 'That's what they all say.'

In the drawing room after dinner, Hattie, Charlotte, Helen, and Emily are sitting back in their comfortable chairs, surfeited with food and very drowsy. Aunt Lucy is frankly asleep. Aunt Katherine has the coffee table in front of her and is sipping her coffee, her eyes on Selma, who is at the piano, playing mechanically. Nora wanders over to the piano, her coffee cup in hand, leans over, and speaks softly to Selma: 'What was it you wanted to tell me?'

Selma stops her playing and is about to answer, when Aunt Katherine calls sharply: 'Nora, will you come here?'

Nora: 'In a minute, Aunt Katherine.' Then turning quickly back to Selma: 'What was it?'

Selma: 'Robert has disappeared.'

Nora: 'Disappeared!'

Aunt Katherine: 'Selma, go on playing!'

Selma, looking over at her aunt desperately: 'I can't play anymore, Aunt Katherine.'

Aunt Katherine: 'Nonsense. Go on.'

Selma tries to control herself for a second and then she suddenly smashes down on the keyboard with both hands: 'I can't! I can't!'

Selma puts her hands to her face and runs from the room to the library beyond, while Aunt Katherine rises to her feet and the other women look wide-eyed and alarmed. Nora says: 'Let me talk to her,' and goes out after Selma.

In the library, Selma is sobbing on a sofa. Nora sits down beside her, puts her arms around her, says: 'Don't, dear. Nick'll find Robert for you. I'm sure he's just—'

Selma sits up, pushing Nora's arms away, crying hysterically: 'Sometimes I hate you and Nick. You're so happy together, and here Robert and I haven't been married half as long and I'm so miserable. I wish he'd never come back. I wish he were dead. I don't really love him. I never did, really. I was a fool to have married him instead of David.' She puts her head on Nora's shoulder and begins to sob again.

Nora strokes Selma's hair, says: 'Well, then, dear, divorce him. Don't let Aunt Katherine keep you from that. If you—'

Selma raises her head again, says: 'But I'm such a fool. This is the first time he's gone off like this without a word—without even telling me lies about where he's going—but there have always been other women and I've always known it. But I've let him twist me around his little finger and made myself believe his lies even when I knew they were lies and—he doesn't love me. He married me for my money. Yet he does horrible things to me and then when I see him I let him smooth everything over and I want to think we love each other and everything will turn out all right. And it won't, it won't. It's all lies and I'm a fool. Oh, why didn't I marry David?' She bursts into tears again.

Meanwhile Aunt Katherine has come into the library and shut the door. Now she says coldly: 'You *are* a fool, Selma, but you might have the decency not to scream so the servants will find out exactly what *kind* of fool you are.'

'Aunt Katherine!' Nora protests. 'Selma's not well. She—'

Aunt Katherine interrupts her, nodding her head grimly: 'I know she's not well. I know better than anyone else—except Dr Kammer—how far from being well she really is.' Selma flinches. Aunt Katherine says to Nora: 'Will you ask Nicholas to come in?' Nora hesitates as if about to say something, then goes out. Aunt Katherine says to Selma: 'Fix yourself up. You look like Ophelia.' Selma flinches again and begins to fix her hair, dress, etc.

The men of the Forrest family stretched out in their chairs, sound asleep. Their waistcoats are open to allow the tremendous meal they have just consumed to settle. There are two good snorers, William and the General, one on either side of Nick. The snoring, like conversation, appears to be going back and forth.

Nick is seated at the dinner table, leaning forward with animated attention. There are empty places on either side of him where the women had been sitting.

Nick: 'No, really! Well, you amaze me! Could you explain that further?'

William lets out a sonorous snore.

Nick: 'I wouldn't go so far as to say that.'

The General, on the other side, is vying with William in his snorts. Nick turns toward his unconscious figure.

Nick: 'What is it?'

As William snores again, Nick turns to him with a restraining gesture: 'Just a minute.'

He turns back to the General, who snorts again. Nick speaks to him, as if amazed at his statement: 'Really!'

He turns to Burton, who is also sound asleep across the table: 'Are you going to let that pass unchallenged? You must have something to say to that!'

Burton's snore tops all of the others, as he turns uneasily in his chair.

Nick: 'That's the boy. I knew you had it in you.'

Nora: 'Nick! Nick!'

Nick looks around at her, rising as he hears her.

Nora: 'Come here—come here!'

Nick turns and addresses the four unconscious figures with great courtesy.

Nick: 'If you gentlemen will forgive me?'

He starts to turn to go to Nora, and then stops to pick up a stiff bunch of flowers from the center of the table and sticks it on the chest of the General, next to him. He turns and joins Nora.

Nick: 'I don't know when I've had a more stimulating evening!'

Nick and Nora walk through the hallway. She is holding his arm and seems worried. She says: 'Aunt Katherine wants to see you.'

Nick: 'What have I done now?'

Nora: 'Do you know why Robert wasn't here tonight?'

Nick: 'Because he's smart.'

Nora: 'I'm not fooling. He's disappeared.'

Nick: 'That's swell. Now if we can get rid of—'

Nora: 'Be nice to Selma, Nickie. She's having such a tough time of it.' Nick stops and turns Nora around to face him, looking at her with suspicion. He says:

'Now come on, tell the old man—what are you getting him into?'

Nora, paying no attention to this: 'And do try to be polite to Aunt Katherine. It'll make it easier for Selma.'

Nick sighs deeply and they go into the library.

Aunt Katherine comes forward to meet them. She is putting up a great show... being very charming to Nick, and speaking as if the whole affair were trifling. Selma is standing in the background, looking out of the window, her hands playing restlessly with the curtain.

Aunt Katherine: 'Oh, Nicholas. I'm sorry to take you away from the boys.'

Nick, remembering the boys: 'That's all right.'

Aunt Katherine: 'But there's a little something that you can do for us.'

Nick: 'How long has Robert been gone?'

Aunt Katherine, as if she couldn't quite remember, it was so unimportant: 'Let me see... about three days.'

Selma turns from the window, and comes toward them, speaking violently: 'Something's happened. I know it has. I can't sleep. I can't eat. Every time anyone comes to the door... every time the phone rings, I know it's someone to say they've found his body.'

Nora crosses quickly to Selma, and puts her arms comfortingly around her: 'Don't, Selma. Nothing terrible can have happened, or you'd be bound to know.'

Aunt Katherine, still keeping up her pretense of treating the matter lightly, in spite of Selma's outburst: 'Selma's exaggerating the whole affair. However, I thought you might like the opportunity to do something for the family. I know that you must have come across situations like this in your previous work as a... er... er...'

She cannot bring herself to say the word 'detective.' Nick realizes, amused, why she hesitates.

Nora, coming out with it: 'As a flatfoot?'

Aunt Katherine, turning to Nora: 'I didn't mean to be as blunt as all that.'

Nick, rubbing it in: 'Why not? It's all in the family.'

Aunt Katherine winces, but goes on bravely: 'Of course, I don't know how to go about such things... I don't know what your methods are. But I thought you might... er... 'snoop' around a little and find out what you can... just to put Selma's mind at ease.'

Nick: 'You haven't notified the police?'

Aunt Katherine is about to answer, when Selma interrupts her, with bitter sarcasm: 'Oh no!'

Selma: 'Our names might get in the papers. People might find out that I'm married to a drunken wastrel, a thief, a man who's already cost me a small fortune getting him out of scrapes with women, a man who has never done a decent thing in—'

Aunt Katherine raps with her cane on the floor and says: 'Selma, stop that nonsense!'

Selma puts her hands over her face and cries: 'I don't care what anybody knows, I don't care what gets in the papers, if I can only be happy again once.'

Nora goes to her to soothe her.

Aunt Katherine, quietly: 'We've kept our private affairs out of the public print up until now, and I hope we shall continue to do so.' She smiles at Nick as if conferring a favor on him. 'I shall leave it in your hands, Nicholas. I know you'll welcome a chance to help us, and I needn't tell you how grateful we'll be if you see that Robert returns home without any scandal.' She smiles at Nora, says: 'If you'll forgive me, I'll go back to my guests. When you've quieted Selma, I think she'd better go off to bed.' She goes out calmly and majestically.

Nick, looking after her half-admiringly, half-disgustedly, says: 'Katherine the Great!'

Selma comes over to Nick, holding out her hands, saying: 'I don't know how to thank you, Nick.'

Nick takes her hands, says: 'You mean you don't know what to thank me for. What is all this fiddle-de-dee?'

Selma: 'Robert hasn't been home—I haven't seen or heard from him for three days.'

Nick: 'Where do you think he might be?'

Selma: 'I don't know. It's some woman, of course. It gets worse and worse. Only last week some Chinese restaurant—Li-Chee or something—sent me a cigarette case they thought I'd left there and I know it was some woman that was there with him, though he swore it wasn't.'

Nick: 'Well, you're at least a cigarette case ahead—or wasn't it worth keeping?'

Nora says: 'Nick,' reprovingly, while Selma, not knowing he is kidding her, says:

'I sent it back, of course, with a note saying it wasn't mine, but I don't—' She breaks off to look at the butler, who is standing in the doorway. The butler says:

'A—ah—gentleman from the police to see you, Mrs Landis.'

Selma screams, and seems about to faint.

Selma's scream brings in Aunt Katherine, followed by the rest of the family. During the ensuing hubbub, while they are bringing her to, asking one another what happened, Lieutenant Abrams comes in. He nods at Nick, says: 'I thought maybe you'd be here,' looks at Selma and asks: 'Is the lady in trouble Mrs Selma Landis?'

Nick says: 'Yes.'

Abrams: 'I thought maybe it was.' Then, to Nora, who is now looking at him: 'Evening, Mrs Charles.'

By this time the others have noticed him. Aunt Katherine looks inquiringly at him. Nick introduces them elaborately.

'Miss Forrest, may I present Lieutenant Abrams of the Police Department Homicide Detail?'

Aunt Katherine asks sharply: 'Homicide?'

Selma pushes past her to put her hands on Abrams's arms, demanding: 'What has happened to him?'

Abrams (as always, in a manner that may come from stupidity or may come from a shrewd pretense of stupidity): 'He was killed this afternoon. Didn't Mr Charles tell you?'

Selma stares at him in dumb horror.

Nora says: 'He doesn't mean Robert, dear. He means Pedro, the gardener we used to have. You remember him.' She helps Selma to a chair, then asks Abrams indignantly: 'Did you do that on purpose?'

Aunt Hattie says: 'I can't understand a thing that's going on.' She points at Abrams: 'Is this man a burglar? Why doesn't someone call the police?'

Abrams addresses Nick: 'You didn't tell 'em about Pedro being killed?'

Nick: 'This is my wife's family. They'd think I did it.'

Abrams: 'I see what you mean. My wife's got relations, too.'

The butler appears in the doorway and says: 'Mr David Graham to see Mrs Landis.' Selma starts up from her chair.

Aunt Katherine says: 'I think it better that we be home to no one but members of the family this evening.'

Selma protests: 'I want to see David. Ask him to come in, Henry.'

The butler remains in the doorway, looking at Aunt Katherine, who says: 'Selma, I don't want to have to—'

Before she has finished this threat, David comes in hurriedly, going straight to Selma and asking: 'What is it? What's the matter?'

Aunt Katherine replies coldly: 'That is exactly what we'd like to know. Something is said about a gardener being killed and Selma becomes hysterical.'

David: 'A gardener? What's that got to do with Selma?'

Lieutenant Abrams: 'Excuse me, but that's what we're trying to find out. This man is killed coming to see Mr and Mrs Charles and a little while later Mrs Landis phones all excited and talking about killing herself and—'

David, angrily: 'And on the strength of that you come here to annoy her?'

Abrams, patiently: 'Not only that. Mrs Charles said she'—indicating Selma—'knew him, and how are we going to get anywhere if we don't talk to the people that knew him?'

Nora says: 'I didn't say she knew him. I said she might remember him.' She turns to David: 'It was Pedro who used to work for Papa when we had the place in Ross.'

David: 'Oh, yes. I remember him, a tall man with a long gray mustache. But what—'

Abrams: 'So you knew him, too. Well, what do you know about him? '

David: 'Nothing. I merely saw him when I was a visitor there, and I've never seen him since.'

Abrams: 'And you, Mrs Landis?'

Selma: 'I may have seen him, but I don't remember him at all.'

Abrams: 'And how about the rest of you?'

None of the Forrests admits knowing Pedro.

Abrams: 'Mrs Charles says Mrs Landis's husband might know him. Is he here?'

Selma: 'No—he—he'll be in later, but I don't think he'll remember the man any better than I do.'

Abrams: 'Did you ever go by the name of Selma Young?'

Selma: 'Certainly not!'

Abrams: 'Anybody here know Selma Young?'

Nobody does.

Abrams: 'Now I got to ask you again about that telephone talk of yours with Mrs Charles.'

Selma says: 'Please, it had nothing to do with this. It was — was a purely personal thing.'

Abrams: 'You mean something to do with your husband?'

Aunt Katherine says: 'Mr—ah—Abraham, you are being impertinent. Furthermore, my niece is under a doctor's care, and—'

Abrams, stolidly: 'What doctor?'

Aunt Katherine: 'Dr. Frederic Kammer.'

Abrams nods: 'I know of him.' Preparing to leave, he says resignedly: 'I can't help it if people don't like me. I got my work to do. Good night.' He goes out.

David leaves the house with Nick and Nora, parting from them in the foggy street.

When Nick and Nora leave, he asks Harold, the chauffeur: 'Where's a good place to get the stink of respectability out of our noses?'

Harold, grinning and chewing his gum, says: 'I get it. Well, there's Tim McCrumb's and there's the Li-Chee and there's the Tin Dipper. None of them three ain't apt to be cluttered up with schoolteachers.'

Nick: 'Suppose we try the Li-Chee.'

Harold says: 'That's a good pick,' while Nora looks at Nick from the corners of her eyes. As they get into the car she says: 'You are going to find Robert?'

Nick: '*I* didn't lose him.'

Nora: 'It would put you in right with the family.'

Nick: 'And *that's* what I'm afraid of.'

In Dancer's apartment at the Li-Chee Club, Robert—drunk and looking as if he has been drunk for several days—is lying back in a chair, holding a drink. Polly is sitting on the arm of his chair, running her fingers through his hair. He is saying: 'Comes tomorrow and we'll be out of this town for good—no more wife squawking at me, no more of her family egging her on, no more of this'—waving his glass around the place—'just you and me off someplace together.' He pulls her down into his lap and asks: 'Good, baby?'

She says: 'Swell.' Then: 'You're sure this—what's his name?—Graham—will come through all right?'

Robert: 'Sure. He's nuts about Selma. He fell all over himself when I put it to him. The only thing is, maybe I was a sucker not to ask him for twice as much for clearing out. Don't worry about the money; he'll have it ready in the morning just as he promised.'

Polly, reassured, asks thoughtfully: 'Does she know about it?'

Robert, scornfully: 'Of course not. He couldn't tell her. She's batty as a pet cuckoo. She'd blow up and make him call off the whole thing.'

Polly: 'Then suppose she finds out about it afterwards and won't marry him.'

Robert: 'Listen. This guy's a sap and he's in love with her. He wants to marry her all right, but even if he knew there was no chance of that, he'd still pay me to clear out. He thinks I'm bad for her and he lo-o-ves her and wants her to be ha-a-ppy.'

Polly laughs and kisses him, says: 'If you want to hear me sing, you'd better come on out and find a table. I go on in a few minutes.'

Outside the door, Phil has been listening. He turns away from the door not quite quickly enough, as Dancer comes up behind him. Dancer says casually: 'Catch a good earful?'

Phil says: 'I wanted to see Polly, but I didn't want to butt in if she was busy.'

Dancer links an arm through Phil's and starts leading him away from the door toward the stairs, saying: 'She's busy. She'll be busy all evening.'

Phil hangs back, saying: 'I got to see her for a minute.'

Dancer jerks him along, says, still casually: 'Not this evening. You shake her down for too much dough, Phil, even if she is your sister. Lay off her a while.'

Phil pulls his arm free, says: 'That's no skin off your face. If she wants to help me out a little, that's her business. Why shouldn't she? I know things that are going on around here that—'

Dancer reaches out, grabs him by the necktie, and pulls him close, saying softly: 'Smart boy. You know things. When are you going to start shaking *me* down?'

Phil says: 'When I want to shake you down, I'll—'

Dancer stops him this time by slapping his face once, not especially hard. Dancer: 'I don't like you, but I've put up with having you around because you're Polly's brother, and she's a nice kid, but don't think you can ride too far on that ticket.' He puts his open hand over Phil's face, and pushes him backwards down the stairs, saying: 'Now stay away for a couple of days.'

Phil tumbles backwards into the arms of Nick, who, with Nora, is coming up the stairs. Nick says: 'Mmmm! Big confetti they throw here.'

Dancer exclaims: 'Ah, Mr Charles! I'm sorry!' and starts down the stairs.

Phil snarls at Nick: 'Why don't you look where you're going, you big clown?'—twists himself out of Nick's arms and goes downstairs out of the place.

Dancer is apologizing again.

Nick says: 'Hello, Dancer. This your place? A neat way you have of getting rid of the customers.'

Dancer smiles professionally: 'Just a kid that hangs around because his sister works here. I get tired of him sponging on Polly sometimes.'

Nick: 'I felt a gun under his left arm when I caught him.'

Dancer, contemptuously: 'Just breaking it in for a friend, I guess.' He ushers them upstairs.

Outside the Li-Chee, Phil finds a dark doorway from which the Club can be watched, and plants himself there. Nick's car is parked near the doorway. Both Harold and a taxi-driver, who is talking to him, see Phil, but neither pays much attention to the boy. Harold is chewing gum and listening with a bored air to the taxi-driver.

'And I said to him, 'You ain't going to give me a ticket, you big flatfoot, and you know it,' I said. I said, 'I got a right to turn there, and you know it,' I said, 'and I ain't got all night to be sitting here gassing, so go polish your buttons and leave me be on my way, you fat palooka,' I said.'

Harold, wearily: 'I know, and then you busted out crying.'

Upstairs in the Li-Chee, Nick is checking his hat and coat while Nora looks interestedly around the place. Suddenly she grabs Nick's arm, says: 'There's Robert!'

Robert and Polly are going into the restaurant.

Nick says: 'The night's bulging with your family.'

Nora starts to pull him toward Robert, saying: 'Come on.'

Dancer to Nick: 'Is Mr Landis a friend of yours?'

Nick, as Nora drags him off: 'On the contrary, a relation.'

Dancer stares thoughtfully after them.

By the time Nick and Nora reach Robert, he and Polly are sitting at a small table near the orchestra. Nora holds out a hand to Robert, saying: 'Hello, Robert,' with a great show of cordiality. He rises drunkenly, mumbling: 'Hello, Nora; hello, Nick,' and shaking their hands. Then he introduces Polly: 'Miss Byrnes, Mr and Mrs Charles.' Nick immediately sits down and begins to talk to Polly, giving Nora a chance to speak aside to Robert.

Nora, in a low voice to Robert: 'You oughtn't to stay away like this.'

Robert: 'I know, but Selma's not easy to get along with, and sometimes I simply have to break loose.'

Nora: 'But you should let her know that you're all right.'

Robert: 'You're right, of course. But sit down. You can talk in front of Polly. She knows about Selma.'

Polly, aside to Nick: 'Tell Mrs Charles not to worry about him—I'll see that he gets home tonight.' She puts her foot under the table and touches Robert's. He starts to laugh, then covers his mouth with his hand, and asks:

'Is—is Selma all right?'

Nora, indignantly: 'You know she's not, and now with the police bothering her—'

Robert: 'The police?' He and Polly both look alarmed.

Nora: 'Yes, the idiots. A gardener we used to have was killed. Remember Pedro Dominges?'

Before Robert can reply, Polly exclaims: 'Killed? Why, he's—' She breaks off with a hand to her mouth.

Nick prompts her: 'He's what?'

Polly, to Nora: 'What was his name?'

Nora: 'Pedro Dominges.'

Polly: 'Oh! I thought you said Peter Dominger—a fellow I used to know.'

Nick looks at her skeptically. Robert asks:

'What's that got to do with Selma?'

Nick: 'Ask the police—they don't know. I wonder if our table's ready.' He stands up.

Polly whispers: 'I'll see he gets home all right.'

Nick: 'Thanks. Pleased to have metten up with you.' He and Nora move off to where Dancer is beckoning them.

Polly leans over to Robert, speaking swiftly: 'Honey, could you get hold of that guy Graham and see if you can get the money right away?'

Robert: 'Maybe. Why?'

Polly: 'I was thinking there's no sense in waiting until tomorrow. I'll tell Dancer I don't feel well and get the night off and we'll blow town right away. Would you like that?'

A waiter comes up with fresh drinks as Robert says: 'I'll try him on the phone now.'

Nick and Nora come up to the table. Dancer stands, holding Nora's chair for her.

Nick: 'Thanks.' He sits down. A Chinese waiter comes to his side, hovering over him.

Dancer: 'This all right?'

Nick: 'Fine.' Then to the waiter, who is handing him his napkin: 'Never mind about that. Bring me two Scotch highballs quick.' The waiter starts away, but Nick stops him. 'No. Better make it three. One for the wife.'

Waiter: 'Yes, sir.'

Dancer leans over toward Nick, adjusting the forks and utensils on the table as he speaks: 'You once sent a friend of mine up... Lum Ying.'

Nick: 'Oh, I remember him. He spread a tong war out to include sticking up a bank.'

Dancer: 'His brother's here now... one of my partners.'

Nick, with a smile: 'Is he a gunman, too?'

Dancer: 'No. But you can't tell how close brothers are. Thought you might like to know.'

Nick: 'Maybe you'd better point him out.'

Dancer: 'I'll call him over. Lum Kee!'

Lum Kee is a plump, middle-aged Chinese man with a round merry face. He is dressed in American clothes.

Dancer: 'Come here.'

Lum Kee: 'You bet you!'

Nick is looking interestedly at Lum Kee, as he comes up to the table.

Dancer, introducing him to Nick: 'I want you to meet a friend of mine... Lum Kee.'

Lum Kee grins, ducking his head.

Lum Kee: 'I'm your friend, you bet you.'

Dancer to Lum Kee: 'This is Nick Charles.'

Lum Kee: 'I hear about you, Mr Charles. Number one detective.'

Nick: 'Thanks. So you're Lum Ying's brother.'

Lum Kee, still grinning: 'You bet you—you catch 'em my brother seven years ago. You play trick on him. You bet you.'

Nick, nodding solemnly: 'No play trick on 'em, no catch 'em. You bet you.' Lum Kee laughs merrily. 'He still in?'

Lum Kee: 'You bet you. Four... five years more.' He ducks his head politely at Dancer, Nick, and Nora and goes off. Dancer looks meditatively after him.

Dancer, as if casually, to Nick: 'That's a good guy to have liking you.' He turns and walks away. As the implication of Dancer's casual words dawns on him, Nick looks after Dancer with humorous dismay.

Dancer goes to the table where Polly is now sitting alone and asks: 'What's the setup?'

Polly: 'They're Bobbie's cousins by marriage and think he ought to go home to his wife.'

Dancer purses his lips thoughtfully for a moment, then says: 'It's all to the good, them seeing him here plastered, but I guess we can't take a chance on them tipping off the wife and having her bang in. Give the customers one song and knock off for the night. Take him up to your place.'

Polly: 'I'm getting kind of tired of him.'

Dancer: 'It's only till tomorrow night. You can turn him loose then. Put a pill in his drink when you get him home, so he'll be sure to stay safe asleep while you run out to do that little errand in the morning.' He pats her shoulder.

Polly, without enthusiasm: 'All right.' She gets up to sing.

Robert at the telephone talking to David. Robert: 'That money you promised me tomorrow—give it to me tonight and I'll be half across the country by daylight.'

David: 'I told you I couldn't raise it till tomorrow.'

Robert, snarling: 'How'd you like it if I changed my mind between now and tomorrow?'

David: 'But, Robert, I—' He breaks off as he thinks of something, then says: 'I've got the bonds I was going to raise the money on—if you'll take them.'

Robert: 'They're negotiable? There's no foolishness about them?'

David: 'Certainly they're negotiable! Do you think I'd—?'

Robert: 'I don't think anything about you. How soon can you turn them over?'

David: 'As soon as you can get here.'

Robert: 'I won't come there for them.'

David: 'All right. Where are you?'

Robert: 'At the Li-Chee.'

David: 'Then I can meet you at the corner of... and... in ten minutes.'

Robert: 'Okay, but don't keep me waiting, or I might change my mind.'

David: 'And you'll give me your word you'll—'

Robert: 'I've got to go home and pack a bag, but I won't bother your sainted Selma. I won't even see her if I can get out of it.' He slams the receiver on the hook, says: 'Boy Scout!' at it, and returns to his table.

(Throughout this scene, waiters, etc. have been passing and repassing Robert at the phone, but none seems to have paid any attention to his conversation.)

Nick and Nora at their table listening to Polly singing. Dancer, intent now on keeping them comfortable until

Polly and Robert are safely away, comes to the table and asks: 'Everything all right, Mr Charles?'

Nick, shuddering at the first taste of his drink and frowning at the glass: 'It's all something.'

Dancer laughs with professional heartiness and addresses the waiter: 'Ling, no check for this table. Anything they want is on the house.'

Nick: 'I can't let you do that.'

Dancer: 'But I insist. You must be my guest—'

Nick, at this point seeing the approach of a group of thugs he knows, and realizing that somebody's going to be stuck for a lot of drinks, says quickly: 'We accept with thanks. That's mighty white of you, Dancer.' He shakes Dancer's hand as the thugs arrive, and says: 'Meet the rest of my party.'

Eddie: 'We don't want to meet him. He's a crumb.'

Nick: 'But he's giving the party. It's all on the house.'

Eddie: 'Well, I'll—well—well!' He turns to his companions, saying enthusiastically: 'Boys! Champagny!'

Nick: 'Certainly champagne.'

Dancer tries to smile as if he likes it. The others crowd him back out of the way as they make room for themselves around the table.

Men: 'Say, this is all right.'

'Hi'yer, Nick.'

'Hello, Nick.'

Eddie, a bull-like thug, looks gallantly at Nora. 'You certainly can pick 'em, Nick.'

He turns to Nora: 'I never seen such a guy. Every time I meet him, he's got another good-looking gal.'

Nick shoots a quick look at Nora.

Nick, to Nora: 'We haven't met in years.'

Nora, looking back at him amused and skeptical: 'No?'

Eddie, to Nora: 'When he gives you the sack, let me know, will yer?'

Nora, smiling up at him, delightedly: 'I certainly will.'

Eddie, turning to another of the men: 'She's hot-looking, ain't she?'

The Other Man: 'Shut up, you lug. It's his wife.'

Eddie winces and sinks down into his chair.

Another Man, stepping into the breach, pushing Willie toward Nick and Nora: 'Come on, Willie.'

'Here's Willie.'

'You remember Willie. He just got out today.'

Nick shakes Willie's hand cordially.

Nick: 'Indeed I do. Glad to see you.'

Willie: 'Likewise.'

Nick, turning to Nora: 'Darling, this is Willie the Weeper.'

Nora, smiling cordially at him: 'Delighted.'

Willie: 'Likewise.'

Nick (introducing the rest to Nora en masse): 'And the boys.'

Nora looks at them and smiles. They sit down, dragging their chairs up. The waiter comes up, listening for their orders.

Nick: 'I feel honored to be at your coming-out party, Willie. What'll you boys have?'

Another Man: 'Champagne!'

Nick: 'Willie?'

Willie: 'Scotch.'

Nora: 'Likewise!'

Eddie: 'Scotch, with a champagne chaser.'

The men all roar with delight.

Polly, nearing the end of her song, looks questioningly at Robert, who nods and points to his watch and the door to indicate that she should hurry. Lum Kee is watching them. He goes over to Dancer, who has left Nick's table.

Lum Kee: 'No trouble, Dancer. I ask you, please.'

Dancer, putting a hand on his partner's arm: 'Stop worrying, Lum. Everything is okay.'

Lum Kee: 'All the time you say everything okay. All the time trouble-trouble.'

Dancer: 'We always get out of it, don't we?'

Lum Kee: 'You bet you, but too much money. Pretty soon money not fix something. Then no more Li-Chee.'

Dancer slaps Lum Kee on the back and says: 'If it's Landis you're worrying about, I'll tell him to stay away. I don't like the guy much either. But you'll find something else to squawk about.'

Lum Kee, cheerfully: 'You bet you.'

Polly, having finished her song, tells the orchestra to play a dance number instead of an encore, and goes toward her dressing room. As she passes Nora, she gives her a reassuring nod. Robert is getting his hat and coat. Dancer crosses to meet Polly at the door and says: 'Just keep him in your apartment till evening and we'll both be cutting ourselves a nice piece of gravy.'

Polly says without enthusiasm: 'I hope so. Has Phil been in tonight?'

Dancer: 'For a minute. He went off like he had a date. Go ahead, kid.' He pats her back, urging her toward the door. She goes out.

At Nick's table, his guests are still applauding Polly deafeningly, pounding the table with bottles, etc. Nora seems to be talking to Nick, but nothing can be heard. He yells back: 'Can't hear you.' The words are barely audible. She puts her mouth to his ear and screams: 'Do you think that girl will really see that he gets home?'

The noise dies suddenly just as she starts, and everybody in the place looks at her—her scream could be heard a block away. Willie, who has been banging on the table with two bottles, nudges the thug beside him and says: 'I don't care whose wife she is, I don't like a dame that gets noisy when she's had a few snifters.'

Nick is trying to recover his hearing in the ear Nora screamed in. She asks again, but in a lower voice: 'Do you?'

Nick: 'She'll see that he gets to somebody's home. You can phone if you want, when he's had time to get there.'

Outside, the fog is thicker. Polly starts for a taxi, but Robert says: 'It's only three blocks.' They turn down the street. Phil comes out of his doorway and follows them. Harold is slumped down in the seat of Nick's car asleep, though his jaws still move a little with his gum. The taxi-driver is saying: 'And I said to this truck-driver, 'All right, tough guy, if you don't like me cutting in on you, how would you like to climb down off that hearse and get bopped in the nose?' I said.'

At a corner three blocks from the Li-Chee, Robert points to David, waiting in his car, and says: 'There's our honeymoon money!' Polly holds back as he goes toward the car, but he takes her arm, saying: 'Come on. I want him to see how much better I'm doing.' They go up to the car.

Robert: 'Have you got the bonds?'

David slowly looks from one to the other of them as he takes a thick sheaf of bonds from his pocket. He hands them to Robert, who eagerly examines them, then says: 'Thanks, Sir Galahad,' as he puts them into his pocket.

David: 'You'll keep your promise?'

Robert: 'Don't worry about that—and I wish you as much luck with your bargain as I got with mine.' He pulls Polly toward him and kisses her on the mouth. David turns his head away in disgust. Robert laughs at him, says: 'There's only one thing. I'm going home to pack a bag. Stay away till I've cleared out. Fifteen minutes oughtn't to mean anything to a man who's waited as long as you have. Ta-ta!' He and Polly turn away. David looks after them for a moment, then sighs as if with relief, and slowly starts his car.

At Nick's table in the Li-Chee, Eddie is complaining: 'Where's Polly? I want to hear Polly sing. We come up here and spend all this dough'—indicating the champagne bottles—'and what does she do? She sings one song and quits.' Joe, earnestly: 'You can't say anything against Polly. She's all to the good.'

Another thug, very drunk, his eyes almost shut, asks: 'She still live in that place on White Street with the ghosts running up and down the halls?'

Nora, very interested: 'A haunted house?'

The drunk, opening his eyes: 'Did I say ghosts? I'm drunk, lady. I meant goats.' He puts fingers up to his head to imitate horns and says: 'Ba-a-a!'

Nora: 'Well, that's *almost* as good.'

Nick, as if not very interested: 'What part of White Street?'

The Drunk: 'Three forty-six. I can always remember that number because my old man used to have a livery stable there.'

At the mention of the number Nora puts her hand quickly on Nick's and looks at him with a frightened face. Nick pats her hand without taking his attention from the drunk, and asks: 'In the place with the goats?'

The drunk, who is going back to sleep, shakes his head and says: 'No, that was back in Baraboo, Wisconsin.'

Nick: 'You know the fellow who owns the house?'

The Drunk: 'In Baraboo?'

Nick: 'The one Polly lives in.'

The drunk shakes his head again: 'Nope, but he ought to keep the front door shut so the goats can't get in.'

Nick: 'He was killed today.'

The Drunk: 'It don't surprise me. Stands to reason no tenants weren't going to put up with those goats forever.' The other thugs exchange glances, then begin to regard Nick with suspicion.

Nora: 'Nick, I'm going to phone.'

Nick: 'He's had time enough to get home.' He holds out a handful of change.

Dancer, not far away, sees Nora take the nickel (if necessary, he can have overheard some of the conversation), and he goes quickly over to one of the hatcheck girls and says: 'Get on the phone and stay there.' She goes to the phone, drops in a coin, and when Nora arrives the girl is in the middle of a long description of a dress that can be written much more accurately by Miss Goodrich than by Mr Hammett. Nora waits impatiently.

At Nick's table his guests are no longer having a good time; his questioning the drunk looks too much as if he is working on a murder job. Eddie clears his throat, says: 'Well, boys, I guess we better be trucking along.'

Willie: 'I guess we better.' Only the drunk seems comfortable.

Nick: 'What's the matter? It's early. Don't you like the party?'

Eddie: 'Sure we like it. It's swell. But—well, we got to get up early in the morning.'

Nick: 'Surely you haven't become an early riser in your old age, Eddie.'

Eddie squirms, says: 'Well, no, but—' He gets a bright idea: 'You see, we're giving Willie a picnic. He's nuts about picnics and he's been locked up a long time, so we thought we'd take him out in the country early tomorrow morning and throw a picnic for him. Ain't that right, Willie?'

Willie: 'I'm sure nuts about picnics!'

The drunk has opened his eyes and is staring at the others in surprise. He says: 'What's the matter with you dopes? What can you lift out in the country?' Then more indignantly: 'I ain't gonna ride in the backseat with no *cow*!'

Eddie laughs, says to Nick: 'Ain't he a card!' and with Willie's help begins to haul the drunk to his feet.

Dancer, going into his apartment, says to a passing waiter: 'Bring me a glass of milk.' In his apartment, he goes to the telephone and calls Polly's number. Lum Kee is lying on a sofa reading a book. Dancer waits patiently at the phone until the waiter comes in with his milk; then he puts down the phone and says: 'That bum! I told her to take him straight to her place.'

Lum Kee, not looking up from his book: 'Mr Landis?'

Dancer: 'Uh-huh. I wanted her to get him in shape so he could go home.'

Waiter: 'Mr Landis on phone I hearum say go home pack bag.'

Dancer's eyes narrow; then he says: 'Oh, sure, that's right. I had forgotten.'

The waiter goes out. Dancer stands idly spinning an ashtray on a table for a moment, then yawns, and says: 'I think I'll go out for a couple of minutes and get a little air in one of my lungs.' Lum Kee nods without looking up. Dancer takes his hat and coat from a closet, says: 'That last batch of Scotch we got from Monty's pretty bad.'

Lum Kee: 'I tell him.'

Dancer goes out. Lum Kee puts his book down, takes his hat from the closet and goes out.

The girl at the telephone is now talking about hats, while Nora fidgets with increasing impatience.

In his room, Robert is finishing packing a bag, with occasional glances at the bathroom that connects his room with Selma's. He does not make much noise, but is still too drunk to be completely silent. He has changed his clothes.

Selma turns in bed and makes a faint moaning noise, but does not open her eyes.

In another room a bedside light goes on, and Aunt Katherine sits up in bed, listening. Grim-faced, she unhurriedly gets out of bed and reaches for her slippers.

His bag packed, Robert puts it out in the hall, then turns out the lights and tiptoes through the connecting bathroom into Selma's room, going to a dressing table, pulling a drawer open, and taking out a jewel case. He has transferred part of its contents to his pocket when Selma suddenly sits up in bed and screams: 'Robert!' He turns, pushing the case back into the drawer as she snaps on the light.

Robert, with taunting mildness: 'Hello, Selma, how are you?'

She runs toward him, crying: 'Oh, where have you been? Oh, why do you do these things?'

He takes her in his arms, says: 'There, there, darling.'

For a moment she relaxes in his arms, then she puts her hands on his chest, pushing herself free, and cries: 'No, I won't this time. I won't forgive you. I won't let you make a fool of me again.'

Robert, as if to an unreasonable child: 'All right, all right, darling. As a matter of fact, I only stopped in for a minute, anyhow, to change my clothes.'

Selma: 'Where are you going?'

Robert: 'A trip, a little trip.'

Selma: 'You're not. I won't have it. I won't.'

Robert, smiling: 'Oh, won't you?' He takes a step toward the door, then stops to ask: 'Want to kiss me goodbye?' She flies at him in insane rage. He catches her wrists, kisses her lightly on the mouth, says: 'Thanks, darling,' releases her wrists, and goes out. She stands staring after him with wild eyes, scrubbing her lips with the back of one hand, then runs into his room and pulls a table drawer open.

FLASHES: Robert, smiling, bag in hand, going out the front door into the foggy street.

Polly standing in a small store dooway, straining her eyes trying to see through the fog.

Phil, at the entrance of a narrow alley, his collar up, his right hand under his coat near his left armpit.

Dancer at the wheel of a black coupé, his eyes searching the street.

Lum Kee in a car driven by a Chinese chauffeur.

On a street corner a policeman is hunkered down on his heels scratching the back of a gaunt alley cat. He hears a pistol shot—not too loud—straightens up, and starts across the street.

Robert lies on his back on the sidewalk, his head and one shoulder propped up a little by the wall he has fallen against—dead. Selma stands looking down at him. Her face is a blank, dazed mask. In her right hand, hanging down at her side, is a pistol. Brakes scream and a car comes to a jarring halt at the curb. She does not move. David jumps out of the car and runs over to her, exclaiming: 'Selma!' She does not move until he turns her to face him and even then her face does not change. He shakes her, cries: 'Selma! What—' He sees the pistol and takes it from her, stepping back a little. As he does so, her eyes lose their blankness and she looks at the pistol.

In a monotone she says: 'He was going away. I took that from his room—to try to stop him.' She begins to tremble and her face works convulsively—she is about to go to pieces.

David has put the pistol in his pocket. He glances quickly up and down the foggy street, then takes her by the shoulders and shakes her again, putting his face close to hers, speaking very clearly, as if to one who understood English poorly: 'Listen, Selma. You're going back to the house. You never had a pistol. Hear me? You haven't been out of the house. Understand? You know nothing about this. Understand?' She nods woodenly. With an arm around her, he leads her quickly to the corner, only a few steps away. There he says: 'Now hurry! Back in the house. Up to your room. You know nothing about this. Run!' Automatically obeying his command, she runs blindly back toward her front door. David dashes back to his car, jumps in, and drives off with reckless speed.

In the Li-Chee, the girl at the telephone is now talking about shoes. Besides Nora, half a dozen other people are waiting to use the phone. Nora goes up to the girl and says: 'Please, it's awfully important that I—'

The girl, dropping another nickel into the slot: 'I can't help it if there's only one phone here. Why don't you carry around one of them portable shortwave sets if you got so many important things to call people about.' She goes on with her phone conversation.

Nora goes back to Nick, who is engaged in rearing on his table one of those old-fashioned towers of bottles, salt shakers, oranges, forks, etc., all carefully balanced atop one another. Waiters and customers stand around with bated breath watching him admiringly. He is getting along fine until Nora comes up and says: 'Nick!'' Then the whole pile comes crashing down on the table. The audience applauds.

Nick bows, then turns to Nora and says: 'The divorce is Wednesday.' She doesn't laugh.

She says: 'Nick, I can't get to the phone. One of the hatcheck girls has been talking for hours.'

Nick: 'You've come to the right place. Old Find-a-Phone Nick, the boys around the drugstore used to call me.' He offers her his arm and they go across the floor and out of the restaurant. As they pass the pay phone—where the hatcheck girl is now talking about underwear and a dozen customers are angrily waiting—Nick says loftily: 'Mere amateur phone-finding!' He opens a door, shakes his head, and shuts it. He starts to open the next door, but stops when he sees it is labeled LADIES. The third door opens into Dancer's apartment. He bows Nora in, ushers her to the sofa, hands her the book Lum Kee had been reading, goes to the phone, and calls Selma's number.

The door opens and Dancer, in hat and coat, comes in.

Nick: 'Hello, Dancer. Nice men's room you have.' He waves a hand to indicate the room and the rather elaborate bath that can be seen through an open door, then suddenly frowns at Nora and asks: 'What are *you* doing in here?'

Dancer stands inside the open door looking at Nick with cold eyes, and when he speaks his voice is cold and level: 'Once a gum-heel always a gum-heel, huh? I don't like gum-heels, but I thought you'd quit it when you married a pot of money and—'

Nora, indignantly: 'Did he call me a pot?'

Nick pays no attention to either of them; Aunt Katherine is on the other end of the wire. She says: 'You'd better come over, Nicholas. Robert has been killed.'

Nick's expression does not change as he says: 'I will,' and slowly hangs up.

Dancer, jerking a thumb at the open door behind him: 'Well, now, if you're through in here.'

Nick, leaning back comfortably in his chair: 'Still foggy out?'

Dancer, very deliberately: 'Have you ever been thrown out of a place, Mr Charles?'

Nick, to Nora: 'How many places was it up to yesterday, Mrs Charles?'

Nora: 'How many places have you been in, Mr Charles?'

Dancer: 'Look here!'

Nick, raising a hand: 'Wait, wait! As I was about to say, it's not for me to tell any man how to run his business—though I *could* give you a few hints—but just the same it doesn't look right for you and your partner and your chief entertainer and one of your best customers all to go out at about the same time. It gives the place a—a—a quite vacant look. Did you notice it, Mrs Charles?'

Nora: 'Oh, decidedly, Mr Charles. Quite barn-like.'

Nick: 'Thank you, Mrs Charles. Now there's another thing. If Mr Robert Landis came here with a lady who left a cigarette case, you shouldn't have sent it to his *wife*. You know what a fellow Mr Landis was.'

Dancer: 'That wasn't me. Lum didn't know.'

Nora leans toward Nick, her face strained: 'Did you say 'was'?' Nick nods slowly, his face serious now. Nora, softly: 'Poor Selma.'

Dancer, angrily: 'I've had enough of this. I—' He breaks off as through the open door comes the sound of Polly's singing.

Nick: 'Ah! Another of our travelers has returned. Now if only—no sooner said than done,' he says as Lum Kee comes in. Nick looks from one to the other of them and says thoughtfully: 'I wonder which of you would be most frightened if Robert Landis walked in now.' Neither man says anything. Nick: 'But *you* know there's no chance of that, don't you, Dancer?'

Dancer: 'I don't know what you're talking about, and I don't care.' He advances threateningly. 'Get out!'

Nick smiles, shakes his head, says: 'You said that before and it's foolish. We're not going to get out—we're going to have more people come in.'

He picks up the phone. Dancer, grabbing at the phone: 'Give me that phone!'

Nick: 'Certainly.'

He raps Dancer on the jaw with it. Dancer staggers back, holding his jaw.

Nora, proud of Nick, says to Dancer: 'See?'

Nick dials a number, says: 'Nick Charles speaking. I want to get hold of Lieutenant Abrams of the Homicide Detail. If he's not on duty, will you give me his residence number?'

Lum Kee crosses to the closet and carefully puts his hat away.

On a dark and seemingly deserted part of the waterfront, David gets out of his car, walks to the edge of a small pier, and throws Selma's pistol as far out into the water as he can.

Through the fog comes a man's voice shouting: 'Hey, what are you doing there?' followed by the sound of feet running toward David. David races back to his car and drives off.

In Dancer's apartment, Nick is saying into the phone: 'Sure, I'll wait for you, Abrams... Well, I'll *ask* them to wait, but sometimes I think they don't like me well enough to do me favors... Yes. I'll tell them.' He puts down the phone and tells Lum Kee and Dancer: 'The Lieutenant said something about boiling you in oil if you budged before he gets here. The fellow probably exaggerates.'

Polly has finished her song: the sound of applause comes through the door. Dancer turns on his heel and goes out.

A still larger and angrier group of customers is waiting to use the phone. The hatcheck girl is talking about pajamas. Dancer takes the receiver roughly from her and slams it on the hook, snarling: 'Get back to work. What are you going to do? Spend the whole night here?' He goes on toward the restaurant.

In Dancer's apartment, Lum Kee says: 'Dancer not mean anything, please, Mr Charles. Good man—only excited. Sometime make a little trouble—not mean anything.' He smiles cheerfully at Nick and Nora, as if he had explained everything, and says: 'Now we have little drink, you bet you.'

Nora rises, saying to Nick: 'I ought to go to Selma's. She'll need somebody.'

Nick: 'Right. I'll put you in the car.' To Lum Kee: 'Hold everything.' Nick and Nora go downstairs.

Harold is sound asleep now. The taxi-driver is saying: 'So I said to these two gobs, I said, 'Maybe you boys are tough stuff back on Uncle Sam's battle-wagon, but you ain't there now,' I said, 'you're on land,' I said, 'and you're either gonna pay that fare or I'm going to take it out of your—" He breaks off as Nick and Nora come to the car, and opens the door for them. Harold wakes up.

As Nora gets in, Nick asks Harold: 'Did you see Robert Landis leave?'

Harold: 'No, I would've only—' He breaks off, leans past Nick to push the taxi-driver violently with one hand, saying angrily to him: 'Putting me to sleep with them yarns about where you told everybody to get off at! I ought to—' He jerks his cap off and turns to Nora, saying earnestly: 'Aw, gee, I'm sorry, Mrs Charles!'

Nick: 'Did you see anybody you knew?'

Harold: 'Nope, I didn't notice nobody coming out particular—except there was a kid come out right after you went in, and I only noticed him because he was kind of hanging around'—he indicates the doorway Phil stood in—'for a little while. Why? Something up?'

Nick: 'What did the kid look like?'

Harold gives a rough description of Phil, adding: 'Why?'

Nick: 'What happened to him?'

Harold: 'I don't know.' He calls to the taxi-driver, who is standing back against a wall, looking resentfully at them: 'Hey, Screwy! What happened to the kid that was hanging around here?'

The Taxi-Driver: 'I don't know. I guess he went down the street half hour ago.'

Harold warns Nick: 'Maybe he never even seen him. What's up, Nick?'

Nick: 'Plenty. Drive Mrs Charles back to her aunt's,' then to Nora: 'Going to stay all night?'

Nora: 'I think I ought to.'

He nods, says: 'I'll stop over in the morning.' He stands at the curb staring thoughtfully after the car as it drives away.

Upstairs in the Li-Chee, Dancer meets Polly as she leaves the floor and asks her: 'What are you doing back here?'

Polly: 'It wasn't my fault, Dancer. You know how drunks are. We got outside and he insisted on going home—his home—and I couldn't talk him out of it. I couldn't strong-arm him, could I? So I thought I'd better come back and tell you. I couldn't stop him.'

Dancer: 'Okay, sister, dress your dolls the way you want to.'

Polly: 'I don't understand what you mean, Dancer.'

Dancer: 'A cluck, huh? All right. I'll tell you so you can understand. Somebody cooled off Landis tonight, and the heat's on plenty—right here. You're in it with me, and you're going to be in it with me, because the first time you step out of line—get the idea?'

Polly: 'You don't have to try to scare me.' (But she is scared.) 'I'm shooting square with you.'

Dancer, sneering: 'You mean starting now? That'll help some. Where's the paper?'

Polly: 'In my bag. Shall I tear it up?'

Dancer: 'Maybe you *are* as dumb as you act sometimes. Listen. Try to understand what I'm telling you. Landis is killed—dead. Maybe we're going to need that paper bad. So you don't let anything happen to it—be sure you don't.'

Polly: 'All right, but I still don't get it. I don't know what you—' Dancer: 'Shut up and do what you're told.'

At this point, as they move toward Dancer's apartment, they pass the head of the stairs and are joined by Nick, returning from the street.

Nick: 'Now let's have that little drink Lum Kee was talking about.'

Dancer: 'Swell! And, Mr Charles, I want to apologize for losing my temper like that.'

Nick, linking arms with them: 'Don't give it a second thought. Some people lose one thing, some lose another, but they all like a drink afterwards.'

To Polly, sympathetically: 'Tough you couldn't do a better job of seeing Landis got home all right.'

Polly, sullenly: 'It wasn't my fault. I did the best I could.'

Nick says: 'I'm sure you did,' as they go into Dancer's apartment.

Lum Kee is at the telephone saying: 'Better you come right away... You bet you.' He hangs up, explaining blandly to Nick:

'Mr Caspar. He our lawyer. Sometimes good thing when you have trouble.'

Nick: 'You bet you.'

Dancer: 'Maybe, but I think you're going to a lot of trouble over nothing. It's a cinch none of us shot Landis—so what do we need a lawyer for?'

Nick: 'Maybe to help you explain how you know he was *shot*'

Dancer: 'Well, whatever way he was killed, it's still a cinch we didn't have anything to do with it.'

Nick yawns, says: 'A cinch is no defense in the eyes of the law,' and makes himself comfortable on the sofa.

Dancer smiles ingratiatingly at Nick and says: 'I don't blame you for thinking maybe we're tied up in this somehow. It's our own fault for starting off with you on the wrong foot, but—let's have that drink first and talk things over. We can show you we're in the clear.' He pushes a button for a waiter.

Nick, indifferently, lying back and looking at the ceiling: 'Don't worry about me. Talk it over with the police.'

Dancer catches Polly's eye and jerks his head a little toward Nick. She nods and moves as if aimlessly over to the sofa. Lum Kee looks from Dancer to Polly, then goes over and sits on a chair not far from the sofa, but behind Nick.

Dancer calls: 'Come in,' as the waiter knocks, and moves over so that he is between Nick and the door. (None of these movements should be definitely threatening, though it should seem to the audience that Nick is being surrounded.)

Dancer, to Nick: 'What'll you have?'

Nick: 'Scotch.'

Polly and Lum Kee say: 'Same.'

Dancer: 'And a glass of milk.'

The waiter goes out. Polly sits down on the sofa beside Nick and says: 'Do you suppose that David Graham could have killed Robert?'

Nick blinks in surprise, then says: 'I'm no good at supposing. What do *you* know about David Graham?'

Dancer is regarding the girl with a puzzled look.

Polly: Only what Robert told me—that he was in love with his wife.'

Nick: 'Oh.'

Polly, putting a hand on one of Nick's as if unconsciously: 'Wasn't he?'

Nick: 'Everybody's in love with *somebody's* wife—I guess.'

Polly, moving a little closer to him on the sofa: 'Are you?'

Nick, still looking at the ceiling, takes his hand out of Polly's and puts his arm around her, making himself more comfortable. He says: 'Everybody doesn't *admit* it.'

Polly, bending over him a little, smiles and says admiringly: 'I bet you could admit a lot—if you wanted to.'

The waiter comes in with drinks, but halts in the doorway at a signal from Dancer. Nick pats Polly's shoulder and says lightly: 'My dear, for a girl who's had so much practice giving men the works for Dancer, your technique is remarkably—ah—unpolished.'

She jerks away from him angrily.

Nick: 'There's the fellow with the drinks. That's what we're waiting for, isn't it?' None of the others moves.

Harold begins to apologize again as Nora gets out of the car in front of Selma's: 'I feel like busting myself in the nose for that—'

Nora: 'That's all right, Harold. Go back for Mr Charles.'

Harold stands looking after her, scratching his head and putting three fresh pieces of gum into his mouth, as she goes to the front door.

The door is opened immediately by one of the detectives who was with Abrams earlier that day. He touches the brim of his hat with one finger; she smiles at him without saying anything and goes down the hall to the open drawing-room door. Aunt Katherine, Abrams, and Dr Klammer are standing in the drawing room. Dr Kammer is a powerfully built middle-aged man with very pale skin, thick, short-cut black hair, and large, dark, staring eyes. He speaks very precisely, with a barely noticeable accent, and, though he does not use a cane, one of his legs is stiff at both ankle and knee. His dress is dandified, more European than American, and—except for the dragging of his lame leg when he walks—he has a decidedly military carriage.

As Nora reaches the door, Abrams is saying gloomily to Dr Kammer: 'Okay, Doc—if you still want to take the responsibility for not letting me talk to her.'

Kammer: 'My dear sir, it is not a case of responsibility. Mrs Landis has suffered a great shock. It was necessary to give her something to quiet her. Can she talk to you in her sleep? She will not be awake for hours.'

Abrams: 'And then?'

Kammer: 'And then we shall see.'

Abrams sighs, says: 'This is making it pretty tough for me. Well, let me ask you—'

Nora, coming into the room, interrupts him impatiently: 'What are you wasting time here for? Nick's waiting for you at the Li-Chee. Robert was there tonight and left with a girl who lives in that apartment house Pedro owns. Pedro Dominges, the man who was killed at our place. She's back there now, and Dancer and the Chinaman, and Nick's with them waiting for you.'

Abrams, stolidly: 'Good evening, Mrs Charles—or I guess it's good morning. Did you see him there? I mean Robert Landis.'

Nora: 'Yes.'

Abrams: 'What happened?'

Nora: 'Nick knows. Go down there. He can tell you everything.'

Abrams, not very hopefully: 'I hope somebody can tell me something. These people!' He looks gloomily at Aunt Katherine and Kammer, and shakes his head, then continues: 'Anyhow, I got to ask a couple more questions. Dr Kammer, do you often have to give Mrs Landis things to quiet her?' Kammer stares at him. Abrams turns to Nora for sympathy, saying: 'You see—that's the way it's been going.'

Nora: 'But surely you don't think Mrs Landis—' She breaks off, looking from one to the other in amazement.

Abrams, patiently: 'How do I know what to think if nobody'll tell me anything. Well, Dr Kammer, let's put it plain: does she take dope?'

Aunt Katherine: 'Mr Abraham, you're insulting.'

Kammer: 'Certainly not.'

Abrams, paying no attention to Aunt Katherine: 'Okay. Check that off. Then is she crazy?'

Kammer: 'My dear sir, why should you think that?'

Abrams: 'Easiest thing in the world. I've seen you three times in my life before this, and all three times you were on the witness stand testifying that somebody was nuts.' He begins to count on his fingers. 'First it was that guy Walter Dabney that killed a guy in a fight; then it was that Harrigan woman'—he opens his eyes a little wider—'by golly, she shot her husband, too; and then it was—'

Nora goes up to Abrams as if she were about to smack him, and says angrily: 'Too! What right have you to say a thing like that?'

Dr. Kammer bows to Aunt Katherine and says: 'Miss Forrest, in view of this definite accusation of the gentleman's'—he bows to Abrams— 'I think you would be justified in insisting that your attorney be present at any further interviews members of your family may have with the police.'

Aunt Katherine continues to regard Abrams in stony silence, as she has throughout this scene except for her one speech.

Abrams groans wearily and says, though not apologetically: 'Anybody's tongue's liable to slip.' Nobody says anything. He addresses Nora as if he were disappointed in her: 'It's what you'd expect out of them—but you ought to know better.' When she does not reply, he shrugs his shoulders and goes out.

Nora wheels to face Aunt Katherine and Kammer, asking: 'Where's Selma?'

Aunt Katherine: 'She's sleeping, my dear,' adding quickly as Nora starts toward the door: 'Don't disturb her. Dr Kammer says she must not be disturbed.'

Nora looks at them for a moment, then says very deliberately: 'I won't disturb her, but I am going to be with her until she wakes up,' brushes past them, and goes out of the room.

Aunt Katherine puts a hand on Kammer's arm and in almost a whisper asks: 'Well?'

Kammer says: 'I think there is as yet no reason for alarm.'

Nora goes into Selma's bedroom, where a dim night-light is burning, and stands for a moment by the bed, looking down at Selma. When she turns away to take off her coat, one of Selma's eyes opens cautiously; then she sits up in bed and whispers: 'Nora!'

Nora runs to her, exclaiming: 'But they told me you were—'

Selma: 'I know.' She unwads a handkerchief while she speaks, showing Nora two white tablets. 'They gave me these to put me to sleep, but I didn't take them. I wanted to see you. I knew you'd come.' Selma and Nora go into a clinch. Then Selma asks: 'Has David come back yet?'

Nora: 'I don't think so. He's not here now.'

Selma: 'Will you phone him for me—see if he's home?'

Nora: 'Of course.' She puts out a hand toward the bedside phone.

Selma, catching her arm: 'No, not here. That's why I was afraid to phone. The police might be listening in. Go to a drugstore or something. Or—better—go to his apartment—it's a only a few blocks.'

Nora, puzzled: 'But I don't understand.'

Selma: 'He took the pistol and told me to come back and not say anything and I want to know if he's all right.'

Nora: 'The pistol!'

Selma, explaining rapidly, unconscious of the effect her words have had on Nora: 'Yes. I took it and ran out after Robert when he said he was going away—you know, to scare him into not going—and he'd insulted me so terribly. And he turned the corner before I could catch up with him, and then there was a shot, and then when I turned the corner, there he was dead, and after a while David came and took the pistol and told me to come back home and not say anything to anybody. And now I don't know whether he's all right or—'

Nora: 'Then you didn't shoot Robert?'

Selma, amazed: 'Shoot Robert? Nora!'

Nora puts her arms around Selma, saying: 'Of course you didn't, darling. That was stupid of me.'

Selma: 'And you'll go find out about David? I was in such a daze or I wouldn't have let him do it; and I'm so afraid he may have got into trouble.'

Nora: 'I'll go right away.'

Selma: 'And you'll hurry back to tell me?'

Nora: 'Yes, but do try to get some sleep.'

Selma: 'I will.'

They kiss and Nora goes out.

Nora goes softly downstairs and out of the house without seeing anybody, but as she hurries up the foggy street a man comes out of a dark doorway and follows her.

Aunt Katherine and Dr Kammer are sitting in silence, as if waiting for something, when they hear the street door close behind Nora. In unison, they look at each other, then in the direction of Selma's room. Neither speaks. They rise together, and slowly—he dragging his lame leg, she leaning on her cane—they go to Selma's room. Selma lies as if sleeping. Kammer feels her pulse, then picks up her handkerchief and finds the tablets. He does not seem surprised. He pours a glass of water and says, not unkindly: 'Come, why must you be so childish? Take these now.' Selma, very sheepishly, sits up in bed and takes the tablets and water.

In David's apartment, he is distractedly walking up and down. He looks at his watch, goes to the telephone, but puts it down without calling a number. He lights a cigarette, puts it out immediately, goes to the window; then repeats his performance with watch and telephone. He is wiping his face with a handkerchief when the phone rings. He picks it up quickly. Nora, on the other end of the wire, says: 'David, this is Nora. I'm downstairs. I want to—'

David: 'Come up! Come up!' He goes to the door and waits impatiently for her.

As soon as Nora appears, David asks: 'Have you come from her?'

Nora: 'Yes. She—'

David, excitedly: 'Where's Nick? What'll I do, Nora? It's my fault. I'm all to blame. If I hadn't given Robert those bonds, he wouldn't have been going away, and she wouldn't have'—his voice breaks and he almost whispers the last words—'shot him.'

Nora: 'But she didn't, David!'

David: 'What? She told me.'

Nora: 'She told you what?'

David: 'That she took the gun and ran out after him to try to keep him from going away and—'

Nora: 'But she didn't shoot him. She hadn't turned the corner when she heard the shot, and when she got there he was already dead. She told me herself, and she was perfectly calm when she told me.'

David sinks back into a chair, his eyes wide and horrified. He tries to speak twice before the words will come out, and when they do his voice is hoarse with anguish. 'I've killed her, Nora! I've sent her to the gallows! I thought she shot him. I took the gun and threw it in the bay. I'm a fool and I've killed her.'

Nora, frightened, but trying to soothe him: 'Perhaps it's not that bad, David. We'll see what Nick says. He'll know how to—'

David: 'But, don't you see? If I hadn't thrown the gun away, the fact that it hadn't been fired—and the police could've fired a bullet from it and seen that it didn't match the one he was killed with—don't you see?—it would have been absolute proof that she didn't do it. But now—' He breaks off and grabs one of Nora's hands, asking: 'How is she? Do the police—do they think she—' He seems unable to finish the question.

Nora: 'Selma's all right. She's lying down. The police haven't talked to her yet. Dr Kammer wouldn't let them.'

David, a little sharply: 'Kammer! Is he there?' Nora nods. David, frowning: 'I wish he'd stay away from her.' He shrugs off his thoughts about Kammer and asks: 'Do the police suspect her?'

Nora: 'I'm afraid they suspect everybody.'

David: 'But her especially—do they?'

Nora, hesitantly: 'I'm afraid they do—a little.' Then, more cheerfully: 'But they didn't know about the Li-Chee Club and those people then. We were there tonight and saw Robert, and Nick found out a lot of things about Robert's running around with a girl who lives in the same house as Pedro Dominges, oh! a lot of things, and I'm sure by this time he knows who killed Robert—so there's nothing to worry about.'

David, not sharing her cheerfulness: 'I hope so. I'll kill myself if—'

Nora, sharply: 'Don't talk like that, David. They'll find out who killed Robert—Nick'll find out.'

David: 'Tell me the truth, Nora, does Nick think she, Selma, killed him?'

Nora: 'Oh, he knows she didn't. He knows—' She breaks off, staring with frightened face past David and pointing at the window. David turns, in time to catch a glimpse of Phil's face outside the window. He rushes to the window, but has some trouble with the fastening, so that by the time he gets it open, the fire-escape is empty. As he turns back to Nora, she says in a surprised voice: 'Why, that was—'

There is a sharp, triple knock on the door. David goes to the door and opens it. The man who shadowed Nora from Selma's house is there. He asks: 'Mr Graham?'

The man takes a badge in a leather case from his left pants pocket and shows it to him briefly, saying: 'Police—'

Nora says: 'There was a man on the fire-escape! The brother of that girl at the Li-Chee.'

The policeman says: 'Yeah?' as if not believing her. He goes to the window and looks out for a moment, then turns back and says: 'He's gone.' Then he scowls at Nora and asks: 'What girl at the Li-Chee?'

Nora says: 'Polly Byrnes—the girl Robert Landis went out with just before he was killed.'

The policeman says: 'Say, you know a lot, don't you, sister? What does all this make you out to be?'

Nora says, with great dignity: 'I'm Mrs Nick Charles!'

The policeman says, apologetically: 'I didn't know. I guess then maybe there was somebody on the fire-escape.'

Nora asks, indignantly: 'Well, what are you going to do—stand here and wait for them to come back?'

The policeman says: 'No, I reckon not.' He goes to the phone.

David takes Nora out of the policeman's hearing and asks, in a low voice: 'Should I tell him about the gun—about Selma?'

Nora says: 'No, don't tell anybody until we see Nick.'

Dancer's apartment—at the Li-Chee. Nick is lying on the sofa, as before. Lum Kee is sitting in the corner, reading a book. In another chair, Polly is sitting, manicuring her fingernails. Dancer is sitting astride a chair, chewing a toothpick, and looking angrily at Nick. Nick is in the middle of an apparently long and pointless anecdote.

Dancer spits toothpick out on the floor and says, angrily: 'Listen, we're putting up with you, but do we have to put with all this talk?'

Nick sits up and looks at him in surprise, saying: 'But I thought I was entertaining you.'

A Chinese waiter opens the door and says: 'Mr Caspar here—'

Caspar comes in. He is a little man, almost a dwarf, sloppily dressed, with bushy hair, and is addicted to Napoleonic poses. He comes into the room bowing and smiling to everyone and saying: 'Well, well—what is it?'

Dancer, grouchily: 'Do I know? So a guy comes in and buys a drink. He goes out and somebody kills him. What are we supposed to do, give the customers insurance policies with the drinks?'

Nick says: 'Wouldn't be a bad idea—with the kind of stuff you're serving.'

Caspar advances toward Nick with his hand out, saying: 'I didn't recognize you for a moment, Mr Charles. You remember me— Floyd Caspar?'

Nick says: 'Oh, yes,' and pats his pockets as if to make sure he hasn't lost anything.

Caspar goes on: 'A man killed! Surely you don't think these people—' he looks at the three others in the room as if they were saints '—would have anything to do with a thing like that!' He puts a hand on Dancer's shoulder and says: 'Why, I've known this boy since he was—'

Dancer pushes the hand off roughly and says: 'Save it for the district attorney. What're you wasting your voice on this gum-heel for?'

Through the closed door comes the sound of men arguing. Then the door is swung open by Lieutenant Abrams, pushing a Chinese waiter against it. Two other detectives are with Abrams. He looks very tired and very dissatisfied with all the people in the room. When he sees Caspar, he groans and says: 'I knew it would be like this. I knew there would be some shyster around to slow things up.'

Caspar draws himself up to his full five feet and begins, pompously: 'Lieutenant Abrams, I must ask you—'

Abrams pays no attention to him, walks over and sits down on the sofa by Nick, asking, not very hopefully: 'Is it right you know something about what's been happening?'

Nick says: 'A little.'

Abrams says: 'It can't be any littler than anybody else seems to know. Do you want to say it in front of them—or do we go off in a corner?'

Nick says: 'This suits me.'

Abrams asks: 'Is this the dame Mrs Charles was telling me about—that lives in Dominges's apartment and was with Landis tonight?'

Nick says: 'Yes. She sings here, but she took time off to see that he got home all right.'

Abrams says, gloomily: 'She certainly did a swell job." Then asks Polly: 'And what did you do after he got home?'

Polly says: 'I came back here. I work here.'

Abrams says: 'When did you find out he was killed?'

Polly says: 'After I came back—maybe half an hour. Dancer told me. I guess Mr Charles told him.'

Abrams says: 'Never mind guessing... I guess you know your landlord was killed this afternoon?'

Polly exclaims: 'What!'

Nick says: 'I told her earlier tonight, but she seemed to think it had to do with some fellow named Peter Dufinger, or Duflicker, or something.'

Polly says, earnestly, to Nick: 'I honestly didn't know, Mr Charles. I never knew what his name was, except Pedro.'

Abrams asks: 'What did you know about him besides that?'

Polly says: 'Nothing. I've only lived there a couple of months and I never even seen him more than half a dozen times—'

Abrams asks Nick: 'You believe her?'

Nick says: 'I believe everybody. I'm a sucker.'

Abrams asks Polly: 'Who do you think would kill Landis?'

She says: 'I haven't the faintest idea. Honest I haven't.'

Nick says: 'Miss Byrnes has a brother who carries a gun. Dancer was chucking him out when I came in. I hear he hung around for a while outside... perhaps until just about the time that Polly and Landis left.'

When Nick says, 'Dancer was chucking him out,' Polly looks sharply at Dancer, but when Nick finishes his speech, Polly jumps up and comes over to him, saying earnestly: 'Phil didn't have anything to do with it, Mr Charles. He wouldn't have any reason.'

Nick says: 'I'm not accusing anybody. I'm just talking.' Then he tells Abrams: 'Dancer says he threw him out because he was bothering Polly for money.'

Polly turns to Dancer, angrily, exclaiming: 'That's a lie! You had no right to—'

Little Caspar interrupts her, saying: 'Take it easy—take it easy. That's the idea of this police clowning—to get you all at each other's throats. Just answer any of their questions that you want to and don't let 'em get under your skin.'

Abrams complains to Nick: 'That's the way it goes. I leave that little shyster stay in here because I got nothin' to hide and he keeps buttin' in. If he don't stop it, I'm going to put them where he'll need a court order to get to them.'

Caspar smiles and says: 'Well, that's never been much trouble so far.'

Abrams turns to Polly again, asking: 'Where is this brother of yours that didn't kill anybody?'

Polly says: 'I don't know. I haven't seen him today.'

Abrams asks: 'Does he live with you?'

Polly says: 'No. He lives in a hotel on Turk Street. I don't know just where.'

Abrams says: 'You don't know much about anybody, do you?'

Polly says: 'I honestly don't know what hotel. Phil's always moving.'

Abrams says: 'What's the matter—does he have to move every time he don't kill somebody? What does he do for a living—besides not killing anybody?'

Polly says: 'He's a chauffeur, but he hasn't been able to get much work lately.'

Abrams asks if anybody knows Selma Young. Nobody does.

Abrams asks Nick: 'What do you think of it now?'

Nick says: 'My dear lieutenant, you wouldn't expect me to question a lady's word.'

Abrams says: 'It's all right for you to kid. Nobody jumps on your neck if you don't turn up a murderer every twenty minutes.' He sighs and, indicating Dancer and Lum Kee, asks: 'Well, what about them?'

Nick says: 'They seem to have disappeared not long after Polly and Landis went out. Then showed up again with their hats on around the time I heard about the murder.'

Abrams asks Dancer: 'Well?'

Dancer says: 'I went out to get some air. What city ordinance does that break?'

Lum Kee, who has continued to read all through the scene so far, puts down his book and says: 'I went with him.'

Dancer tries not to show surprise.

Abrams says: 'Yeah? Where'd you go for all this air?'

Lum Kee says, blandly: 'Air pretty much same everywhere. We go in my car—ride around. Ask chauffeur.'

Nick says: 'There was another little point: I told Dancer Landis had been killed but he seemed to know that he'd been shot.'

Abrams asks Dancer: 'How about that?'

Dancer says, disagreeably: 'This is the twentieth century—in a big city. How do most people get killed—battle-axes? I just took it for granted, like you would when you don't know you're on the witness stand.'

Abrams asks: 'Have you got a gun?'

Dancer takes an automatic out of his pocket and gives it to Abrams. From a card case he takes a slip of paper and gives it to Abrams, saying: 'Here's my permit.'

Abrams asks Lum Kee: 'You?'

Lum Kee brings Abrams an automatic and a permit.

Caspar says: 'If you're going to take those, Lieutenant, we should like a receipt.'

Abrams complains to Nick: 'I can't stand that shyster.'

Nick: 'I was beginning to suspect that.'

Abrams asks Polly: 'Have you got a gun?'

Polly shakes her head no.

Abrams: 'What'd you do with it?'

Polly: 'I never had one.'

Abrams, wearily: 'Nobody has anything, nobody knows anything. I don't see why I don't give up this racket and go farming.'

Dancer, to Caspar: 'Everybody thought he did a long time ago.'

Abrams: 'I'm laughing. Did you know this Pedro Dominges?'

Dancer: 'No.'

Abrams looks at Lum Kee, who says: 'No.'

Abrams stands up wearily, saying: 'Come on, we're going down to the Hall of Justice.'

Caspar: 'On what charge?'

Abrams, disgustedly: 'Charge, me eye! Witnesses. You ask 'em questions—where were you when you were over there?—and you have a stenographer take it down. You ought to know. Your clients spend nine-tenths of their time doing it.' He looks at his watch, nods at the door through which the sound of music comes, says: 'Or maybe for staying open after hours. Didn't you ever tell 'em about the two o'clock closing law?'

Caspar: 'I'm going with 'em.'

Abrams: 'And you can bring the wife and kiddies for all I care.'

The door opens and Nora and David come in accompanied by their detective. David and Polly look at each other with startled recognition, but neither says anything. Nora goes quickly over to Nick, who asks: 'What are you up to now?'

Nora: 'Have they found out who did it? Who did it, Nick?'

Nick: 'Sh-h-h, I'm making Abrams guess.'

Abrams looks from David to the detective and asks: 'Where'd you find him?'

Detective: 'You told me to shadow anybody that left the Landis house. Well, Mrs Charles did, and went over to his apartment, and I knew you wanted to talk to him, so as soon as I found out who it was I went on up and got him. There's something about a fellow on the fire-escape, but they can tell you better than I can.'

Abrams looks questioningly at Nora, who says: 'Yes, it was—' She looks at Polly, hesitates, says: 'It was her brother,' then to Dancer: 'The one you threw down the stairs when we came in.'

Everybody looks expectantly at Polly, who seems dumbfounded. After a long moment she exclaims: 'I don't believe it!'

Nick says: 'That's certainly a swell answer.'

Abrams asks Nora: 'What was he doing on the fire-escape?'

Nora: 'I don't know. He went away as soon as we saw him and by the time we could get the window open there was no sign of him. You know how foggy it is. And then this man came'—indicating the detective—'and by the time we could persuade him to do anything it was too late.'

The detective, apologetically: 'I reckon maybe I wasn't up on my toes like I ought to've been, Lieutenant, but it sounded kind of screwy to me at first.' He addresses Nick: 'I didn't know she was *your* wife then.'

Nick: 'You never can tell where you're going to find one of my wives.'

The sound of music suddenly stops. Out in the restaurant, the customers, complaining about this unaccustomed early closing, are being shooed out.

Polly flares up, saying angrily: 'What are you picking on Phil for? What's the matter with Robert's wife killing him? He told me himself she was batty as a pet cuckoo and would blow up and gum the whole thing if she found out that this guy—she points at David—was paying him to go away. Maybe she did find out about the bonds. What's the matter with that?'

Abrams looks thoughtfully at David and says: 'Hmmm, so that's where the bonds came from?'

Dancer is watching Polly with hard, suspicious eyes. Nick, surprised, asks David: 'Bonds?'

David nods slowly.

Abrams says to Polly: 'This is no time to stop talking—go on, tell us more about this bond deal.'

Caspar comes forward importantly, saying to Polly: 'No, no, I think this is a very good time to stop talking at least until you've had some sort of legal advice—'

Polly says: 'They know about it. Anyway, he does' (indicating David). 'Besides, you're Dancer's and Lum's mouthpiece, not mine. How do I know you won't leave me holding the bag?'

Abrams looks pleased for the first time since he's come into the room. He says to Polly: 'Now just a minute—that's fine!' He turns to Caspar and says: 'So you aren't her lawyer? Well, that'll give us a little rest from your poppin' off. You and your two clients are going outside and wait until we get through talking to the little lady—'

Caspar starts to protest, but Abrams nods to his detectives and two of them take Caspar, Lum Kee, and Dancer out. At the door, Dancer turns to warn Polly: 'Don't get yourself in any deeper than you have to.'

When the door is closed behind him, Abrams sits down with a sigh of relief and says: 'It's a lot better in here without them—especially that little shyster. Now maybe we can get somewhere!' He turns and sees that Nick, Nora, and David are huddled together whispering in a far corner of the room. David is telling Nick about Selma and the gun. Abrams says, gloomily: 'There it is again. If people got anything to say, why don't they say it to me?'

The huddle breaks up, Nick saying: 'Just a little family gossip.'

Abrams says: 'I'd even like to hear that.' He asks Polly: 'Did you ever see Mr Graham before?'

Polly says: 'I saw him tonight, when we went to get the bonds.'

Abrams asks: 'You and Robert Landis went to get them?'

Polly says: 'Yes. He was waiting for us on the corner of—Street—and he gave them to Robert.'

Abrams asks: 'And then what?'

Polly says: 'And then nothing. We left him and Robert went home.'

Abrams asks: 'And what did you do?'

Polly, after a moment's hesitation, says: 'I went with him.'

Abrams asks: 'He took you home with him?'

Polly says: 'Well, not in the house. I waited for him a block away—around the corner.'

Abrams asks: 'And then what?'

Polly says: 'I waited a long time and then I heard a shot—only I thought it might be an automobile backfire—it was foggy and I was too far away to see anything—and I didn't know what to do—then after a while a policeman went past the doorway where I was standing—and a police car came—then I honestly didn't know what had happened, but I thought I'd better get out of the neighborhood if I didn't want to get in trouble—so I came back here—'

Abrams says: 'Phooey!' and looks at Nick.

Nick says: 'I think somebody ought to ask her where she was too far away from—'

Polly stammers: 'From wherever it was it happened. If I hadn't been too far away, I'd have known where it was, wouldn't I?'

Nick says: 'I give up.'

Abrams: 'All right—we'll come back to that later. So you were waiting for him? What were you going to do if he hadn't been killed?'

Polly glances uneasily at the door through which Dancer went, then shrugs and says: 'We were going away.'

Abrams: 'Where to?'

Polly: 'New York first, I suppose—then Europe, he said.'

Abrams (looking at her evening gown): 'Dressed like that?'

Polly: 'We were going to stop at my place for me to change.'

Abrams: 'Dancer know you were going?'

Polly: 'No.'

Abrams: 'Think he found it out, and knocked Landis off?'

Polly, shaking her head quickly from side to side: 'No!'

Abrams: 'You're supposed to be Dancer's gal, aren't you?'

Polly: 'I work for him.'

Abrams: 'That's not what I asked you.'

Polly: 'You've got it wrong—honest. He knew I was running around with Robert—ask anybody.'

Abrams: 'How long?'

Polly: 'A month—three weeks anyhow.'

Abrams: 'Get much money out of Landis?'

Polly, hesitantly: 'He gave me some.'

Abrams: 'How much?'

Polly: 'I don't know exactly. I—I can tell you tomorrow, I guess.'

Abrams: 'Did you split it with Dancer?'

Polly: 'Why, no!'

Abrams: 'Maybe you're lying. Maybe Dancer found out you were going away where you could keep all the sugar to yourself—and he put a stopper to it.'

Polly: 'That's silly!'

Abrams: 'Sure. And hanging up in the air with a hunk of rope around your neck is silly, too.'

After a little pause to let that sink in, he says: 'Landis hadn't been home for a couple of days. Was he with you?'

Polly: 'Most of the time.'

Abrams: 'Drunk?'

Polly: 'Yes.'

Abrams: 'In your apartment?'

Polly: 'There and here.'

Abrams: 'Anybody else with you in your apartment?'

Polly: 'No.'

Abrams: 'Let's get back to the money. How much did you get out of him—roughly?'

Polly stares at the floor in silence.

Abrams: 'As much as a grand or two? Or more?'

Polly, not looking up: 'More.'

Abrams: 'More than five grand?' (Polly nods.) 'All right, kick through—about how much?'

Polly shrugs wearily, opens her bag, takes out a check, and gives it to Abrams, saying: 'A couple hundred dollars besides that, I guess.'

Abrams looks at the check, then up at the girl and asks: 'What'd he give you this for?'

Polly: 'Well, I was chucking up a job and everything to go away with him, and I didn't want to take chances on being stranded somewhere off in Europe.'

Abrams: 'Looks like you didn't all right.' He beckons to the others, who come to look over his shoulders at the check. It is to the order of Polly Byrnes for $10,000 and is signed by Robert Landis. They look at one another in amazement.

Nick says: 'Where do you suppose he got hold of that much?'

Abrams: 'Why? Aren't they rich?'

Nick: 'The money is his wife's, and she found out some time ago that she had to stop giving him too much at a time—just on account of things like this.'

Abrams: 'Yeah? How about the signature?'

Nick: 'Looks all right to me.'

David: 'And to me.'

Abrams (as if thinking aloud): 'But he don't usually have this much money, huh?' He asks Polly: 'Sure you didn't take this to the bank today and find out it was no good?'

Polly: 'I did not.'

Abrams: 'That's something we can check up. You know you're not going to have any easy time collecting this—unless his wife's as big a sap as he was.'

Polly: 'Why? He gave it to me.'

Abrams: 'Maybe. But his bank account's automatically tied up now till the estate's settled, and then I got an idea you're going to have to do a fancy piece of suing—taking a drunk for his roll!'

Polly: 'I'll take my chances. Just the same, if his dying makes all that trouble, that shows we didn't have anything to do with killing him, doesn't it? Why wouldn't we wait till after we'd cashed it?'

Abrams: 'We, we, we! So Dancer *was* in on it! How about the Chinaman?'

Polly: 'Nobody was in on it. There was nothing to be in on.'

Abrams: 'Phooey!' He addresses the remaining detective: 'Okay, Butch. Take her and her two playmates down to the hall and let the district attorney's office know you've got 'em there. We'll be along in a little while.' He turns to Nick: 'Or do you want to ask her something?'

Nick: 'Yes. Did Robert Landis know Pedro Dominges?'

Polly shakes her head and says: 'Not that I—' She remembers something. 'Once when Robert and I were going out together we passed him and he said good evening to both of us by name and we couldn't figure out how he knew Robert's, and Robert made some joke about nobody being able to hide anything from a landlord.'

Nick: 'Thanks.'

Polly and the detective go out.

Abrams: 'That mean anything to you?'

Nick: 'Not too much.'

Abrams: 'Now, Mr Graham, I've got to—' He breaks off to look at Nora and Nick, saying thoughtfully: 'I don't know whether you two ought to be in here while I'm doing this or not.'

Nick, yawning, says: 'I know where we ought to be. Come on, darling.'

Abrams: 'Maybe you *ought* to stay. Now, Mr Graham, I got to ask a lot of questions that you're not going to like, but I got to ask 'em.'

David: 'I understand.'

Abrams: 'First off, you're in love with Mrs Landis. Right?' David starts to protest, then simply nods. 'She in love with you?'

David, trying to speak calmly in spite of the painfulness of this inquiry: 'You'll have to ask her.'

Abrams: 'I will. Did she ever say she was?'

David: 'Not—not since she was married.'

Abrams: 'Before?'

David: 'We were once engaged.'

Abrams: 'Until Landis came along?'

David, in a very low voice: 'Yes.'

Abrams: 'Ever ask her to divorce him and marry you?'

David: 'She knew how I felt—it wasn't necessary to—'

Abrams: 'But did you ever ask her?'

David: 'I may have.'

Abrams: 'And what did she say?'

David: 'She never said she would.'

Abrams: 'But you hoped she would. And you thought with him out of the way she would.'

David looks Abrams in the eye and says: 'I didn't kill Robert.'

Abrams: 'I said you did? But you did pay him to go away.'

David: 'Yes.'

Abrams: 'Did she know about it?'

David: 'No, not unless he told her.'

Abrams: 'Were you and Landis on good terms?'

David: 'Decidedly not.'

Abrams: 'On very bad terms?'

David: 'Very bad.'

The lights go out. In complete darkness Abrams's voice is heard saying: 'Stay where you are—everybody!'

From the distance come the sounds of doors crashing, of glass breaking, of feet running, of men shouting; then close at hand furniture is knocked over, a door is slammed open, feet pound on the floor, two shots are fired, bodies thud and thrash around on the floor. Presently a cigarette lighter snaps on, held in Nick's hand. Behind him, in the dim light, Nora's and David's faces can be seen. The three of them are looking down at their feet. Abrams lies on the floor on his back. On top of him, mechanically chewing gum, his face serene, is Harold. One of his feet is on Abrams's throat; both his hands are clamped around one of Abrams's feet, twisting it inward and upward in the old Gotch toehold.

Nick says gently: 'Harold, Harold, get up from there. Lieutenant Abrams isn't going to like this.'

Harold, cheerfully: 'You're the boss.' He jumps up.

As Abrams gets up, a hand to his throat, Nick says: 'My chauffeur. Stout fellow, eh?'

Abrams goes toward Harold saying: 'What do you think you—'

Harold sticks his face into the Lieutenant's and says: 'What am I supposed to do? I'm sitting out there and I see the lights go off. Nick and Mrs Charles are up here and I know what kind of dump it is. Think I'm going to sit out there like a sissy till they throw the bodies out? How do I know you're a copper?' Then, more argumentatively, as he goes on: 'Suppose I did know it? How can I tell Nick ain't got hisself in a jam with the police?'

Nick: 'All right—but don't you boys think you'd better stop wrangling long enough to find out who turned out the lights and did the shooting?' He asks Harold: 'Did you run into anybody else on your way up?'

Harold: 'Only the copper, here.'

The lights go on.

They are standing in the passageway outside of Dancer's apartment. As they start toward the front of the building, out of the restaurant comes one of Abrams's men with Polly, Lum Kee, and Caspar, and behind them another detective, dragging a Chinese waiter.

Abrams asks in a complaining voice: 'Well, now what have you been letting them do?'

One of the detectives, indicating the waiter, says: 'Dancer had this monkey pull the switch and beat it out a window. Butch is hunting for him now.'

Abrams asks: 'And what was that shooting?'

The other detective says sheepishly: 'I guess it was me, I thought there was somebody running at me but I guess it was only me in the mirror.'

Abrams says wearily: 'All right—but this time take them down to the Hall like I told you.'

David has taken Nick a little aside and is asking: 'Should I tell him about Selma and the gun?'

Nick: 'It depends on whether you think she did it.'

David: 'Of course not—do you?'

Nick: 'No. Then the only thing to do is to tell him everything.'

At this point, Abrams, returning from seeing his men off, says: 'I asked you people not to go off whispering in corners all the time.'

David: 'Lieutenant Abrams, I've something to tell you. I happened—'

Abrams interrupts him: 'All right—but we're all going down to the Hall where we can talk in peace. I don't like the high jinks that come off here.'

Nora yawns.

Abrams: 'Sorry, Mrs Charles. I won't keep you any longer than I have to but we've got to do things regular.'

* * *

A CHEAP HOTEL ROOM

Phil is sitting at a table playing solitaire with a gun on the table. He is smoking nervously and there is a pile of cigarette butts on a saucer near him. Presently there is a knock on the door. He picks up the gun and stares at the door with frightened eyes but doesn't answer. The knock is repeated, louder. After a little pause, Dancer's voice comes through, saying: 'This is Dancer—will you open the door or will I kick it in?'

Slowly, as if afraid to open the door and afraid not to, Phil gets up and, holding the gun behind him, goes to the door and unlocks it. Dancer pushes the door open violently, knocking Phil back against the wall, then kicks the door shut; and standing close to Phil, says with threatening mildness: 'What did I tell you about trying to cut yourself in on somebody else's game?'

OUTSIDE THE HALL OF JUSTICE—BROAD DAYLIGHT

Harold is asleep in Nick's car. Nick, Nora, and Abrams come out of the building surrounded by a flock of reporters.

Abrams is saying to the reporters: 'Lay off us. I told you anything you get, you'll have to get from the D.A.' He then says to Nick and Nora: 'I could use a lot of breakfast. How about you folks?'

Nick looks at his watch and says: 'I could use a lot of sleep.'

Nora is too sleepy to say anything.

Abrams insists: 'Yeh, but you got to eat anyhow, don't you, and there's a pretty good place not far from here.'

Nick asks: 'You mean you want to ask some more questions?'

Abrams: 'No, not exactly, but there are a couple of points.'

Nick: 'We'll drop you wherever you're going and you can ask them on the way—but if you get wrong answers it's because I'm talking in my sleep.'

As they are about to get into Nick's car, a taxi-cab drives up and Dancer gets out. Abrams goes over and grabs him by the shoulder, asking: 'Where have you been?'

Dancer: 'Hiding—where'd you think I've been? The lights go out and somebody starts shooting—I haven't even got a gun—I don't know whether somebody's trying to get me or if I'm being framed by you people, or what—so I did the only smart thing I could think of and played the duck and waited for daylight so I can at least see who's shooting at me.'

Abrams turns to Nick and Nora and says: 'Phooey! I won't be more than a minute. I'm going to turn him over to the boys. I'm afraid to trust myself with him this morning—I'm liable to slap him around too much.' He and Dancer go back into the Hall of Justice.

Abrams returns almost immediately, gets into the car with Nick and Nora complaining: 'What stories these guys think up.' They drive off.

INTERIOR NICK'S CAR

Nick, Nora, and Abrams are sitting together. Nora is nodding sleepily, her head keeps bobbing in front of Nick, interfering with his vision. Whenever Nick turns to speak to Abrams, her head falls back, concealing him.

Abrams: 'Sure I believe David Graham—I guess, but how do I know he ought to have believed Mrs Landis? Well, I'm going to talk to her today if I have to lock up that lame 'nut' doctor while I do it. On the level, Mr Charles, what's she doing with him around if she isn't at least a little bit punchy?'

Nick: 'I don't think she is—just very nervous. You know how idle wives get—look at Mrs Charles, for instance.'

Abrams looks at Nora, who by this time is sound asleep, her chin resting on her chest.

Nick goes on: 'And then, living with Robert wasn't doing her any good.'

Abrams: 'You honestly don't think she did it?'

Nick: 'No.'

Abrams: 'She had the best reason. Graham had paid him to go away and he was going away, so *he* didn't have much reason—Dancer and the Chinaman and the Byrnes gal were taking him all right, but killing him made it tough for them on the check. Besides, why didn't they grab the bonds and that jewelry of his wife's that he had on him? And that goes for the Byrnes gal even if she was double-crossing the others.'

Nick asks: 'How about Phil—her brother?'

Abrams: 'There's no telling exactly until we get hold of him, but he figures to be out for the dough, too—so why don't he grab the bonds? He don't sound to me like a lad who would kill somebody just because he was running off with his sister.'

Nick: 'Lots of stickups go wrong—perhaps he had to leave before he could get the stuff.'

Abrams: 'You mean on account of Mrs Landis running around the corner with a gun in her hand like she said she did? If he saw her, why didn't she see him, and she didn't say anything about that, did she?'

Nick: 'Back in the office, you said Landis and Pedro were killed with bullets from the same gun. She doesn't fit in very well with Pedro's killing; but Polly lived in his house, which ties his killing up at least a little with her and the others.'

Abrams: 'That's right enough and I guess there's not much doubt that he was killed because he was on his way to tell you something. It's a fair bet that that something he was going to tell you had to do with Robert Landis, but there's something funny about that house that I want to show you. Maybe, if you've got a few minutes—'

Nick: 'You don't mean the goats in the hallway?'

Abrams, surprised: 'What goats?'

Nick: 'Never mind—but Mr and Mrs Charles aren't going anywhere but home—to sleep. Think you'll be able to fish Mrs Landis's gun up from where David threw it?'

Abrams: 'I guess so. Anyway, the boys are down there working now.' He pauses. 'And when we get that, then we'll know. It will only take a few minutes to go over to that apartment house.'

Nick: 'Call me later. We've been on a train for three days and look what kind of a night we've had.'

Abrams: 'All right—I could use a little sleep myself but I've got to talk to Mrs Landis and got to stop at the bank and see about that check.'

Harold pulls over to the curb and Abrams gets out. Nora almost falls out after him as he withdraws his support. Abrams helps Nick put her back on the seat and, placing her head on his shoulder, Nick nods goodbye to Abrams, who waves to him as they drive off.

NICK AND NORA IN THEIR CAR GOING HOME

She is sleeping on his shoulder. With his free hand he unties his necktie and takes off his collar. When he twists around a little to unbutton his shirt in back, Nora wakes up and asks:

Nora: 'What are you doing?'

Nick: 'I'm getting as few clothes as possible between me and bed.'

Nora: 'That's cheating.' She begins to loosen her clothes. They arrive at the house. As they go up the front steps, Nora: 'Last one in bed is a sissy!' They run into the house pulling off clothes.

From the living room to meet them come Asta and the reporters that they left at the Hall of Justice, the reporters asking questions: 'Do the police suspect Mrs Landis?' 'What connections did Pedro Dominges have with the Landis killing?' etc., etc.

Nick insists he knows nothing about it and has nothing to say as they go back into the living room, winding up with:

'I'm going to give you boys one drink apiece and then put you out.'

One of the reporters asks: 'Well, answer another question for us and we won't print it if you don't want us to. Is it true that you actually didn't retire as a detective but are working undercover?'

Nick, starting to pour drinks: 'No, it's not true, but don't print it, because I don't want my wife's relatives to know I'm living on her money.'

A stone with a piece of paper wrapped around it crashes through the glass of the window and knocks the bottle out of his hand. Asta joyfully grabs the stone and runs under a sofa with it, and starts to chew the paper off while Nick and the reporters scramble after him. By the time Nick recovers the stone with the paper, the note has been pretty well chewed up. He spreads it out, glances at it, and puts it in his pocket before the reporters, who are crowding around him, can read it.

Nick: 'Silly little woman. I told her to stop writing me.'

The reporters, failing to get anything else out of Nick, rush out to see if they can find out who threw the stone. Nick smoothes the note out and he and Nora, patching it as well as they can where Asta's teeth have torn it, read it. It is crudely printed:

MR CHARLS PHIL BYRNES ALIAS RALPH WEST
IS A EX CON AND WAS MARRIED TO POLLY IN
TOPEKER THREE YERS AGO. HE LIVES AT THE MIL

The rest of the note has been chewed off by Asta.

Nick, indifferently: 'Well, what are we supposed to do, send them an anniversary present?'

Nora: 'Nick, phone Lieutenant Abrams!'

Nick: 'And have him up here to keep us awake some more?'

Nora insists: 'Phone him, Nick. Don't you see, if Phil was her husband...'

Nick grumbles: 'I guess you're right,' and goes out of the room.

Nora plays with Asta for a minute or two and then goes to the door of the next room, where the phone is. Not seeing Nick, she calls him. There is no answer. After a little hesitancy, she goes up to the bedroom. Nick, in pajamas, is asleep. On her pillow is a sign: SISSY.

AUNT KATHERINE AT TELEPHONE AT HER HOME

Dr. Kammer is sitting in a chair nearby. She calls a number and asks: 'Mr Moody. This is Miss Forrest calling.'

STRING OF SHORT SHOTS

Printing press running off extras with enormous headlines about 'MEMBER OF PROMINENT FAMILY KILLED.'

Editorial Room of newspaper office—men being assigned to cover this story.

Then up to Publisher's Office, where Peter Moody, a very dignified old man with a grave and courteous manner, is picking up the phone, saying: 'Yes, Katherine, how are you? I'm awfully sorry to hear about Robert's death.'

Aunt Katherine: 'Thank you, Peter. It's terrible and that's what I called you about. The police, it seems, are trying to make a great deal of mystery out of what must have been—it couldn't have been anything else—simply an attempted holdup. I hope I can count on you to do your best to give the whole terrible affair no more publicity than is absolutely necessary.'

Peter Moody: 'Of course, of course, Katherine. But you must understand that if the police make it news we must print it.'

Aunt Katherine: 'I understand, but you will handle it as quietly as possible?'

Moody: 'Certainly, I can promise you that. And will you please convey my sympathy to poor Selma.'

Aunt Katherine: 'Thank you, Peter.'

As Peter Moody puts down the phone, a man comes into the office bringing an early copy of the extra that had been run off with the enormous headlines seen in the previous shot.

Moody looks at it and nods with approval, saying: 'Very good.'

Aunt Katherine phones her brother, the General, who is having his whiskers trimmed by a valet almost as old as he is. The valet hands him the phone, saying: 'Miss Forrest, sir.'

The General hems and haws between his words a good deal: 'It's terrible, Katherine—I just heard—I'm on my way over.'

Aunt Katherine: 'Yes, terrible, Thomas, and I want to see you—but first will you see if you can get in touch with the mayor?'

General: 'The mayor?' He clears his throat some more.

Aunt Katherine: 'Yes. I'm sure poor Robert was killed by a robber but the police seem determined to make as big a mystery out of it with as much resultant notoriety for all of us as possible. I wish you would ask him to do what he can.'

General: 'Certainly, my dear,' clearing his throat again, 'I shall look after it immediately.'

As Katherine hangs up, he gives the valet the phone, saying: 'Get me the mayor' in the tone one says: 'Get me the newspaper.'

As Aunt Katherine turns from the phone toward Dr Kammer, the butler appears at the door to announce Lieutenant Abrams.

Several hours later the General arrives at Nick's house. He hands his hat to the Butler, who opens the door and says: 'Take me to Mr Charles immediately.'

Butler: 'But he's still asleep, sir.'

The General snorts, saying: 'Yes, yes, so you said when Miss Forrest phoned. Devilish inconsiderate of all of you.'

The Butler says apologetically: 'But we never disturb him when he's asleep, sir.'

The General snorts some more: 'You said that over the phone, too. Now stop this silly nonsense and take me to him.'

The butler, overawed by the General, takes him up to Nick and Nora's room. They are sleeping soundly. The General prods one of Nora's shoulders with his fingers and says: 'Here, here, wake up.'

Nora stirs a little and mumbles something but doesn't open her eyes.

The General prods her again, saying: 'Come—this is no time to be sleeping. Devilish inconsiderate of all of you.'

This time Nora opens her eyes and stares up at him in amazement.

General: 'Wake up your young man, my dear. Why doesn't the fellow sleep at night?'

Nora asks: 'But what's the matter, Uncle Thomas?'

General: 'Matter? We've been trying to get you for hours. Wake him up.'

Nora shakes Nick, who says without opening his eyes: 'Go away, Porter, I told you not to call me till Sacramento.'

Nora: 'Wake up, Nick, Uncle Thomas wants to talk to you.'

Nick: 'Tell the white-whiskered old fossil to do his snorting in somebody else's ear—I'm busy.'

Nora: 'But Nick, he's here, standing beside you.'

Nick sits up blinking and says: 'Why, Uncle Thomas, how nice of you to drop in on us like this.'

General: 'Come—enough of this nonsense. Selma has been arrested and you lie here snoring.'

Nora looks horrified.

The General snorts some more: 'The mayor did nothing to stop it—the bounder.'

Nick: 'Maybe he didn't know.'

The General asks: 'Didn't know what?'

Nick: 'That I was snoring.'

General: 'Come, get up. You know about these things—Katherine is counting on you.'

Nick, putting on his robe and slippers, says: 'You don't need me now, you need a lawyer.'

The General says contemptuously: 'A lawyer—old Witherington is running around in circles, completely at sea; no ability at all— that fellow.'

Nick: 'Then why don't you get another lawyer?'

The General draws himself up: 'Witherington has been our family attorney for years.'

Nick: 'Well, what do you expect me to do?'

General: 'To make the police stop being so silly—to get Selma out of there right away—to put an end to all this beastly notoriety.'

Nick asks: 'Is that all?'

General: 'Come—we're wasting time—get into your clothes.'

In a barely furnished office in the Hall of Justice, Nick is talking to Abrams.

Abrams: 'I know how you feel about it, Mr Charles. I guess I'd feel the same way if it were one of my family; but what can we do? Everything points to her.'

Nick asks: 'You mean you found out some things I don't know about?'

Abrams: 'Well, not much maybe, but there's that check thing.'

Nick asks: 'What check thing?'

Abrams: 'Maybe the district attorney isn't going to like this much, but I'll tell you: I went down to Landis's bank and that $10,000 check he gave the girl is perfectly okay. It was okay because his wife had put $10,000 in there for him just the day before.'

Nick looks surprised. He asks: 'Are you sure?'

Abrams: 'Sure, I'm sure. I saw it myself.'

Nick: 'Did you ask her about it?'

Abrams replies wearily: 'Yes, and there's some kind of hanky-panky there, too, but I can't figure out just what it is. She started to say she didn't and then the old lady, Miss Katherine'—he breaks off to add—'that one's a holy terror—'

Nick: 'Make two copies of that.'

Abrams: '—she spoke up and said: 'You did, Selma, you told me so yourself,' and then Mrs Landis said yes, she did.'

Nick asks: 'So where does that fit in?'

Abrams: 'So maybe she gave it to him and found out he was passing it on to the girl—how do I know? Every time I tried to pin her down she gets hysterical.'

Nick asks: 'Find out anything else at the bank?'

Abrams: 'No. He had given the Byrnes gal a check for $100 and one for $75 like she told us.' He takes the checks out of a desk drawer saying: 'Here, if you want to see them.'

Nick looks at them and asks: 'Have you got the $10,000 check he gave her?'

Abrams: 'Yes.' He gives it to him.

Nick stands up, tilting back a light-shade, holds one of the small checks with the $10,000 check over it up against the light and tries the big check with the other small one. Abrams stands up to look over his shoulder. Nick fiddles with the checks until the signature of the top one is exactly over the bottom one.

Abrams exclaims: 'A forgery!'

Nick nods, saying: 'Yes, a tracing. Nobody ever writes *that* much the same twice.'

Abrams picks up the telephone and says: 'Give me Joe,' then says: 'Joe, go out and pick up that Polly Byrnes for me.' When he puts down the phone, Nick asks: 'You aren't holding any of them?'

Abrams shakes his head and says: 'No. The guns we got from the Chinaman and Dancer are .38s all right like he was killed with, but the experts say they are not the guns that did it. I'm still not sure this forgery is going to help Mrs Landis much. I already told you I knew there was some hanky-panky about those checks.'

Nick asks: 'You haven't found her gun yet?'

Abrams: 'I got a couple of men in diving suits working over the bottom down around where David Graham threw it. But it was night, you know, and we can't be too sure of the exact spot.'

Nick: 'And you think you are going to convict her if you don't find the gun?'

Abrams: 'Maybe I do and maybe I don't. It's what the district attorney thinks.'

Nick: 'Does he think she killed Pedro Dominges?'

Abrams: 'That's not funny, Mr Charles. Her alibi covering that time is just no good at all. She claims a cigarette case had been mailed to her from the Li-Chee and she sent it back saying it wasn't hers; but she thinks it belongs to some woman who was there with Robert, so that afternoon when she's kind of nuts over him not being home for a couple of days, she goes down there to see if she can find out about him. Of course that joint don't open till evening and so she didn't see anybody that could tell us she was there. She says she went back home again and that just about covers the time that Dominges was being killed. On the level, Mr Charles, we had nobody else but her that we could hold.'

Nick: 'Found your Selma Young yet?'

Abrams: 'No.'

Nick: 'How about Phil?'

Abrams: 'Sure, maybe, if we can find him.'

Nick takes out the note that was thrown through the window, gives it to Abrams.

Abrams reads it carefully, then asks: 'And where did this come from?'

Nick: 'Somebody wrapped it around a dornick and heaved it through my window.'

Abrams asks: 'Where's the rest of it?'

Nick: 'Somewhere in my dog's intestines.'

Abrams reads slowly: '—lives at the Mil—'

Nick pushes the telephone book over to him and says: 'Maybe that won't be so tough. Polly said he lived in a hotel on Turk Street.'

Abrams: 'That's right,' and opens the telephone book to the hotel classification and runs his finger down the Mi's, finally coming to the Miltern Hotel, Turk Street.

Abrams: 'That could be it—want to give it a try with me?'

Nick: 'Right!' They get up. As they go toward the door, Nick says: 'You noticed that whoever wrote the note misspelled easy words like my name and years, but did all right with 'alias' and 'married'?'

Abrams: 'Yeah, I noticed.'

EXTERIOR OF MILTERN HOTEL

A small, shabby, dirty joint with a door between two stores, and stairs leading up to an office on the second floor. Abrams, Nick, and two other detectives get out of a car, which draws up with no sound of sirens. One of the men remains at the outer door. Nick, Abrams, and the other detective start up the stairs. They go up to a small and dark office. Nobody is there. Abrams knocks on the battered counter. After a little while, a man in dirty shirt sleeves appears.

Abrams: 'Is Mr Phil Byrnes in?'

The Man says: 'We ain't got no Mr Byrnes—not even a Mrs Byrnes.'

Abrams: 'Have you got a Ralph West?'

The Man: 'Yep.'

Abrams: 'Is he in?'

The Man: 'I don't know—room 212—next floor.'

Abrams says to the detective with him: 'Get on the back stairs.'

Abrams and Nick walk up the front stairs and down a dark hall until they find 212. Abrams knocks on the door—there is no answer. He knocks again, saying in what he tries to make a youthful voice: 'Telegram for Mr West.' There is still no answer. He looks at Nick. Nick reaches past him and turns the knob, pushing the door open.

Nick: 'After you, my dear lieutenant.'

Sprawled on his back across the bed, very obviously dead, is Phil, fully dressed as when we last saw him.

Nick points to something on the floor between them and the bed. It is a pair of spectacles, the frame bent, the glass ground almost to a powder. Abrams nods and comes into the room, stepping over the glasses, and leans over Phil.

Abrams: 'Dead, all right—strangled and he was beaten up some before the strangling set in.' He looks down at one of Phil's hands, then picks it up and takes half a dozen hairs from it. Turning to show them to Nick, he says: 'Somebody's hair in his hand.'

Nick looks at the hairs, then at the broken glasses on the floor. He says nothing. It is obvious he is trying to figure something out.

Abrams goes out saying: 'Wait a minute—I'll have one of the boys phone and then we'll give the room a good casing.'

Nick moves around the room looking at things, opening and shutting drawers and looking into a closet, but apparently not finding anything of interest until he sees an automatic on the floor under one corner of the bed. He bends down to look at it but doesn't touch it.

While Nick is looking at the gun, Abrams returns to the room.

Nick: 'Here's another .38 for your experts to match up.'

Abrams: 'Hmm, what do you think?'

Nick: 'I don't think—I used to be a detective myself.'

Abrams: 'Nobody downstairs seems to know about any visitors, but I guess the kind he had wouldn't have gone to the trouble of knocking on the counter like we did.'

He leans over Phil and begins to go through his pockets.

Abrams straightens up and says: 'I guess the heater's his. He's wearing an empty shoulder holster.' He holds up a flat key and adds: 'And I guess this is the key to the Byrnes gal's apartment. It's got her number stamped on it.'

Nick: 'Another good guess would be that Selma Landis didn't do this.'

Abrams: 'Fair enough, but he wasn't killed the way the other ones were, either.'

Policemen enter, some in plain clothes, some in uniform, and Abrams starts to give them instructions about searching the room, looking for fingerprints, questioning the occupants of adjoining rooms, etc., etc.

Nick: 'And I think you ought to have your laboratory look at that hair and the cheaters,' indicating the broken glasses.

Abrams: 'Okay.' He looks curiously at Nick.

Nick: 'And the sooner the better.'

Abrams, again: 'Okay.' He addresses one of the men standing and listening to them. 'Do it.' He hands him the hair. Then turning back to Nick, says: 'Anything particular on your mind?'

Nick: 'Ought to be on yours, with three murders tied together in just about twenty-four hours. Now that we've been told he's her husband and he's dead, don't you think we ought to see Polly as soon as possible?'

Abrams says: 'There's something in that,' and tells one of his men, 'Don't let these lugs dog it while I'm gone.' He and Nick go downstairs. In the office he uses the telephone. When he's through, he grumbles: 'They haven't picked her up yet.' He scratches his chin, then says: 'I've got a man waiting up in her apartment. Want to take a run up there? I told you there's something funny about the place that I'd like you to see.'

Nick: 'All right. Don't you think now we've got something more to talk about to Dancer?'

Abrams says in a hurt tone: 'I think of things sometimes. I told them to pick up him and the Chinaman both.'

They go downstairs to the street.

* * *

At Aunt Katherine's, all the Forrests except Selma are assembled. They are very excited and keep moving around so that Asta, who obviously doesn't like any of them, has a great deal of difficulty keeping out of their way. Nora and Dr Kammer are also there.

The General is standing, glaring down at Nora, and asking indignantly: 'Do you mean to say that this—ah—husband of yours actually advised David to tell the police about Selma and the pistol?'

Nora says defiantly: 'Yes.'

The General starts to walk up and down the floor, sending Asta into hiding again, and rumpling his whiskers and growling: 'Why, the fellow's a scoundrel—an out and out scoundrel.'

Nora: 'Nick's not—he knows what he's doing.'

The General snorts and says angrily: 'Nonsense—nobody knows what they're doing. The whole country is full of incompetents and scoundrels nowadays.'

Aunt Hattie nudges Aunt Lucy and asks: 'What is Thomas saying now—he mutters so.'

Aunt Lucy, who has been sniffling into her handkerchief, sobs: 'Poor Selma. This is a terrible thing to happen to me—only a week after my eighty-third birthday.'

Nora jumps up and says: 'Nick's not incompetent and he's not a scoundrel. You're all acting as if you thought Selma really killed Robert.'

Aunt Katherine and Dr Kammer exchange significant glances. The General clears his throat and says: 'It's not a case of anybody killing anybody—it's a case of his being so devilish inconsiderate of the family. Has the fellow no feelings?'

William, who is considered not too bright by the family, runs his finger inside his too-tight collar and asks: 'Does anyone know if the police have considered the theory that Robert might have committed suicide?'

Aunt Katherine snaps at him: 'That will do, William,' while the rest of them glare at him.

Burton, his tic working overtime, asks: 'Well, where is this Nicholas? Why isn't he here to explain himself?'

Nora: 'Because he's out trying to clear Selma while you all sit around here and criticize him.'

The General says: 'I'd never have asked him if I'd known what the fellow'd been up to.'

Nora rises with great dignity and calls Asta. She faces the family and says: 'I'm sure he doesn't care what any of you think. He's not doing it for you—he's doing it for Selma. Goodbye.'

What would otherwise have been a dignified exit is spoiled by her bumping into the antique butler as she goes through the door. After the butler has gotten his breath, he says: 'Mr Graham on the phone for you, Mrs Charles.'

She goes to the phone and says: 'Hello, David.'

David, at the other end of wire, asks excitedly: 'Where is Nick? I tried your house and the detective bureau but he wasn't there. Lieutenant Abrams wasn't in either.'

Nora: 'They're probably out together. Oh, Lieutenant Abrams said something about wanting Nick to go over to that apartment house with him. Maybe they're there. What is it, David?'

David: 'Something's happened—I've got to see Nick. What apartment house?'

Nora: 'I'm leaving here now. I'll meet you and take you there. Where are you?'

David: 'I'm in a drugstore at Mason and Bush Streets.'

Nora: 'Wait for me—I'll be right over.'

They hang up and she, after making a face at the direction of the room where she left the family, goes out and gets into her car.

Abrams and Nick arrive at the building where Polly has an apartment. It is a large, shabby building, set at the foot of Telegraph Hill. Across the street from it the hill rises steep and unpaved, with winding, wooden steps leading up between scattered frame houses. The end of the street, even with the house's left-hand wall, is closed by a high board fence. From the fence, as from the house wall, the ground falls perpendicularly fifty or sixty feet to a rock-strewn vacant lot covering several blocks. In the street and on the hill above, goats are roaming. As they approach the door a goat runs out and dodges past them and goes to join the others. The front door is open. Abrams and Nick go in. Abrams knocks on a door on the left side of the corridor. The door is opened by a plain clothesman, who says: 'Nary hide or hair of her yet.'

A policeman in uniform and another in plain clothes are bent over a table doing a crossword puzzle together. They rise hastily as Abrams comes in but he pays no attention to them.

Abrams, as they go in: 'This is Polly's apartment. There's nothing much here except you'll notice the rug's new.'

Nick looks at the rug and says: 'Oh, I saw a new one once in a store window.'

Abrams, patiently: 'All right, but wait—maybe it don't mean anything, maybe it does.'

Nick asks: 'What do you think it means?'

Abrams sighs and says: 'If I knew, do you think I'd be wasting your time dragging you up here? We'll go back here, now.' He leads the way out of Polly's apartment down the hall to an apartment on the same floor in the rear, unlocking it with a key from his pocket, saying as he opens the door: 'This is the fellow's that was killed—that Pedro Dominges.'

Nick says quickly: 'Another new rug—I said it first.'

Abrams, pointing to the other end of the living room where there is a rug rolled up and lying against the wall: 'There's another one.'

Nick asks: 'What is this rug racket? Are we hunting for an Armenian?'

Abrams: 'Maybe you're right in kidding me—maybe none of this means anything, but just the same, he brought twelve rugs only a couple of days ago and that's just how many apartments he's got in the place.' He walks over to the table and says: 'Here's the bill. And the one apartment that didn't get a rug was rented only last week to somebody named Anderson. No front name—no Mr or Miss or Mrs according to his books here. I want to show you that next.'

Nick asks: 'What have you found out about him?'

Abrams: 'Nothing. This guy Dominges ran this place by himself. We haven't found anybody who ever saw this Anderson.'

There is a terrific uproar from the corridor. They go to the door to see Asta, a goat, and Nora (at the other end of Asta's leash) all tangled up together, while David is trying to untangle them. When the goat has finally been chased out, they all return to Pedro's apartment.

As Nick helps Nora brush off her clothes, she says: 'Why, that drunken man was right—there *are* goats in the hall.'

Nick: 'You can always trust my friends, drunk or sober. Is that what you came down here to find out?'

Nora: 'No. David has something to show you.'

David takes from his pocket a sheet of paper, on which in the same crude printing as on Nick's note is:

> IF YOU WANT TO SAFE THAT DISSY
> DAME OF YOURN YOU BETER MAKE
> DANCER TELL HOW HE FOWND OUT
> LAST NIGHT PHIL BYRNES WAS
> POLLY'S HUSBIND
> A FRIEND

After they read it, Abrams asks: 'How'd it come to you?'

David: 'It was under my door when I woke up today.'

Nick: 'The same half-smart attempt at illiteracy as the one I got.'

Abrams: 'Yeah—but that don't have to mean that what it says is wrong. Running out yours got us something, so why don't we run out this?'

Nick: 'We'll have to wait until you pick up your people. Now how about this Anderson?'

Abrams: 'To tell you the truth, Mr Charles, I don't believe there ever was any Anderson, but you can—'

Nick: 'Tut-tut—don't be so skeptical; you read his fairy tales when you were a child.'

Abrams, patiently: 'Okay, kid me—but what I mean is—I don't believe *this* Anderson ever was and I'll show you why when we get upstairs. As a matter of fact I don't believe anybody took that apartment.'

Nora: 'I took that.'

They look at her in surprise. She has gotten up from the chair and has gone over to an enlarged snapshot hanging on the wall.

Abrams: 'You did what, Mrs Charles?'

Nora: 'I took that picture. They're the servants we had at Ross.' She points them out: 'There's Pedro, Elle, Ann, etc.'

Pedro looks much as he did before except that he is six years younger, and his mustache, while not small, is not definitely long nor is it as white as it was when we saw him.

They all get up to look.

Nick asks: 'You're sure that place you had wasn't on Coney Island?' He turns to Abrams and says: 'I apologize for the domestic comedy. Let's go up and look at the apartment that you say wasn't rented by a fellow whose name wasn't Anderson.'

Abrams leads the way up to the next floor, unlocks the door, leading them into the apartment over Polly's, saying to Nick: 'See the rug—' The rug is stained and very worn.

Nick: 'I get it—it's *not* a new rug.'

Abrams: 'Yeah, that's one of the things I meant. I've got something else to show you—' He points to a corner of the room where there is a pile of old and battered iron pipe. 'But the chief things that we found was that Pedro had the lock changed on the door only yesterday and all the fingerprints we found in here are his.'

Nick walks to a window, raises it, and looks down the side of the cliff. He says: 'A nice drop from here. Would I be guessing wrong if I said that this apartment was right over Polly's?'

Abrams: 'No, I guess not.'

Nick asks: 'Well?'

Abrams: 'I don't know, Mr Charles, for a fact, but not putting a new rug in and only his fingerprints here makes it look to me like he was kind of using the place and not figuring on renting it.'

Nick asks: 'And you think he changed the lock so he couldn't get in again to keep tenants out?'

Abrams, patiently, as usual, says: 'I told you there was something funny here. I told you I didn't know what it was all about.'

Nick: 'Pedro was killed first. What are you picking on him for?'

Abrams: 'Do I know from nothing? If you can think of anything, play your string out.'

Nick: 'No hard feelings. Don't take me too seriously. Suppose you were going to put a rug down, what would you do first?'

Abrams: 'I don't know—I guess I'd get somebody to lug it upstairs.'

Nick: 'Swell. And then what?'

Abrams: 'Then you start at one end of the room and roll it across the floor.'

Nick asks: 'On top of this one?'

Abrams scratches his head and says: 'No, I guess not.'

Nick: 'All right—let's take this one up first, then.'

Abrams: 'Okay. You take that corner and I'll take this one.'

Nick: 'Who, me? Haven't you got hired men downstairs?'

Abrams. 'Sure.' He goes outside the door and yells: 'Hey, Francis—you and that other cutie who was trying to find a three-letter word for ape, come up here.'

Nora in a hoarse whisper asks: 'What is it, Nick?'

Nick: 'Do I know? Men are dying all around and you ask me riddles.'

There is a clumping on the stairs and the plain clothesman and the uniformed policeman who were working on the crossword puzzle come in.

Abrams says to them: 'You boys roll this three-letter word meaning rug down to the other end of a four-letter word meaning room.'

They say 'sure' very eagerly, push furniture out of the way, and start to roll the rug up. They roll it halfway when Nick says:

'Maybe that'll do for the time.' He walks over to a spot they have uncovered where six floor boards have been cut across in two places to make about a square foot. 'Let's look at this.'

Abrams, followed by his two men, goes to the spot Nick has indicated. Abrams opens a pocketknife, puts the blade in, and the sawed boards come up in a section, leaving a foot-square hole. He looks down, then puts his hand in and brings up a pair of flat ear pieces on a steel band such as telephone operators wear, attached to a wire running down into the hole.

Nick: 'I suppose we know what this is. Send one of the boys downstairs to recite the alphabet in Polly's place.'

Abrams jerks a thumb at the plain clothesman and says: 'Go ahead, Francis.'

Francis goes out. Presently, from down below through the ear pieces comes Francis's voice: 'A,B,C,D,E—' A moment of hesitation, then: 'A,B,C,D—'

Nick: 'Okay for sound. It was for listening in, all right.'

Abrams: 'Yeh, that's that. What do you guess this Pedro was up to?'

[Note: all through this scene, Asta shows that he is very fond of David, ignoring both Nick and Nora in favor of him.]

Nick: 'Well, there's still this junk to figure—' He turns toward the pile of iron pipe in the corner. Asta is busy chewing it. 'Get away from the evidence, Asta.'

Abrams: 'He won't be hurting it much—there was only Pedro's fingerprints on it. What do you guess it was for? I couldn't be thinking anybody would pipe gas through it.'

Nick: 'Why not? With a layout like this you can pipe gas in several directions at once.' He sits down on the floor and begins to screw sections of the pipe together.

[This is actually a ladder, but he keeps the rungs sticking out in all directions and keeps it from being recognizable until suddenly when he puts the last piece on and turns it around.]

Nick, holding the finished ladder up, says: 'Fifty will get you two-fifty that it will just about reach to Polly's window below, with this piece left over—' he picks up an extra part from the floor 'for good measure when he got there.'

He takes the ladder to window, lowers it, and hangs it on the sill. It reaches exactly to the sill of Polly's apartment below.

Abrams: 'What do you guess he wanted to do that for?'

Francis sticks his head in the door and says: 'We got Byrnes. Do you want her up? And we got Dancer and Lum Kee, too.'

Abrams looks at Nick and asks: 'Will they clutter it up for you? Do you think you got as much out of this place as you want?'

Nick: 'The more the merrier. Perhaps not as much as I want, but as much as I think I'm going to get.'

Nick asks Abrams: 'What kind of clothes did you find in the place?'

Abrams: 'None—not a stitch. Nothing to show anybody ever lived here. That's why I told you I don't believe anybody ever did.'

Nick asks: 'Where does that fit in? Do you think Pedro was using the place himself—spying on the people downstairs? He's killed first and, half a day later, Robert Landis, who visits downstairs, is killed and the next day, the brother or husband or something of the gal he visits is killed. How are you going to blame all that on Pedro?'

Abrams, wearily: 'Mr Charles, how many times have I told you there was something funny here I don't understand; and some hanky-pank about the checks I don't understand? Did I ever pretend I knew what all this led to?'

Nick: 'Oh, yes—about the checks. We've got to ask these people about them when they come upstairs and maybe they won't want to say right out. What would be wrong with getting Mrs Landis over so we'd have her here to chuck at them if they think we're fooling?'

Abrams: 'I don't know, the D.A.'s kind of—'

Nick: 'What—with a police escort?'

Abrams: 'Okay—I'll send for her.'

Nick: 'God will reward you.'

Three policemen, one in uniform, bring in Polly, Dancer, and Lum Kee.

Abrams: 'Francis, phone the Hall and tell them to bring up Mrs Landis.'

Francis goes to the phone.

Nick, aside to Abrams: 'Maybe they don't know. Throw it hard enough to bounce.'

Abrams says to Nick: 'Okay.' Turns to Polly: 'Your husband was killed this afternoon. What do you know about it?'

Polly: 'I—what?'

Abrams, to Dancer: 'Her husband was killed this afternoon.'

Dancer: 'Her what?'

Abrams: 'Cut it out! We're not playing charades.'

They look at him blankly.

Abrams, counting out syllables on his fingers, says: 'Pol-ly had a hus-band named Phil e-ven if he was sup-posed to be her bro-ther and he was found dead on Turk Street this af-ter-noon.'

Polly and Dancer turn to face each other at the same moment, exclaiming simultaneously: 'You—!!!' and then breaking off as they realize each is saying the same thing.

Abrams: '*You*—*you*—you what?'

Neither of them says anything.

Nick says to Abrams: 'Simple enough—she started to accuse *him* of killing Phil because he found out he was her husband and he started to accuse *her* of double-crossing him by not telling him Phil was her husband.'

Abrams says to Polly: 'He was your husband, wasn't he? Married three years ago in Topeka?'

She nods, glancing sidewise at Dancer. 'But I didn't want to have any more to do with him and so when he showed up last week I didn't say anything about it.'

Abrams: 'What did he go to the pen for?'

Polly: 'Blackmail.'

Abrams: 'And what did he have on you that he was hanging around shaking you down for?'

Polly, hesitantly: 'Well, he knew about me and Robert and I didn't want Robert to find out I was married and then I was kind of sorry for Phil. He was broke and had come out of the pen with bad lungs.'

Abrams: 'And why did you keep it from Dancer?'

Polly: 'It was nobody else's business and a girl in this racket gets along better without people knowing about things like that.'

Abrams: 'You didn't know Dancer found out about it, did you?'

Polly: 'Not until—' and breaks off with a frightened look at Dancer. Abrams: 'Go ahead—not until what?'

Dancer: 'I never found out about it up to now.' Then to Polly: 'I wish I had, baby.'

Abrams says to Dancer: 'Stick your mouth out of this until you get your invitation. You'll get it.' Then to Polly: 'And now you think he killed Phil because he found out?'

Polly stammers: 'No—I don't—I—'

Abrams breaks in very sharply: 'Isn't it the truth, sister, that you and this husband of yours were working together on Robert Landis and something went wrong and you had to kill him?'

Polly shakes her head and says: 'No.'

Abrams, paying no attention to her answer: 'And then isn't it just as true that Dancer found out about it and killed Phil?'

Dancer interrupts again: 'Listen, I never found out about it till I come to this room.'

Abrams: 'Whenever you found out about it, what do you think now—don't you think they were double-crossing you?'

Dancer shrugs and says: 'Maybe I do, now, but I didn't know anything about it till you told me.'

Abrams asks him: 'Do you think Phil tried to stick Landis up and had to kill him?'

Dancer replies contemptuously: 'I don't know what a punk like that would do.'

Abrams's manner has become increasingly irritable through this scene so that when, as he starts to ask Dancer: 'Now do you—' and Nick interrupts him by saying: 'Let's go into the check business—' Abrams turns around and says, sharply for him: 'Who's doing this?'

Nick says very mildly: 'It's hardly ever been my party. Come on, Nora.'

Abrams says very earnestly: 'Aw listen, Mr Charles, I'm not getting any rest out of this at all and I'm kind of jumpy. What were you going to say?'

Nick: 'I thought I said it—about those forgeries?'

Dancer says to Nick: 'I've put up with your gum-heeling for a day or two, but I got a business to run. I better be down there running it than barbering here with you. Why don't the two of us just go out in the hall and see who smacks who in the nose and call it square?'

Nick: 'No, let's do it the hard way. The ten-grand check Landis is supposed to have given Polly is a forgery.'

Dancer: 'So what's it to me?'

Nick: 'The signature was traced from one of the other checks he gave her.'

Dancer: 'I'm still asking you—what's that to me?'

Nick: 'Maybe Polly can answer that.' He asks her: 'Did you do the tracing or did he?'

While Polly is hesitating, Dancer says very distinctly: 'I told you before, I don't know anything about that check. Whatever was between Landis and Polly was between them.'

Nick says to Polly: 'You were right—they *are* letting you hold the bag.' Before Polly can answer, Dancer, addressing Nick, but talking for Polly's benefit, asks: 'What bag? This check you're talking about—has anybody tried to pass it yet? What kind of charge have you got against her until she does?'

Nick and Abrams look at each other and Abrams says: 'Wise guy.' Then to Polly: 'Come on, answer that question now.'

Polly says hesitantly: 'Well, I don't know—I—' and breaks off, looking all the time at Dancer, hoping for a cue.

Dancer says nothing and gives Polly no sign.

Polly: 'Honestly, Lieutenant Abrams, I don't think that check is a forgery.'

Abrams asks: 'Where did you get it?'

Polly: 'Well, I—' and breaks off again.

Abrams: 'What are you covering this lug up for, sister?' He takes the note David had given him out of his pocket and shows it to her, saying: 'See, he had already found out Phil was your husband.'

Polly reads the note and her eyes widen. She looks at Dancer.

Dancer: 'If you're helping to frame me, Polly, okay; I'll have to figure out what I do about that. But if you haven't made a dicker for yourself with the police, I don't see where you'll be getting anywhere just running off at the head for the fun of it.'

Abrams starts toward Dancer, saying angrily: 'Listen, you—'

The door opens and Caspar comes in. He bows very formally to everybody in the room, then says to Dancer: 'I just heard a moment ago.' Then very pompously, to Abrams: 'Lieutenant, I cannot permit you to—'

Abrams turns to Nick and groans: 'Now look—we got this five- and-ten-cent-store Darrow with us again.'

Caspar says to Nick: 'Good evening, Mr Charles.'

Nick bows, buttoning up his coat and patting his pockets to see if he's lost anything.

Caspar goes over to Dancer, puts a hand on his shoulder, and says: 'My dear boy—I'm entirely at your service.'

Dancer shakes the hand off his shoulder and snarls: 'You ought to be—for the dough you charge me.'

Caspar tries to smile as if he thought Dancer were joking. He asks Lum Kee: 'What are these policemen doing now?'

Lum Kee, bland as usual, says: 'Trouble, trouble—they want to see us—we go—why not? They police, we innocent, you betcha.'

Abrams growls: 'Aw, cut it out. Hold your conferences on your own time. We've got work to do. Has anybody here ever been in this apartment before?'

Some of those there say 'No,' some shake their heads.

Abrams looks questioningly at Nick. Nick says: 'Perhaps Polly could help us if we told her what it's all about.'

Polly: 'What?'

Nick: 'You know this place is right over yours?'

Polly: 'Yes.'

Nick, indicating the ear pieces: 'With that dingus you can hear a pin drop in your place.' She stares at the ear pieces in surprise. Nick goes on. 'And if you'll go to the window, you'll see a ladder running down to your window.' She goes to the window, looks at the ladder, then turns back to Nick, still more bewildered. Nick picks up the extra piece of pipe and says: 'And nobody's head would be helped much by being patted with this.'

Polly: 'But I don't understand—'

Nick, looking at Dancer and Lum Kee, says: 'Is there anybody here that *does* understand?'

Dancer looks sullenly at him but doesn't say anything.

Lum Kee says cheerfully: 'We run restaurant—you detective.'

Nick, to Polly: 'Even if you don't understand, who can you think of that would have this much interest in you?' hefting the pipe in his hand.

Polly: 'Nobody.'

Nick: 'Phil had a key to your apartment. Has Dancer?'

Before she can reply, Dancer takes a key out of his pocket and tosses it on the floor, saying: 'Yes. So what would I need that trick ladder for?'

Nick asks: 'Has Lum Kee?'

Polly: 'No. of course not.'

Nick: 'Who else?'

Polly: 'Nobody.'

Nick: 'Did Robert have one?'

Polly: 'No. What do you think I did, put them around under doors?'

A policeman opens the door and Selma comes in. She and Nora immediately run to each other, uttering exclamations of affection.

David exclaims: 'Selma,' and goes over to them asking, 'are you all right, dear?'

She exclaims: 'David!' and holding out her hands to him, she starts to ask him a question. 'Did you—' and then breaks off, glancing nervously at Lieutenant Abrams. 'Oh, it's been terrible,' she tells Nora and David.

Nora: 'I know, dear, but it'll soon be over. Nick will have everything cleared up in no time. He's wonderful.'

Nick: 'Nice of you to say so, darling.' He goes over to greet Selma.

Selma: 'Oh Nick, I'm so grateful to you. Have you really—?'

Nick: 'Now don't start asking us questions. The game is for us to ask you. Have you ever seen any of these people before?' indicating in turn, Polly, Dancer, and Lum Kee.

To each Selma replies 'No.'

Nick asks: 'Have you ever been in this building before?'

Selma: 'No.'

Nick: 'Did you know that Robert and Miss Byrnes were friends?'

Selma: 'No.'

Nick: 'All right. Now this next question you've answered before, but the police weren't altogether satisfied with the way you answered it. I want you to remember that Robert's dead, so whatever you say isn't going to hurt him though it may help us find his murderer and get you out of this mess.'

Selma: 'What is it, Nick?'

Nick: 'That $10,000 check of yours that was deposited in Robert's account. Did you or didn't you write it?'

Selma hesitates, looks from Nick to Abrams then down to the floor, and in a very low voice, says: 'I didn't.'

Abrams, who has been a very interested listener up to this point, now takes his hat off and throws it angrily on the floor. But when he crosses to confront Selma, his voice and manner are more hurt than angry. He asks: 'Why couldn't you have told us that before? Whatever got into you to—' He breaks off as her lips begin to tremble, and grabs a chair, saying: 'Now, now, sit down, Mrs Landis, be comfortable. One of you boys get Mrs Landis a glass of water.' Then again to her: 'Now, now, maybe there's not a great deal of harm done anyhow.' Then aside to Nick, as she sits down: 'If this dame gets hysterical again I'll go nuts.'

Selma: 'Thank you. I'm quite all right.'

Abrams mumbles in Nick's ear: 'You ask her the rest. She always blows up on me.'

Nick says to Selma: 'Since you've gone this far, I think you'd better tell the police why you didn't tell them the truth before.'

Selma: 'I started to, but Aunt Katherine wouldn't let me.'

Abrams growls: 'That old battle-axe.'

Nick asks: 'Why wouldn't she?'

Selma: 'She said there was enough scandal with Robert being killed that way, without this.'

Nick: 'Thanks. That's fine.' Pats her on the shoulder, turns away.

Abrams: 'Maybe that's fine for you, but it could stand a little more explaining for my part.'

Nick: 'The explaining room is out there,' indicating the kitchen. 'Shall we try it now?' He and Abrams go into the kitchen. Nick continues: 'The gadget is that Aunt Katherine thought Robert forged the check and she was willing to let the $10,000 go to keep people from knowing there had been a forger in the family as well as a murdered man—"Then as an afterthought, he adds: 'Especially since it was Selma's $10,000.'

Abrams asks: 'Had he ever done anything like that before?'

Nick, earnestly: 'That boy had done everything.'

Francis comes to the door and says: 'Telephone for you,' to Abrams.

Abrams goes out.

Nick spies a battered cocktail shaker on the shelf, and begins to look through the closets for something to put in it. The closets are absolutely bare. He disgustedly throws the cocktail shaker in the garbage can as Abrams comes back.

Abrams: 'The laboratory says those red hairs were probably from a wig and that the broken specs were only window-glass. Were you kind of expecting something like that?'

Nick: 'Kinda.'

Abrams: 'And the gun's not the one those people were killed with. Expect that?'

Nick: 'Kinda.'

Abrams: 'But what's really good is, the boys picked up some pretty nice fingerprints of Dancer's in the joint. Let's go in and see how he likes that.'

Nick: 'All right, but mind if I get in a question first?'

Abrams: 'Go ahead, help yourself.'

They return to the room where the others are.

Nick asks Lum Kee: 'Did you ever mail to Mrs Landis a cigarette case that you thought she left in the restaurant about a week ago?'

Lum Kee: 'Maybe yes, maybe no. All the time people leave things.'

Nick to Dancer: 'I know he didn't. You sent it to her pretending you thought it was hers and when she sent it back with a note saying it wasn't, you traced her signature on the bottom of a $10,000 check payable to Robert, and sent it over for deposit in his account because you knew the bank wouldn't question that and when they eventually found out it was a forgery, he'd be blamed for it because he'd done things like that before. Then you were all set to forge a check on his account for the same $10,000 while Polly kept him busy so that the bank couldn't reach him to ask him about it if they got suspicious. And so then if he's killed, who's going to be able to prove that he didn't forge his wife's name to the check to get money to give to this girl he was in love with?'

Dancer asks scornfully: 'And then I suppose I knock him off and stir up all this fuss before I get the dough? What kind of a stumble-bum does that make me out to be?'

Nick: 'I'll let you know in a little while. Take the witness, Lieutenant Abrams.'

Abrams: 'I'll tell you what kind of a stumble-bum you are. You're the kind that left fingerprints all over Phil Byrnes's joint when you killed him.'

Caspar comes forward between Dancer and Abrams, saying: 'Lieutenant Abrams, I cannot allow—'

Dancer takes him by the back of the neck and pushes him out of the way, snarling: 'Shut up! Everything *you* say is used against *me?* Then to Abrams: 'Yeah, I was at Phil's place last night and when I left he was on the floor with a split lip and a goog and a couple of dents in him here and there but he was just as alive as you are, if that means anything.'

Abrams: 'You mean you went up there when you had the switch pulled in your place?'

Dancer: 'Yeah.'

Abrams: 'What for?'

Dancer looks thoughtful for a moment, then says: 'Okay, I don't know what I'm letting myself in for, but I'm not going to let you hang any murder rap on me. This Robert was a sucker and Polly and I were taking him. Maybe it was some kind of check razzle-dazzle like he (jerking a thumb at Nick) said, maybe it wasn't. Even if it had been, what would be the sense of killing him? Nobody'd have believed him if he'd said he hadn't forged his wife's name. Maybe we even talked him into doing it; anyways, he's cooled before we get anything. This guy,' jerking his thumb again at Nick, 'says Phil followed Robert and Polly down the street. Knowing Phil, I figured he tried to stick Robert up that night and had to kill him. I don't like having a punk gum things up for me that way, so why shouldn't I go over and push him around a little to learn him manners. But I didn't kill him.'

Abrams asks: 'Did you ever wear a wig?'

Dancer seems completely surprised. Then he says: 'No, but you ought to see my collection of hoopskirts.'

Abrams asks Lum Kee: 'Did you?'

Lum Kee says: 'No,' pulling a lock of his hair. 'Good hair—see?'

Abrams groans and says to Nick: 'I *hate* comedians.' Then he asks Polly: 'Did you?'

Polly: 'No.'

Abrams: 'Have you thought of anything that might have something to do with this layout?' indicating the window from which the ladder is hanging and the earphones.

Polly: 'No. But maybe this was all just a gag. Nobody came down and hit me on the head with that pipe and Robert wasn't killed in my place.'

Nick asks her: 'You know why that was, don't you?'

Polly: 'No.'

Francis says to the detective standing beside him: 'What a swell gal she'd be to take out—all she can say is 'No."

Nick: 'I'll tell you. This mysterious Anderson, probably in a red wig, phony glasses, and gloves to keep from leaving fingerprints, was sitting up here at his listening post waiting for a good chance to come down and polish off Robert, and hearing most of the things that were said down there between you and Phil and you and Dancer and you and Robert until he knew more about all of you than any of *you* did. But for one reason or another, he put off the killing until he learned that you and Robert were going away the next day. It was that night or never with him, but he got a bad break. Pedro came up and wanted to put a new rug down. That would have exposed the listening post and spoiled everything; so when he tries to talk Pedro out of it—'

Asta, who has been playing with David over by the open window, now lifts his leg against the chair.

Nora yells: 'Asta!' then complains, 'Now I'll have to take you out just when I was so interested. Couldn't you wait until I get back, Nickie?'

David: 'I'll take him out for you.'

Nick to Abrams: 'Murderers get funnier every year, don't they?'

Abrams: 'Huh?'

Nick: 'Just when you get ready to arrest them they want to take dogs out walking!'

Everybody looks at Nick in surprise.

Nick: 'David is Anderson. He didn't recognize Pedro any more than Robert or I did, but in spite of the disguise, Pedro finally recognized him just as Polly told us he'd recognized Robert. I suppose David gave him some hocus-pocus story, but Pedro, knowing Robert was spending a lot of time in the apartment just below this, probably knowing that Robert married Selma and knowing that David had been engaged to her when Pedro was working for Nora, and knowing Nora married a detective, thought he'd better change the lock and keep David out until he could come over and ask Nora's and my advice. He was foolish enough to tell David what he was going to do and David followed him over and shot him in the vestibule.'

David turns to Nora, who is standing beside him by the window, and asks: 'Nora, is he fooling?'

Nora says nothing. She is too busy listening to Nick, as are the others.

Nick: 'Sure. And *you* were fooling when you said you hadn't seen him since he worked for Nora and pretended you remembered him as a man with a long, gray mustache. He's got one now all right, but if you'll look at that picture downstairs, you'll see that it was neither very long nor very gray then. And what was Phil doing on your fire-escape except to try to shake you down because we know he'd followed you and Polly that night? We know the boy liked to shake people down; but you weren't alone that night, so he beat it and made a date with you for the next night and got himself killed.'

David protests: 'But—'

Nick, paying no attention to him, continues: 'And what do you suppose Pedro was trying to say when he died? That he'd been killed by *Miss Selma's young man*, which would be a servant's language for your status back when he worked for Nora.'

Selma says: 'But Nick, why should David have killed him? He'd given him the bonds and Robert was going away.'

Nick: 'He didn't want Robert to go away—he wanted to kill him. That's why he had to do it that night; otherwise he'd have had to hunt all over the world for him. Promising to pay him, with Polly knowing it, would make it look as though he had no reason for killing him. He intended killing him that night he met him, but Polly was along, so he couldn't. But he followed him and shot him when he came out of the house.'

Selma: 'I can't believe—'

David grabs Nora and forces her backwards out of the window so that only her legs are inside and she is held there only by his arms. His face has become insane; his voice, high-pitched and hysterical. He screams: 'I'm not going to the gallows! Either you give me your word that I go out of here with a five-minute start, or Nora goes out of the window with me.'

The policemen's guns are in their hands, but everyone is afraid to move except Lum Kee, who, standing by the corridor door, softly slips out, and Selma, who starts toward David, crying: 'David!'

David snarls: 'Keep away, you idiot!'

Nick, talking to gain time, trying not to show how frightened he is, says to Selma: 'See, he's not in love with you. He was, but when you turned him down for Robert, he probably came to hate you almost as much as he did Robert. But playing the faithful lover let him hang around until he could get a crack at Robert. That's why when he saw you hop around the corner with a gun in your hand right after he'd shot Robert from the car, he circled the block and came back in time to frame you while he pretended he was covering you up. He had probably meant to frame Phil or Dancer—which he did after he'd had to kill Phil while you were in jail.'

David, from the window, says: 'You're stalling for time, Nick, and it's no good. Five minutes' start or another of your lovely family goes down on the rocks with me.'

Nick: 'Don't be a sap, David. The chances are they'd never hang you. You ought to be able to get off with a few years in an asylum. What jury's going to believe a sane man did all this?'

David: 'That's a good idea! So I won't have to jump out the window with her. Either I get my five minutes or she goes down alone.'

Nick turns to Abrams and says: 'Lieutenant, I—'

There is a commotion at the window. Nora goes farther out backwards. David turns and leans out of the window, looking at something below. Outside, Lum Kee, in his stocking feet, is hanging by his toes and one hand to the rungs of the ladder, with his other around Nora's waist, and his head bent down, trying to avoid David's blows. Inside, Nick snatches a pistol from the nearest policeman and shoots David. David somersaults out of the window and crashes to the rocks some sixty feet below. Nick has gone to the window and is pulling Nora in. He shakes her violently by the shoulders and says:

'You numbskull, why didn't you keep away from him after I told you he was a murderer?'

She says just as sharply: 'You fool, why didn't you—'

They both break off and go into each other's arms.

Abrams turns from looking out of the window and says: 'Some of you boys go down and gather him up. A good enough ending for it. I guess that Doc Kammer would have had no trouble at all getting *him* off.'

Lum Kee climbs over the sill. Nick and Nora turn to him together to thank him for saving her, Nora adding that it was especially wonderful of him, inasmuch as Nick had once sent his brother to the pen.

Lum Kee says: 'Sure. Mr Charles send him over—number one detective—I no like my brother—I like his girl—thank you many times—you betcha.'

He moves uncomfortably and looks down at his stocking feet. He is standing in a puddle. He smiles blandly and says: 'I go down and get my shoes,' while Nora exclaims reproachfully, 'Asta!'

Another Thin Man

ANOTHER THIN MAN

May 13, 1938

AN ELABORATE SUITE IN A NEW YORK HOTEL

It is late afternoon in September. Hotel maids, valets, etc., pass through, unpacking, bringing flowers, etc. Nora in negligee is at telephone with an open address book before her.

Nora into phone: 'No we can't, dear—we've got to go on down to Colonel MacFay's for the weekend as soon as we get unpacked. Colonel MacFay—you remember—used to be my father's partner.... No, I really can't, darling. If it were anything else I could persuade Nick to get out of it, but this is something about our financial affairs and you know how mercenary he is.... Yes, we had a lovely trip; Nick was sober in Kansas City. I'll give you a ring Monday as soon as we get back, darling. I'm dying to have you see the baby.... We kind of like him.' She puts the phone down and makes a face at it.

Nick, bringing Nora a drink, says: 'You're a bitter woman, Mom.'

The phone rings again and Nora answers it, speaking to another friend.

A bellboy, a youngish man with a small, cheerful, wizened face, comes in carrying an enormous bunch of flowers. When he turns from putting them on the table, he and Nick recognize each other.

Nick frowns disapprovingly at the boy's uniform and says: 'God help honest folk in a hotel like this. How are you, Face?'

Face grabs Nick's hand saying: 'Gee, I'm glad to see you, Nick, even if it does spoil one of the prettiest jobs I ever lined up for myself.' He unbuttons his coat, sighs, and says: 'Oh well, if I could have thought of this, I'll think up something else.'

Nora hangs up the phone again and turns toward them.

Nick says: 'You remember Face Peppler? He came to a party of ours the last time we were in New York.'

Nora says: 'Of course.' She holds out her hand.

Face: 'Gee, I'm glad to see you, Mrs Charles.'

Nora looks at his unbuttoned uniform coat.

Face: 'I was hopping bells here until a minute ago when Nick seen me.'

Nora says to Nick: 'But, Nick, if he's trying to go straight now, I don't think you ought to—'

Face interrupts her by laughing heartily: 'Aw, Mrs Charles, it was nothing like that. Give me two days more and I'd have had a million dollars. Well, anyway, I'd have had a pretty bank roll.'

An assistant manager comes in, bowing primly to Nick and Nora, asking: 'Is everything satisfactory? Is there anything we could do to make you more comfortable?' He sees Face and says sharply: 'Thirtle!'

Face takes off his coat and hands it to the assistant manager. 'I've quit. I'm visiting here.' He starts to unbutton his pants. 'These are my friends.'

Nora says sweetly: 'Oh yes, Mr Peppler—Thirtle is an old friend of ours.'

Nick puts his arm on Peppler's back and says: 'You must have a drink, old chap. I have some incredible Scotch.'

The assistant manager bows himself out in a daze.

Face shakes hands warmly with Nick and Nora, saying: 'You people are okay for my money.'

A nervous man in chauffeur's livery comes in and says: 'Mr Charles?'

Nick says: 'Yes?'

Chauffeur: 'Colonel MacFay's car, sir.'

Nick says: 'Thanks. Be down in a little while.'

The Chauffeur fidgets with his cap, then says: 'Excuse me for saying so, but it's getting a little late.'

Nick: 'I'll try to hurry.'

Chauffeur: 'Thank you, sir.' He goes out.

From the rear of the suite comes Asta's voice raised in deafening complaint.

Nora says: 'Nicky's doing something.' She hurries toward the noise, Nick and Face following her.

In the kitchen Nick Jr. is sitting on the floor calmly chewing on a bone that he has taken from Asta. Asta is not trying to snatch the bone back, but is walking around and around the baby complaining noisily.

Nick Jr. is a fat, year-old boy who is interested in very little besides eating and sleeping. He eats anything that comes to hand and can sleep anywhere. His vocabulary is limited, consisting chiefly of two words— 'Drunk' for things he does not like and 'Gimme' for things he does. He seldom laughs and never cries and does not think his parents are amusing. He ordinarily regards them with the same sort of mild curiosity or tolerant boredom with which he regards the rest of the world. He is calmly chewing his bone, playing no attention to Asta.

Nora picks him up, takes the bone out of his hand, and gives it to Asta, who runs off with it. The baby watches Asta out of sight without any particular expression on his face.

Face says: 'Gee, a baby! Yours?'

Nick and Nora say: 'Yes,' trying not to look proud of themselves.

Face wiggles a finger in front of the baby's nose, saying: 'Googoo, googoo!'

The baby looks at him blankly.

Nick and Nora try to stir the baby into some semblance of liveliness, but with no success. After watching their antics for a moment, the baby says, 'Drunk,' and turns to Face again.

Face, a little abashed by the baby's patient stare, asks: 'A boy?'

Nora says: 'Certainly!'

Face: 'That's great. How old is he?'

Nora says: 'Be a year next Tuesday.'

Face: 'Tuesday? Swell. Say, we'll give him a party... Tuesday afternoon! I'll get my brother to let me bring his kids over. He's got two of the cutest little monkeys—leave it all to me. Tuesday afternoon— that's a date.'

Nora says confusedly: 'Well, I don't—'

Face pats her on the back: 'You leave it all to Facie, Mrs Charles. I'll give you a baby party you never seen the like of.'

He goes out, picking up Nora's address book from beside the telephone as he passes without their seeing him.

Nora looks at Nick in consternation.

Nick says: 'We can stay down at MacFay's until Tuesday night.'

Nick, Nora, the nurse, Nick Jr., and Asta go down to the street, where the nervous Chauffeur is standing beside a car into which a bellboy and the doorman have just finished putting their bags.

The Chauffeur, looking at the two women and the baby, asks Nick in a somewhat surprised tone: 'Are you going to take them?'

Nick says: 'I don't know how to get rid of them. Maybe we can ditch them somewhere on the road.'

The Chauffeur says: 'I'm sorry, Mr Charles, I didn't mean to—' and breaks off to look at his watch and then at the sky. It is now early twilight, although the streetlights have not yet been turned on.

They get into the car. The nurse sits in front with the Chauffeur; Nick, Nora, the child, and dog sit in the rear.

Nora, looking at the Chauffeur, asks: 'What's the matter with him?'

Nick replies: 'We had a couple of girls lined up.'

DISSOLVE THROUGH THE NEWYORK STREETS, OVER THE TRIBOROUGH BRIDGE, ALONG LONG ISLAND ROADS

As darkness closes down, the chauffeur drives faster and faster until, by the time they have turned off the highway into a dark, tree-lined side road, Nick, Nora, the baby, and Asta are bouncing around on the backseat. The baby bounces peacefully without opening its eyes.

Nick calls to the chauffeur: 'You're working too hard. If we don't get there in three minutes, it'll still be all right.'

The chauffeur pays no attention to him. Nick leans forward, touches the chauffeur's shoulder. The chauffeur jumps, jerks his head around, and almost sends the car off the road. His face and the back of his neck are covered with sweat.

Nick says: 'Not so fast, son, the baby has a hangover.'

The chauffeur mumbles: 'Yes, sir—I'm sorry,' then almost immediately begins to step up the speed again.

Suddenly he emits an ear-piercing scream of terror and sends the car hurtling ahead. Through a window, Nick catches a glimpse of a Negro man lying on his back on the side of the road. The man's body is arched so that its weight rests on heels and head. The five-inch handle of a knife sticks up from the left side of his breast.

Nick yells to the chauffeur to stop. The chauffeur pays no attention, and, when Nick touches him on the shoulder, he screams again but does not slow up.

Nick, standing up in the lurching car, puts his forearm around the chauffeur's throat, his other hand on the wheel, finally chokes the chauffeur into submission, and stops the car. Nick Jr. opens his eyes once to look at this and then goes back to sleep.

Nick says to the nurse: 'Come back here.'

She jumps out and gets in the rear of the car. Nick pushes the chauffeur over into the nurse's seat and climbs in behind the wheel. The chauffeur jumps out of the car and runs off into the woods.

Nora asks: 'What happened?'

Nick says: 'You wouldn't believe me if I told you,' turns the car around, and drives back to where he saw the Negro.

There is no body there, and, with the help of the car's lights, he can find no signs that one has been there.

Nora asks: 'What are you hunting for?'

Nick says: 'I thought I knew, but now I'll take anything I can find. Listen, I'm willing to call the whole thing off and drive right back to New York.'

The nurse says: 'Oh yes, sir, that would be fine.'

Nora says: 'We can't do that, Nick. Colonel MacFay expects us. What was the matter with the chauffeur, Nick?'

Nick answers: 'He was scared and now I am. Let's go somewhere and get a drink and think this over.'

Nora says: 'The nearest drink would be at the MacFays', but I wish you would tell me what is going on—what we came back here for.'

Nick says: 'You're a stubborn woman, Mom.'

He turns the car around again and drives on. Presently they come to a high grilled gate that blocks the road. When Nick has honked the horn, a gangling youth appears on the other side of the gate holding a double-barreled shotgun partly out of sight behind the gatepost. His manner is half-frightened, half-sullen.

He asks: 'What do you want?'

Nick says: 'We're bringing back Colonel MacFay's car.'

The youth says: 'I can see that all right, but how do I know what you want?'

Nick says: 'This is the Charles family. We have come down to spend the weekend.'

The youth says: 'Anybody can say that, but wait—I'll see,' and vanishes into a cottage set beside the gate. His voice can be heard talking over the telephone. 'He says their name is Charles—I don't know—He looks like a pool parlor dude and he's got a couple of ladies and a baby and a dog. Oh, all right.'

He comes back without his shotgun and swings the gate open. They drive on to a large house set in the middle of extensive grounds.

The front door is opened by a neat, elderly woman with a placid face. This is Mrs Bellam, the MacFay housekeeper.

Nick says to her: 'I'm sorry, but we lost your chauffeur somewhere along the road.'

She replies serenely: 'Oh, bless you, it's quite all right. Thomas,' indicating the servant who has appeared behind her, 'will bring up your bags. I suppose you'll want to wash up. Colonel MacFay is waiting dinner for you, but you don't have to hurry.'

She leads them upstairs into their rooms. One is for Nick and Nora, with a connecting bath leading to the nurse and Junior's room.

MACFAY LIVING ROOM

In the MacFay living room are four people.

Colonel Burr MacFay is a tall, scrawny man of seventy, actually still vigorous, but a hypochondriac and suspicious of those around him, though his bark is worse than his bite.

Lois, his adopted daughter, is a girl of twenty—very pretty, with a sweet and simple manner.

Dudley Horn, her fiancé, is a large man in his thirties. He is an engineer, MacFay's right-hand man, rather good-looking, and affects a candid, open-faced, man's-man manner.

Freddie Coleman is MacFay's secretary, a nice boy of twenty-two or twenty-three, who is very much in love with Lois and is writing a play in his spare time.

Colonel MacFay is complaining over a glass of sherry, his voice a nasal whine: 'I won't have it. I won't put up with it. I'm not a child and I won't have it.'

Horn, leaning against the mantelpiece, holding a Scotch and soda, says good-naturedly: 'What's the good of saying we won't put up with it when we are putting up with it?'

Freddie, leaning forward in his chair, frowning earnestly, says: 'But maybe he did kill him.'

MacFay, glaring at Freddie, whines impatiently: 'Him! Him! *I'm* the one that doesn't want to be killed.'

Lois, patting a collie that is standing with its head on her knee, looks anxiously at her foster-father and starts to say: 'But, Papa dear, you—' as Nick, Nora, and Asta come in. Asta goes over to investigate the collie.

MacFay greets Nick and Nora: 'Come in! Come in! You're late.'

Nick: 'Had a little trouble. Did your chauffeur tell you about the black man in the road?'

MacFay presses his lips together, says nothing.

Nick: 'He wasn't there when we went back.'

MacFay, explosively: 'I don't care about your black men and your roads. I care about what happens to me. I—' He breaks off, pushes his face into what is meant for a smile. 'You know Dudley.'

Nick and Nora say: 'Yes,' and shake hands with Horn.

MacFay: 'And this is my adopted daughter, Lois, and my secretary, Mr Coleman.'

When the introductions have been acknowledged and Lois has given Nick and Nora each a drink, MacFay says: 'Dinner is waiting. Come on, bring your drinks in.'

As they go into the dining room, Lois tells the servant to feed the dogs.

Dinner is served by two badly trained servants who keep looking over their shoulders as if frightened, and jump at every unexpected sound. One of them, turning from putting soup on the table, knocks Nick on the elbow with the butt of a pistol in his pocket.

MacFay, who attacks his soup hungrily, complains after each spoonful. 'They know this isn't good for my stomach. I ought to have some kind of light broth, but they don't care—nobody cares what happens to me.' He empties his plate before the others are half through and has a second helping. When he has finished that, between complaints that it is so badly cooked that it wouldn't be food for him even if it weren't too heavy, he bangs his spoon down on a plate and says to Nick: 'I'm not a child—I won't be frightened.'

Nick asks: 'What is there to be frightened of?'

MacFay replies: 'Nothing, nothing but a lot of idiotic and very pointless trickery and play-acting.'

One of the servants grumbles sullenly over the dish he is taking from the table: 'You can call it anything you want to call it, but I seen what I seen.' Nobody pays any attention to him.

Nick says: 'What kind of trickery and play-acting?'

MacFay puts his arms on the table, leans over them toward Nick, and says: 'Suppose you had a man working for you and he did something they put him in jail for. He did it, you didn't do it, and you even tried to get him off and to get his sentence cut down, but you couldn't. And now, after he gets out, he comes to you and says it's all your fault and wants you to give him a lot of money. And when you're not fool enough to do that, he says he hopes you're not going to be pig-headed about it because he's dreamed twice about your dying, and the third time he dreams things, they come true. He says he hopes you're not going to die before your conscience makes you do the right thing by him. What would you think?'

Nick says: 'I wouldn't think I ought to hurry up my dying on his account.'

MacFay stares at Nick blankly for a moment, then says: 'You'll excuse me, but that's just about as stupid an answer as I've ever heard.'

Nora nods brightly at Nick and assures him: 'Yes it is.'

One of the servants says to the other: 'A fat lot of help this new guy's going to be to us.'

MacFay taps his glass with a knife and says angrily to the servants: 'Shut up! Where's the roast?' He points to Nora's glass. 'Her glass is empty.' He holds up the knife and complains: 'See how they take care of my silverware. It hasn't been cleaned decently in a month.' He puts the knife down, pushes back his plate, and leans over the table. 'Listen,' he whines to Nick, 'this isn't April-foolery, this man means to murder me. He came here to murder me, and he will certainly murder me unless somebody does something to stop him.'

Nick asks: 'But what has he done so far?'

MacFay shakes his head impatiently. 'That isn't it. I don't ask you to undo anything that he's done. I ask you to keep him from killing me. What has he done? He's terrorized the whole place—that's what he's done.'

Nick asks: 'How long has this been going on?'

MacFay says: 'A week, ten days.'

Nick asks: 'Do you think the black man on the road is part of it?'

MacFay retorts: 'I don't think anything about it. You used to be a detective. I asked you down here to help me, not to bring me more wild stories.'

Nick asks: 'Have you said anything to the local authorities?'

MacFay whines: 'I'm not altogether a fool. Of course I have, but what good did it do? Has he threatened me? Well, he told me he has dreams about me dying, and I know him well enough to know that's a threat. But to the sheriff it isn't a threat.

Have I any proof that he is responsible for all these things that have happened—that he's turned this place upside down? The sheriff says I haven't. As if I needed proof! So it comes to this: The sheriff promises to keep an eye on him. 'An eye,' mind you. Here I have, with my family and servants and the guards I've hired, twenty people with forty eyes, and he comes and goes when he wants, so what good's the sheriff's 'eye'?'

Nick asks: 'Who is this fellow?'

One of the servants mutters: 'It's not him, it's that black devil.'

MacFay says: 'Church is his name—Sam Church. He's an engineer— worked for me ten years ago.'

Nick asks: 'How long was he in jail?'

MacFay says: 'Ten years. He got out a month ago.'

Nick: 'You think he really means to kill you?'

MacFay bangs on the table and shouts: 'No! No! No! I don't *think* he means to kill me, I *know* it!'

Lois tries to soothe MacFay, saying: 'Mr Charles is only trying to get it straight in his mind, Papa.'

MacFay: 'There's nothing to get straight. This man means to kill me and I am asking Mr Charles not to let him do it. That's simple enough, isn't it, even for Mr Charles?'

Nora shakes her head, no.

Mrs Bellam, the placid housekeeper, puts her head in at the door and says: 'The swimming pool is on fire.'

Everybody jumps up from the table. The servants disappear.

Nora exclaims: 'Nicky!' She starts upstairs to the baby.

Nick tells Freddie: 'Better stay here with the Colonel and Miss MacFay.'

Nick and Horn go out, Horn picking up a heavy walking-stick in the vestibule. They go out the front door, separating a little as they go around the side of the house toward where a wooden bathhouse is burning fiercely at one end of a large swimming pool.

The muzzle of a double-barreled shotgun is suddenly jabbed into Nick's face from a clump of bushes and a voice roars: 'One move out of you and I'll blow your head right off the end of your neck. Hey, Barney! Hey, Slim! I got him!' A big man comes out of the bushes, holding the end of the shotgun within half an inch of Nick's nose.

Two other men with shotguns, yelling: 'Hold him! Kill him if he bats a eye!' come running toward Nick and his captor.

Horn comes around the clump of bushes and says to the man with the shotgun: 'Take that gun out of Mr Charles's face and stop bellowing.'

Nick: 'I'm mighty glad to see you, Mr Horn.'

The man with the shotgun steps back, mumbling: 'How was I going to know who he was?' He turns to his mates, who have arrived by then, and says: 'It ain't the right one. It beats all how that fellers come and go without nobody seeing hide nor hair of them.'

The three men with shotguns move off toward the fire.

Horn says to Nick: 'The Colonel's guards. They've never seen anything and never will.'

Nick spies Lois's collie lying on its side a short distance from the burning building and goes over to it.

Horn, following him, asks: 'Dead?'

Nick: 'Yes. Its head almost cut off.'

Horn says in a somewhat choked voice: 'He was a swell dog. This is going to be tough on Lois.'

Nick: 'Is this the kind of thing that's been going on?'

Horn, still looking gloomily down at the dog: 'More or less. I don't know how seriously you're going to take it. Most of it's pretty silly, but it's nasty, too.'

Lois comes running up and kneels beside the dead dog. Horn squats with an arm around her, trying to console her.

Nick goes over to where the three men are standing looking at some faint blurred prints in a damp patch of ground.

Nick: 'Find anything?'

One of the guards: 'Only them, and they don't look like nothing and don't lead nowhere.'

Nick, looking at the prints: 'Our man wore rags wrapped around his shoes.'

The guard, suspiciously: 'You know a lot about them things, mister.'

Nick: 'Back home I'm a scoutmaster.' He suddenly thinks of something and goes back to Lois and Horn, asking them: 'Wasn't Asta with this dog?'

Lois: 'Yes, they were fed and let out together.'

Nick begins to whistle and call to Asta, who after some time is found hiding in a folded beach umbrella with only the tip of his nose showing.

When Nick, Lois, and Horn return to the house, MacFay is still at the table, eating a meringue glacé. Nora has returned to her place, holding Nick Jr. on her lap, and Freddie is awkwardly trying to play with him without any cooperation from the baby.

MacFay looks up as they come in and says: 'If it's any more of that foolishness, I don't want to hear a single word about it. It'll only upset my stomach and these frozen desserts are unwholesome enough anyway.'

Lois says: 'Papa, they killed Sandy,' and explains to Nora: 'I've had him ever since he was a puppy.' Then she sees Nick Jr., and goes over to play with him.

Nick Jr. regards her with his usual complete lack of interest.

Horn says: 'They set fire to the bathhouse, too.'

MacFay slams his spoon down on the table and stands up whining: 'I'm tired of hearing about these things. I'm an old man and I'm sick and you should have some consideration for me. Freddie, bring the Consolidated Transportation correspondence upstairs. Good night! Good night! Good night!' He goes out, followed by Freddie.

Nick says: 'He's a cheerful old fellow.'

Horn laughs and Nora rises, saying: 'I'm going to put Nicky to bed.'

Lois says: 'Let me help you!' and goes out with her.

In the living room, Nick and Horn are given coffee and brandy by a frightened servant.

Nick asks: 'Is this Sam Church staying in the neighborhood?'

Horn answers: 'Yes, he's rented the Kennedy cottage at the foot of the Hill Road.'

Nick asks: 'Have you tried talking to him?'

Horn says: 'Yes, but *that* didn't do any good. I used to work under him and he seems to think I had a hand in sending him over. We never got along very well anyhow.'

Nick asks: 'What's he like?'

Horn replies: 'He's all right, I suppose, but don't think you can frighten him off with rain on the roof. He's a tough baby.'

Nick says: 'Does MacFay really owe him anything?'

Horn says: 'Not the way we look at it. His job was to get results without bothering the Colonel with too many details. We were trying to put over a, well, call it a public utilities enterprise—and some details that were pretty illegal were traced as far as Church, but not as far as the Colonel, and so Church went to jail.'

Nick says: 'In other words, if everything goes okay, the Colonel gets the profits, and if they go wrong, Church gets the blame.'

Horn says cheerfully: 'That's about it.'

Nick continues: 'And that's your job with the Colonel now?'

Horn answers: 'Something like it.'

Nick: 'This deal that Church got tripped up on—where did it happen?'

Horn, beginning to smile: 'Out West—California.'

Nick: 'Ten years ago, huh?'

Horn: 'Closer to twelve; it took a little while to catch him and convict him.' His smile broadens. 'I know what's worrying you.

Your wife's father was alive then. You'd like to know whether he was in on it with the Colonel or whether the Colonel was playing a lone hand.'

Nick: 'Well?'

Horn: 'I don't know the answer. I don't suppose anybody does but the Colonel. There were no records to show anything—that's why Church took the fall alone.'

Nick, after a thoughtful pause: 'What do you think is behind all these Halloween tricks? What do you think Church is really up to?'

Horn says: 'Trying to scare the Colonel into coming across with money.'

Nick asks: 'Do you think he'll do it?'

Horn says: 'I don't know. The Colonel scares easily, but I've never seen it cost him anything.'

Nick asks: 'If he doesn't come across, will Church kill him?'

Horn replies: 'That's hard to say. He'd kill you—like that—' he snaps his fingers, 'for profit, and he might do it for fun, but I can't see him brooding much over revenge.'

Nick asks: 'Could any of the people on the inside here be working with him?'

Horn says: 'I don't think so. The servants aren't much good, but I imagine they're honest.'

Nick asks: 'How about the secretary?'

Lois, coming into the room behind them, says lightly: 'I won't have you suspecting Freddie of things. He's a nice boy.'

Horn, rising to give her his chair, says: 'All men who are in love with you are nice,' and explains to Nick, 'He's my rival. He only puts up with the Colonel's nonsense so he can be around Lois.' He sits on the arm of her chair and puts his arm around her.

Lois asks Nick: 'Do all fiancés have these pet jokes, and does the girl have to keep on laughing at them?'

Nick says: 'Only until she gets him to the altar. Did you and Nora get the Charles offspring tucked in?'

Lois says: 'Oh yes—isn't he the loveliest baby?'

Nick says modestly: 'We'll do better when we've had more practice,' and rises adding: 'I'd better go up and see him. He never closes an eye until I say good night to him.'

Nick goes up to his bedroom, where Nick Jr. is peacefully sleeping beside Nora, who is reading in bed.

Nick asks: 'What's he doing in here?'

Nora says: 'You don't suppose I'm going to have him out of my sight again in this place? And we're going back to New York tomorrow morning.'

Nick says: 'That's all right with me. I ought to get hold of some accountants and maybe we should cut the trip short and go back to the Coast.'

He begins to undress.

Nora asks: 'What are you talking about?'

Nick says: 'Money—your property—our property—that Colonel's been managing. A day like this begins to make you lose faith in your fellow man. I'd hate to wake up some morning and find that I'd married you for a fortune that MacFay had either stolen or got messed up so that somebody could take it away from us by due process of law.'

Nora: 'I love you, but you're an awful silly man sometimes.'

Nick: 'I'm not silly, I'm just timid. Some men are afraid of airplanes and some are afraid of thunderstorms—I'm afraid of losing money. I'd better go have a talk with this Church fellow in the morning.'

Nora: 'What for?'

Nick: 'He worked for MacFay back when your father was alive. Maybe he can tell me whether your father was mixed up in this—'

Nora, interrupting him indignantly: 'Of course he wasn't mixed up in it if it was anything wrong! My father was just as honest as yours!'

Nick laughs. 'Some day you'll find out what a hot recommendation that is. But, sweetheart, I'm not trying to write dirty words on your old man's tombstone. I've just got to find out where we stand.'

Nora: 'All right, but leave my father out of it. You're a fine one to talk, anyway. I still remember when you were working for Father as a private detective, every time you took me out you charged it up to him on your expense account, and he never knew it till after we were married.'

Nick: 'Ah, I was a *brilliant* young man!'

The next morning Nick takes a walk accompanied by Asta. A countryman they meet on the road tells him how to find the Kennedy house. 'You can't miss it,' he says, 'it's got a terracotta roof and sits back from the road to the left on the other side of the hill.'

Nick and Asta climb the hill and as they start down the other side, pass an expensive coupé parked a little off the road, partly hidden by foliage. Nick starts to go on, then stops and goes cautiously over to examine the parked car. Finding nothing of interest there, he looks around and discovers that twigs have been broken by someone forcing his way through the bushes. He pushes the bushes aside and sees a man lying facedown on a rock on the hillside, looking through field glasses at a house at the foot of the hill. The house has a terracotta roof.

The man is large, tough-looking, middle-aged, wearing very thick rimless spectacles. He takes the field glasses from his eyes and rolls over on one elbow to scowl at Nick, asking in a hoarse voice: 'Now what are you sticking your pretty nose in here for, chum?'

Nick says: 'Sorry. The door was open.'

The hoarse-voiced man says: 'All right, you made your joke. Now pull your freight.' He takes a police badge in a leather case from his pants pocket, shows it to Nick briefly. 'Get going.'

Nick salutes, says: 'Just as you say, Chief,' and backs out through the bushes again, takes a step or two on his way, stops to write down the license number of the automobile, and then continues on to the cottage at the foot of the hill.

When he knocks on the door, it is opened by a good-looking young Negro (the one he saw in the road the previous night), who smiles, and, speaking with a Spanish accent, says: 'Good morning, sir. Mr Church waiting breakfast for you.' He bends down to scratch Asta's head.

Nick says: 'You're going to catch pneumonia lying in damp roads after dark.'

The Negro laughs and says: 'No sir—I dress warm in this country.'

He ushers Nick into a room where a man and woman put down newspapers and rise to meet him.

The man is perhaps forty years old, big, hard-faced, sunburned.

The woman is twenty-seven, quite six feet tall, muscular, and attractive.

There are a couple of partially packed traveling bags in the room and through a door a trunk can be seen.

The man says: 'I'm Sam Church. Sit down. Breakfast will be ready in a few minutes.' He indicates the woman. 'This is Smitty—you can talk in front of her.'

Nick says: 'Thanks, I've had breakfast.' He looks at the traveling bags. 'Going away?'

Church says: 'Sure. Back to Cuba. We were just waiting to see you. It would be nice if you would give us the gory details first, though. What'll you drink?' He claps his hands and calls: 'Dum-Dum.'

Nick asks: 'What gory details? You don't mean the dead dog and the burning bathhouse?'

Church says: 'No—afterwards.'

Nick says: 'Nothing happened afterwards.'

Church says in a surprised tone: 'But I dreamed—' He breaks off and looks suspiciously at Nick, asking: 'You're not tricking me, are you?'

Nick says: 'No.'

Church says: 'Will you give me your word that nothing happened afterwards?'

Nick says: 'My word.'

Church sinks back in his chair, shaking his head in bewilderment. He says to the Negro who has appeared in the doorway: 'Give Mr Charles a drink, and you'd better give me one, too—a big one.'

Nick looks from Church to the woman.

She smiles reassuringly at Nick and says: 'He's nuts, and, if you listen to him, he'll have you nuts, too.'

Nick asks her: 'Do you know what this is all about?'

Church says: 'It's all simple enough. Some years ago the Colonel and I got in a jam and I took the fall for him on his promise that he'd see I didn't lose by it. But he ran out on me and when I got out of prison last month I went to see him to give him a chance to make good in a financial way, which is the only way that means anything to me. He said no soap, so I went on down to Cuba, knowing sooner or later I'd figure out some way to collect from him. My first night there I had a dream about him being killed. You can laugh if you want, and Smitty will laugh with you, but *I* don't laugh at my dreams. So I came on back, hoping to make the Colonel listen to reason before it was too late. And on the way back I had the dream again. I went to see the old boy and told him about the dreams, hoping to shake him loose from a few dollars, but you know how pig-headed he is, so there was nothing else for me to do but hang around on the off-chance that something would happen to loosen him up before I had the third dream, because the third one's the end on my schedule.' He takes a deep breath. 'Well, last night I had the third dream.'

Nick: 'How does he die in those dreams?'

Church: 'Oh, he's all battered up, throat cut from ear to ear—it's all very messy—just the kind of death you'd expect the slob to have.'

Nick: 'It would be funny if it happened that way.'

Church: 'It's funnier that it didn't, though I'm glad enough to know I don't have to say goodbye yet to my chances of getting money out of him. Listen, are you sure he was all right this morning?'

Nick: 'He wasn't up when I left.'

Church, somewhat excitedly: 'Had anybody else seen him?'

Nick: 'Not that I know of.'

Church jumps up, exclaiming: 'That's it, then!' He puts his hands in his pockets and walks the length of the room, scowling thoughtfully at the floor.

Smitty smiles at Nick, putting a forefinger up to her temple and making little circular movements with it.

Nick: 'You've got a lot of faith in your dreams.'

Church, absent-mindedly: 'Why not?' He sits down again, studying Nick. 'Well, that's the end of *him* as a possible gold mine. Now we've got to think about you.'

Nick: 'Me?'

Church, still thoughtfully: 'He was a hard man to do business with and I've got a hunch you're going to be even harder.'

Nick: 'Then why bother with me? I can introduce you to a lot of rich people.'

Church, ignoring this suggestion: 'On the other hand, you look like a reasonable chap. Do you think we could talk business?'

Nick: 'You'd have to show me why we should first.'

Church: 'Don't kid me. Your wife's father was MacFay's partner back in the days when my foot slipped.'

Nick: 'He was MacFay's partner in some deals, not in others. Prove to me that he had anything to do with this deal, and I'll give you a check right now for whatever you think is reasonable pay for your time in the pen.'

Church sighs. 'Yes, that's always the catch in it—proof. Nobody but me was putting anything on paper, Charles. That's why nobody but me went over. I expected this. I knew you were going to be tough to deal with. And I can't honestly tell you I've ever dreamed about you'—a pause—'or about your wife'—another pause—'or about your baby'—a longer pause—'yet.'

Nick, starting his punch before he leaves his chair, jumps up and hits Church in the eye, knocking Church and his chair over backwards. Dum-Dum whips a wooden-handled knife from his waistband (the same one seen sticking from his chest when he lay in the road the previous night) and throws it at Nick. The knife slits Nick's coat in passing and sticks in a wall.

Church, on the floor, says sharply: 'Stop it, Dum-Dum!'

Smitty, shaking her head in disapproval, says: 'Men are such rowdies,' and raises her skirt to return her pistol to its holster on her thigh.

Asta, always a great help, charges across the room after the knife, jumps up, pulls it from the wall, takes it to Dum-Dum, and then backs away from him, barking happily, tail wagging, waiting for him to throw it again.

Church stands up patting his eye. His face is calm.

Nick: 'That's to remind you *not* to dream about my family.'

Church: 'Oh, I'll remember all right.' He addresses Dum-Dum: 'Finish packing. We'll catch the noon train.'

Nick: 'Still heading for Cuba?'

Church: 'Still Cuba. I need time to think you over, and that's a good place to think. If you get down that way before I come back to see you, look me up. Sometimes I dream about roulette wheels.'

Nick: 'You're coming back to see me sometime?'

Church: 'Yep. I think as time goes on you'll see your way clear to do business with me.'

Nick, indicating Church's bruised eye: 'You mean *continue* doing business with you.' He calls Asta and goes to the door, where he turns and bows to Smitty, saying: 'Thanks for not shooting me.'

Smitty smiles good-naturedly, says: 'It would've only made things worse.'

The coupé and the hoarse-voiced man are no longer on the hilltop.

At MacFay's, Nora—with the baby—Lois, Horn, and Freddie are swimming. They come out of the pool as Nick approaches.

Nora, looking at the rip in Nick's coat: 'What have you been doing now?'

Nick: 'Asta plays too rough.'

Nora: 'It's not a tear, it's been cut.'

Nick: 'Uh-huh. A very peculiar thing happened. We were going down the hill to see Church, walking along, minding our own business, not bothering anybody, when who should we meet but three very old women, all bent over like this, walking along—'

Nora: 'Minding their own business, not bothering anybody. Did you see Church?'

Nick: 'Yes, ma'am.'

Nora, after waiting a moment for him to go on: 'Well, don't be so coy. Speak up. What did he say and what clever replies did you make?'

Nick: 'You're a tough audience, Mrs Charles.'

Horn: 'How *did* you make out with him?'

Nick says: 'He had his third dream last night and was packing to head for Cuba on the noon train when I left.'

Horn laughs.

Lois turns to look up at the house, saying in a frightened voice: 'You mean he dreamed Papa was—'

Nick finishes the sentence for her—'Dead.'

Horn puts his arm around Lois: 'Come, darling, don't be foolish.' Then he looks uncertainly at Freddie, who clears his throat nervously.

Lois looks from one to the other and insists: 'Has anybody seen Papa this morning?' None of them had. Without another word, she turns and runs toward the house, with the others following.

They go to Colonel MacFay's room. He is huddled on the bed in a grotesque position, with the covers in disarray over him. Horn peers down at MacFay's face while Nick bends over to feel his pulse.

MacFay sits up in bed and says angrily: 'The first decent sleep I've had in weeks and you have to come in like a pack of wet Indians and spoil it! What do you want?'

Leaving Lois to pacify him, the others sneak out sheepishly.

Nick and Nora are in their room packing when MacFay comes in and asks: 'What is this Lois tells me about your going back to the city today?'

Nora says: 'We have to, Colonel MacFay. We—well, this is no place for the baby the way things are.'

'The baby?' MacFay glares at Nick Jr.—'He's big enough to—' then breaks off and begins to whine: 'Nobody's doing anything to the baby. It's me that's in danger—it's me you're deserting.' He turns to Nick. 'Besides, I haven't had a chance to talk to you. There are things you ought to know about the business—about your investments.'

Nick, interested: 'What things?'

Horn appears in the doorway and says: 'I phoned the village to check up, and they really did leave on the noon train.'

MacFay says irritably: 'What are you talking about?'

Horn explains: 'Church told Charles this morning that he was leaving for Cuba, and he got off all right, with a trunk and a lot of bags, and the Negro and a tall woman.'

MacFay turns to Nora: 'See, my dear, they've gone. There'll be no more trouble.'

Nora looks undecidedly from MacFay to Nick.

MacFay pats her on the cheek and says: 'There, there, my dear, as a favor to an old man—an old friend of your father's.'

He goes out.

Nora looks at Nick, asks: 'What do we do?'

Nick, staring after MacFay, says: 'It's a shame the way I'm beginning to distrust that old duffer.'

Nora: 'Stop being so silly. He was Father's partner. He wouldn't—'

Nick: 'Maybe it wasn't so smart leaving him in control of the businesses our money is invested in all these years. He might've come to look on our money as practically his own.'

Nora: 'Stop it!'

Nick: 'I don't care about myself. I can always make a good living as a detective. But what are you and Nicky going to live on? That's what I worry about at night.'

Nora kicks him.

MacFay and Horn go into a room furnished as an office, where Freddie is sitting at a typewriter.

Freddie jumps up on his feet and says: 'Good morning, Colonel MacFay.'

MacFay walks past Freddie and fishes a discarded piece of carbon paper from the wastebasket. 'You could have used this a time or two more.'

Freddie says: 'I'm sorry, I—'

MacFay cuts him short. 'Being sorry doesn't bring back money that's wasted.' He sits down at his desk. 'Tell Lois I want to see her.'

Freddie goes out.

MacFay starts to look at his mail, complaining: 'That boy's not worth the room he takes up. Do you know what I found him doing yesterday? Practicing a kind of tap-dance with the typewriter keys.'

Horn, standing at the window, says casually: 'I think Freddie's mind is more on Lois than it is on his work.'

MacFay says: 'Lois? Ridiculous! I'll kick him out so fast it'll make his head swim.'

Horn, still casually, says: 'I've got a young cousin that might suit you if you are going to make a change—a smart boy just out of law school.'

MacFay looks suspiciously at Horn and whines: 'I've had enough of people's relations. None of them are ever any good.' He returns his attention to his mail.

Horn shrugs and looks out of the window at Lois crossing the lawn with Freddie.

She is asking: 'Is Papa in a very bad humor this afternoon?'

Freddie answers: 'You won't like me to say it, but not much worse than usual.'

She pats his arm and says: 'Be a little patient, Freddie. He's not well, and he hasn't had an easy life, and now that he's getting old I know that he is difficult sometimes. But if you knew him as well as I do, you'd know he doesn't mean one-tenth of the things he says.'

Freddie exclaims: 'Be a little patient? Good lord! When I think of the things I've had to put up with. If it hadn't been for you—'

She puts her hand on his arm and says: 'I know, I know, and I'm grateful.'

They go into the house.

When they come into the room where MacFay and Horn are, MacFay looks up from his correspondence and asks point-blank: 'See here, Lois, has this young nitwit been making googoo eyes at you?'

Lois and Freddie look at him dumbfounded.

Horn says good-naturedly: 'Come, come, Colonel MacFay, if there was anything like that, it seems to me I ought to be the one to ask questions.'

MacFay, ignoring Horn, says to Lois: 'Answer me. Has he been making love to you?'

Horn, scowling at MacFay, says bluntly: 'This is pretty damned insulting to all three of us.'

Lois cries: 'Papa—how can you say things like that?'

Freddie, the last to recover his speech, says, half in tears: 'This is too much. I'm through—I'm leaving!' He starts out the door, then turns back and yells: 'I know Lois is engaged to Dudley, but my feelings for her are my own business!'

MacFay, thus outnumbered, whines: 'How am I going to know what's going on if I don't ask? Everybody hides everything from me. You all think I'm just a useless old fool.'

Lois goes over to him, runs her hand over his head, and says: 'No we don't, but sometimes you are a problem. Won't you ever learn not to say these terrible things to people?'

Horn goes out after Freddie, who has left the room, and catches him at the head of the stairs, saying: 'You're not going to be foolish, are you?'

Freddie says: 'I'm going away.'

Horn says: 'Don't do it, kid. Lois is going to feel that it's partly her fault. You ought to know what to expect from the old man by now.'

Freddie says: 'But I couldn't stay—I feel too ashamed.'

Horn says: 'So do Lois and I, and so does the old man if he'd admit it. Try it a little longer, kid. We don't want you going like this.'

While Freddie hesitates, MacFay's voice comes through the open doorway. 'Freddie!'

Freddie looks at Horn, nods, and starts back to the office. Horn puts his arm around Freddie's shoulder. They go into the office.

MacFay says: 'Where's that bill from Nichols and Brackett?'

Lois says gaily: 'I know what's coming and you needn't bother. A sports dress for $62.50. I haven't worn it yet, so I can send it back tomorrow and there'll be no hard feelings.'

MacFay says: 'That's not it. I don't begrudge you the dress, but it's for your own good—you're too extravagant.'

Lois: 'I guess you're right. I guess that's why I didn't wear it before you saw the bill—so I wouldn't have to keep it if you didn't want me to.'

MacFay whines: 'Oh, you can keep it, but I wish you'd be a little more careful.'

Nick and Nora come in.

Nick, briskly: 'Shall we have that little business chat now, Colonel?'

MacFay: 'Whenever you're ready. There's no particular hurry.'

Nick: 'But you wired us to come straight down as soon as we got to New York. We thought—'

MacFay: 'You'll forgive an old man's inconsiderateness, children. There's really nothing but routine matters.'

Horn winks at Nick. (Lois and Freddie have left the room.)

Nick: 'I get it. You wanted me down here on account of Church—and used the business angle as bait.'

MacFay: 'Now that it's over, perhaps I should confess that there may be a little truth in what you say.' He pinches Nora's cheek. 'You'll forgive the old scoundrel, won't you?'

Nick: 'I wouldn't be too sure it's over.'

MacFay: 'What do you mean?'

Nick: 'My guess is that whatever Church meant to do in the first place, he still means to do.'

MacFay starts up from his chair, then sinks down with a little laugh and relaxes again. 'You're trying to frighten me as punishment for bringing you down here on the run. You can't do it, son. As soon as Church found out you were here, he lit out, and that's all there is to it.'

Nick: 'I hope you're right, but his talk to me didn't sound like that.'

MacFay shakes his head from side to side. 'The years it takes young men to learn not to pay any attention to what other young men say!'

Nick: 'He wants to include Nora and me in this shakedown on the grounds that her father was your partner. Was he tied up in this mess?'

MacFay: 'What difference can all that make now?'

Nora, reproachfully: 'Colonel MacFay!'

Nick: 'If Church went to jail to shield Nora's father, we want to settle with him.'

Nora nods vigorously.

MacFay, angrily: 'You want to settle with him! Sure! Neither of you know what it means to have to scrape together your dollars. You don't have to work for money! People die and leave it to you! What's a few thousand here, a few thousand there? It grows on trees!'

Nick: 'That's not answering my question. Was Nora's father in with you on this deal?'

MacFay to Horn: 'Run along, Dudley.'

Horn goes out, shutting the door behind him, and stands there listening.

MacFay, patiently to Nick: 'You knew Nora's father, son. Did you think he was a crook?'

Nick: 'No.'

MacFay: 'Do you think I'm a crook?'

Nick, hesitantly: 'No-o.'

MacFay: 'Can you pretend you think I'm a crook?'

Nick: 'Yes, I can do that all right.'

MacFay: 'I thought you could. Well, Nora's father knew mines and he knew timber as well as anybody in the world, but he didn't know the first thing about finance. I did. I built his fortune for him. If it hadn't been for me, he'd never have had a hundred thousand dollars in his life.'

Nick, pityingly: 'As poor as that!' To Nora: 'You'd never have got a first-rate husband that way.'

MacFay: 'So if I'm a crook, and my partner's an honest man who doesn't know anything about finance, why should I give him a share in the profits from any crooked deal I put over? I have to do all the work myself, don't I? Even if I use his money now and then, why should I let him know it? Isn't it enough to give him his share of the profits from straight deals, where he knows what's going on and where I need his honest knowledge of mining and timber?'

Nick, blinking at MacFay: 'There's probably a catch in that somewhere, but you certainly make it sound reasonable.'

Nora goes over and kisses MacFay on the cheek. She says: 'I don't understand it, but I know you've said something nice.'

MacFay pats Nora's hand, says: 'So you needn't worry about your father ever having been mixed up in anything like that.'

Nora: 'And if you hadn't told us this, we'd have paid Church and he'd probably never have bothered you anymore.'

MacFay: 'You young idiots! Money's not to pass out to the first person that asks for it.'

Nora: 'But it would have been our money and you—'

MacFay: '*Your* money? Yes, but *I'm* the one that slaved getting it together for you and I feel about it just as I do about my own.'

Nick and Nora exchange suspicious glances.

Nick clears his throat, says: 'That's swell of you. Now about those routine business matters you mentioned. Don't you think we may as well—uh—you know—kind of go over them now that we're here?'

MacFay: 'If you want to.' He puts his hand on a desk drawer.

Nick, trying to speak casually: 'I sometimes feel ashamed of myself for not knowing more about business than I do. I think a man ought to—well, I'm going to try to take more of an interest in things. For instance, if a man's money is invested in—say in any kind of business—he should know something about it; he should be able to understand—uh—balance sheets and things.'

Nora: 'Why, Mr Charles, I'm proud of you!'

MacFay, dryly: 'You're not still pretending you think I'm a crook?'

Nick laughs insincerely. 'Oh, of course not! But seriously, my conscience hurts me sometimes. Here we are, going along not bothering about anything, just okaying—uh—routine matters when you show them to us. Kind of like butterflies, you might say. And there you are, having to shoulder all the responsibilities, look after all the details for us. It's not right. Is it hard to learn to—uh—you know—make heads or tails of these rows of numbers and things?'

MacFay: 'No, all it takes is a little application.'

Nick: 'Well, suppose instead of just skimming the surface the way we usually do, would it take too long if we—uh—went into things a little more thoroughly this time?'

MacFay: 'An excellent idea, and I've all the time in the world. Pull your chairs up.' He smiles maliciously. 'We'll take our lumber company first. It's a little simpler than the others.' He takes a bale of papers from a drawer and puts it on the desk, selecting one sheet of paper from the bale and putting it on the desk in front of them. 'To start at the beginning, this graph shows the production of lumber, seasonally adjusted, for our company—that's the solid line—for all other companies in the United States combined—that's the dotted line—for all Canadian companies—the double lines, and for all Canadian and United States companies, exclusive of our company—the chain line—from January 1929, to the present month, both inclusive. Here'—passing them another sheet of paper covered with columns of typewritten figures—'are the figures, if you wish to check them.'

Nick: 'Not at all.'

MacFay: 'Study them. Don't fall back into your habit of skimming over things again.'

Nick and Nora bend their heads over the figures.

MacFay: 'You'll notice that production, seasonally adjusted, has been falling off since June.' He fishes out another sheet of paper. 'You can see by this that new business in the last couple of months has slowed up and unfilled orders are some 20 percent below last year's figure, while gross stocks are considerably higher than they were a year ago.'

Nick, trying to pretend he knows what it is all about, asks: 'How large a stock of grosses do we usually have on hand?'

MacFay dives into his bale of papers again.

Nora, who has been counting on her fingers under the desk, nudges Nick and whispers: 'The first row of figures in that left-hand column is added up right.'

Nick, whispering: 'But are they seasonally adjusted?'

Nora nods: 'Like a watch!'

Nick: 'Good!'

MacFay gives them a still larger sheet of paper with still more figures on it. 'Now here are our yearly figures from 1929 to 1936, both inclusive. You'll find them very interesting.' He leans over to point out the various columns to them. 'Here are the Sales, here Depreciation and Depletion, here Net Income—you'll notice that the figure for 1931 excludes unrealized inventory loss—then Interest, Interest Times Earned, Earned Per Share, Cash Dividends, Surplus For Year—you'll notice there were deficits for the years 1931 to 1934, both inclusive; and here below are Invested Capital—the 1934 figure is after drastic adjustments in the value of land and development—then Percentage Earned on Capital, Properties, Percentage Earned on Properties, Cash and Equivalent, Working Capital, Current Ration, and, last of all, Profit and Loss Surplus. Now here's a statement of...'

We leave Nick and Nora nodding determinedly, but groggily, at each item the Colonel shows them.

IN A SHABBY SALOON

Face Peppler is standing at the bar with a big thug.

Face, giving the bartender a dollar bill: 'Give me twenty nickels—twenty.'

The big thug, plaintively: 'I want to go to Nick's party, Face. I love Nick.'

Face, as if repeating something he had said before: 'It's a *kid's* party, Whacky. Nobody can't go unless they bring a kid.'

Whacky: 'But Pete and Larry are going.'

Face: 'Larry's got a kid, and I'm lending Pete one of my brother's brats.'

Whacky: 'I'll bring a kid.' He buttons his coat with an air of determination. 'What kind of kid do you want?'

Face grabs his lapel. 'Wait a minute, Whacky! No snatch, for God's sake! We don't want to put the big heat on this party!'

Whacky mumbles: 'Well, I want to go.'

Face: 'Okay, but borrow a kid legitimate. Don't show with no hot tot.'

Face carefully counts the nickels the bartender gives him, then, with the nickels in one hand, Nora's address book in the other, goes into the telephone booth and dials the first number in the address book.

Face, into the phone: 'Is Miss Adams there?... This is Nick Charles's society sekkatary. Put her on the wire.'

At the other end of the wire, Miss Adams is being handed a telephone by a maid. Miss Adams: 'Hello.'

Face: 'This is Nick Charles's society sekkatary. We're throwing a binge for Nick's kid Tuesday afternoon. Can you make it?'

Miss Adams: 'Nick Charles? Are they in town?'

Face: 'Are they in town? *You* ought to be in town like they are! But, hey!—wait a minute. Have you got any kids?'

Miss Adams: 'Kids? Why, no!'

Face: 'Then don't bother. Give it a skip.' He hangs up muttering, 'That dame wasting my nickels!' dials another number, says into the phone: 'Is Mrs Alliston there? This is Nick Charles's society sekkatary...'

MACFAY'S OFFICE

The lights have been turned on.

MacFay, straightening up from the last sheet of paper in his bale, is saying: 'And now I think I've given you a pretty good rough picture of the situation.'

Nick and Nora rise with deep sighs of relief. Nora seems to be having trouble focusing her eyes. Nick's hair is rumpled, his tie askew, and his face tired.

Nick, pulling himself together and trying to sound hearty: 'This has been awfully nice of you, Colonel MacFay, and we've learned a lot. It's—uh—it's opened up—uh—new vistas to us. Hasn't it, Nora?'

Nora: 'It's been marvelous!'

MacFay: 'But sit down. That's only the lumber company. You'll find the railroad much more interesting. It's more complicated.' He takes a larger bale of papers from another drawer. 'And after that, we'll take the mining properties.'

Nora strikes a pose with a hand to one ear and says: 'I hear Nicky crying.' She moves toward the door. 'Isn't that like him—to make a fuss just when I've found something so fascinating!'

Nick: 'I'll go with you.'

Nora: 'Oh, no! I'll be right back, and you must show me afterwards what Colonel MacFay explained to you while I'm gone, because I don't want to miss a thing.'

Nick, glaring at her: 'Well, at least send me in a Scotch and soda.'

MacFay: 'No, son. I want to give you a piece of advice. A lot of men say liquor and business don't mix. I don't say that, but I do say there's one time they don't mix. Drink all you can handle any other time, but don't touch it while you're checking up the figures.'

Nora: 'That sounds like mighty sound advice to me.'

As she goes out, MacFay is beginning: 'First, I must tell you that the courts have authorized us to make payments of 20 percent of the principal amount on equipment trust certificates, series D, maturing December 15th.'

Nora goes to her room, blows a kiss at Nick Jr., who is sleeping, smiles at the nurse, and begins to change for dinner.

LIVING ROOM OF SMITTY'S APARTMENT IN NEW YORK

It is a typical middle-class furnished apartment, to which Smitty has added feminine touches in the shape of some beribboned cushions, a doll or two, etc.

Dum-Dum is sitting on his heels in one corner of the room eating a dish of ice cream.

Smitty, at the telephone, is saying: 'I want to speak to Lieutenant John Guild, Homicide Bureau. This is Mrs R. Culver Smith speaking.' She gets Guild on the phone. 'This is Mrs R. Culver Smith.'

He asks: 'Who?'

She says disgustedly: 'This is Smitty.'

He says: 'Oh, Smitty—how are you? What do you hear from Tip?'

She says: 'He's still kicking about wanting a larger cell—but that ain't what I called you about. I don't know whether it's one of those half-smart tricks that you people think up, or what it is, but some guy phoned me a little while ago, all excited. He won't tell me who he is except he claims he's a friend of Tip's, and he wants to know if I'm going to be home after midnight.

He won't tell me what it's all about except that it's something that won't get me in a jam if I give him a square break, but he said he don't want any monkey business, because he's got two murder raps hanging over his head and he's playing for keeps. That wouldn't be some kind of charade you boys thought up, would it?'

Guild says: 'It's all news to me. What are you going to do about it?'

Smitty says: 'I ain't going to do anything but keep as far away from trouble as I can until Tip gets out of Sing Sing.'

Guild says: 'That's showing sense. I think the best thing for you to do is to stick around home after midnight and give us a chance to see what this setup is.'

Smitty says: 'Yeh, but I don't want to get into any trouble with people thinking I'm rattling on them either.'

Guild says: 'Oh, it's nothing like that. We'll keep your nose clean both ways.'

Smitty says hesitantly: 'Oh, all right then,' and puts up the telephone as Church, in his shirt sleeves, comes in from the adjoining room, holding ice wrapped in a towel to his black eye.

Church asks: 'Oke?'

Smitty says: 'Oke. But I'm afraid of these fancy rackets. There are too many things can go wrong.'

Church laughs at her fears. 'It's airtight—we can't miss.'

She smiles ruefully. 'If that don't sound like Tip. I guess I'm just a sucker for men who are too slick for their own good and mine. Seven years I've been married to *him*, and he's so slick that he ain't been out of the can long enough to finish our honeymoon.'

Church says: 'You like that guy, don't you?'

Smitty says: 'No foolin'.'

Church says thoughtfully: 'So do I.' Then he asks: 'Going back to him when he gets out?'

Smitty says: 'Yep! I like you a lot, Sam, but Tip's my boy.' She laughs reminiscently. 'Living with him you never know what kind of a jam you're going to get into from one minute to the next. Did I ever tell you about the time I had my operation and he gave the hospital a rubber check that bounced back before they got me on the table? Was I burned up! Another time in Boston he was fooling around on the side with a little hatcheck girl...' She breaks off saying, 'But you don't want to listen to all this.'

Church kisses her lightly and says: 'I like to hear you talk about Tip.'

She says: 'But on the level, I don't like these schemes where a lot of pieces have to fit in together.' She dovetails her fingers. 'If I was a man and wanted to steal, I'd rather take my chances just socking somebody with a hunk of pipe.'

Church says good-naturedly: 'You'd miss a lot of fun.'

Smitty says: 'Fun? It's no fun to me. Anyway, if we've got to go in for all this razzle-dazzle, why don't you do something about pulling that Nick Charles away from there? I don't trust him. He looks like a guy with insomnia to me'—she smiles at Church's eye—'and a fast punch.'

Church: 'I don't want him around, but I don't see how he can gum our game. It was airtight without him, and it'll be airtight with him.' He touches his black eye. 'Don't let this goog bother you. A lot of winners have had them.'

Smitty: 'All right, if you say so, but maybe I ought to know more about the ins and outs of what you're doing.'

Church: 'Losing confidence in me since I stopped that punch?'

Smitty: 'No, I *still* haven't got that much sense.'

The doorbell rings. Smitty looks at Church.

Church wriggles a thumb at Dum-Dum, who gets up swiftly and carries his ice-cream dish into the next room, putting it on a table, and flattening himself against one side of a connecting doorway. Dum-Dum's hand pushes his coat aside a little to rest a handle of the knife in his waistband.

Church nods his head and Smitty goes to the door.

Diamond-Back Vogel, the man Nick saw watching Church's cottage from the hilltop that morning, is there.

Vogel says in his hoarse voice: 'Hello, Smitty! Busy?'

She says: 'Never too busy to see a friend. Come on in. What do you know?'

Vogel says: 'Nothing much.' He follows her into the living room. He says: 'Hello, Church' without much warmth.

Church says casually: 'How are you, Diamond-Back?'

Smitty says: 'Sit down.'

Vogel sits down, says: 'No, I've only got a minute. A guy came in from up the river this morning with a line from Tip.'

Smitty asks: 'What is it? What does he say?'

Vogel stares at Church.

Smitty says: 'Go ahead—Sam's all right. What did Tip say?'

Vogel says: 'For you he's all right maybe, but I don't know if he's all right for Tip. Come on out in the kitchen.'

Smitty says to Church: 'You don't mind, do you?'

Church says: 'No.'

Smitty and Vogel go into the kitchen.

'What did Tip say?' Smitty asks. 'Is he all right?'

Vogel growls: 'He's okay, but he's been thinking again. He sent down a lot of forms, orders for material and stuff, with the warden's signature forged on them, and he wants you to get hold of somebody that can pass himself off as the warden's go-between and collect a rake-off for placing these phony orders with business houses. He says make a fifty-fifty deal with whoever you get.'

Half-laughing, half-angry, Smitty exclaims: 'Nothing can stop that boy!' She holds out her hand. 'Have you got the stuff he sent?'

He takes some papers from his pocket and gives them to her. She tears them up.

Vogel nods approvingly, asks: 'You spend a lot of time with Church, don't you?'

Smitty says: 'Don't start that again. He's just a good friend like I told you.'

Vogel growls: 'And a guy can get to be too good a friend, too, like *I* told *you*. Be seeing you.'

He goes out. Smitty returns to the living room.

Church says: 'I'm going to skin a knuckle on that four-eyed gent some day.'

Smitty laughs and says: 'Take big sister's advice and—A, don't try it; and B, if you think you have to try to catch him without the cheaters on, because I've heard experts say he's plenty good as long as he can see.'

Church says: 'But he can't see very well without—?' He holds thumbs and forefingers up in circles to indicate glasses.

Smitty says: 'So they tell me.'

Church says: 'Maybe that's something to remember.' He looks at his watch and calls: 'Dum-Dum.'

The Negro comes in.

Church says: 'It's time to get going, son.' He holds out his hand. 'Good luck.'

Dum-Dum, smiling broadly, shakes Church's hand and says: 'Thank you, sir,' pulls a wadded cap from his pocket, says: 'Adios' to Church and Smitty, and goes out.

AT MACFAY'S

Lois and Horn are sitting on the shore of a lake, looking out over the water. His arm is around her; she is leaning back against his shoulder.

Horn: 'Happy, darling?'

Lois: 'M-m-m!'

Horn: 'It's not too chilly?'

Lois: 'I'd never be chilly this way.'

In the living room, Freddie is fooling with the dial of a radio. After a moment, he turns the radio off impatiently and goes to a window, where he stands looking out, biting a fingernail.

In a linen closet, Mrs Bellam, the housekeeper, is placidly counting sheets.

In Nora's bedroom, she is lying in bed reading, with Nick Jr. sleeping beside her. She turns her head once to smile in the direction of MacFay's office, then goes back to her reading.

In the office, Nick's collar is open and he has taken off his coat. A tray on a table near the desk holds the remains of their dinners. The desk is piled high with papers now.

MacFay is saying: '...showing a consolidation net profit of thirty-one thousand, eight hundred sixty-four dollars and twenty-two cents after all charges and normal federal income taxes, but before provision for surtax, equal, after preferred dividend requirements, to fifty-eight cents a share on the combined class A and B common stock.

Nick, trying to prop his eyes open: 'I wouldn't've believed it.'

MacFay: '*But*, production in August showed a substantial decline, though part of the sharp July increase was retained, and the average for the two months is well above that for the second quarter.'

Nick: 'Wait till Nora hears that!'

STREET IN HARLEM, NIGHT

Dum-Dum walks briskly up the street, looks around, then goes into the dark entrance of a building. He takes a pint bottle from one of his pockets, drinks from it, and sits down comfortably on the vestibule floor, legs sprawled, back against the wall, chin down on his chest, cap down over his eyes. After a little while, a man comes out of the building, glances timidly at him as he passes, goes on, then returns cautiously to fumble at Dum-Dum's pockets.

Dum-Dum remains motionless except to raise one foot and kick the man in the face. The man tumbles out of the doorway, jumps up, and hurries off. Dum-Dum takes another drink from his bottle, then slumps there as before.

AT MACFAY'S

Nick is lying in bed with his eyes shut, his back to Nora's bed.

Nora: 'Aw, stop sulking.'

Nick: 'You've no loyalty. There isn't another wife in the world who would have left her husband in there to be seasonally adjusted like that.'

Nora: 'What do you suppose 'seasonally adjusted' means?'

Nick: 'I wouldn't tell you. But if you'd stuck around a little longer you would have met 'adverse long-run consequences' and 'major cyclical downswing.' There's a sweetheart!' He repeats, softly and fondly: 'Major Cyclical Downswing. Can't you see him? A little threadbare and shiny at the elbows, but still hale and hearty, with a booming, if somewhat whiskey-roughened, voice, and a contemptuous snort for those bounders who want to know what army he was ever in. Dear old fellow!'

He tries to go to sleep again.

Nora: 'It's too early to go to sleep, Nick.'

Nick: 'What time is it?'

Nora, looking at the clock beside the bed: 'One o'clock.'

Nick: 'Sh-h-h! Colonel Both-Inclusive MacFay will hear you. No numbers are that simple. It must be one point three one six two at least.'

Fingers tap lightly on the door.

Nora: 'Come in.'

Lois enters. She is wearing nightgown, robe, and slippers.

Lois: 'I saw your light and wondered if you couldn't sleep, too.'

Nick: 'Some of us could and some of us couldn't.' He gets out of bed saying: 'Old Major Cyclical Downswing Charles has just the thing for you.' He pours her a drink.

Nora says: 'I don't think there's anything to worry about now, dear. They—'

Lois says: 'Oh, it's not that. I'm not worried. I—' She laughs. 'I guess I'm too happy to sleep.' She goes to the window and looks out. 'It's lovely out. Dudley and I took a long walk over by the lake, and then I couldn't get to sleep for thinking about—' She goes over to Nora's bed, sits down, and hugs her. 'I guess you think it's silly to be this happy about getting married, but Dudley really, really is so marvelous.'

Nick, starting to offer Lois her drink, quickly gulps it down himself.

Nora pats the girl's shoulder and asks: 'When are you getting married?'

Lois says: 'The first of the month.'

There is the sound of a shot and the lights go out. There are distant sounds of doors slamming, of a man's voice calling out in alarm, of a piece of furniture being upset, and of a body falling.

Nick strikes a match and lights candles on a dressing table. Nora is sitting up in bed clutching Nick Jr., who does not wake.

Lois gasps: 'Papa! See if he's all right.'

Nick says: 'Stay here.'

He goes out into the hallway carrying one candle. From the other end of the hall, Horn, barefooted, in pajamas, is approaching with a flashlight. Freddie, dressed, comes out of his room with a candle. There are sounds of people moving in other parts of the house. The three men come together at MacFay's bedroom door.

The door is ajar. Horn pushes it open and throws the beam of his flashlight on the bed. MacFay's bare legs protrude from a wadded pile of blankets that cover the rest of him, except his right arm, which, grotesquely bent, dangles down to the floor.

Nick goes to the bed, lifts enough of the covers to look at MacFay's face. Freddie and Horn look over his shoulder. They stare at the dead man in horror for a moment; then Nick puts the covers back gently over his face. He touches the dangling hand to feel its temperature and straightens up as the housekeeper comes into the room.

Mrs Bellam is fully dressed and carries a small Bible with one finger marking her place in it. Her face and manner are placid as ever.

Freddie says: 'I'm going to be sick,' and goes out of the room hurriedly.

The housekeeper says with no sign of excitement: 'I heard the noise.'

Horn says hoarsely: 'MacFay's been murdered.'

Mrs Bellam says quietly, as if to herself: ' 'The Lord giveth and the Lord taketh away.' Do you want me to phone the sheriff?'

Nick says: 'Yes.'

She goes out as Lois comes in.

Just inside of the doorway, Lois halts and stands trembling with fear and grief. She says: 'Dudley, is he—' She breaks off and tries again: 'Is he—' but still cannot finish the sentence.

He goes to her, puts his arm around her, keeping his body between Lois and the bed. He says gently: 'Yes, he's dead.'

She tries to go past him to the bed, but he holds her, saying: 'Not now, darling. You can't look at him now.'

Horn leads Lois out.

Nick, left alone in the room, tries the light-switch beside the door, and the wall-lights go on as Freddie returns.

Both windows are open. The bedside lamp is lying on the floor with the wire torn out of it. Neither of its light bulbs is broken. On the bedside table a glass has been upset, spilling water on the table and on the crumpled newspaper, telephone, cigarette box, matches, etc. on the floor below. In one corner of the room an old-style Frontier model .44-caliber revolver lies on the floor. There is a bullet hole high in one wall.

Nick asks: 'Ever see the gun before?'

Freddie says: 'Yes, it's Colonel MacFay's.' He points to an open drawer at the bedside table. 'He kept it there.'

By this time there are three or four partially dressed servants crowded in the doorway, looking into the room with excited faces.

One of the servants says: 'He went out the front door.'

Nick asks: 'Who?'

The servant says: 'I didn't see nobody. I just seen the front door was open when I went down to fix the fuse.'

Nick: 'What fuse?'

The servant: 'The one that was blowed out.'

Nick: 'How did you know it was blowed out?'

Servant: 'I didn't know nothing. I was just doing what Mrs Bellam told me. When she come out of here she told me to see if any fuses was blowed out and I went down and there was and I put in a new one and that's when I seen the front door was open.'

Freddie: 'Here's Mrs Bellam now.'

The housekeeper comes in carrying a tray with two cups of coffee and some toast on it. She says: 'I don't suppose you'll be getting back to sleep again tonight, so maybe you'll feel better for this.' She puts the tray down, looks at the bed, shakes her head, and says mildly: 'Poor soul—seems he always expected to be murdered like this.'

She goes out, driving the servants away from the door as she goes.

Horn comes in.

Freddie asks: 'How's Lois?'

Horn says: 'She'll be all right. I left her with Mrs Charles.' He looks at the bed. 'That's a mean way to die.'

Nick asks: 'Know any good ways?'

The sound of cars and motorcycles arriving comes through the open windows.

The arriving party consists of the assistant district attorney, the examining physician, three deputy sheriffs, a photographer, a fingerprint expert, and three state troopers on motorcycles. From time to time more troopers, deputies, etc., come until there are altogether some fifteen or twenty of them. These are well-trained men who go to work immediately with a minimum of noises and confusion. Floodlights are turned on the grounds around the house and men afoot and on motorcycles set off to examine every part of the estate. Servants and outer guards are rounded up for questioning.

The assistant district attorney, followed by a deputy sheriff, photographer, medical examiner, and fingerprint man go up to MacFay's room.

VanSlack, the assistant district attorney, is a tall, stooped, colorless young man with a vague face; the same vagueness characterizes his words and manner.

He looks uncertainly around the room and says: 'I am Assistant District Attorney VanSlack.'

Horn says: 'How do you do. This is Nick Charles, Freddie Coleman, and I'm Dudley Horn, and here is—' He finishes the sentence by motioning with his hand toward the bed.

The photographer, setting up his camera, says to the medical examiner: 'You can have it in a minute, Doc.' He asks Horn: 'Anything been moved?'

Horn looks at Nick, who says: 'Only this doesn't belong here.' He takes up the tray with the cups of coffee and toast on it.

VanSlack says: 'If you gentlemen will, eh—' and steps back out of the room.

The others follow him out into the corridor. Nick puts the tray on the floor.

VanSlack asks: 'Do you know who found him?'

Nick says: 'The three of us. We met at the door.'

VanSlack, clearing his throat again, says: 'I don't suppose you saw anything.'

Nick says: 'Just what you see in there now.'

VanSlack asks: 'Was there any special reason for you three meeting here? I mean had you heard anything—perhaps—'

Nick answers: 'A shot.'

VanSlack says: 'Oh—there was a shot? Did it—do you mind telling me where you were when you heard it?'

Nick says: 'I was in my bedroom at the other end of the hall with my wife and MacFay's daughter.'

VanSlack says: 'That is MacFay in there, isn't it?'

Nick says: 'I'd hate to think anybody was playing that kind of joke on us.'

Horn says: 'I was asleep.'

VanSlack looks at Freddie, who says: 'I was in my room. I was—' he hesitates '—writing.'

This dialogue is punctuated from time to time by the flare of the photographer's flashlights through the open bedroom door.

VanSlack says: 'I don't suppose any of you know who saw him last?'

After a moment of hesitancy, Freddie says: 'I guess I did. I was in there a little after midnight, to have him sign some mail.'

VanSlack asks: 'Did you happen to notice what he was doing when you left?'

Freddie says: 'Yes, he was reading the afternoon paper. That is— he picked it up as I went out.'

VanSlack asks: 'Was he in bed?'

Freddie says: 'Yes. I turned off all except the bedside light when I left.'

The photographer looks out to say: 'It's all yourn, Doc.'

The doctor goes in to the bed and starts to examine the body.

VanSlack says: 'If any of you gentlemen happen to think of anything that might help us, just tell one of the boys, will you? I oughtn't to be very long in here.'

He, the deputy sheriff, and the fingerprint man go into the bedroom and shut the door behind them.

Horn says: 'He's not exactly my idea of a human bloodhound.'

Nick says: 'Maybe that's nothing against him.'

VanSlack opens the door and says: 'Mr Charles, eh—could you— that is, have you a minute?'

Nick says: 'Sure.'

He goes into MacFay's room and VanSlack shuts the door.

VanSlack says: 'I thought perhaps—of course everybody knows your reputation—perhaps you wouldn't mind sort of looking at things with us. It's pretty confusing, isn't it?'

Nick says: 'I'll be glad to do anything I can, but the way you people are going at it, it doesn't look as if you need much of anybody's help.'

He looks around the room. The deputy sheriff and photographer are measuring the height of the bullet hole from the floor, the distance of the gun from the bed, etc.; the fingerprint man is at work on the window sills, and the examining physician is busy with the body.

VanSlack says modestly: 'Well, we try to keep up to date. You see, not having very much of this sort of thing ourselves we have plenty of time to keep in touch with what progress crime detecting agencies are making in other places. Of course that doesn't take the place of practical experience.' He points to the gun. 'You don't happen to know who that belongs to?'

Nick says: 'The secretary said it was MacFay's. He kept it in the drawer there.'

VanSlack says: 'I thought maybe it would be.'

The medical examiner turns from the bed and says: 'Throat cut from ear to ear with a fairly large, heavy blade. Death instantaneous. Bruise on left temple, blunt instrument. Right wrist broken. That ought to be enough to go on. If there is anything else, I'll give it to you after I go over him more thoroughly tomorrow. Been dead half an hour.' He looks at Nick. 'Does that check with the time you found him?'

Nick says: 'Check.'

VanSlack says: 'Thank you, Doctor.'

The medical examiner goes out.

VanSlack looks worriedly at the bullet hole, at the gun, at the bedside lamp, glass, etc., at the dead man, and then at Nick, and says uncertainly: 'We'll say, for instance, that MacFay heard the murderer—he could have come in through either the door or the window—we ought to be able to find out which—and grabbed the gun.' He turns to the deputy sheriff and says: 'From the looks of that hole, Les, where would you say the bullet was fired from?'

Les says: 'I figure it had to come from pretty close to the floor there alongside the bed.'

VanSlack: 'Then the murderer was already bearing down on his arm when MacFay got the shot away; or it could be, with one of those old guns, that it went off when it hit the floor after the murderer had broken his arm and made him drop it.' He says to Nick: 'I hope this sounds reasonable to you.'

Nick says: 'It does—and a paraffin test would tell you whether MacFay pulled the trigger or the gun went off after it hit the floor, if that point's worth bothering about.'

VanSlack says: 'Well, we always try to be as thorough as we can. So next, our murderer would have knocked MacFay back on the pillow with that blow on the temple, perhaps stunning him, and then cut his throat, pulling the bed-clothes over him to keep the blood from spurting around. Now we've got to try and figure out how he entered and left. What do you think on that point, Mr Charles?'

Nick says: 'One of the servants said the front door was open.'

VanSlack says: 'But if you and the other gentlemen came as soon as you heard the shot, wouldn't you have seen or heard, or—you know what I mean?'

Nick says: 'This room's right at the head of the stairs. I didn't get here that quick. The lights were out, you know, and I had to stop to find a candle.'

VanSlack says vaguely: 'Oh, the lights went out.'

Nick says: 'Yes, the servant says a fuse blew out. An electrician ought to be able to tell you whether it could have happened when the wires were torn out of that upset lamp.'

VanSlack says: 'Oh yes—an electrician. Certainly.'

Nick says: 'You know about Sam Church?'

VanSlack says: 'Yes—and the Negro. We're doing everything we can to catch them, of course. But sometimes it's so hard to find people. Now there are a couple of other things I'd like to ask your help on.'

Nick, imitating VanSlack: 'My help—oh yes—certainly.'

Elsewhere in the house, other members of the household are being questioned separately.

In the living room a uniformed trooper is saying to Dudley Horn: 'So you were asleep, huh? How long had you been asleep?'

Horn, who has put on some clothes, answers: 'Half an hour—maybe three-quarters.'

The Trooper asks: 'What were you doing before that?'

Horn says: 'Miss MacFay and I had taken a walk.'

The Trooper says: 'Miss MacFay, huh? The daughter?'

Horn says: 'Yes. But if you'd stop wasting time here and start looking for Church—'

The Trooper interrupts him: 'I got a *lot* of time to waste. Did MacFay know you and his daughter were out walking?'

Horn says: 'Of course. I don't know. What difference does that make? Miss MacFay and I are engaged.'

Trooper: 'Oh! So you're marrying the heiress? She *is* the heiress, isn't she?'

Horn says: 'I suppose so. I don't actually know.'

The Trooper says: 'Hmm! A while back you said you used to work with this fellow Church. Are you and he still pretty close?'

Horn says: 'We were never pretty close.'

The Trooper says: 'Oh! You didn't like each other much, huh?'

Horn says: 'That's right.'

The Trooper says: 'Well, are you unfriends enough that it wouldn't make you mad to see him go back to the can or maybe to the chair?'

Horn stands up, saying indignantly: 'If you're suggesting that I would frame him—'

The trooper puts a hand on Horn's chest and pushes him back into his chair, saying: 'Don't get sore over a little thing like that. Wait'll you hear what I'm really going to suggest.'

In another downstairs room, Mrs Bellam, the housekeeper, is being questioned by a little, plump man in clothes that need pressing.

The Plump Man says: 'Ain't that pretty late for a lady your age to be up?'

Mrs Bellam: 'I don't think so.'

The Plump Man: 'What time do you mostly go to bed?'

Mrs Bellam: 'Not often before two o'clock, and sometimes it's three or four.'

The Plump Man: 'Got things on your mind that worry you, keep you awake?'

Mrs Bellam: 'No, it's just that I don't sleep very much.'

Plump Man: 'What were you doing when you heard the shot?'

Mrs Bellam: 'Reading.'

Plump Man: 'Reading what?'

Mrs Bellam: 'The Bible.'

Plump Man: 'Oh!' then, after a pause: 'Well, that's all right. How long had you been in your room?'

Mrs Bellam: 'I went up there about eleven o'clock.'

Plump Man: 'Were you undressed?'

Mrs Bellam: 'No.'

Plump Man: 'And you were in your room all the time from around eleven till you heard the shot?'

Mrs Bellam: 'That's right.'

Plump Man: 'And you didn't see or hear anything out of the ordinary till you got to his room and saw the others there?'

Mrs Bellam: 'Not a single thing except the shot.'

Plump Man: 'What did you think when you found out the old man had been killed?'

Mrs Bellam: 'I was sorry.'

Plump Man: 'You and the Colonel get along pretty well?'

She says: 'Yes. I always know what to expect from Colonel MacFay and I never expected anything different.'

The Plump Man thinks that over for a moment, then gives it up and asks: 'Who gets the old man's money?'

She says: 'I'm sure I don't know except I always thought it would go to Miss Lois.'

He asks: 'Will you get any of it?'

She answers: 'I'd be mighty surprised if I did.'

He says: 'You've been working for the old man a long time, haven't you?'

Mrs Bellam: 'Sixteen years.'

The Plump Man: 'And you used to know this Sam Church when *he* worked for the old man?'

Mrs Bellam: 'Yes, indeed, I knew him.'

The Plump Man: 'All right, then, make yourself comfortable and we'll have a long talk about what you know about him.'

In his bedroom, Freddie is being questioned by an elderly detective who from time to time jots down notes on pieces of paper he takes from various pockets, apparently never using the same piece twice.

The Detective says: 'Now, son, when you left the old man in his room after midnight, what did you do?'

Freddie says: 'I came here.'

Detective: 'Straight here?'

Freddie: 'Yes, sir.'

Detective: 'You didn't hear or see anything until the shot came?'

Freddie: 'That's right.'

Detective: 'Where were you when you heard it—in bed?'

Freddie: 'No, sir.'

Detective: 'Where were you?'

Freddie: 'Sitting at that table.'

Detective: 'Undressed yet?'

Freddie: 'No sir.'

Detective: 'Well, you must have been doing something.'

Freddie: 'I—I had some work to do. I was writing.'

Detective: 'Writing what?'

Freddie stammers and finally says: 'A play. I'm trying to write a play.'

Detective, in a tone of slight surprise, says: 'Oh, go on!' Then: 'What's it called?'

Freddie: "The Minute-Hand."

Detective: 'Yes? Let me see it.'

Freddie goes to the table and gives him a handful of manuscript pages written in longhand.

The Detective says: 'You're a private secretary—how is it you don't write this on one of those typewriters?'

Freddie: 'I only get a chance to work on it late at night and I was afraid the typewriter would disturb people. Besides, when you're writing your first play, you kind of don't like people to know about it.'

The detective, puzzled by this, looks at Freddie for a moment, then begins to read the play.

Presently, the Detective puts the manuscript down on his knee and says: 'So you write about murders, huh? Do you think much about murders?'

Freddie says: 'It's a mystery play. Lots of people write mystery plays.'

The Detective says: 'They do? You wouldn't happen to make a hobby of what they call criminology?'

Freddie: 'No sir.'

Detective: 'Well, I'll have to show this to VanSlack. He might think it kind of shows how your mind works—what they call psychology.' He looks down at the manuscript. 'This isn't all of it, is it?'

Freddie says: 'No sir. I haven't finished the second act.'

The Detective says: 'Hmmm! And how many acts now would a play have?'

Freddie: 'Three.'

Detective: 'Maybe you can write the rest of it while VanSlack's reading this. Who is MacFay's lawyer?'

Freddie: 'Floyd Tanner.'

Detective: 'The one that's always in some jam with the income tax people?'

Freddie: 'I don't know about that.'

Detective: 'When's the last time MacFay made a will?'

Freddie: 'About seven months ago, I think.'

Detective: 'Well, who gets the money?'

Freddie: 'I don't know whether I ought to—'

Detective: 'This is a murder we're trying to clear up, lad, and the more you can tell us the better. So don't let's hang up over who's going to tell what.'

Freddie: 'According to the memorandum I typed, Miss MacFay was to get everything except a hundred thousand dollars. That went to Mrs Bellam, the housekeeper.'

Detective: 'How much do you figure everything but a hundred thousand would amount to?'

Freddie: 'I don't know. It would certainly be several million, but I don't suppose anybody but Colonel MacFay knew exactly what property he had.'

Detective: 'Where do these Charles people fit in?'

Freddie: 'Why, they—they have money invested in some properties with the Colonel.'

Detective: 'And they never had any trouble with the Colonel over their money?'

Freddie: 'No—nothing—nothing to pay any attention to. Of course not.'

Detective: 'What was there not to pay any attention to?'

Freddie: 'Nothing. It was just a joke. He was laughing tonight about their wanting to examine the accounts for the first time and how he kept Mr Charles up to his neck in figures for eight solid hours without Mr Charles being able to tell a decimal point from a debit.'

Detective: 'How do you tell a—never mind. What came up that Charles wanted all of a sudden to examine the accounts?'

Freddie: 'Nothing. It was just a joke. Even Colonel MacFay thought it was funny.'

Detective: 'A sense of humor. That's got men killed before.'

Freddie: 'But you can't—'

Detective: 'Take it easy, lad. I'm going to give you a little rest now, but don't be going out of the house.'

The detective goes down to the living room, where the uniformed trooper is still questioning Horn. The detective and the trooper whisper together for a moment in a corner of the room, then go back to Horn.

Trooper: 'You been working for MacFay a long time; so has this Bellam woman. What's the connection?'

Horn: 'Between her and me? None.'

Detective: 'She gets a hundred grand in his will.'

Horn: 'What's that got to do with me?'

Trooper: 'You're marrying his daughter who gets the rest of his dough.'

Horn: 'What's that got to do with Mrs Bellam?'

Detective: 'It's a coincidence.'

Trooper: 'What makes Bellam rate a hundred gees?'

Horn: 'It's none of my business, but I'll tell you. Years ago she was MacFay's girl. Then they drifted apart and she got married, and then after her husband died and left her without a nickel the old man took her in as housekeeper.'

Trooper: 'Just as housekeeper?'

Horn nods.

Detective: 'That's kind of sweet.'

Trooper: 'He adopted this Lois: could she be Bellam's daughter?'

Horn: 'No. He took Lois from an orphanage. Her mother's name was Shelley and she died when Lois was born. You can check that.'

Detective: 'We will. What's the tie-up between Charles and Church?'

Horn: 'There's no tie-up! Church had threatened him, too.'

Trooper: 'Yeah? Well, do you think Charles is the type of man that might have killed the Colonel to frame Church?'

Horn stares open-mouthed at the trooper.

IN MACFAY'S OFFICE

VanSlack is keeping in touch with New York City and the surrounding country by telephone, meanwhile receiving information from and giving instructions to men who pass in and out of the room. Nick is sitting on a corner of the desk; a couple of VanSlack's men are lounging by the window.

Nick: 'Did you people have a man watching Church?'

VanSlack: 'No. The sheriff's office was keeping an eye on him in a way, but we didn't have anybody actually watching him. I suppose there will be a lot of complaining about that now. People will be saying we should have covered Church day and night after Colonel MacFay came to us, but I didn't see how we could have guessed it was going to turn out like this. You know yourself it was all pretty ridiculous in a way and could have turned out to be just a kind of bad practical joke. Couldn't it?'

Nick nods.

VanSlack: 'Did you have any special reason for thinking we had a man on Church's tail?'

Nick says: 'When I went down to see Church yesterday morning, there was a chap up on the hill keeping tabs on him with field glasses and, when I tried to strike up a conversation with him, he showed me a buzzer and told me to go chase myself.'

VanSlack: 'Really? What kind of looking man was he?'

Nick describes Vogel.

VanSlack looks questioningly at the other men in the room. They all shake their heads.

VanSlack says: 'That's peculiar, because I don't know of anybody around here who looks like that.'

Nick says: 'I thought it was peculiar—I'd never seen a country cop with a new six-thousand-dollar coupé before, so I wrote the license number down.'

VanSlack says: 'That's splendid. Will you get it?'

Nick goes to his bedroom. Nick Jr. is asleep on one of the beds. Lois, sitting in a chair by the window, has recovered some of her composure. Nora is encouraging her to drink a cup of coffee.

They both turn to Nick as he comes in and Nora asks: 'Have they found anything?'

Nick says: 'They haven't found Church or his black man yet, if that's what you mean, but he can't have much of a start.'

Lois says: 'Do you suppose he did it?'

Nick looks at her in slight surprise, asking: 'Don't you?'

She says: 'Oh yes—he must have. Don't pay any attention to me.'

Nick has crossed to a closet and is hunting through his coat for the paper on which he wrote the license number.

He asks: 'Did you have your session with the police?'

Nora says: 'Yes. They were very sweet. I think detectives' manners have improved since your day.'

He finds his piece of paper.

Lois asks: 'Could I—do you think they'd let me see Papa now?'

Nick shakes his head at Nora, who begins to explain to Lois why it is best not to see her father now, as Nick escapes.

In the hall, at the head of the stairs, Nick meets Freddie.

Freddie: 'Is she all right?'

Nick says: 'Lois? I think so.'

Freddie: 'Do you think she'd like to see me?'

Nick: 'You could try.'

Freddie: 'Will these policemen be here long?'

Nick says: 'Most likely. They tell me they don't often get a chance to play at being scientific detectives, so they'll probably make the most of it. Why? Do they bother you?'

Freddie: 'No, but I wish they'd clear out.'

Horn and the trooper who was questioning him come up the stairs together.

Nick, holding out the slip of paper with the license number on it to the trooper: 'Will you give this to Mr VanSlack for me and tell him I'm taking time out to dress?'

The Trooper, taking the paper: 'Sure thing.'

Horn, going over to Lois: 'How are you now, darling?'

Lois: 'I'm all right.'

Freddie hovers over them, smiling an aimless smile that is meant to be cheering.

Nick moves between bedroom and bathroom, dressing.

Lois: 'I think I would feel better if somebody told me whether Papa—did he die without—'

Horn: 'There was no pain, dear; he died instantly.'

Lois: 'Where—where was he shot?'

Horn: 'Your father fired that, at the murderer. Don't let's talk about it now.'

Lois: 'But I want to talk about it. I want to face it. I don't want to baby myself. Do you think the police are enough, or should we get somebody to help them?'

Horn, bitterly: 'From my experience with them, I'd say they were being thorough enough anyway.'

Lois: 'Do you mean they questioned you?'

Horn: 'They did everything but jail me, and that can still happen.'

Lois: 'Don't be unreasonable, dear. You know they have to suspect everybody.'

Horn grumbles: 'I don't know it. I think Church would be enough.'

Lois: 'Did they question you, Freddie?'

Freddie: 'Yes. They haven't much respect for anybody's privacy, but I really didn't mind.' He sits down on the baby.

Nick, Nora, Lois, and Horn all yell warnings at Freddie, but too late. Nora runs over to pick up the baby. Nick Jr. does not cry, but scowls unpleasantly at Freddie, and says: 'Drunk.'

Freddie: 'I'm sorry! I'm—did I—'

The door bursts open and half a dozen detectives and troopers with guns in their hands come running in bawling: 'What is it? What's the matter? What's going on here?'

Reporters try to crowd into the room behind the police.

Nora, indignantly: 'How would you like somebody to sit on your baby?'

One of the troopers: 'If you're talking about my baby, it would do her plenty of good.'

The reporters, seeing Nick, begin to call: 'There he is. Hello, Nick. These mugs didn't want to let us see you,' etc.

The police herd the reporters out of the room as VanSlack comes in.

One of the detectives: 'It's nothing, Van. They're just horsing around.'

VanSlack, vaguely: 'Is that so?' Then to Nick: 'That license number belongs to a man named Vogel, a gambler-racketeer, and his description seems to fit the man you saw. The New York police think they can get hold of him for us. Do you—that is, I'm going in to see him and that Smith woman you told me about. Would you care to go along?'

Nick: 'If you think I'd be any help.'

Nora: 'Then I'm going, too. I'm not going to keep Nicky down here with nothing but a lot of country pol—' She breaks off in consternation, staring at the country policemen around her, gulps, says, 'country pol—' again while hunting desperately for an out, finds it, and finishes triumphantly '—country poultry to eat. You know he's on a diet.'

Nick goes over and kisses her, saying: 'Sweetheart, you are wonderful. I wouldn't have believed anybody could get out of that one.'

Nora, with mock modesty: 'It was nothing really.'

One policeman to another: 'How do you like them to do until a couple of real screwballs come along?'

VanSlack to Nora: 'I can appreciate your feelings, Mrs Charles. Naturally you think—with everything that's happened—I understand. But—well—we'd like to get away without attracting the attention of the newspaper men and we'll be in pretty much of a hurry. It might not be so comfortable for—and you'll be perfectly safe here with—or if you want you can follow us in as soon as you're ready and a couple of my men will ride in with you.'

Nick, imitating VanSlack: 'Yes, dear, you can—I think it would give you time—there's always another—and there you are.'

A trooper comes in panting: 'There's a dog running around outside with a knife in his mouth.'

Nick and Nora exclaim: 'Asta!' together.

Outside it is still night. With the help of lights that range in size from searchlights mounted on automobiles to flashlights carried in hands, policemen are trying to corner Asta, who, holding in his mouth a knife similar to the one seen in Dum-Dum's possession, dashes across an open space and disappears into darkness behind a row of shrubs.

At an upstairs window, Freddie and Mrs Bellam can be seen looking down at the men chasing the dog.

As Nick and VanSlack come up, one of the troopers says: 'We're going to have to shoot that mutt; we'll never catch him this way.'

VanSlack: 'First we'll see if Mr Charles—it's Mr Charles's dog—perhaps he can help us.'

Nick: 'Where did he find the knife?'

Trooper, pointing: 'We don't know. He came around thataway with it.'

Nick: 'Where is he now?'

Trooper, pointing in the opposite direction: 'We don't know. He went around thataway with it.'

Nick whistles and calls to Asta, with no result.

Trooper: 'A guy that can't make his dog mind ought to trade it in for goldfish or something.'

Nick, pretending he hasn't heard the trooper, calls again, then says: 'He's not going to come running up to a lot of strange men with lights. What do you think he is, a moth? Call your men back and give me a flashlight.'

VanSlack sends a trooper to call back the men who are trying to corner Asta, and Nick, armed with a flashlight, whistling and calling as he goes, moves off into the darkness. Presently he finds Asta in the same folded beach umbrella in which the dog hid after the killing of Lois's collie.

As Nick takes the knife from Asta and straightens up, he hears somebody approaching stealthily. He switches off his light, moves a little to one side, and crouches there with his hand on his gun.

Lois's voice comes through the darkness, whispering: 'It's Lois, Mr Charles. I want to—'

Nick, as she comes up to him: 'What are you doing running around out here?'

Lois: 'I had to see you away from the police.' She stands so that Nick, to face her, must turn his back toward a dark clump of bushes not far away. Then she starts as she sees the knife in Nick's hand, and asks: 'Is that the—is that the one?'

Nick: 'Probably.'

Lois: 'Oh, Mr Charles, I've got a horrible question to ask you. Will you tell me the truth?'

Nick: 'If I can.'

Lois: 'You've got to. There's nobody else I can turn to. I don't know what to—' Looking over Nick's shoulder, she sees a man with a gun in his hand emerge from the clump of bushes behind Nick. Lois gasps, 'Look out!' and pushes Nick to one side as the man fires. (It must be obvious that she does save Nick from being shot.)

Nick, upset by the girl's push, yanks his gun out as he falls, and fires as the man near the bushes shoots a second time. The man staggers back into the bushes and from time to time fires again, with Nick, circling the bushes, returning his fire.

Police come running up, pouring bullets into the bushes. The grounds are flooded with lights again. Presently the firing stops, and Nick and the police force their way into the clump of bushes.

Dudley Horn is lying there dead, the ragged condition of his clothes suggesting that he has been nearly shot to pieces. The police stare at him in surprise.

Trooper: 'Him! Can you beat that?' Then he suddenly looks sharply at Nick and demands: 'Say, what were you shooting at him for?'

Nick: 'Because he was shooting at me. What were you shooting at him for?'

Trooper, scratching his head: 'Well, everybody else was.'

VanSlack arrives, stares at Horn, says: 'This is a surprise in a way. Do you mind telling me what—how it happened?

Nick: 'I was taking the knife'—he hands the knife to VanSlack— 'away from the dog when Lois MacFay came up and started to tell me something. Then she yelled and pushed me out of the way just as this fellow started snapping caps at me.'

VanSlack: 'Lois MacFay, hum? Do you—the question will surprise you no doubt—but do you think she might have been—you know?'

Nick: 'Putting me on the spot? The first bullet would have caught me if she hadn't pushed me out of the way. I felt it go past.'

VanSlack: 'It was just a thought. Where is she?'

Nick looks around. 'I don't know.'

Police throw the beams from their lights across the grounds. Lois is lying on the grass back where Nick was first shot at, apparently unconscious, with blood staining her clothes.

Nick kneels beside her, feeling for a pulse, then says: 'She's alive.'

Another of the men says: 'It's just her arm,' and opens a knife to rip her sleeve.

Lois's eyes open. She sees Nick and asks: 'Was it—Dudley?'

Nick: 'Yes.'

Lois shudders, then asks: 'Did they catch him?'

Nick: 'He's dead.'

Lois shuts her eyes.

The man who has been examining Lois's arm says: 'She'll be okay. The bullet only took a hunk of flesh out.'

VanSlack: 'Well, let's carry her up to the house. I want to talk to her when she comes to.' Then to Nick: 'What was it she started to tell you?'

Lois opens her eyes again and sits up, saying: 'I'm not badly hurt. It was the shock. Oh, Nick, it was true then!'

Nick: 'What was true?'

Lois: 'What I tried to tell you, about Dudley.' She begins to cry. 'Oh, it can't be true. I loved him so.'

Nick: 'He killed Colonel MacFay?'

Lois: 'That's what I wanted to ask you.'

VanSlack: 'I don't want to seem unkind, Miss MacFay, but surely you can see that all this might have been avoided if you had come to us with your suspicions, whatever they were.'

Lois: 'I know, but how could I believe it? I can't believe it now.'

VanSlack: 'It's not a matter of what you believe, Miss MacFay, it's more—well—what happened that you wanted to talk to Mr Charles about? '

Lois: 'It was about Dudley. He—it started right after Papa was killed. Dudley suggested that we say we were together at the time Papa was killed—so the police wouldn't bother me, he said. I told him we couldn't do that, but I didn't think anything of it until later when he began to act funny.

VanSlack: 'Funny in just what way?

Lois: 'Nothing that anyone who didn't know him so well would notice, but I noticed it. And then after that policeman said the knife had been found, and you and Mr Charles went out, he acted still funnier, and when he went out of the room I followed him to ask him what was the matter, I saw him in his room putting a pistol in his pocket, and then I didn't know what to think except that I'd better find Mr Charles as soon as possible and ask him what he thought.'

(Those of Horn's actions which fit in with her story may be shown in their proper place if necessary, depending on whether it is thought better to bolster up her story than to keep the audience in doubt as to who Nick's assailant is until the last moment.)

* * *

Nick and VanSlack are together in the rear of a car being driven toward New York City. The sun is not yet up, though it is fairly light.

VanSlack: 'It's amazing the obstacles one runs into in this work, isn't it?'

Nick: 'Oh, quite.'

VanSlack: 'It's so unfortunate that your dog should have found the knife with nobody around to see where he found it. Now we'll probably never know.'

Nick: 'I'm apologizing. No fingerprints on the knife?'

VanSlack: 'There'd hardly be, after the dog had been playing with it for nobody knows how long. Though there are plenty of his tooth prints on it. But I daresay we can safely assume it was the knife used for the murder. Don't you think so?'

Nick: 'I think so.' After a pause. 'How do you fit Horn into all this?'

VanSlack: 'I should ask you that. After all, you're the one who killed him.'

Nick: 'Maybe I am, maybe not. A lot of you people were shooting at him, too. All we know is that I am the one he was trying to kill.'

VanSlack: 'Doesn't that come to the same thing in a sense?' Looks at his watch. 'Now that you have had time to think, perhaps you can remember something—something that happened or was said—that might have slipped your memory in the excitement... if you know what I mean.'

Nick: 'I know what you mean. You mean if I've been holding out on you, you'll make it easy for me to come clean now.'

VanSlack: 'Not at all, Mr Charles. Well, not exactly. But perhaps Miss MacFay's story was not...'

Nick: 'Miss MacFay may be a liar but that was a truthful bullet she pushed me out of the way of.'

VanSlack, sighing: 'I suppose it was, but it makes the whole thing more confusing, doesn't it?'

Nick, shrugging: 'Maybe yes, maybe no. All we've got to find out is why Horn should try to kill me when I found the knife that killed MacFay and that belonged to Church's henchman.'

VanSlack: 'That's exactly it, and I must say that from my viewpoint everything would be clearer if it were not for your statements that Miss MacFay was with you and Mrs Charles at the time of her father's murder and that she did save you from being killed by Horn.'

Nick: 'What do you want me to do? Confess that Horn killed me?'

VanSlack, his voice and manner for the first time cold and menacing: 'What I want you to do, Mr Charles, is to tell me the truth.'

Nick stares at him a moment, then laughs. 'You know, I am beginning to think you've really got hold of something, even if you don't know what it is or what to do with it. My guess is you are bouncing around not more than six inches away from the answer to the whole thing.'

VanSlack looks down at the space between him and Nick on the seat of the car. The space is about six inches.

Back at MacFay's Lois is lying on her bed with her eyes shut. Mrs Bellam sits in a chair beside the bed, placidly knitting.

Mrs Bellam: 'Whatever Mr Horn did in this world, he is now answering for in the other world and it is not for us to judge him.'

Lois, opening her eyes, sitting up: 'But why did he kill Papa?'

Mrs Bellam: 'Lie down, dear. Men's hearts are incomprehensible.'

Lois: 'But Papa was so good to Dudley. He—'

Mrs Bellam: 'How are we, with our limited understandings, to say what is good and what is not good?' She pauses to count a row of stitches. 'It would be easy for us in our worldliness to say that Colonel MacFay was the most wicked man that ever lived, but how can we look into his inner soul?'

Lois: 'But nobody could say that. He wasn't. He wasn't.'

Mrs Bellam, quietly as before: 'Only by human standards, my dear.'

Lois: 'But look how good he was to me, and to Dudley.'

Mrs Bellam: 'Colonel MacFay was afraid of Dudley Horn. Dudley Horn knew too much about him, even knew how he was robbing that nice Mr and Mrs Charles.'

Lois: 'Oh, he wasn't!'

Mrs Bellam, calmly nodding: 'I'm only telling you that because I imagine it will come to light anyhow. Dudley Horn would most surely have taken the precaution of leaving a statement somewhere to be published in case he was killed. He would have thought that would tie Colonel MacFay's hands.'

Lois: 'But then why should Dudley have tried to kill Mr Charles?'

Mrs Bellam: 'If Mr Charles had discovered his losses in going over the accounts yesterday, the estate would have had to make them good, my dear.'

Lois: 'Go away, please, Mrs Bellam.' She turns over, burying her head in the pillow. 'Go away.'

Mrs Bellam: 'Try to rest, my dear.' She gathers up her knitting, rises, and goes quietly out.

Freddie, listening outside the door, jumps back in confusion as Mrs Bellam comes out of the room.

Mrs Bellam smiles tranquilly at Freddie, shuts the door behind her, and goes upstairs.

Freddie stares after Mrs Bellam for a moment, biting a fingernail, then looks at Lois's door in indecision, hears footsteps coming up the stairs from the ground floor, and goes off to his own room.

The man coming up the stairs is a detective. He goes into Nora's room, where she is being questioned by two detectives. Nick Jr. has gone to sleep holding Asta's tail. Asta is very uncomfortable, but afraid to try to pull away.

Detective: 'One o'clock in the morning's a funny time to have a alibi down here in the country—unless you were expecting something to happen. Were you?'

Nora: 'Of course not.'

The Detective: 'Nobody else had a alibi—just you and your husband and this Lois.'

Nora: 'It's a habit with Nick. He's had an alibi for everything that's happened since I married him.'

Detective: 'And a lot of things happen every place he goes, don't they?'

Nora: 'Never a dull moment is what all our friends say.'

Detective: 'Wasn't there a killing in your family that he was mixed up in out on the Coast a year or two ago?'

Nora: 'Do you mean wasn't there a killing that he solved while policemen were suspecting the wrong people?'

Detective: 'You can put it any way you want, but he was mixed up in it; and there was another woman mixed up in it, too, wasn't there?'

Nora: 'My cousin.'

Detective: 'I don't know anything about that. I just remember seeing her picture in the papers, and she was kind of young and pretty. Then he was mixed up in that Wynant murder last time he was in New York, and there was some women in that that he used to know before he was married, wasn't there?'

Nora: 'Just what are you getting at?'

Detective: 'Looks to me like every time he gets in with a gal the insurance companies take an awful beating. Say, that guy's deadlier than the Bourbon plague.'

Nora: 'But what has that got to do with Colonel MacFay's murder?' Detective: 'Lois. It's nice for a wife to trust her husband—in reason—but don't you ever get to wondering about him sometimes?'

Nora: '*Some*times?'

Detectivc: 'We're not just dishing the dirt on your husband for the fun of it. We're trying to show you what you're up against. It ain't in the book that any man that's had that many numbers would settle down to one, and you are too fine a lady to get that kind of runaround.'

Nora: 'Was he really like that? I thought he was just bragging.'

Detective: 'I suppose you never heard about the coalman's widow in Cleveland that wanted to set him up in a detective agency of his own.'

Nora, leading him on: 'Was that Louella?'

Detective: 'No, her name was Belle Spruce.'

Nora, delighted: 'I mustn't forget that one. Tell me more.'

Detective: 'Well, then there was a lighthouse keeper's daughter in—'

Nora: 'A what?'

Detective: 'A lighthouse keeper's daughter.'

Nora: 'What was her name?'

Detective, exasperated by her facetiousness: 'What it all comes down to is this Lois. You're wrong to think there couldn't be anything between them. They're just making a monkey of you covering up for them.'

A New Arrival: 'Hey.' The second detective turns to him. 'Are you getting anywhere?'

Detective: 'Naw, she's bats.'

Second Detective: 'I wouldn't mind my old lady being bats that way.'

New Arrival to Nora: 'There's a telephone call for you.' He winks at the others.

First Detective to Nora: 'Go ahead, take it. We're through with you.'

Nora: 'I'm sorry. You've no idea how interesting this sort of thing can be to a wife. Please tell me the lighthouse keeper's daughter's name.'

As the three men go out, the Detective says, 'Letty Finhaden,' and slams the door.

Nora, happily, to the sleeping baby: 'And Letty Finhaden. Isn't your papa going to be surprised at the things your mama knows?' She goes to the telephone.

In New York City Nick and VanSlack buy morning papers with screaming headlines—ANOTHER THIN MAN MURDER MYSTERY—LONG ISLAND MILLIONAIRE KILLED—NICK CHARLES GUEST OF SLAIN CAPITALIST EX-CONVICT AND NEGRO SOUGHT BY POLICE, ETC. Nick's photograph occupies the chief position on most front pages, with MacFay's and Church's (a rogues' gallery photograph) flanking it.

As Nick and VanSlack prepare to drive on, a bundle of extras is thrown to the newsdealer from a passing truck. They buy copies of the extras, whose headlines say—SECOND SLAYING IN LONG ISLAND THIN MAN MYSTERY–ENGINEER KILLED IN ATTACK ON NICK CHARLES, etc. There are more pictures of Nick, and one of Nora.

As they get out of their car in front of Smitty's apartment, they are joined by Lieutenant John Guild.

Nick: 'Hello, Guild.'

Guild, shaking Nick's hand warmly: 'I'm glad to see you back with us. Say, things sure pop when you're in town, don't they? Remember last time when folks were being killed all over the—'

Nick: 'Don't say that! I'm having enough trouble with VanSlack now. I've been on the wrong end of a third degree all morning.'

VanSlack looks reproachfully at Nick.

Guild: 'How are you, Mr VanSlack? I came over as soon as I heard you were trying to get a line on Smitty. But if your killing was at one o'clock this morning, she's in the clear. We had a plant on this joint from before midnight till way after three and we know she was in it all the time.'

VanSlack: 'Are you sure she couldn't—'

Guild: 'Dead sure. I saw her two-three times myself between twelve and three and it would take her easy an hour or an hour and a half each way to get down to MacFay's and back.'

Nick, beginning to grin: 'How did it happen you were watching her place?'

Guild: 'It turned out to be a false alarm, but she phoned me yesterday—' He breaks off as Nick's grin widens. 'Could she have been stringing me—using *me* to give her an alibi?'

Nick nods.

Guild, indignantly: 'She can't do that to me!' He leads the way into the apartment building.

They go up to Smitty's apartment and knock on the door. After a little while it is opened by Smitty in pajamas and robe.

Smitty, yawning: 'Good morning, Nick; good morning again, Lieutenant.' Then to VanSlack: 'Pleased to meet you.' She yawns again. 'Come on in and have some coffee before you tell me what Tip's been doing now.'

Guild: 'So you pick me to give you an alibi, huh? I've got to lose a night's sleep so you can duck a murder rap. Well, you're not ducking it. There's such a thing as complicity and—'

Smitty: 'Murder?'

Guild: 'What did you think was going to happen down at MacFay's after midnight?'

Smitty, holding up her right hand: 'I never thought it was going to be murder.'

VanSlack, edging in between her and the angry lieutenant: 'But you did expect something to happen down there.' Then, when she does not reply: 'Where is Church?'

Smitty: 'I don't know.'

VanSlack: 'When is he coming back?'

Smitty: 'He isn't coming back. He said he was going to Cuba.'

Guild, who has been looking in the closet, turns with a man's overcoat in his hand. 'Who does this belong to?'

Smitty: 'Sam.'

Guild empties the contents of its pockets on the table. They are a handkerchief, a pair of gloves, crumpled package of cigarettes, and a book of paper matches. 'What is his coat doing here if he ain't coming back?'

Smitty: 'It's been here two or three weeks.'

Guild, indicating the things he's taken from the coat pocket to Nick and VanSlack: 'There's nothing else in it.'

VanSlack to Smitty: 'Where is his servant, Dum-Dum?'

Guild continues to look around the apartment, opening drawers, looking under cushions, etc.

Smitty: 'I don't know. They went out of here around ten o'clock last night and that's the last I've seen or heard of them.'

VanSlack: 'Where were they going?'

Smitty: 'I don't know.'

VanSlack: 'But they left together.'

Smitty: 'No. Dum-Dum left first, and Sam went out maybe ten or fifteen minutes afterwards.' She turns to Nick. 'Please tell me on the level—was MacFay murdered?'

VanSlack, before Nick can reply: 'Why do you think MacFay was murdered?'

Smitty, holding up her right hand again. 'I knew Sam was trying to get dough out of MacFay, but I never knew he meant to kill him.'

VanSlack: 'But you know it now, don't you?'

Smitty: 'I don't know anything that's got anything to do with murders.'

VanSlack: 'Murders! Who else's murder was planned besides MacFay's?'

Smitty: 'I don't know about anybody's murder being planned.'

Guild: 'You're psychic, huh? You get yourself alibis for murders you don't know are going to happen.'

Smitty: 'I'll never need an alibi for murder because I'll never have anything to do with any murder.'

VanSlack: 'You know Mr Charles, don't you?'

Smitty: 'Sure.'

VanSlack: 'Were you present at a meeting between Church and Mr Charles yesterday morning?'

Smitty: 'That's right.'

VanSlack: 'Exactly what happened at that meeting?'

Smitty looks at Nick in bewilderment.

Nick, cheerfully: 'I'm a suspect, too. We must get together sometime and swap experiences.'

Smitty: 'What do you know about that? You cops don't even trust yourselves.'

VanSlack: 'What happened at that meeting?'

Smitty: 'They didn't get along very well. There was a lot of talk about who ought to give Sam some money and about Nick's father-in-law, who's dead as far as I could make out, and it wound up with Nick slugging Sam.'

VanSlack: 'Why did he slug him?'

Smitty: 'You know how men are.'

VanSlack: 'Did Church threaten Nick—and Nick's wife and kid?'

Smitty: 'Nick seemed to think so—and I guess he was right. Sam's likely to say anything when he gets going: he's the loosest-talking man.'

VanSlack: 'How long have you known Church?'

Smitty: 'Just since they sprung him. He was Tip's cellmate.'

VanSlack: 'It didn't take you long to tie up with him, did it?'

Smitty: 'We weren't playing for keeps. He said he needed a girl to stooge for him. I'm small-time stuff and it wasn't costing him much, but I'm not fronting for murder. If he's innocent, he can come clean, and if he's guilty I'm getting out from under.'

VanSlack: 'Just what do you mean by stooging for him?'

Smitty: 'There's a lot of rackets where it's handy to have a girl around.'

VanSlack: 'You mean in various blackmail rackets, for instance?'

Smitty: 'I mean in a lot of kinds of rackets—except murder.'

As VanSlack starts to ask his next question, the doorbell rings. Guild goes to the door and opens it.

Vogel, coming in: 'What are you doing here, Guild?' He looks at Nick and VanSlack.

Guild: 'Diamond-Back, I want you to meet Mr Nick Charles and Mr VanSlack, an assistant district attorney from the Island. This is Mr Vogel.' His manner toward Vogel is that of a policeman toward an influential politician whom he doesn't trust too much. 'We were asking Smitty some questions.'

Vogel: 'About Church, huh? I always figured he was a wrong gee.'

VanSlack: 'What do you know about him?'

Vogel: 'Me? Nothing except he was spending too much time hanging around Smitty.' He scowls at the woman. 'You haven't been unloading to these people yet, have you?'

Smitty, touching her knee: 'Only from here up.'

Vogel: 'I ought to take a smack at you.'

Smitty: 'But I'll not be the goat for any—'

Vogel: 'Shut up. Didn't you ever hear about talking through a lawyer? That's why mugs have got a slang name for them!'

VanSlack: 'I may as well tell you, Mr Vogel, that the lady has told enough to justify us holding her as a material witness at the very least.'

Vogel: 'Okay, hold her as long as you want, ask her all the questions you want, but let's have her lawyer there; and if you want to let her out on bail afterwards, make it any amount you want, but let's do it regular.'

VanSlack: 'Just what is your relationship to the people involved?'

Vogel: 'None. Call me a friend of the family.'

VanSlack, to Nick: 'Is this the man you saw watching Church's house?'

Nick: 'Yes.'

Smitty to Vogel: 'Why, you big ape!'

VanSlack: 'Well, what's the matter?'

Vogel: 'It won't get you very far. Tip's married to this baby and you know how it is when a guy's hanging on the wall upstate—he gets to worrying about things. So I been kind of keeping an eye on her for him. Well, I hear Church is going away and for all I know this cluck might think she's going away with him.'

VanSlack: 'Suppose she had gone away with Church.'

Vogel: 'That's supposing too much.'

VanSlack: 'You mean you would have stopped her? But just as a friend of the family.'

Vogel: 'Listen, chum. So Tip's a crummy little coffee-and-doughnut crook, but when I hit this town strickly on my insteps ten years ago he was the only guy in it that would give me a stake. Well, that boy can call on me for anything I got—money, time, or the gun.' He jerks a thumb at Guild. 'He can tell you I got a permit to carry *that*.'

VanSlack clears his throat and begins to slip back into his former vagueness: 'I think I can understand your feelings. Now in the course of—uh—watching over Mrs Smith, just what did you learn about Church that might help us?'

Vogel: 'Just nothing. You can get whatever you want to know out of Smitty—as soon as she gets her lawyer.'

Smitty to Vogel: 'So that's the way it's been.'

Vogel: 'What did you think was going on? Did you think I was hanging around because I was nuts about you?'

Nick: 'Don't let's quarrel with one another. The police are our natural enemies.'

VanSlack looks reproachfully at him again.

There is a noise from the direction of the kitchen. Guild dashes toward the kitchen, with the others following him, except for Nick, who stands looking after them. Through the open door Dum-Dum can be seen running down the service entrance. Guild and VanSlack dash out in pursuit of him with Smitty and Vogel following them more slowly.

Nick walks over to the table where Guild put the articles taken from Church's coat pocket, pokes at them with a finger, picks up the paper of matches, reads the advertisement on it—'West Indies Club'— tosses it back on the table, picks up his hat, and goes out.

He pauses at the top of the back stairs, looks down the well at a landing several floors below where Guild and VanSlack have caught Dum-Dum and are searching him. Guild finds the wooden-handled knife in his waistband.

VanSlack, staring at it in amazement, says: 'This is the knife MacFay was killed with, dog's tooth prints and all. It can't be.'

Nick smiles and turns away to descend by the other staircase.

Nick walks up a street in the Latin American section of Harlem. It is now broad daylight and the street is almost empty except for eight or ten men planted in doorways watching the West Indies Club. These men are obviously detectives, but Nick gives no sign that he notices them.

Nick goes into the West Indies Club, a not too Broadwayish establishment fairly full at this hour; its patrons are chiefly Latin American, with a sprinkling of New York underworld characters. On the small dance floor a West Indian boy and girl are singing and dancing a beguine to the music of a noisy native orchestra. Many of the customers are reading the newspaper accounts of MacFay's murder and discussing them: Church and Dum-Dum are well-known habitués of the place. At a large table a group of men is extremely interested in something that is hidden from us and from Nick by their backs.

As Nick appears in the doorway, one of the men looking at the newspapers sees him, nudges his neighbor, points to Nick's picture in the paper, then at Nick. Others recognize him by the same means.

The proprietor goes over to Nick, bowing, saying: 'Ah, Mr Nick Charles, is it not? And you are alone?'

Nick, accepting recognition as his due: 'The good are often alone.'

The proprietor, smiling: 'I fix it so you will not be good long.'

He leads Nick to a table near the orchestra where two or three girl entertainers are seated. Nick is welcomed with that special cordiality reserved for liberal spenders in Harlem late-spots.

The beguine over, one of the girls at the table signals the orchestra and gets up to do a special number for Nick. While she is working at it a waiter brings Nick a note, which reads:

Darling Nickie,

If you still remember poor little me and my little coal-yard in Cleveland, and can tear yourself away from your charming little playmates, won't you come over and have a little drinkie for old times' sake.

Adoringly,
Belle Spruce

Nick, to the waiter: 'Where did this come from?'

Waiter indicates the table men are crowded around.

Nick, seeing nothing but men: 'Is there a lady there?'

Waiter, enthusiastically: 'A lady? What a lady! If I didn't have to work for a living carrying drinks to these pigs!' He throws a kiss toward the hidden lady.

Nick, rising, straightening his tie, eluding the detaining hands of his tablemates: 'Well, well, old Belle Spruce.' He crosses to the crowded table, pats the shoulder of one of the men standing in his way, and, when the man steps aside, is face-to-face with Nora.

Nora, brightly: 'Why, Nickie, are you looking for somebody?'

Nick, looking at her, speaking as if with carefully controlled anger: 'Tonight, two nights ago, three times last week. How much longer did you think I was going on believing you had to sit up with your sister's sick baby?' Then sharply: 'Which is the man?' Then craftily, as he begins to look in turn at each of the men at the table: 'They tell me he limps a little.'

Each man, as Nick looks at him, walks away from the table with exaggerated agility, or firmness, or gracefulness, to show he is not lame. Nick quickly sits down at the table and says to the waiter: 'Take the rest of those chairs away and bring us two Bacardis and a menu. I'm starving.'

Nora, looking regretfully at her departed admirers: 'They were such nice men, Nick. One of them promised to teach me a new dance. And another was telling me how much I'd like Buenos Aires.'

Nick: 'With a blond wig? What are you doing here anyhow?'

Nora, putting a finger up beside her nose: 'I have a clue.'

Nick, with complete loss of interest: 'Oh, well, if that's all it is.'

Nora: 'I oughtn't to tell you.'

Nick, agreeably: 'Go ahead and don't.' Then, as the waiter arrives with their drinks and menus: 'What do you want to eat?'

Nora, sulking: 'I don't care. Anything you want.'

Nick, to the waiter: "Two more Bacardis, two orders of oysters on the half shell, two...' etc., etc. He orders two enormous and complicated meals. The waiter goes away.

Nora: 'You're going to feel very silly if you don't solve this mystery just because you were too smart-alecky to listen to my clue.'

Nick: 'Don't get mad—I'll listen.'

Nora: 'You don't have to listen. Just give me the fourteen dollars and seventy-five cents.'

Nick: 'What fourteen dollars and which seventy-five cents?'

Nora: 'For the man.'

Nick, patiently: 'What man?'

Nora: 'The man who phoned me.'

Nick: 'Let's get this straight. A man phoned you and—'

Nora: 'No, he phoned *you*.'

Nick: 'A man phoned me and I promised him fourteen dollars and seventy-five cents?'

Nora: 'Yes. I did. You weren't there.'

Nick: 'I wasn't where?'

Nora: 'You're just trying to get me mixed up. At MacFay's, after you left, a man phoned you, a man with an accent, and when you weren't there he talked to me, and he said he'd seen in the paper that you were hunting for Church and Dum-Dum and he could tell you where to find Dum-Dum if you met him here. He said not to bring the police because he was not a stool-pigeon and he only wanted fourteen dollars and seventy-five cents because that was what Dum-Dum owed him and wouldn't pay and the whole thing was between gentlemen. He kept saying the whole thing was between gentlemen.'

Nick: 'That must have made you feel pretty much an outsider. Where did he say Dum-Dum is?'

Nora: 'He didn't say.'

Nick: 'Is that why we're going to give him fourteen dollars and seventy-five cents?'

Nora: 'No. He hasn't had a chance to speak to me yet. All those nice men came over and began to talk to me, so there wasn't much privacy.'

Nick, as the waiter brings their fresh drinks and the oysters: 'I'm sorry I chased them away. For fourteen seventy-five they can come back.'

Nora, rising as the orchestra begins to play again: 'They don't have to. I'm going to dance with my new teacher.' She goes over to one of the men who had been at her table, and they dance.

The girl entertainer who had done a number for Nick, now seeing him alone, comes over to his table. Her face lights up when she sees the two orders of oysters in front of him and she asks: 'What are you doing later?'

Nick starts to answer her, then breaks off as he sees Dum-Dum coming into the Club. Dum-Dum is making a smiling entrance, bowing to acquaintances right and left, and when he sees Nick he comes straight to his table.

Dum-Dum, to the entertainer: 'Mr Charles my friend. You sharpen the teeth someplace else. Scram, scram.'

The girl goes away.

Nick: 'Make out all right with the police?'

Dum-Dum: 'Always I do. Last night I get drunk and go to sleep in a vestibule and they lock me up until a couple hours ago I get sober. Those policemen from Long Island, they don't believe me, but they believe policemen in station-house when I take them there.'

Nick: 'How about Church? Is he making out all right?'

Dum-Dum, shaking his head: 'That I come to ask you. I do not know.'

Nick: 'Where do you think he is?'

Dum-Dum: 'I do not know.'

Nick: 'Think he killed MacFay?'

Dum-Dum, grinning: 'Does any man say he think his friend killed?'

Nick: 'MacFay was killed with a knife just like yours.'

Dum-Dum: 'The police tell me that. I think they tell lie to trick me. I never see another knife like that up here.'

On the dance floor, Nora has just begun to learn the new step when, each time she comes around close to the orchestra, she is thrown off by one of the musicians going, 'ps-s-s-s!' in her ear. She doesn't succeed in learning which musician it is, or why he is 'ps-s-sing' in her ear until the music stops. Then, as she moves off the floor, one of the musicians catches her eye and makes a double gesture—indicating Dum-Dum with a jerk of his thumb, rubbing the fingers of his other hand with that thumb to say 'Pay me.'

Nora nods and goes back to her table, accompanied by her dance partner. Thus encouraged, the other men who had been at her table begin to drift back to it, bringing chairs with them.

Nora, whispering to Nick: 'The man wants his money.'

Nick: 'All men want money. Greed, greed! It's the curse of the age.'

Nora: 'But he did help us find Dum-Dum.'

Nick: 'If he helped you, you pay him.' He turns to find his table is crowded with Nora's admirers, most of them busy just now ordering drinks on him of course.

Nora takes advantage of Nick's preoccupations with his guests to pick his pocket.

Sitting opposite Nick is a fat man the others call Cookie. He is very tight and talkative and none of the others seems to like him.

Cookie: 'I could tell you right now who killed most of the guys that get themselves killed in this man's town. A fellow that gets around as much as I do and keeps his eyes open and can put two and two together don't have to wait to read things in newspapers.'

One of the men, contemptuously: 'Okay, big lard, who knocked off A. R.?'

Cookie: 'Don't think I don't know, but you don't have to think I'm putting the finger on guys. Listen, I could ...' As he goes on, the orchestra begins to play again; one of the men at the table rises and bows to Nora, who gets up and goes off with him to dance, the money she took from Nick wadded in one hand. Dancing past the musician who had signaled her, she drops the money into his instrument.

Back at the table, Cookie is telling Nick: 'And I could tell you plenty about Sam Church, too. Many's the bottle him and me killed in this joint and over in that gal's flat he run around with, too.'

Nick: 'What girl? Smitty?'

Cookie: 'No—Linda Mills—the one he ditched, or got ditched by, before he took up with Smitty. A cute-looking kind of doll, I guess, under all that war-paint, but too plenty tough for me. Too plenty tough, I guess, for most guys—the way she didn't hold on to any of 'em very long. Lives over in the Chestevere Apartments.'

Nick: 'He must move around fast. I thought he'd only been back from Cuba ten days or so.'

Cookie: 'If you call this Cuba. He's been around these joints ever since he got out of stir. Say, you don't know no more about him than the police; and it's a cinch they're plenty wrong about him if they say Sam was mixed up in anything down on the Island last night. I seen him going in Vogel's at—'

Dum-Dum suddenly jumps up, reaches for his knife, which is not in its usual place at his waistband, then hits Cookie in the face with his fist. A waiter swings his tray high in the air with both hands and bangs it down on Cookie's head. As Cookie falls down on all fours another man hits him with a bottle, and then half a dozen are making flying leaps at him as the lights go out.

The orchestra, in the manner of a well-trained orchestra in a joint, continues, playing a little louder than usual. When the lights go on, Nora is one half of the only couple still dancing. Nick is the other half of the couple. Nora's former partner is coming out from under a table. Police are coming into the place. Cookie has disappeared.

Nick: 'Shall we rejoin our guests, Mrs Charles?'

Before Nora can reply, her former partner comes up to her holding one side of his jaw, saying: 'Are you all right? Something bumped into me something terrible.'

Nick looks down at the knuckles of his right hand, but does not say anything.

They return to their table. Their uneaten dinner is a smeary mess. The police are trying to find out what happened.

Dum-Dum: 'It is that Cookie. Always he want to start something—always a fight.'

Nick: 'I didn't see him do anything.'

Waiter: 'Aw, you can't wait till he does anything. It's too late then. You got to get the jump on him.'

Another man: "That's right. It's a kind of look he gets in his eye.'

Nick gives it up. He and Nora start to leave. Nick gets his hat and they start down the stairs.

Nora, stopping: 'Oh, Asta. I checked Asta.'

Nick returns to the hatcheck room and gets Asta, who has been sleeping on a pile of coats. When Asta gets up from them the hatcheck girl calmly begins to pick them up one at a time to hang them carefully on hangers.

As Nick and Nora go downstairs, Nick: 'Before we get outside, darling. We have a baby—remember? You didn't check that, did you?'

Nora: 'I left Nicky home with the policemen.'

Nick, as they go into the street: 'Oh, the policemen, of course. What policemen?'

Nora: 'That Lieutenant Guild sent up to the hotel to guard him. Oh, there's the park. Let's give Asta a little run in it before we go home.'

Nick, as they walk toward the park: 'Did you have a chance to count the policemen?'

Nora: 'I counted both of them.'

Nick: 'I'm glad there are only two.'

Nora: 'So am I, because they said they were going to stay with us till things quieted down if it took six months, and that they wouldn't be any trouble at all—we could just treat them like members of the family.'

They turn Asta loose in the park and sit down wearily on a bench, where Nora immediately falls asleep. Nick is thinking. He makes up his mind, calls Asta, ties him to the bench, gets up quietly, and leaves Asta and Nora there.

At the Chestevere Apartments Nick knocks on Linda Mills's door. There is the sound of movement in the apartment, but nobody opens the door. Nick knocks again.

The Chestevere landlady comes out of another apartment. She is a frowsy, middle-aged woman with the sniffles. In one hand she carries a newspaper, in the other a handkerchief.

Landlady: 'At this time of morning, mister, she's either asleep or ain't home yet.'

She peers sharply at Nick, then down at the newspaper in her hand.

Nick cranes his neck to see his picture in the paper, then strikes the pose shown in the picture.

Landlady, all agog: 'Say, you're him, ain't you?'

Nick bows.

Landlady, dabbing her nose with her handkerchief: 'Well, I declare. What are you—' She lowers her voice to a noisy whisper. 'Say, is she involved?'

Nick: 'Who?' he whispers. The next seven lines are spoken in whispers that would be audible at a distance of twenty feet or more.

Landlady, gesturing toward the door with her handkerchief: 'Mills.'

Nick: 'What makes you think she might be—involved, as you put it?'

Landlady: 'You being here—and then that friend of hers.'

Nick: 'What friend?'

Landlady, raising paper to show Church's picture—rogues' gallery picture: 'Him.'

Nick: 'Do you know him?'

Landlady: 'I seen him coming in and out.'

Nick: 'When's the last time you seen him?'

Landlady: 'I don't know. Maybe a couple of weeks. But that don't mean nothing. Sometimes I don't see my tenants for that long—them that ain't behind in their rent.'

Nick: 'What does Linda Mills do for a living?'

Landlady: 'What do you think these girls do? I don't run no Y.M.C.A. She's been here a couple of years and she's good pay. That's all I care about. That's what I tell some of the others when they kick about her throwing noisy parties sometimes and having fights in her flat.'

Nick: 'How's chances of finding out whether she's in now?'

Landlady: 'I'll see.'

She knocks on the door, then knocks louder, calling in an unnaturally sweet voice: 'Miss Mills. Miss Mills. It's me, Mrs Dolley.'

There is no answer. She dabs her nose with the handkerchief and takes a bunch of keys from her belt, unlocks the door, sticks her head in, and calls again: 'Miss Mills.' Then to Nick: 'I guess she ain't in all right.'

Nick, stepping into the apartment, pushing the door back against the wall and standing with a heel against it, holding it there: 'That's too bad. Will you do me a favor?'

Landlady: 'What?'

Nick: 'I left the district attorney sitting out front in my car. Will you ask him to come up?'

Landlady, impressed: 'Yes, sir.' She hurries away.

Cookie comes out sheepishly from behind the door. He has a black eye, a swollen ear, and his clothes are torn.

Cookie: 'I can explain everything if you just give me a chance.'

Nick: 'That's dandy. How about explaining that bag of nails at the West Indies.'

Cookie: 'Oh, that! Those guys get too excited.'

Nick: 'I agree with you, but the point is, what was it they got too excited about this morning?'

Cookie: 'I don't know—unless maybe they thought I hadn't ought to dragged Linda's name in.'

Nick: 'You mean they're old-fashioned gentlemen who think a woman's name shouldn't be bandied about a pub?'

Cookie: 'No, not exactly, but—I don't want to do the gal no harm. She and Sam Church don't pal around no more, so I don't see how I was tying her up in anything. That's what I came over here for after they threw me out of that dump—to tell her about it and see what she said.'

Nick: 'And?'

Cookie: 'No soap. She ain't home.'

Nick: 'How did you get in?'

Cookie: 'The door's unlocked. Try it yourself.'

Nick tries the door, finds it unlocked.

Nick: 'I've misunderstood the whole thing. I thought the boys ganged up on you when you mentioned Vogel's name.

Cookie: 'Vogel? What Vogel?'

Nick, patiently: 'You said Church wasn't down on the Island last night because you saw him going into Vogel's. And then the shindig was on.'

Cookie: 'Oh, sure, I remember now. I started to say I saw Sam going in Vogel's Delicatessen down on Third Avenue last night and he told me he was catching a 'leven o'clock train south, so I knew he couldn't have been down on Long Island way around one.'

Nick: 'Unless he was lying to you.'

Cookie, earnestly: 'But why would he lie to *me*?'

Nick: 'I give up. What Vogel is this that has the delicatessen?'

Cookie: 'Do I know? Sol Vogel or something.'

Nick: 'Not Diamond-Back Vogel?'

Cookie: 'You mean the gambler? What would he be doing with a delicatessen?'

The Landlady comes back, saying: 'I couldn't find no car out front with or without a district attorney.'

Nick: 'I'm sorry. He's such a restless fellow. Have you met Cookie?'

Landlady: 'I seen him somewhere, but I never met him.'

Nick: 'Cookie's a friend of Linda Mills.'

Landlady: 'Maybe. I seen him somewhere.'

Nick: 'Mind if I look around?'

He goes into the living room without waiting for the landlady's reply, then into the kitchen, and finally into the bedroom. The apartment is not dirty, but there are signs that Linda Mills is a careless housekeeper. The landlady complains about cigarette burns on a table and when she touches them, she gets dust on her fingers. The bed has not been made; its two pillows are on a chair beside the bed.

Nick notices an unfaded rectangle of wallpaper the size and shape of a nearby picture, looks behind the picture, and sees that the wallpaper behind it is faded the same shade as the uncovered paper—except where a small patch of white paper has been pasted over a small hole.

He goes over to the bed. On the floor beside the bed there is a scorched spot on the rug.

Nick: 'How long since either of you have seen this Mills girl?'

Cookie: 'Oh, I'd say ten days anyways, maybe longer.'

Landlady: 'I ain't seen her in a couple of weeks, but that ain't unusual. I don't see my people much most of the time—them that ain't behind with their rent.'

Nick: 'What does she look like?'

The landlady and Cookie collaborate in giving him a description that would fit either Lois MacFay or the nurse, Ella Waters, with allowances for heavy makeup, flashy clothes, a tougher manner, etc.

Nick, wandering around, opening drawers: 'She get much mail?'

Landlady: 'Not that I know anything about.'

Nick stops by a small table and, as if idly, thumbs the phone directory there.

Cookie, coming over to him, eagerly helping him turn the pages: 'See, there is Sol Vogel, the delicatessen on Third Avenue. See, I didn't lie to you. See.'

Nick, skeptically: 'I see it's in the book and I believe it's on Third Avenue, but I don't know how much further I can go with you.'

Cookie begins long-winded protestations of his trustworthiness, which continue while Nick leaves the apartment and walks down the street. Cookie trots along beside him, chattering away until they are in front of an electrical appliance shop.

(Nick then drops back, the CAMERA PANNING WITH COOKIE until he suddenly realizes he is alone, turns to look back, cannot see Nick, and, crestfallen, goes on alone.)

Presently Nick comes out of the electrical appliance shop, saying 'A million thanks' to someone inside, and goes off down the street.

When Nick returns to Nora and Asta in the park, she is still asleep. He starts to rouse her, then sits down beside her, starts once more, hesitates, his eyelids drooping, lifts his hand a couple of inches in another attempt, and goes to sleep beside her.

When they are finally awakened it is early afternoon.

In their suite at the Normandie, Nick and Nora find Nick Jr.'s guards — Detectives Dan Schultz and Red Jensen — playing cards. Nick Jr. is sitting under the table playing with a pistol.

Nora cries out in consternation.

Jensen: 'It's all right, lady. I took the bullets out. He can't hurt anything.'

Nick Jr. bangs the pistol down on Jensen's foot.

Schultz falls out of his chair laughing, gasping between laughs: 'That kid's a humdinger. I never seen anything like him.' He points at the child, who is staring with calm interest at Jensen holding his injured foot, and goes off into further roars of laughter.

Nora picks up Nick Jr., separates him from the pistol, and goes toward the bedroom. Asta grabs the pistol and heads for the kitchen with it, Jensen running after him.

Nick, to Schultz: 'We live like this.' He follows Nora into the bedroom, where he takes the child from her and begins to play with it.

Nora: 'Sh-h-h. You'll wake her up.'

Nick: 'Who?'

Nora, indicating door opposite the one they came in through: 'Didn't I tell you I brought Lois up with me?'

Nick: 'No, you didn't. Are you telling me now?'

Nora: 'But, Nick, I couldn't leave her down there alone with all those terrible things happening.' She puts a finger to her lips and goes over to open the other bedroom door. Nick goes with her.

In the next room Lois is lying in bed apparently asleep. There are no pillows on the bed.

As Nora softly shuts the door a commotion breaks out in the living room, that door opens, and Schultz sticks his head in.

Schultz: 'Hey! Gangrene's setting in out here.'

They go into the living room. The corridor door is open. Jensen is blocking the doorway, trying to keep out Creeps, Whacky, and six or eight of their friends, each with a child of some sort in tow.

Nora: 'The baby party!'

AN HOUR LATER, WITH THE BABY PARTY IN FULL BLAST. THE SCENE:

1. Creeps and Whacky tend the door, insisting that 'You can't come in unless you got a kid.'
2. Gilbert Wynant is slugged when Mimi tries to pass him off as a kid.
3. Bootleg business in kids being passed out at service chute at a dollar a head to be used as tickets of admission. Nick Jr. used for this purpose, as his guards have trouble telling one child from another and are satisfied to be guarding any child that is about the same age and size as Nick Jr.
4. Children of Nora's more social friends, some terrified by the thugs' brats, some delighted.
5. Mrs Bellam and Freddie come to see Lois, but are drowned in party before they see her. She is still asleep.
6. Assortment of gifts brought for Nicky, ranging from costly dolls to homemade blackjacks.
7. Creeps, with his collection of keys to fit every door in the hotel, throws open adjoining suites to the guests as Nick and Nora's suite becomes crowded. A very dainty young girl from one of the higher social levels follows him around in admiration, and when, in one of the suites they open, a man sits up in bed, she snarls at him: 'Nick Charles has brought his mob on from the Coast and we're taking the dump over for a little while, but you'll be okay if'n you stay

in bed with your head under the covers.' The man quickly takes her advice.

8. A drunk staring at the party in two layers—bending down, he sees a room full of children, playing, squabbling on the floor, with everything above them a hazy blur; standing erect he sees a riotous adult party, with the children blotted out by the haze.
9. Creeps and a thug near a telephone. Nick comes to phone, says to operator: 'Hello, darling, will you get me ....'s candy store.' Then: 'This is Nick Charles at the Normandie Hotel. Can you send me over [some candy suitable for children] right away? Thanks.' He hangs up, starts away from phone, then remembers something, and says: 'Creeps, will you phone the drugstore and order some... 'Creeps says: 'Sure, Nick,' picks up the phone and tells the operator: 'Sweetheart, will you get me the drugstore?' Then: 'Will you send... to Nick Charles at the Normandie Hotel?' The Thug, curiously: 'What do they do, send it up C.O.D.?' Creeps: 'No, these rich people don't have to bother about things like that. They pay for it downstairs and put it on the bill.' The Thug: 'Say, that ain't bad.' He picks up the telephone and says: 'Snooky, will you get me Tiffany's jewelry store?' Creeps takes the phone away from him.

FLASHES:

1. Smitty at her phone, saying heatedly: 'He's gone to the Normandie? He can't get away with that.' (It should seem that she may be speaking threateningly, though she is not.)
2. Dum-Dum, at drugstore phone, speaking to Smitty, saying softly but menacingly: 'Maybe you're right, but you stay away from there.' He hangs up, thinks for a moment, then leaves the store, steps into a taxi, and says to the driver: 'Drop me around the corner from the Normandie, Ted.'

3. Smitty getting up from phone, grabbing hat and coat, and leaving apartment.
4. Nick Jr.'s nurse walking up and down the street opposite the Normandie, starting toward it, then walking on a little way.
5. Vogel getting out of a car in front of the Normandie.
6. Church, his hat pulled down over his face, walking swiftly toward the Normandie.

Nora, in her bedroom, picks up the telephone and asks the operator: 'Will you ring my living room, please?'

In the living room, Nick answers the phone. The ensuing conversation is interrupted from time to time by one or another of his guests falling over him, etc.

Nora, in a disguised voice: 'Mr Charles?'

Nick: 'Yes.'

Nora: 'Oh, Nickie. Guess who this is.'

Nick: 'Oh, hello! It's good hearing your voice again. I didn't recognize it for a moment. How have you been?'

Nora: 'Who is it, then?'

Nick: 'Now you don't think I'd ever forget your voice.'

Nora: 'Yes, I do. Who am I?'

Nick: 'Okay, who are you?'

Nora: 'Oh, Nickie, to think you'd forget poor little me in just a few years.'

Nick: 'I know your voice as well as I do my own, but I just can't place it at the moment.'

Nora: 'It's Letty, Nickie!'

Nick: 'Who?'

Nora: 'Letty Finhaden. Don't you remember? My papa used to have a lighthouse.'

Nick: 'Of course... This connection is so bad and there is so much noise I can hardly hear you. How are you, darling?' He takes the Belle Spruce note from his pocket and nods at it.

Nora: 'I'm fine, but you had forgotten me completely.'

Nick: 'No, no. It's all this noise. I often think about you. How is your father?'

Nora: 'He's all right, except that he gets a little giddy climbing up and down those ladders. Can you meet me for lunch, Nickie?'

Nick: 'Not today, honey. I've been up all night and—'

Nora: 'How about tomorrow?'

Nick: 'Well, you'd better phone me in the morning. I've been so—'

Nora: 'I know what's the matter. That awful rich woman you married won't let you out. Tell me, Nickie, is she really as ghastly as everybody says?'

Nick: 'She's not as ghastly as *everybody* says.'

Nora, after a moment's struggle to stay in character: 'Hold the line a minute, Nickie. I hear Papa coming in his rowboat and I know he'd love to talk to you.' She hangs up gently.

In the living room, Nick makes a face at the telephone and hangs up, then goes over to straighten out a disagreement between a couple of his guests, after which he goes into the bedroom.

Nora, at the telephone, is saying: 'Will you ring my living room again, please?'

Nick: 'Who are you this time? That cooch dancer I used to run around with in Juarez? You have to do that with a Greek accent.'

Nora puts the phone down and turns toward him, then gasps and looks over his shoulder. Nick spins around.

Church is coming into the room from the fire-escape, one hand in his coat pocket as if pointing a pistol at Nick.

Church: 'I got no time to waste. Get your hands up.'

Nick puts them up, backing away until he is against the door leading to Lois's room. Church walks over to him.

Church: 'I missed connections and need getaway money. Come across.'

Nick, somewhat loudly: 'How much do you need, Church?'

Church: 'I'll take what you've got.' He runs his hand over Nick's clothes, finds his wallet, and takes it. He is very careless, giving Nick ample opportunity to grab him, but Nick makes no move in that direction.

Nora, watching her husband in proud anticipation at first, begins to look puzzled as he makes no attempt to disarm Church, even when Church's attention is centered on counting the money in the wallet.

Church, too, seems puzzled. He stands there awkwardly for a moment, until it is apparent that Nick is not going to grab him; then he says: 'If you're smart, you'll wait five minutes before you blow any whistles,' and goes out the window and up the fire-escape.

Nick, still standing with his back to Lois's door, says in a clear voice: 'I never saw anybody trying so hard to get caught as this Sam Church. And now look at the clown, going *up the fire-escape in broad daylight*'

Nora, who has been looking at Nick with almost tearful disillusionment, asks: 'But why would anybody want to get caught?'

Nick: 'Maybe because he thinks he could beat the rap now—and then he couldn't be tried again no matter what came out later.'

Nora: 'But—'

Nick: 'That's the law. What fooled all of us was our not thinking there was anything serious between him and Smitty, that they were just playing around.' Nick is sweating.

Nora: 'But what's—'

Nick: 'They're a couple of no-goods, but what I've got hold of now shows they're certainly two people in love with each other, if two people ever were. Wait till he gets off the fire-escape. I'll show you a—'

There is a sound of a shot from outside.

Nick starts and goes to the window. Nora goes with him. On the sidewalk below, Church is lying dead. Not far from him stands Smitty, staring at him. Near her on the sidewalk is a pistol. Dum-Dum is running away; as he reaches the corner a policeman jumps out and grabs him.

As Nick and Nora see these things from the window, Lois joins them, asking: 'I heard a shot—what is it?'

Nora leads Lois away from the window, then exclaims, 'Nickie!' and the three of them go into the living room.

There is a mad scramble of departing guests; thugs are grabbing their ticket-kiddies and hurriedly departing. Vogel, coming in, is caught in a jam of departers, and his glasses are knocked off and broken. He takes another pair from an inner pocket and puts them on.

Schultz and Jensen are standing guard over a child sleeping on a sofa. Nick and Nora do not see the child's face, though Lois does. Jensen assures them: 'This is our job and we're sticking with it, no matter who gets killed where.'

Police begin to come in, bringing Smitty, Dum-Dum, and Ella Waters. VanSlack and Guild arrive. Vogel does not try to leave. Mrs Bellam and Freddie try to go, but are detained.

VanSlack takes Nick into the bedroom and, after a bit of preliminary hemming and hawing, says: 'Look here, Mr Charles. You kidded me unmercifully about suspecting you, but I want to tell you right now that if Church did come here to make good his threats in connection with your wife and child and you killed him, I don't think any jury in the world would or should convict you.'

Nick: 'Let's go back with the others. They'll think we're talking about them.' He returns to the living room, followed by VanSlack.

Guild is questioning Smitty: 'What were you doing around here anyhow?'

Smitty: 'I knew Sam was coming to see Nick Charles and I wanted to head him off.'

Guild: 'Why?'

Smitty: 'I knew Sam would be up to some trick too slick for his own good and I knew he'd wind up in trouble—but I never expected this.'

Guild: 'How'd you know he was coming here?'

Smitty: 'Dum-Dum told me.'

Guild turns to Dum-Dum, who has been crying since he came in. He does not sob and his face is not contorted; it's simply that tears keep running down his cheeks.

Guild: 'Come on—talk.'

Dum-Dum: 'Mr Church told me he coming here. He did not say why. I did not ask. When Miss Smitty ask me, I tell her, and then I am sorry when she get excited, and I afraid she come over and butt in maybe, so I come to maybe stop her.'

Guild: 'And then what?'

Dum-Dum: 'I just had seen her and was going cross the street to talk to her—a truck get in my way—and when it pass I see her—and Mr Church.'

Guild: 'Didn't you hear the shot?'

Dum-Dum: 'No, sir. I am dodging noisy truck.'

Guild, to Smitty: 'What did you see?'

Smitty: 'I heard the shot, I think, though I didn't know what it was at the time.'

Guild: 'I didn't ask you what you heard. What did you see?'

Smitty: 'Just—I looked up and there was Sam falling down right in front of me. I didn't know who it was at the time. I—I don't think I knew until the copper grabbed me.'

Guild: 'Oh, you didn't? And you didn't know about the gun you dropped?'

Smitty: 'I didn't drop that gun. I heard it fall right after he fell, but I didn't drop it.'

Guild turns to Ella Waters: 'And what's your unlikely story, Hilda?'

Ella, turning to Nick and Nora: 'My name's really not Ella Waters. I took that after I got out of jail for shoplifting, but I was honestly trying to go straight, but I knew the police wouldn't believe it after Colonel MacFay was killed, and would find out from my fingerprints who I was, so I ran away; but I felt bad about it and was coming back to tell you about it, because I knew you'd understand, when there was all that excitement downstairs and a policeman that knew me grabbed me and brought me up here, but I—'

Guild stops her by putting a hand over her mouth, growling: 'You still talk more and say less than anybody I ever ran into.' He turns to Vogel: 'And what were you here for, Diamond-Back?'

Vogel: 'I had a couple of questions I wanted to ask Charles.'

Guild: 'Such as for instance?'

Vogel: 'Is that monkey Church really dead?'

Guild: 'He'll never be any deader. Somebody shot him off the fire-escape from below with a .38, and if the slug hadn't done the job, the fall would—he must've dropped twenty storeys.'

Vogel: 'Okay. I didn't trust that guy, and when it looked like he was going out of his way to do folks a favor I thought I'd better come over and see what I could angle out of Charles.'

Guild: 'Could you come to the point now—you can fill in the details afterwards.'

Vogel: 'You're getting it all. I got a place I run uptown that gets a high-class trade that wouldn't want their connections to know they're there. Get what I mean? Or do you want me to wait till I can talk through a lawyer?'

Guild: 'I get it. You don't admit you run gambling joints.'

Vogel: 'That's right. Last night there was—say—a bank vice- president in my place and a couple of other customers like that—big and respectable—and Sam Church comes in and sits in with them for an hour or two—including the time MacFay was being killed down on the Island. Well, when I see in the morning papers that coppers are hunting for him, I don't feel so good about it, and I don't think my customers are going to feel so hot either—having to give him that kind of alibi. And just when I'm stewing about it, he phones and says tell them not to worry. He knows what it'll cost them to come to the front for him, and he says even if he's picked up and things look pretty black, he won't call on them unless it's only that between him and the chair—so they can sleep pretty, because he don't think things'll ever get that far.'

VanSlack: 'I don't understand. Do you mean he had an alibi—a genuine one?'

Nick: 'That's what he means. And he didn't want to use it—yet. A man who saw Church going into Vogel's last night was slugged all over Harlem by Church's friends for trying to tell me about it.'

VanSlack: 'That's incredible.'

Nick: 'Not as incredible as if Church *had* killed MacFay, after going to all that trouble before and after to advertise himself as the murderer and coming here trying to get himself pinched.'

VanSlack: 'But if he were innocent—'

Nick: 'I didn't say he was innocent. I'm saying—drew all the attention to himself while his accomplice did the dirty work—and when the accomplice thought Church was working a double cross, the accomplice killed Church.'

Dum-Dum draws a deep breath, stops crying, smiles as if to himself.

VanSlack, looking at Smitty and Dum-Dum: 'But they have alibis, too.'

Nick: 'So then they didn't kill MacFay, huh? Maybe Dum-Dum's knife that didn't do the killing had Asta's tooth prints in it from when he pulled it out of the wall of the cottage yesterday—huh?'

Guild: 'All right. Who did it?'

VanSlack: 'Yes, who?'

Nick, aside to Nora, indicating VanSlack and Guild: 'A couple of schoolboys,' then: 'Didn't you think it was funny that nobody heard any sounds of a struggle before the shot at MacFay's—in spite of the signs of a row in which a lamp had been upset and his arm broken—though all of us had heard noises of people moving around afterwards?'

VanSlack: 'I don't know. That is—what do you mean?'

Nick: 'Let me show you a trick.' He sets up the electric-cord-gun- paper-water trick as it was used by the murderer, saying as he arranges it: 'I figured this out by myself, but I had an electrician check up the details for me. Lend me a gun, somebody... Will you switch on the lights... Get me a glass of water, etc.'

The trick works perfectly, even to blowing out the fuses. Nick takes a bow as they all stare at him.

Dum-Dum, who has been held tightly by a policeman up to this point, takes advantage of the policeman's attention being on the trick to suddenly dive across the floor after the pistol that has been hurled into a corner by the recoil, grab it, and begin shooting. Nick has leapt upon Dum-Dum, grappling with him, so that the bullets go wild. As he succeeds in disarming Dum-Dum, a policeman knocks the Cuban cold.

VanSlack, bewildered: 'But he had an alibi.'

Nick: 'Then he's still got it. All he was trying to do just now was to kill the accomplice that killed his Mr Church.'

VanSlack: 'And who is that?'

Nick looks at VanSlack and at the others who are impatiently awaiting his reply.

Nick: 'You people haven't been paying any attention to what I'm saying or doing. Listen to me now. There was no struggle in MacFay's room. He was stunned—probably with a blow from the hilt of the knife—then his throat was cut and his wrist broken, and it's easy enough to break a dead man's wrist—to pretend there was a struggle in which the lamp and stuff was upset. The trick I just showed you gave the murderer between five and ten minutes to get an alibi before the water soaked through and set the gun off. Get it?'

Nora: 'But who, Nick?'

Nick: 'Who is the only person that used that particular alibi?'

Nora stares at Nick in bewilderment.

Nick, answering his own question: 'Lois, of course. Everybody else had real alibis or none at all.' He steps close to Lois, speaking swiftly:

'Church, the engineer, planned it, and you carried it through; that's why he needed Smitty to stooge for him, so folks wouldn't suspect him of being mixed up with any other woman. You were friends with Church and Dum-Dum; that's why your dog was friends with them and let them come and go on the grounds as they wanted, and that's why your dog stood up with his paws on his killer's shoulders—as the prints showed—and let his throat get cut.'

Lois: 'But why should I kill Papa?'

Nick: 'For money. But don't interrupt the maestro when he's exposing criminals. I don't get the Horn killing exactly, unless he had found out you killed MacFay and you told him I had you cold or would have when I came back from getting the knife from the dog. He'd have covered you up and would have tried to kill me for those millions he would have when he married you. You had to get him going quick, because once he saw it was Church's knife you'd used, he'd have seen through you. So you put me on the spot, even moving around so I had to turn my back toward where he was standing, and then pushed me off the spot so there was nothing for me to do but kill him in self-defense.'—

Lois: 'But Papa gave me everything I wanted. He—'

Nick: 'That wasn't your kind of life and he looked good for years. Your kind of life was the Linda Mills life you had been leading ever since you got old enough to sneak out after the folks went to bed.'

Lois: 'Linda Mills?'

Nick: 'Yes—L. M. for Linda Mills and Lois MacFay. Linda Mills, the girl whose description fits you with allowance for makeup and flashy clothes. Linda Mills, who sleeps without pillows, just as you do. Linda Mills, in whose apartment there is a scorched spot beside the bed and a bullet hole in the wall where the lamp-trick was rehearsed. Linda Mills, who disappeared a couple of weeks ago when you and Church started planning MacFay's murder.'

Lois stares stonily at him.

Nick: 'This is going to be easy enough to prove, you know. We'll make you up for the people who knew you as Linda Mills and see what they say. Or maybe you'd rather be left alone with Dum-Dum after he comes to.'

Lois: 'But he can't think I killed Sam Church. They said he was shot from the street.'

Nick: 'Nonsense. They said he was shot from below. Well, he ran *up* the fire-escape from here, and you leaned out the window and shot him from below, and dropped the gun down after him.'

Lois: 'But why?'

Nick: 'Why? I'm still hoarse from standing close to your door bellowing that he was trying to get himself arrested and tried, so he would be in the clear forever after, and in a spot to shake you down if he wanted to double-cross you; and telling you how nuts he was about Smitty and—'

Smitty: 'That's a lie and you know it.'

Nick: 'I don't know anything. Anyhow I thought it would sound good at the time. I didn't know how sweetness here would kill Church, but I wanted to stir her up as much as I could.'

Lois, horrified: 'Sam wasn't—' Then she pulls herself together, shrugs slightly, says: 'Can I talk to you and Nora alone?'

VanSlack and Guild look at Nick, who nods.

Guild: 'Okay, but slap her down if she gets funny.'

Nick, Nora, and Lois go into the bedroom and shut the door.

Lois to Nick, coolly: 'You're right. I'm Linda Mills at heart. I hated having to play Little Red Riding Hood to that horrible old man. So when Sam was fooling around trying to find a way of getting money out of him and picked me up, we found out we talked the same language. I'm not sorry for any of it—except your lying to me about Sam and Smitty—it was a chance and I took it. Having to get rid of Horn that way—and you guessed it right—made things tough—gummed the works pretty bad—but what could I do? Then when I thought Sam was crossing me up for that big tramp—well, I let him have it. I'd always figured he was safe because he was nuts about me, but—oh, well, I still think you gave me a raw deal on that, but the chances are he was playing me for a sap anyway, even if not with Smitty. So far, so good or bad, whichever way you look at it. What I'm getting at is, I'll make a deal with you.'

Nick: 'What'll you give us? The moon?

Lois, calmly: 'You like that brat of yours, don't you?'

Nick and Nora stare at her, alarmed.

Lois: 'Let me walk out of here and I'll send the kid back in an hour.'

Nick and Nora start for the door together, then Nick checks himself and says to Nora: 'You look. I'll stay here with angel.'

Nora goes into the living room and looks at the sleeping child. It is not Nicky. Paying no attention to the others in the room, she runs back to Nick, leaving the door open. She cannot speak, but one look at her tells Nick the child is gone. He grabs Lois by the shoulders.

Lois, wincing, but smiling coolly: 'Now you know. Make up your minds. Try to send me to the chair, or get your child back all in one piece. Whichever you like best.'

As the others start to come in from the living room, there is a terrific pounding on the corridor door. A policeman opens it.

Into the room comes an enormous unkempt woman carrying Nick Jr. under one arm, holding one of Creeps's friends by the ear with her other hand.

Woman, loudly and angrily: 'My beautiful Raphael. Give me back my beautiful Raphael and take this toad-frog you try to palm off on me. Where is my lovely boy?'

Nora runs to her and takes Nick Jr., while the woman, spying the child who has been awakened by the noise and is sitting up on the sofa, goes over and gathers him into her arms, crooning over him: 'Mama's darling. Did they try to swap that awful hideous dwarf for Mama's darling? Never again will your mama lend you to go to a party.'

Raphael is a truly, deeply, and offensively ugly child.

Jensen and Schultz stare at each other, Schultz muttering: 'Kids are like Chinamen—how can you tell 'em apart?'

Lois says philosophically to Nick: 'Oh, well, all you can do is try to play the breaks as far as you get them.'

Sequel to the Thin Man

'SEQUEL TO THE THIN MAN'

Metro Goldwyn Mayer Script Dept.
December 7, 1938

Nick, Nora, Tommy, and Dorothy arrive in San Francisco and are met by reporters who want to know about 'new developments' in the Macaulay case. Nick ignores their questions as he has ignored the telegrams he has been receiving en route. They are driven to his house and have settled down with signs of relief at being in a quiet place once more when a mob of surprise party guests comes out from behind furniture at them.

While the party is going on, Mimi phones from New York to say that Macaulay has escaped and she is afraid he will kill her, since she was the chief witness against him. Nick, uninterested, hangs up and tells Nora it was a man trying to sell him something.

Nick and Nora are asleep when Mimi—fresh from a plane—crashes their bedroom to demand Nick's protection. She is followed by Gilbert, complaining about the cost of taxis in San Francisco. He has become a miser since inheriting money. Nick and Nora unwillingly tell them they can stay.

In New York, Macaulay—disguised as a middle-aged woman—learns Mimi has gone to San Francisco and dashes for a plane, being helped aboard by Guild, who is at the airport hunting for him.

Next day Mimi phones Chris in New York, begging him to come out. He pretends indifference until his first wife, Georgia, comes in, overhears the conversation, and starts a quarrel, saying she will never let Mimi have him unless she gets some money out of it. Chris laughs at her threats and leaves for the West. Georgia goes out to keep a date with Morelli, who has been in love with her since Nick's dinner, and tells him about the dirty deal she is getting. He is having the first 'clean' love affair of his life and thinks this slut is Joan of Arc. He offers to take her to San Francisco and see that her wrongs are righted.

In San Francisco Nick and Nora have been leading dogs' lives for a couple of days. In addition to Mimi—who keeps complaining about Gilbert's stinginess—and Gilbert—with his complaints about her extravagance—they have an antique uncle and aunt of Nora's visiting them, people who never trusted Nick very much and now suspect him of everything down to being Mimi's lover and Gilbert's father.

Chris arrives on the Coast and phones a man called Dancer—a man of Chris's type but much more dangerous—who tells Chris, 'Yeah, I remember you,' and hangs up. Chris calls him back and with promises of easy money persuades Dancer to meet him.

Nick and Nora, fed up with their guests, sneak out the back way, run into Tommy and Dorothy doing the same thing, and they all set out for a peaceful evening somewhere away from home.

In a Chinatown joint Chris tells Dancer he knows he can get a lot of money from Mimi, because she is crazy about him, but he is afraid of Nick, Georgia, Morelli, etc., as well as having no local connections. Dancer is skeptical, especially since Chris has no cash now. Nick and his party come in, are greeted warmly by the proprietor, and Dorothy sees Chris; she's angry at his having followed Mimi to San Francisco and tells him so. When Chris starts to tell her what he thinks of her, Tommy hits him, and as much riot as we want is on—winding up with Chris and Dancer out on the sidewalk. Dancer says: 'If you're on the level, now's your chance. Let's go up and see the dame while these people are here and collect.' Chris agrees to call on Mimi.

Across the street from Nick's house Macaulay, still in disguise, sees Morelli and Georgia arrive and go in.

Inside Mimi and Georgia have a grand row, Georgia demanding money for giving up Chris, Mimi saying she wouldn't give her a cent if it meant losing him forever, throwing threats at each other and at Chris—'Even if I can't have him, you won't,' etc.

Chris and Dancer arrive and after a bit of five-handed quarreling Chris gets Mimi aside and tries to get some money out of her but she is too afraid Georgia will get some of it, so she gives him very little. He tells her she has till the next morning to make up her mind and they rejoin the others for another battle-royal that lasts until Nick arrives and puts Chris, Dancer, Morelli, and Georgia out.

Macaulay follows Chris and Dancer down the street and waits outside when they go into a saloon. When they come out Dancer says to Chris: 'If the idea is for me to keep you from being hurt maybe it's better I stick a little ways behind you,' so he follows Chris while Macaulay follows him. Meanwhile Nick and Nora have gone to bed; Mimi, after trying to get Chris on the phone, has sneaked out of the house, shadowed by the ever-spying Gilbert; and downtown, Morelli and Georgia, making lame excuses and a date for later, have separated and each is headed for Chris's hotel.

At Chris's hotel—a small one in a dark and now foggy street—Mimi is told that he has not come in yet. She leaves the hotel. Morelli and Georgia arrive separately, neither aware of the other's presence, and conceal themselves in darkness. (For reasons that will be obvious the audience should not know too much about their positions in relation to the hotel; they should simply be hiding in darkness.)

As Chris, walking down the street, approaches a dark alley on one side of the hotel, Dancer silently moves up closer behind him. Macaulay is half a block down the street. A policeman standing on that farther corner hears two shots and turns toward the hotel. Dancer dashes into the dark alley and there are scuffling sounds, his voice grunting in surprise, the sound of running feet in the alley. Macaulay, scampering down the street, trips himself on his skirts and falls, losing hat and wig. The approaching policeman grabs him, drags him up to the entrance of the alley next to the hotel, and turns his light down on Chris, who lies dead on the sidewalk.

In an all-night lunchroom Morelli and Georgia keep their date and immediately each knows the other was at the scene of the killing. They leave to find a place to hide.

In the morning Guild and some local detectives call on Nick and tell him about Chris's murder and Macaulay's arrest. Nick tells them of the meeting between Chris, Dancer, Morelli, Georgia, and Mimi the previous night and arrangements are made to try to pick up Dancer, Morelli, and Georgia. Then Guild asks, 'And how about this Mimi?' Nick says he thinks she is out of it—she was in the house. Guild says the clerk at Chris's hotel described a woman like her calling for Chris not half an hour before he was killed. Nick sends for Mimi, who comes in followed by Gilbert. When asked about her whereabouts she says she was at home of course but Gilbert interrupts her. He tells her it is silly to lie at a time like this; he knows she went to Chris's hotel because he shadowed her there and back again to Nick's. Questioned, he places the time of her return early enough to make it impossible for her to have been in the neighborhood of the hotel at the time of the shooting, though the police do not altogether believe him.

Macaulay is brought in and questioned again. He says he accidentally ran into Chris on the street, was surprised to know he was in the city, and shadowed him in an attempt to learn where he lived so he could avoid that part of town until he could board a boat for the Orient. He said he heard the shot and ran because as an escaped convict he could not afford to be around trouble, but he did not see the flash and could not tell whether the man walking behind Chris had killed him or not.

Dancer phones Mimi, saying: 'This is the fellow who was with your boyfriend. Can you meet me now?' She says she can and he gives her careful instructions. When she goes out a detective shadows her, with the result that both she and the sleuth have walked a couple of inches off their heights before Dancer can safely pick her up in his car.

Later that afternoon, in a room behind drawn blinds, Morelli and Georgia see their pictures in an afternoon paper, with WANTED over them; Dancer looks at his as he leans carelessly against a police-call box on crowded Market Street.

Morelli suggests that now her husband's dead, Georgia should marry him so neither can be made to testify against the other in case they are caught, but she thinks it is simpler for them just to lie, and besides how could they walk into the City Hall with their faces spread over all the papers? Morelli has to go out, his only explanation being that he's 'got a job to do.'

At cocktail hour Nick and Nora, with Mimi, Gilbert, Dorothy, and Tommy, are drinking in a front room in his house when somebody firing through the window from the street shoots a glass out of his hand. Nick digs the bullet out of the wall and takes it to headquarters, where the expert says it was from the same gun Chris was shot with.

Dancer comes into headquarters and gives himself up, saying he had just seen in the papers that he was wanted. He tells of the proposition Chris made him, but said he had no intention of getting hurt, at least until Chris paid him something, which is why he walked behind Chris—he didn't want to stop a bullet meant for the other fellow. He didn't see the flash and as soon as he saw Chris fall he ran up the alley and away from there, taking no chances on being next. Nobody can prove he ever owned a gun or had the slightest reason for killing Chris, whom he had never known well and had not seen for years. Macaulay sends for Nick and makes a complete confession to having shot Chris over Dancer's shoulders, involving Mimi in both the murder and his escape from prison. Nick says: 'Hooey! Just a fellow who'd rather stall through a long, drawn-out murder trial here than go back to be burnt in a few days,' and tears the confession up.

'Having,' as he says, 'not only been shot at, but also insulted by yaps,' Nick decides to go to work. He goes down into Chinatown and gets a line on Dancer's friends and habits and digs into them; he combs the waterfront; he has practically exhausted the city before he, also exhausted, returns home looking fairly satisfied with himself.

Meanwhile Morelli, returning from his 'job,' has arrived in the neighborhood of his hideout just in time to see Georgia being taken away by the police, so later that night he comes calling on Nick again, asking him to help save the little woman. Grilled, he admits that both of them were near the hotel when Chris was shot but swears both are innocent and didn't even see the flash.

Nick makes Morelli a proposition. He says he's got everything he needs to convict Dancer except an eyewitness. If Morelli and Georgia can find it in their hearts to change their testimony just a little bit, even if only enough to swear there was nobody except Dancer within ten feet of Chris when he was killed (he was shot under one ear and there were plenty of powder-marks), Nick will promise to save them. Morelli balks; he would never frame anybody and he hadn't thought Nick would. Nick insists that it's not really framing to add a little needed evidence against a man you're positive is guilty and keeps talking about 'saving the little woman' until Morelli agrees.

The next day Nick assembles everybody and goes to work on Dancer. He has a mob of witnesses: a bellboy to swear Dancer had a gun for years; a longshoreman to swear he saw him throw what looked like a gun off a dock the previous afternoon; a newsboy to swear he had seen him running from the direction of Nick's house right after the shot had been fired through the window; a pool-room attendant to swear he had once told him when drunk that there was one guy in the world he wanted to get, a guy named Chris Something. He has more witnesses, but the most effective are Morelli and Georgia, who now almost remember seeing the gun in Dancer's hand.

Dancer gives up. 'All right,' he tells Nick, 'you win. I'll take what's coming to me but I don't want a murder rap. It was all just as I told you till we got to the alley. I was closing in then, wanting to get some few pennies anyway from Chris before he went in his hotel, and then that gun came out and was almost under my nose when it went off, and I didn't want to be the next on the list, so I grabbed it and then I see what I've got besides the gun. Real dough, if what Chris said was right. So I helped in the getaway and the next day I called her [nodding at Mimi] up and—'

Mimi screams: 'That's a lie, you double-crossing—' and a copper grabs her and puts handcuffs on her wrists.

Dancer shakes his head coolly and goes on talking: 'Not her, you mug. I went to her and told her if she wanted the kid kept off the gallows I'd have to be fixed up regular and so—after a little trouble: she was kind of tough at first—we made the deal.' He scowls at Nick. 'And a fine deal you turned it into.'

Nick says excuse me and goes out to pay off his witnesses, one of whom suddenly looks up and asks: 'Mister, was it just a joke like you said?' Nick assures him it was and goes back into the room where Gilbert was assuring the detectives very seriously that he *did* feel that now he was the head of the house he had a right to protect his mother from ravenous males, and after all the money she would waste on Chris was actually *his* money, since it was doubtful if she would get anything out of his father's estate, and...

The First Thin Man

The unfinished draft included in this collection was the first draft of Hammett's last novel *Thin Man*. The only apparent connection between both is that the name of the missing thin man is Wynant, and that the name Guild is used for the investigators.

The protagonists—Nick and Nora Charles—in the novel published in early 1934 are a married couple who solve crimes while exchanging sharp and witty repartee. (Hammett reportedly based Nora's character on his longtime partner, Lillian Hellman, whom he had dated in the period between the two thin men.) In this draft, the protagonist, John Guild is a working investigator who is similar to Hammett's Continental Op. In the version published in 1934, the setting is primarily New York, and Guild is a police lieutenant working on the case.

The manuscript of *Thin Man* is neatly typed and 65 pages long. Hammett gave away the original in 1942, so it could be auctioned off in connection with a War Bonds drive, for which he wrote an explanatory note:

'In 1930 I started writing a book entitled *The Thin Man*. By the time I had written these 65 pages my publisher and I agreed that it might be wise to postpone the publication of The *Glass Key*—scheduled for the fall—until the following spring. This meant that *The Thin Man* could not be published until the fall of 1931. So—having plenty of time— I put these 65 pages aside and went to Hollywood for a year. One thing and/or another intervening after that, I didn't return to work on the story until a couple of more years had passed—and then I found it easier, or at least generally more satisfactory, to keep only the basic idea of the plot and otherwise to start anew. Some of the incidents in this original version I later used in *After The Thin Man,* a motion picture sequel. But, except for that and for the use of the characters' names Guild and Wynant, this unfinished manuscript has a clear claim to virginity.'

BY DASHIELL HAMMETT

1

The train went north among the mountains. The dark man crossed tracks to the ticket-window and said: 'Can you tell me how to get to Mr Wynant's place? Mr Walter Irving Wynant's.'

The man within stopped writing on a printed form. His eyes became brightly inquisitive behind tight rimless spectacles. His voice was eager. 'Are you a newspaper reporter?'

'Why?' The dark man's eyes were very blue. They looked idly at the other. 'Does it make any difference?'

'Then you ain't,' the ticket-agent said. He was disappointed. He looked at a clock on the wall. 'Hell, I ought to've known that. You wouldn't've had time to get here.' He picked up the pencil he had put down.

'Know where his place is?'

'Sure. Up there on the hill.' The ticket-agent waved his pencil vaguely westward. 'All the taxi-drivers know it, but if it's Wynant you want to see you're out of luck.'

'Why?'

The ticket-agent's mien brightened. He put his forearms on the counter, hunching his shoulders, and said: 'Because the fact is he went and murdered everybody on the place and jumped in the river not more than an hour ago.'

The dark man exclaimed, 'No!' softly.

The ticket-agent smacked his lips. 'Uh-huh—killed all three of them—the whole shooting match—chopped them up in pieces with an ax and then tied a weight around his own neck and jumped in the river.'

The dark man asked solemnly: 'What'd he do that for?'

A telephone-bell began to ring behind the ticket-agent. 'You don't know him or you wouldn't have to ask,' he replied as he reached for the telephone. 'Crazy as they make them and always was. The only wonder is he didn't do it long before this.' He said, 'Hello,' into the telephone.

The dark man went through the waiting-room and downstairs to the street. The half dozen automobiles parked near the station were apparently private cars. A large red and white sign in the next block said *Taxi*. The dark man walked under the sign into a small grimy office where a bald fat man was reading a newspaper.

'Can I get a taxi?' the dark man asked.

'All out now, brother, but I'm expecting one of them back any minute. In a hurry!'

'A little bit.'

The bald man brought his chair down on all its legs and lowered his newspaper. 'Where do you want to go?'

'Wynant's.'

The bald man dropped his newspaper and stood up, saying heartily: 'Well, I'll run you up there myself.' He covered his baldness with a sweat-stained brown hat.

They left the office and—after the fat man had paused at the real-estate-office next door to yell, 'Take care of my phone if it rings, Toby'—got into a dark sedan, took the left turn at the first crossing, and rode uphill towards the west.

When they had ridden some three hundred yards the fat man said in a tone whose casualness was belied by the shine in his eyes: 'That must be a hell of a mess up there and no fooling.'

The dark man was lighting a cigarette. 'What happened?' he asked.

The fat man looked sharply sidewise at him. 'Didn't you hear?'

'Only what the ticket-agent told me just now'—the dark man leaned forward to return the lighter to its hole in the dashboard—'That Wynant had killed three people with an ax and then drowned himself.'

The fat man laughed scornfully. 'Christ, you can't beat Lew,' he said. 'If you sprained your ankle he could get a broken back out of it. Wynant didn't kill but two of them—the Hopkins woman got away because it was her that phoned—and he choked them to death and then shot himself. I bet you if you'd go back there right now Lew'd tell you there was a cool half dozen of them killed and likely as not with dynamite.'

The dark man took his cigarette from his mouth. 'Then he wasn't right about Wynant being crazy?'

'Yes,' the fat man said reluctantly, 'but nobody could go wrong on that.'

'No?'

'Nope. Holy hell! Didn't he used to come down to town in his pajamas last summer? And then when people didn't like it and got Ray to say something to him about it didn't he get mad and stop coming in at all? Don't he make as much fuss about people trespassing on his place as if he had a gold mine there? Didn't I see him with my own eyes heave a rock at a car that had gone past him raising dust once?'

The dark man smiled meagerly. 'I don't know any of the answers,' he said. 'I didn't know him.'

Beside a painted warning against trespass they left their graveled road for an uneven narrow crooked one of dark earth running more steeply uphill to the right. Protruding undergrowth brushed the sedan's sides and now and then an overhanging tree branch its top. Their speed made their ride rougher than it need have been.

'This is his place,' the fat man said. He sat stiffly at the wheel fighting the road's unevennesses. His eyes were shiny, expectant.

The house they presently came to was a rambling structure of gray native stone and wood needing gray paint under low Dutch roofs. Five cars stood in the clearing in front of the house. The man who sat at the wheel of one of them, and the two men standing beside it, stopped talking and watched the sedan draw up.

'Here we are,' the fat man said and got out. His manner had suddenly become important. He put importance in the nod he gave the three men.

The dark man, leaving the other side of the sedan, went towards the house. The fat man hurried to walk beside him.

A man came out of the house before they reached it. He was a middle-aged giant in baggy worn clothes. His hair was gray, his eyes small, and he chewed gum. He said, 'Howdy, Fern,' to the fat man and, looking steadily at the dark man, stood in the path confronting them squarely.

Fern said, 'Hello, Nick,' and then told the dark man: 'This is Sheriff Petersen.' He narrowed one eye shrewdly and addressed the Sheriff again: 'He came up to see Wynant.'

Sheriff Nick Petersen stopped chewing. 'What's the name?' he asked.

The dark man said: 'John Guild.'

The Sheriff said: 'So. Now what were you wanting to see Wynant about?'

The man who had said his name was John Guild smiled. 'Does it make any difference now he's dead?'

The Sheriff asked, 'What?' with considerable force.

'Now that he's dead,' Guild repeated patiently. He put a fresh cigarette between his lips.

'How do you know he's dead?' The Sheriff emphasized 'you.'

Guild looked with curious blue eyes at the giant. 'They told me in the village,' he said carelessly. He moved his cigarette an inch to indicate the fat man. 'He told me.'

The Sheriff frowned skeptically, but when he spoke it was to utter a vague 'Oh.' He chewed his gum. 'Well, what was it you were wanting to see him about.?'

Guild said: 'Look here: is he dead or isn't he?'

'Not that I know of.'

'Fine,' Guild said, his eyes lighting up. 'Where is he?'

'I'd like to know,' the Sheriff replied gloomily. 'Now what is it you want with him?'

'I'm from his bank. I want to see him on business.' Guild's eyes became drowsy. 'It's confidential business.'

'So?' Sheriff Petersen's frown seemed to hold more discomfort than annoyance. 'Well, none of his business is confidential from me any more. I got a right to know anything and everything that anybody knows about him.'

Guild's eyes narrowed a little. He blew smoke out.

'I have,' the Sheriff insisted in a tone of complaint. 'Listen, Guild, you haven't got any right to hide any of his business from me. He's a murderer and I'm responsible for law and order in this county.'

Guild pursed his lips. 'Who'd he kill?'

'This here Columbia Forrest,' Petersen said, jerking a thumb at the house, 'shot her stone dead and lit out for God only knows where.'

'Didn't kill anybody else?'

'My God,' the Sheriff asked peevishly, 'ain't that enough?'

'Enough for me, but down in the village they've got it all very plural.' Guild stared thoughtfully at the Sheriff. 'Got away clean?'

'So far,' Petersen grumbled, 'but we're phoning descriptions of him and his car around,' He sighed, moved his big shoulders uncomfortably. 'Well, come on now, let's have it. What's your business with him?' But when Guild would have replied the giant said: 'Wait a minute. We might as well go in and get hold of Boyer and Ray and get it over with at one crack.'

Leaving the fat man, Guild and the Sheriff went indoors, into a pleasantly furnished tan room in the front of the house, where they were soon joined by two more men. One of these was nearly tall as the Sheriff, a raw-boned blond man in his early thirties, hard of jaw and mouth, somber of eye. One was younger, shorter, with boyishly rosy cheeks, quick dark eyes, and smoothed dark hair. When the Sheriff introduced them to Guild he said the taller one was Ray Callaghan, a Deputy Sheriff, the other District Attorney Bruce Boyer. He told them John Guild was a fellow who wanted to see Wynant.

The youthful District Attorney, standing close to Guild, smiled ingratiatingly and asked: 'What business are you in, Mr Guild?'

'I came up to see Wynant about his bank-account,' the dark man replied slowly.

'What bank?'

'Seaman's National of San Francisco.'

'I see. Now what did you want to see him about? I mean, what was there about his account that you had to come up here to see him about?'

'Call it an over-draft,' Guild said with deliberate evasiveness.

The District Attorney's eyes became anxious.

Guild made a small gesture with the brown hand holding his cigarette. 'Look here, Boyer,' he said, 'if you want me to go all the way with you you ought to go all the way with me.'

Boyer looked at Petersen. The Sheriff met his gaze with noncommittal eyes. Boyer turned back to Guild. 'We're not hiding anything from you,' he said earnestly 'We've nothing to hide.'

Guild nodded. 'Swell. What happened here?'

'Wynant caught the Forrest girl getting ready to leave him and he shot her and jumped in his car and drove away,' he said quickly. 'That's all there is to it.'

'Who's the Forrest girl?'

'His secretary.'

Guild pursed his lips, asked: 'Only that?'

The raw-boned Deputy Sheriff said, 'None of that, now!' in a strained croaking voice: 'She's dead and you might just as well talk decently about her.'

Guild moved his shoulders a little. 'I didn't know her,' he said coldly. 'I'm trying to find out what happened.' He stared for a moment longer at the raw-boned man and then shifted his gaze to Boyer. 'What was she leaving him for?'

'To get married. She told him when he caught her packing after she came back from town and—and they had a fight and when she wouldn't change her mind he shot her.'

Guild's blue eyes moved sidewise to focus on the raw-boned Deputy Sheriffs face. 'She was living with Wynant, wasn't she?' he asked bluntly.

'You son of a bitch!' the Deputy Sheriff cried hoarsely and struck with his right fist at Guild's face.

Guild avoided the fist by stepping back with no appearance of haste. He had begun to step back before the fist started towards his face. His eyes gravely watched the fist go past his face.

Big Petersen lurched against his Deputy, wrapping his arms around him. 'Cut it out, Ray,' he grumbled. 'Why don't you behave yourself? This is no time to be losing your head.'

The Deputy Sheriff did not struggle against him.

'What's the matter with him?' Guild asked the District Attorney. There was no resentment in his manner. 'In love with her or something?'

Boyer nodded furtively, then frowned and shook his head in a warning gesture.

'That's all right,' Guild said. 'Where'd you get your information about what happened?'

'From the Hopkinses. They look after the place for Wynant. They were in the kitchen and heard the whole fight. They ran upstairs when they heard the shots and he stood them off with the gun and told them he'd come back and kill them if they told anybody before he'd an hour's start, but they phoned Ray as soon as he'd gone.'

Guild tossed the stub of his cigarette into the fireplace and lit a fresh one. Then he took a card from a brown case brought from an inner pocket and gave the card to Boyer.

John Guild
Associated Detective Bureaus, Inc.
Frost Building, San Francisco

'Last week Wynant deposited a ten-thousand-dollar New York check in his account at the Seaman's National Bank,' Guild said. 'Yesterday the bank learned the check had been raised from one thousand to ten. The bank's nicked for six thousand on the deal.'

'But in the case of an altered check,' Boyer said, 'I understand—'

'I know,' Guild agreed, 'the bank's not responsible—theoretically—but there are usually loopholes and it's—Well, we're working for the insurance company that cover's the Seaman's and it's good business to go after him and recover as much as we can.'

'I'm glad that's the way you feel about it,' the District Attorney said with enthusiasm. 'I'm mighty glad you're going to work with us.' He held out his hand.

'Thanks,' Guild said as he took the hand. 'Let's look at the Hopkinses and the body.'

2

Columbia Forrest had been a long-limbed smoothly slender young woman. Her body, even as it lay dead in a blue sport suit, seemed supple. Her short hair was a faintly reddish brown. Her features were small and regular, appealing in their lack of strength. There were three bullet-holes in her left temple. Two of them touched. The third was down beside the eye.

Guild put the tip of his dark forefinger lightly on the edge of the lower hole. 'A thirty-two,' he said. 'He made sure: any of the three would have done it.' He turned his back on the corpse. 'Let's see the Hopkinses.'

'They're in the dining-room, I think,' the District Attorney said. He hesitated, cleared his throast. His young face was worried. He touched Guild's elbow with the back of one hand and said: 'Go easy with Ray, will you? He was a little bit—or a lot, I guess—in love with her and it's tough on him.'

'The Deputy?'

'Yes, Ray Callaghan.'

'That's all right if he doesn't get in the way,' Guild said carelessly. 'What sort of person is this Sheriff?'

'Oh, Petersen's all right.'

Guild seemed to consider this statement critically. Then he said: 'But he's not what you'd call a feverish manhunter?'

'Well, no, that's not—you know—a sheriff has other things to do most of the time, but even if he'd just as life have somebody else do the work he won't interfere.' Boyer moistened his lips and leaned close to the dark man. His face was boyishly alight. 'I wish you'd—I'm glad you're going to work with me on this, Guild,' he said in a low earnest voice. 'I—this is my first murder and I'd like to—well—show them'—he blushed—'that I'm not as young as some of them said.'

'Fair enough. Let's see the Hopkinses—in here.'

The District Attorney studied Guild's dark face uneasily for a moment, started to say something, changed his mind, and left the room.

A man and a woman came with him when he returned. The man was probably fifty years old, of medium stature, with thin greying hair above a round phlegmatic face. He wore tan trousers held up by new blue suspenders and a faded blue shirt open at the neck. The woman was of about the same age, rather short, plump, and dressed neatly in grey. She wore gold-rimmed spectacles. Her eyes were round and pale and bright.

The District Attorney shut the door and said: 'This is Mr and Mrs Hopkins, Mr Guild.' He addressed them: 'Mr Guild is working with me. Please give him all the assistance you can.'

The Hopkinses nodded in unison.

Guild asked: 'How'd this happen?' he indicated with a small backward jerk of his head the dead young woman.

Hopkins said, 'I always knew he'd do something like that sometime,' while his wife was saying: 'It was right in this room and they were talking so loud you could hear it all over the place.'

Guild shook his cigarette at them. 'One at a time.' He spoke to the man: 'How'd you know he was going to do it?'

The woman replied quickly: 'Oh, he was crazy-jealous of her all the time—if she got out of his sight for a minute—and when she came back from the city and told him she was going to leave to get married he—'

Again Guild used his cigarette to interrupt her. 'What do you think? Is he really crazy?'

'He was then, sir,' she said. 'Why, when we ran in here when we heard the shooting and he told us to keep our mouths shut he was—his eyes—you never saw anything like them in your life—nor his voice either and he was shaking and jerking like he was going to fall apart.'

'I don't mean that,' Guild explained. 'I mean, is he crazy?' Before the woman could reply he put another question to her: 'How long have you been with him?'

'Going on about ten months, ain't it, Willie?' she asked her husband.

'Yes,' he agreed, 'since last fall.'

'That's right,' she told Guild, 'It was last November.'

'Then you ought to know whether he's crazy. Is he?'

'Well, I'll tell you,' she said slowly, wrinkling her forehead. 'He was certainly the most peculiar person you ever heard tell of, but I guess geniuses are like that and I wouldn't want to say he was out and out crazy except about her.' She looked at her husband.

He said tolerantly: 'Sure, all geniuses are like that. It's—it's eccentric.'

'So you think he was a genius,' Guild said. 'Did you read the things he wrote?'

'No, sir,' Mrs Hopkins said, squirming, 'though I did try sometimes, but it was too—I couldn't make heads or tails of it—much—but I ain't an educated woman and—'

'Who was she going to marry?' Guild asked.

Mrs Hopkins shook her head vigorously. 'I don't know. I didn't catch the name if she said it. It was him that was talking so loud.'

'What'd she go to town for?'

Mrs Hopkins shook her head again. 'I don't know that either. She used to go in every couple of weeks and he always got mad about it.'

'She drive in?'

'Mostly she did, but she didn't yesterday, but she drove out in that new blue car out there.'

Guild looked questioningly at the District Attorney, who said: 'We're trying to trace it now. It's apparently a new one, but we ought to know whose it is soon.'

Guild nodded and returned his attention to the Hopkinses. 'She went to San Francisco by train yesterday and came back in this new car at what time today?'

'Yes, sir. At about three o'clock, I guess it was, and she started packing.' She pointed at the traveling bags and clothing scattered around the room. 'And he came in and the fuss started. I could hear them downstairs and I went to the window and beckoned at Willie—Mr Hopkins, that is—and we stood at the foot of the stairs, there by the dining-room door and listened to them.'

Guild turned aside to mash his cigarette in a bronze tray on a table.

'She usually stay over-night when she went to the city?'

'Mostly always.'

'You must have some idea of what she went to the city for,' Guild insisted.

'No, I haven't,' the woman said earnestly. 'We never did know, did we, Willie? Jealous like he was, I guess if she was going in to see some fellow she wouldn't be likely to tell anybody that might tell him, though the Lord knows I can keep my mouth shut as tight as anybody. I've seen the—'

Guild stopped lighting a fresh cigarette to ask: 'How about her mail? You must've seen that sometimes.'

'No, Mr Gould, we never did, and that's a funny thing, because all the time we've been here I never saw any mail for her except magazines and never knew her to write any.'

Guild frowned. 'How long had she been here?'

'She was here when we came. I don't know how long she'd been here, but it must've been a long time.'

Boyer said: 'Three years. She came here in March three years ago.'

'How about her relatives, friends?'

The Hopkinses shook their heads. Boyer shook his head.

'His?'

Mrs Hopkins shook her head again. 'He didn't have any. That's what he would always say, that he didn't have a relative or a friend in the world.'

'Who's his lawyer?'

Mrs Hopkins looked blank. 'If he's got one I don't know it, Mr Gould. Maybe you could find something like that in his letters and things.'

'That'll do,' Guild said abruptly around the cigarette in his mouth, and opened the door for the Hopkinses. They left the room.

He shut the door behind them and with his back against it looked around the room, at the blanketed dead figure on the bed, at the clothing scattered here and there, at the three traveling bags, and finally at the bloodstained center of the light blue rug.

Boyer watched him expectantly.

Staring at the bloodstain, Guild asked: 'You've notified the police in San Francisco?'

'Oh yes, we've sent his description and the description and license-number of his car all over—from Los Angeles to Seattle and as far east as Salt Lake.'

'What is the number?' Guild took a pencil and an envelope from his pockets.

Boyer told him, adding: 'It's a Buick coupé, last year's.'

'What does he look like?'

'I've never seen him, but he's very tall—well over six feet—and thin. Won't weigh more than a hundred and thirty, they say. You know he's tubercular: that's how he happened to come up here. He's about forty-five years old, sunburned, but sallow, with brown eyes and very dark brown hair and whiskers. He's got whiskers maybe five or six inches long—thick and shaggy, and his eyebrows are thick and shaggy. There's a lot of pictures of him in his room. You can help yourself to them. He had on a baggy gray tweed suit and a soft gray hat and heavy brown shoes. His shoulders are high and straight and he walks on the balls of his feet with long steps. He doesn't smoke or drink and he has a habit of talking to himself.'

Guild put away his pencil and envelope. 'Had your fingerprint people go over the place yet?'

'No, I—'

'It might help in case he's picked up somewhere and we're doubtful. I suppose we can get specimens of his handwriting. Anyway we'll be able to get them from the bank. We'll try to—'

Someone knocked on the door.

'Come in,' Boyer called.

The door opened to admit a man's head. He said: 'They want you on the phone.'

The District Attorney followed the man downstairs. During his absence Guild smoked and looked somberly around the room.

The District Attorney came back saying: 'The car belongs to a Charles Fremont, on Guerrero Street, in San Francisco.'

'What number.' Guild brought out his pencil and envelope again. Boyer told him the number and he wrote it down. 'I think I'll trot back right now and see him.'

The District Attorney looked at his watch. 'I wonder if I couldn't manage to get away to go with you,' he said.

Guild pursed his lips. 'I don't think you ought to. One of us ought to be here looking through his stuff, gathering up the loose ends. I haven't seen anybody else we ought to trust with it.'

Though Boyer seemed disappointed he said, 'Righto,' readily enough. 'You'll keep in touch with me?'

'Sure. Let me have that card I gave you and I'll put my home address and phone number on it.' Guild's eyes became drowsy. 'What do you say I drive Fremont's car in?'

The District Attorney wrinkled his forehead. 'I don't know,' he said slowly. 'It might—Oh, sure, if you want. You'll phone me as soon as you've seen him—let me know what's what?'

'Um-hmm.'

3

A red-haired girl in white opened the door.

Guild said: 'I want to see Mr Charles Fremont.'

'Yes, sir,' the girl said amiably in a resonant throaty voice. 'Come in.'

She took him into a comfortably furnished living-room to the right of the entrance. 'Sit down. I'll call my brother,' She went through another doorway and her voice could be heard singing: 'Charley, a gentleman to see you.'

Upstairs a hard masculine voice replied: 'Be right down.'

The red-haired girl came back to the room where Guild was. 'He'll be down in a minute,' she said.

Guild thanked her.

'Do sit down,' she said, sitting on an end of the sofa. Her legs were remarkably beautiful.

He sat in a large chair facing her across the room, but got up again immediately to offer her cigarettes and to hold his lighter to hers. 'What I wanted to see your brother about,' he said as he sat down again, 'Was to ask if he knows a Miss Columbia Forrest.'

The girl laughed. 'He probably does,' she said. 'She's— They're going to be married tomorrow.'

Guild said: 'Well, that's—' He stopped when he heard footsteps running down stairs from the second floor.

A man came into the room. He was a man of perhaps thirty-five years, a little above medium height, trimly built, rather gaily dressed in gray with lavender shirt, tie, and protruding pocket-handkerchief. His face was lean and good-looking in a shrewd tight-lipped fashion.

'This is my brother,' the girl said.

Guild stood up. 'I'm trying to get some information about Miss Columbia Forrest,' he said and gave Charles Fremont one of his cards.

The curiosity that had come into Fremont's face with Guild's words became frowning amazement when he had read Guild's card. 'What—?'

Guild was saying: 'There's been some trouble up at Hell Bend.'

Fremont's eyes widened in his paling face. 'Wynant has—?'

Guild nodded. 'He shot Miss Forrest this afternoon.'

The Fremonts stared at each other's blank horrified faces. She said through the fingers of one hand, trembling so she stuttered: 'I t-t-told you, Charlie!'

Charles Fremont turned savagely on Guild. 'How bad is she hurt? Tell me!'

The dark man said: 'She's dead.'

Fremont sobbed and sat down with his face in his hands. His sister knelt beside him with her arms around him. Guild stood watching them.

Presently Fremont raised his head. 'Wynant?' he asked.

'Gone.'

Fremont let his breath out in a low groan. He sat up straight, patting one of his sister's hands, freeing himself from her arms. 'I'm going up there now,' he told her, rising.

Guild had finished lighting a cigarette. He said: 'That's all right, but you'll do most good by telling me some things before you go.'

'Anything I can,' Fremont promised readily.

'You were to be married tomorrow?'

'Yes. She was down here last night and stayed with us and I persuaded her. We were going to leave here tomorrow morning and drive up to Portland—where we wouldn't have to wait three days for the license—and then go up to Banff. I've just wired the hotel there for reservations. So she took the car—the new one we were going in—to go up to Hell Bend and get her things. I asked her not to—we both tried to persuade her—because we knew Wynant would make trouble, but—but we never thought he would do anything like this.'

'You know him pretty well?'

'No, I've only seen him once—about three weeks ago when he came to see me.'

'What'd he come to see you for?'

'To quarrel with me about her;— to tell me to stay away from her.'

Guild seemed about to smile. 'What'd you say to that?'

Fremont drew his thin lips back tight against his teeth. 'Do I look like I'd tell him anything except to go to hell?' he demanded.

The dark man nodded. 'All right. What do you know about him?'

'Nothing.'

Guild frowned. 'You must know something. She'd've talked about him.'

Anger went out of Fremont's lean face, leaving it gloomy. 'I didn't like her to,' he said, 'so she didn't.'

'Why?'

'Jesus!' Fremont exclaimed. 'She was living up there. I was nuts about her. I knew he was. What the hell?' he bit his lip. 'Do you think that was something I liked to talk about?'

Guild stared thoughtfully at the other man for a moment and then addressed the girl: 'What'd she tell you?'

'Not anything. She didn't like to talk about him any more than Charley liked to have her.'

Guild drew his brows together. 'What'd she stay with him for then?'

Fremont said painfully: 'She was going to leave. That's why he killed her.'

The dark man put his hands in his pockets and walked down the room to the front windows and back, squinting a little in the smoke rising from his cigarette. 'You don't know where he's likely to go? Who he's likely to connect with? How we're likely to find him?'

Fremont shook his head. 'Don't you think I'd tell you if I knew?' he asked bitterly.

Guild did not reply to that. He asked: 'Where are her people?'

'I don't know: I think she's got a father still alive in Texas somewhere. I know she's an only child and her mother's dead.'

'How long have you known her?'

'Four—nearly five months.'

'Where'd you meet her?'

'In a speakeasy on Powell Street, a couple of blocks beyond the Fairmont. She was in a party with some people I know—Helen Robier—I think she lives at the Cathedral—and a fellow named MacWilliams.'

Guild walked to the windows again and back. 'I don't like this,' he said aloud, but apparently not to the Fremonts. 'It doesn't make sense. It's—Look here.' He halted in front of them and took some photographs from his pocket. 'Are these good pictures of her?' He spread three out fanwise. 'I've only seen her dead.'

The Fremonts looked and nodded together. 'The middle one especially,' the girl said. 'You have one of those, Charley.'

Guild put the dead girl's photographs away and displayed two of a bearded man. 'Are they good of him?'

The girl said, 'I've never seen him,' but her brother nodded and said: 'They look like him.'

Guild seemed dissatisfied with the answers he had been given. He put the photographs in his pocket again. 'Then it's not that,' he said, 'but there's something funny somewhere.' He scowled at the floor, looked up quickly. 'You people aren't putting up some kind of game on me, are you?'

Charles Fremont said: 'Don't be a sap.'

'All right, but there's something wrong somewhere.'

The girl spoke: 'What? Maybe if you'd tell us what you think is wrong—'

Guild shook his head. 'If I knew what was wrong I could find out for myself what made it wrong. Never mind, I'll get it. I want the names and addresses of all the friends she had, the people she knew that you know of.'

'I've told you Helen Robier lives—I'm pretty sure—at the Cathedral,' Fremont said. 'MacWilliams works in the Russ Building, for a stockbroker, I think. That's all I know about him and I don't believe Columbia knows—' he swallowed '—knew him very well. They're the only ones I know.'

'I don't believe they're all you know,' Guild said.

'Please, Mr Guild,' the girl said, coming around to his side, 'don't be unfair to Charley. He's trying to help you—we're both trying—but—' She stamped her foot and cried angrily, tearfully: 'Can't you have some consideration for him now?'

Guild said: 'Oh, all right.' He reached for his hat. 'I drove your car down,' he told Fremont. 'It's out front now.'

'Thank you, Guild.'

Something struck one of the front windows, knocking a triangle of glass from its lower left-hand corner in on the floor. Charles Fremont, facing the window, yelled inarticulately and threw himself down on the floor. A pistol was fired through the gap, in the pane. The bullet went over Fremont's head and made a small hole in the green plastered wall there.

Guild was moving towards the street-door by the time the bullet-hole appeared in the wall. A black pistol came into his right hand. Outside, that block of Guerrero Street was deserted. Guild went swiftly, though with many backward glances, to the nearest corner. From there he began to retrace his steps slowly, stopping to peer into shadowy doorways and the dark basement-entrances under the high front steps.

Charles Fremont came out to join him. Windows were being raised along the street and people were looking out.

'Get inside,' Guild said curtly to Fremont. 'You're the one he's gunning for. Get inside and phone the police.'

'Elsa's doing that now. He's shaved his whiskers off, Guild.'

'That'd be the first thing he did. Go back in the house.'

Fremont said, 'no,' and went with Guild as he searched the block. They were still at it when the police arrived. They did not find Wynant. Around a corner two blocks from the Fremonts' house they found a year-old Buick coupé bearing the license-numbers Boyer had given Guild—Wynant's car.

4

After dinner, which Guild ate alone at Solari's in Maiden Lane, he went to an apartment in Hyde Street. He was admitted by a young woman whose pale tired face lighted up as she said: 'Hello, John. We've been wondering what had become of you.'

'Been away. Is Chris home?'

'I'd let you in anyhow,' she said as she pushed the door farther open.

They went back to a square bookish room where a thick-set man with rumpled sandy hair was half buried in an immense shabby chair. He put his book down, reached for the tall glass of beer at his elbow, and said jovially: 'Enter the sleuth. Get some more beer, Kay. I've been wanting to see you, John. What do you say you do some detective-story reviews for my page—you know—The Detective Looks at Detective Fiction?'

'You asked me that before,' Guild said. 'Nuts.'

'It's a good idea, though,' the thick-set man said cheerfully. 'And I've got another one. I was going to save it till I got around to writing a detective story, but you might be able to use it in your work sometime, so I'll give it to you free.'

Guild took the glass of beer Kay held out to him, said, 'Thanks,' to her and then to the man: 'Do I have to listen to it?'

'Yes. You see, this fellow's suspected of a murder that requires quite a bit of courage. All the evidence points right at him—that kind of thing. But he's a great lover of Sam Johnson—got his books all over the place—so you know he didn't do it, because only timid men—the kind that say, 'Yes, sir,' to their wives and, 'Yes, Ma'am,' to policemen—love Johnson. You see, he's only loved for his boorishness and the boldness of his rudeness and bad manners and that's the kind of thing that appeals to—'

'So I look for a fellow named Sam Johnson and he's guilty?' the dark man said.

Kay said: 'Chris has one of his nights.'

Chris said: 'Sneer at me and be damned to you, but there's a piece of psychology that might come in handy some day. Remember it. It's a law. Love of Doctor Johnson is the mark of the pathologically meek.'

Guild made a face. 'God knows I'm earning my beer,' he said and drank. 'If you've got to talk, talk about Walter Irving Wynant. That'll do me some good maybe.'

'Why?' Chris asked. 'How?'

'I'm hunting for him. He slaughtered his secretary this afternoon and lit out for parts unknown.'

Kay exclaimed: 'Not really!'

Chris said: 'The hell he did!'

Guild nodded and drank more beer. 'He only paused long enough to take a shot at the fellow his secretary was supposed to marry tomorrow.'

Chris and Kay looked at each other with delighted eyes.

Chris lay back in his chair. 'Can you beat that? But, you know, I'm not nearly as surprised as I ought to be. The last time I saw him I thought there was something wrong there, though he always was a bit on the goofy side. Remember I said something to you about it, Kay? And it's a cinch this magazine stuff he's been doing lately is woozy. Even parts of his last book—No, I'm being smart-alecky now. I'll stick to what I wrote about his book when it came out: in spite of occasional flaws his 'departmentalization' comes nearer supplying an answer to Pontius Pilate's question than anything ever offered by anybody else.'

'What kind of writing does he do?' Guild asked.

'This sort of thing.' Chris rose grunting, went to one of his bookcases, picked out a bulky black volume entitled, in large gold letters, *Knowledge and Belief*, opened it at random, and read: 'Science is concerned with percepts. A percept is a defined, that is a limited, difference. The scientific datum that white occurs means that white is the difference between a certain perceptual field and the rest of the perceiver. If you look at an unbroken expanse of white you perceive white because your perception of it is limited to your visual field: the surrounding, contrasting, extra-visual area of non-white gives you your percept of white. These are not scientific definitions. They cannot be. Science cannot define, cannot limit, itself. Definitions of science must be philosophical definitions. Science cannot know what it cannot know. Science cannot know there is anything it does not know. Science deals with percepts and not with non-percepts. Thus, Einstein's theory of relativity—that the phenomena of nature will be the same, that is not different, to two observers who move with any uniform velocity whatever relative to one another—is a philosophical, and not a scientific, hypothesis.

'Philosophy, like science, cannot define, cannot limit, itself. Definitions of philosophy must be made from a viewpoint that will bear somewhat the same relation to philosophy that the philosophical viewpoint bears to science. These definitions may be—'

'That'll be enough of that,' Guild said.

Chris shut the book with a bang. 'That's the kind of stuff he writes,' he said cheerfully and went back to his chair and beer.

'What do you know about him?' Guild asked. 'I mean outside his writing. Don't start that again. I want to know if he was only crazy with jealousy or has blown his top altogether—and how to catch up with him either way.'

'I haven't seen him for six or seven months or maybe longer,' Chris said. 'He always was a little cracked and unsociable as hell. Maybe just erratic, maybe worse than that.'

'What do you know about him?'

'What everybody knows,' Chris said depreciatively. 'Born somewhere in Devonshire. Went to Oxfords. Went native in India and came out with a book on economics—a pretty good book, but visionary. Married an actress named Hana Drix—or something like that—in Paris and lived with her there for three or four years and came out of it with his second book. I think they had a couple of children. After she divorced him he went to Africa and later, I believe, to South America. Anyway he did a lot of traveling and then settled down in Berlin long enough to write his *Speculative Anthropology* and to do some lecturing. I don't know where he was during the War. He popped up over here a couple of years later with a two-volume piece of metaphysics called *Consciousness Drifting*. He's been in America ever since—the last five or six years up in the mountains here doing that *Knowledge and Belief*.'

'How about relatives, friends?'

Chris shook his tousled head. 'Maybe his publishers would know—Dale & Dale.'

'And as a critic you think—'

'I'm no critic,' Chris said. 'I'm a reviewer.'

'Well, as whatever you are, you think his stuff is sane?'

Chris moved his thick shoulders in a lazy shrug. 'Parts of his books I know are damned fine. Others parts—maybe they're over my head. Even that's possible. But the magazine stuff he's been doing lately—since *Knowledge and Belief*— I know is tripe and worse. The paper sent a kid to get an interview out of him a couple of weeks ago—when everybody was making the fuss over that Russian anthropologist—and he came back with something awful. We wouldn't have run it if it hadn't been for the weight Wynant's name carries and the kid's oaths that he had written it exactly as it was given to him. I'd say it was likely enough his mind's cracked up.'

'Thanks,' Guild said, and reached for his hat, but both the others began questioning him then, so they sat there and talked and smoked and drank beer until midnight was past.

In his hotel-room Guild had his coat off when the telephone-bell rang. He went to the telephone. 'Hello... Yes... Yes' He waited. 'Yes?... Yes, Boyer ... He showed up at Fremont's and took a shot at him ... No, no harm done except that he made a clean sneak... Yes, but we found his car... Where?... Yes, I know where it is... What time?... Yes, I see... Tomorrow? What time?... Fine. Suppose you pick me up here at my hotel... Right.'

He left the telephone, started to unbutton his vest, stopped, looked at the watch on his wrist, put his coat on again, picked up his hat, and went out.

At California Street he boarded an east-bound cable-car and rode over the top of the hill and down it to Chinatown, leaving the car at Grant Avenue. Rain nearly fine as mist was beginning to blow down from the north. Guild went out beyond the curb to avoid a noisy drunken group coming out of a Chinese restaurant, walked a block, and halted across the street from another restaurant. This was a red brick building that tried to seem oriental by means of much gilding and colored lighting, obviously pasted-on corbelled cornices and three-armed brackets marking its storeys—some carrying posts above in the shape of half-pillars—and a tent-shaped terracotta roof surmounted by a mast bearing nine aluminumed rings. There was a huge electric sign—*Manchu.*

He stood looking at this gaudy building until he had lit a cigarette. Then he went over to it. The girl in the cloak-room would not take his hat. 'We close at one,' she said.

He looked at the people getting into an elevator, at her again. 'They're coming in.'

'That's upstairs. Have you a card?'

He smiled. 'Of course I have. I left it in my other suit.'

She looked severely blank at him.

He said, 'Oh, all right, sister,' gave her a silver dollar, took his hat-check, and squeezed himself into the crowded elevator.

At the fourth floor he left the elevator with the others and went into a large shabby oblong room where, running out from a small stage, an oblong dance-floor was a peninsula among tables waited on by Chinese in dinner clothes. There were forty or fifty people in the place. Some of them were dancing to music furnished by a piano, a violin, and a French horn.

Guild was given a small table near a shuttered window. He ordered a sandwich and coffee.

The dance ended and a woman with a middle-aged harpy's face and beautiful satin-skinned body sang a modified version of *Christopher Colombo*. There was another dance after that. Then Elsa Fremont came out to the center of the dance-floor and sang *Hollywood Papa*. Her low-cut green gown set off the red of her hair and brought out the greenness of her narrowly lanceolate eyes. Guild smoked, sipped coffee, and watched her. When she was through he applauded with the others.

She came straight to his table, smiling, and said: 'What are you doing here?' She sat down facing him.

He sat down again. 'I didn't know you worked here.'

'No?' Her smile was merry, her eyes skeptical.

'No,' he said, 'but maybe I should have known it. A man named Lane, who lives near Wynant in Hell Bend, saw him coming in this place early this evening.'

'That would be downstairs,' the girl said. 'We don't open up here till midnight.'

'Lane didn't know about the murder till he got home late tonight. Then he phoned the District Attorney and told him he'd seen Wynant and the D.A. phoned me. I thought I'd drop in just on the off-chance that I might pick up something.'

Frowning a little, she asked: 'Well?'

'Well, I found you here.'

'But I wasn't downstairs earlier this evening,' she said. 'What time was it?'

'Half an hour before he took his shot at your brother.'

'You see'—triumphantly—'you know I was home then talking to you.'

'I know that one,' Guild said.

5

At ten o'clock next morning Guild went into the Seaman's National Bank, to a desk marked *Mr Coler, Assistant Cashier.* The sunburned blond man who sat there greeted Guild eagerly.

Guild sat down and said: 'Saw the papers this morning, I suppose.'

'Yes. Thank the Lord for insurance '

'We ought to get him in time to get some of it back,' Guild said. 'I'd like to get a look at his account and whatever canceled checks are on hand.'

'Surely.' Coler got up from his desk and went away. When he came back he was carrying a thin pack of checks in one hand, a sheet of typed paper in the other. Sitting down, he looked at the sheet and said: 'This is what happened: on the second of the month Wynant desposited that ten-thousand-dollar check on—'

'Bring it in himself?'

'No. He always mailed his deposits. It was a Modern Publishing Company check on the Madison Trust Company of New York. He had a balance of eleven hundred sixty-two dollars and fifty-five cents: the check brought it up to eleven thousand and so on. On the fifth a check'—he took one from the thin pack—'for nine thousand dollars to the order of Laura Porter came through the clearing house.' He looked at the check. 'Dated the third, the day after he deposited his check.' He turned the check over. 'It was deposited in the Golden Gate

Trust Company.' He passed it across the desk to Guild. 'Well, that left him with a balance of twenty-one hundred sixty-two dollars and fifty-five cents. Yesterday we received a wire telling us the New York check had been raised from one thousand to ten.'

'Do you let your customers draw against out-of-town checks like that before they've had time to go through?'

Coler raised his eyebrows. 'Old accounts of the standing of Mr Wynant—yes.'

'He's got a swell standing now,' Guild said. 'What other checks are there in there?'

Coler looked through them. His eyes brightened. He said: 'There are two more Laura Porter ones—a thousand and a seven hundred and fifty. The rest seem to be simply salaries and household expenses.' He passed them to Guild.

Guild examined the checks slowly one by one. Then he said: 'See if you can find out how long this has been going on and how much of it.'

Coler willingly rose and went away. He was gone half an hour. When he returned he said: 'As near as I can learn, she's been getting checks for several months at least and has been getting about all he deposited, with not much more than enough left over to cover his ordinary expenses.'

Guild said, 'Thanks,' softly through cigarette-smoke.

From the Seaman's National Bank, Guild went to the Golden Gate Trust Company in Montgomery Street. A girl stopped typewriting to carry his card into the cashier's office and presently ushered him into the office. There he shook hands with a round white-haired man who said: 'Glad to see you, Mr Guild. Which of us criminals are you looking for now?'

'I don't know whether I'm looking for any this time. You've got a depositer named Laura Porter. I'd like to get her address.'

The cashier's smile set. 'Now, now, I'm always willing to do all I can to help you chaps, but—'

Guild said: 'She may have had something to do with gypping the Seaman's National out of eight thou.'

Curiosity took some of the stiffness from the cashier's smile.

Guild said: 'I don't know that she had a finger in it, but it's because I think she might that I'm here. All I want's her address—now—and I won't want anything else unless I'm sure.'

The cashier rubbed his lips together, frowned, cleared his throat, finally said: 'Well, if I give it to you you'll understand it's—'

'Strictly confidential,' Guild said, 'just like the information that the Seaman's been nicked.'

Five minutes later he was leaving the Golden Gate Trust Company carrying, in a pocket, a slip of paper on which was written *Laura Porter, 1157 Leavenworth.*

He caught a cable car and rode up California Street. When his car passed the Cathedral Apartments he stood up suddenly and he left the car at the next corner, walking back to the apartment-building.

At the desk he said: 'Miss Helen Robier.'

The man on the other side of the counter shook his head. 'We've nobody by that name—unless she's visiting someone.'

'Can you tell me if she lived here—say—five months ago?'

'I'll try.' He went back and spoke to another man. The other man came over to Guild. 'Yes,' he said, 'Miss Robier did live here, but she's dead.'

'Dead?'

'She was killed in an automobile accident the Fourth of July.'

Guild pursed his lips. 'Have you a MacWilliams here?'

'No.'

'Ever have one?'

'I don't think so. I'll look it up.' When he came back he was positive. 'No.'

Outside the Cathedral, Guild looked at his watch. It was a quarter to twelve. He walked over to his hotel. Boyer rose from a chair in the lobby and came to meet him, saying: 'Good morning. How are you? Anything new?'

Guild shurgged. 'Some things that might mean something. Let's do our talking over a lunch-table.' He turned beside the District Attorney and guided him into the hotel grill.

When they were seated and had given their orders he told Boyer about his conversation with the Fremonts, the shot that had interrupted them, and their search for Wynant that had resulted in their finding his car; about his conversation with Chris—'Christopher Maxim,' he said, 'book-critic on the *Dispatch*'; about his visit to the Manchu and his meeting Elsa Fremont there; and about his visits that morning to the two banks and the apartment-house. He spoke rapidly, wasting few words, missing no salient point.

'Do you suppose Wynant went to that Chinese restaurant, knowing the girl worked there, to find out where she and her brother lived?' Boyer asked when Guild had finished.

'Not if he'd been at Fremont's house raising hell a couple of weeks ago.'

Boyer's face flushed, 'That's right. Well, do you—?'

'Let me know what's doing on your end,' Guild said, 'and maybe we can do our supposing together. Wait till this waiter gets out of the way.'

When their food had been put in front of them and they were alone again the District Attorney said: 'I told you about Lane seeing Wynant going in this Chinese place.'

Guild said, 'Yes. How about the fingerprints?' and put some food in his mouth.

'I had the place gone over and we took the prints of everybody we knew had been there, but the matching-up hadn't been done when I left early this morning.'

'Didn't forget to take the dead girl's?'

'Oh, no. And you were in there: you can send us yours.'

'All right, though I made a point of not touching anything. Any reports from

'None.'

'Anyway, we know he came to San Francisco. How about the circulars?'

'They're being printed now—photo, description, handwriting specimens. We'll get out a new batch when we've got his fingerprints: I wanted to get something out quick.'

'Fine. I asked the police here to get us some of his prints off the car. What else happened on your end?'

'That's about all.'

'Didn't get anything out of his papers?'

'Nothing. Outside of what seemed to be notes for his work there wasn't a handful of papers. You can look at them yourself when you come up.'

Guild, eating, nodded as if he were thoroughly satisfied. 'We'll go up for a look at Miss Porter first thing this afternoon,' he said, 'and maybe something'll come of that.'

'Do you suppose she was blackmailing him?'

'People have blackmailed people,' Guild admitted.

'I'm just talking at random,' the District Attorney said a bit sheepishly, 'letting whatever pops into my mind come out.'

'Keep it up,' Guild said encouragingly.

'Do you suppose she could be a daughter he had by that actress wife in Paris?'

'We can try to find out what happend to her and the children. Maybe Columbia Forrest was his daughter.'

'But you know what the situation was up there,' Boyer protested. 'That would be incest.'

'It's happened before,' Guild said gravely. 'That's why they've got a name for it.'

Guild pushed the button beside Laura Porter's name in the vestibule of a small brown stone apartment-building at 1157 Leavenworth Street. Boyer, breathing heavily, stood beside him. There was no response. There was no response the second and third times he pushed the button, but when he touched the one labeled *Manager* the door-lock buzzed.

They opened the door and went into a dim lobby. A door straight ahead of them opened and a woman said: 'Yes? What is it?' She was small and sharp-featured, grey-haired, hook-nosed, bright-eyed.

Guild advanced toward her saying, 'We wanted to see Miss Laura Porter—three ten—but she doesn't answer the bell.'

'I don't think she's in,' the grey-haired woman said. 'She's not in much. Can I take a message?'

'When do you expect her back?'

'I don't know, I'm sure.'

'Do you know when she went out?'

'No, sir. Sometimes I see my people when they come in and go out and sometimes I don't. I don't watch them and Miss Porter I see less than any.'

'Oh, she's not here most of the time?'

'I don't know, mister. So long as they pay their rent and don't make too much noise I don't bother them.'

'Them? Does she live with somebody?'

'No. I meant them—all my people here.'

Guild turned to the District Attorney. 'Here. One of your cards.'

Boyer fumbled for his cards, got one of them out, and handed it to Guild, who gave it to the woman.

'We want a little information about her,' the dark man said in a low confidential voice while she was squinting at the card in the dim light. 'She's all right as far as we know, but—'

The woman's eyes, when she raised them, were wide and inquisitive. 'What is it?' she asked.

Guild leaned down towards her impressively. 'How long has she been here?' he asked in a stage whisper.

'Almost six months,' she replied. 'It is six months.'

'Does she have many visitors?'

'I don't know. I don't remember ever seeing any, but I don't pay much attention and when I see people coming in here I don't know what apartment they're going to.'

Guild straightened, put his left hand out, and pressed an electric-light-button, illuminating the lobby. He put his right hand to his inner coat-pocket and brought out pictures of Wynant and his dead secretary. He gave them to the woman. 'Ever see either of these?'

She looked at the man's picture and shook her head. 'No,' she said, 'and that ain't a man I'd ever forget if I'd once seen him.' She looked at Columbia Forrest's picture. 'That!' she cried. 'That *is* Miss Porter!'

6

Boyer looked round-eyed at Guild.

The dark man, after a little pause, spoke to the woman. 'That's Columbia Forrest,' he said, 'the girl who was killed up in Hell Bend yesterday.'

The woman's eyes became round as the District Attorney's. 'Well!' she exclaimed, looking at the photograph again, 'I never would've thought she was a thief. Why, she was such a pleasant mild-looking little thing—'

'A thief?' Boyer asked incredulously.

'Why, yes.' She raised puzzled eyes from the photograph. 'At least that's what the paper says, about her going—'

'What paper?'

'The afternoon paper.' Her face became bright, eager. 'Didn't you see it?'

'No. Have you—?'

'Yes. I'll show you.' She turned quickly and went through the doorway open behind her.

Guild, pursing his lips a little, raising his eyebrows, looked at Boyer.

The District Attorney whispered loudly: 'She wasn't blackmailing him? She was stealing from him?'

Guild shook his head. 'We don't know anything yet,' he said.

The woman hurried back to them carrying a newspaper. She turned the newspaper around and thrust it into Guild's hand, leaning over it, tapping the paper with a forefinger. 'There it is.' Her voice was metallic with excitement. 'That's it. You read it.'

Boyer went around behind the dark man to his other side, where he stood close to him, almost hanging on his arm, craning for a better view of the paper.

They read:

MURDERED SECRETARY KNOWN TO N.Y. POLICE

New York, Sept. 8 (A.P.)—Columbia Forrest, in connection with whose murder at Hell Bend, Calif., yesterday the police are now searching for Walter Irving Wynant, famous scientist, philosopher and author, was convicted of shoplifting in New York City three years ago, according to former police magistrate Erie Gardner.

Ex-magistrate Gardner stated that the girl pleaded guilty to a charge brought against her by two department stores and was given a six-month sentence by him, but that the sentence was suspended due to the intervention of Walter Irving Wynant, who offered to reimburse the stores and to give her employment as his secretary. The girl had formerly been a typist in the employ of a Wall St. brokerage firm.

Boyer began to speak, but Guild forestalled him by addressing the woman crisply: 'That's interesting. Thanks a lot. Now we'd like to look at her room.'

The woman, chattering with the utmost animation, took them upstairs and unlocked the door of apartment 310. She went into the apartment ahead of them, but the dark man, holding the corridor-door open, said pointedly: 'We'll see you again before we leave.' She went away reluctantly and Guild shut the door.

'Now we're getting somewhere,' Boyer said.

'Maybe we are,' Guild agreed.

Words ran swiftly from the District Attorney's mouth, 'Do you suppose she handled the details of his banking and forged those Laura Porter checks and juggled his books to cover them? The chances are he didn't spend much and thought he had a fat balance. Then when she had his account drained she raised the last check, drew against it, and was running away?'

'Maybe, but—' Guild stared thoughtfully at the District Attorney's feet.

'But what?'

Guild raised his eyes, 'Why didn't she run away while she was away instead of driving back there in another man's car to tell him she was going away with another man?'

Boyer had a ready answer, 'Thieves are funny and women are funny and when you get a woman thief there's no telling what she'll do or why. She could've had a quarrel with him and wanted to rub it in that she was going. She could have forgotten something up there. She might've had some idea of throwing suspicion away from the bank-account-juggling for awhile. She could've had any number of reasons, they need not've been sensible ones. She could've—'

Guild smiled politely. 'Let's see what the place'll tell us.'

On a table in the living-room they found a flat brass key that unlocked the corridor-door. Nothing else they found anywhere except in the bathroom seemed to interest them. In the bathroom, on a table, they found an obviously new razor holding a blade freshly spotted with rust, an open tube of shaving-cream from which very little had been squeezed, a new shaving-brush that had been used and not rinsed, and a pair of scissors. Hanging over the edge of the tub beside the table was a face-towel on which smears of lather had dried.

Guild blew cigarette-smoke at these things and said: 'Looks like our thin man came here to get rid of his whiskers.'

Boyer, frowning in perplexity, asked: 'But how would he know?'

'Maybe he got it out of her before he killed her and let himself in with the key on the table—hers.' Guild pointed his cigarette at the scissors. 'They make it look like him and not—well—Fremont for instance. He'd need them for the whiskers and the things are new, as if he'd bought them on his way here.' He bent over to examine the table, the inside of the tub, the floor. 'Though I don't see any hairs.'

'What does it mean, then—his coming here?' the District Attorney asked anxiously.

The dark man smiled a little. 'Something or other, maybe,' he said. He straightened up from his examination of the floor. 'He could've been careful not to drop any of his whiskers when he hacked them off, though God knows why he'd try.' He looked thoughtfully at the shaving-tools on the table. 'We ought to do some more talking to her boy friend.'

Downstairs they found the manager waiting in the lobby for them. She stood in front of them using a bright smile to invite speech.

Guild said: 'Thanks a lot. How far ahead is her rent paid?'

'Up to the fifteenth of the month it's paid.'

'Then it won't cost you anything to let nobody in there till then. Don't and if you go in don't touch anything. There'll be some policemen up. Sure you didn't see a man in there early last night?'

'Yes, sir, I'm sure I didn't see anybody in there or come out of there, though the Lord knows they could if they had a key without me—'

'How many keys did she have?'

'I only gave her one, but she could've had them made, all she wanted to, and likely enough did if she was—What'd she do, mister?'

'I don't know. She get much mail?'

'Well, not so very much and most of that looked like ads and things.'

'Remember where any of it was from?'

The woman's face colored. 'That I don't. I don't look at my people's mail like that. I was always was one to mind my own business as long as they paid their rent and don't make so much noise that other people—'

'That's right,' Guild said. 'Thanks a lot.' He gave her one of his cards. 'I'll probably be back, but if anything happens—anything that looks like it might have anything to do with her—will you call me up? If I'm not there leave the message.'

'Yes, sir, I certainly will,' she promised. 'Is there—?'

'Thanks a lot,' Guild said once more and he and the District Attorney went out.

They were sitting in the District Attorney's automobile when Boyer asked: 'What do you suppose Wynant left the key there for, if it was hers and he used it?'

'Why not? He only went there to shave and maybe frisk the place. He wouldn't take a chance on going there again and leaving it there was easier than throwing it away.'

Boyer nodded dubiously and put the automobile in motion. Guild directed him to the vicinity of the Golden Gate Trust Company, where they parked the automobile. After a few minutes' wait they were shown into the white-haired cashier's office.

He rose from his chair as they entered. Neither his smile nor his bantering 'You are shadowing me' concealed his uneasy curiosity.

Guild said: 'Mr Bliss, this is Mr Boyer, District Attorney of Whitfield County.'

Boyer and Bliss shook hands. The cashier motioned his visitors into chairs.

Guild said: 'Our Laura Porter is the Columbia Forrest that was murdered up at Hell Bend yesterday.'

Bliss's face reddened. There was something akin to indignation in the voice with which he said: 'That's preposterous, Guild.'

The dark man's smile was small with malice. 'You mean as soon as anybody becomes one of your depositors they're sure of a long and happy life?'

The cashier smiled then. 'No, but—' He stopped smiling. 'Did she have any part in the Seaman's National swindle?'

'She did,' Guild replied and added, still with smiling malice, 'unless you're sure, none of your clients could possibly touch anybody else's nickels.'

The cashier, paying no attention to the latter part of Guild's speech, squirmed in his chair and looked uneasily at the door.

The dark man said: 'We'd like to get a transcript of her account and I want to send a handwriting man down for a look at her checks, but we're in a hurry now. We'd like to know when she opened her account, what references she gave, and how much she's got in it.'

Bliss pressed one of the buttons on his desk, but before anyone came into the room he rose with a muttered 'Excuse me' and went out.

Guild smiled after him. 'He'll be ten pounds lighter before he learns whether he's been gypped or not and twenty if he finds he has.'

When the cashier returned he shut the door, leaned back against it, and spoke as if he had rehearsed his words. 'Miss Porter's account shows a balance of thirty-eight dollars and fifty cents. She drew out twelve thousand dollars in cash yesterday morning.'

'Herself?'

'Yes.'

Guild addressed Boyer: 'We'll show the teller her photo on the way out just to be doubly sure.' He turned to the cashier again: 'And about the date she opened it and the references she gave?'

The white-haired man consulted a card in his hand. 'She opened her account on November the eighth, last year,' he said. 'The references she gave were Francis X. Kearny, proprietor of the Manchu Restaurant on Grant Avenue, and Walter Irving Wynant.'

7

'The Manchu's only five or six blocks from here,' Guild told Boyer as they left the Golden Gate Trust Company. 'We might as well stop in now and see what we can get out of Francis Xavier Kearny.'

'Do you know him?'

'Uh-uh, except by rep. He's in solid with the police here and is supposed to be plenty tough.'

The District Attorney nodded. He chewed his lips in frowning silence until they reached his automobile. Then he said: 'What we've learned today seems to tie him, her, the Fremonts, and Wynant all up together.'

'Yes,' Guild agreed, 'it seems to.'

'Or do you suppose she could have given Wynant's name because she knew, being his secretary, she could catch the bank's letter of inquiry and answer it without his knowing anything about it?'

'That sounds reasonable enough,' the dark man said, 'but there's Wynant's visit to the Manchu yesterday.'

The District Attorney's frown deepened. 'What do you suppose Wynant was up to—if he was in it with them?'

'I don't know. I know somebody's got the twelve thousand she drew out yesterday. I know I want six of it for the Seaman's National. Turn left at the next corner.

They went into the Manchu Restaurant together. A smiling Chinese waiter told them Mr Kearny was not in, was not expected until nine o'clock that night. They could not learn where he might be found before nine o'clock. They left the restaurant and got into Boyer's automobile again.

'Guerrero Street,' Guild said, 'though we ought to stop first at a booth where I can phone the police about the Leavenworth Street place and the office to pick up canceled checks from both banks, so we'll know if any of them are forgeries.' He cupped his hands around the cigarette he was lighting. 'This'll do. Pull in here.'

The District Attorney turned the automobile in at the Mark Hopkins.

Guild, saying, 'I'll hurry,' jumped out and went indoors. When he came our ten minutes later his face was thoughtful. 'The police didn't find any fingerprints on Wynant's car,' he said. 'I wonder why.'

'He could've taken the trouble to—'

'Uh-huh,' the dark man agreed, 'but I'm wondering why he did. Well, on to Guerrero Street. If Fremont's not back from Hell Bend we'll see what we can shake the girl down for. She ought to know where Kearny hangs out in the daytime.'

A Filipino maid opened the Fremonts' door.

'Is Mr Charles Fremont in?' Guild asked.

'No, sir.'

'Miss Fremont?'

'I'll see if she's up yet.'

The maid took them into the living-room and went upstairs.

Guild pointed at the broken window-pane. 'That's where the shot was taken at him.' He pointed at the hole in the green wall. 'That's where it hit.' He took a misshapen bullet from his vest-pocket and showed it to Boyer. 'It.'

Boyer's face had become animated. He moved close to Guild and began to talk in a low excited voice. 'Do you suppose they could all have been in some game together and Wynant discovered that his secretary was double-crossing him besides getting ready to go off with—'

Guild jerked his head at the hall-door. 'Sh-h-h.'

Light footsteps ran down the stairs and Elsa Fremont in a brightly figured blue *baori* coat over light green silk pajamas entered the room. 'Good morning,' she said, holding a hand out to Guild. 'It is for me anyway.' She used her other hand to partly cover a yawn. 'We didn't close the joint till nearly eight this morning.'

Guild introduced the District Attorney to her, then asked: 'Your brother go up to Hell Bend?'

'Yes. He was leaving when I got home.' She dropped down on the sofa with a foot drawn up under her. Her feet were stockingless in blue embroidered slippers. 'Do sit down.'

The District Attorney sat in a chair facing her. The dark man went over to the sofa to sit beside her. 'We've just come from the Manchu,' he said.

Her lanceolate eyes became a little narrower. 'Have a nice lunch?' she asked.

Guild smiled and said: 'We didn't go there for that.'

She said: 'Oh.' Her eyes were clear and unwary now.

Guild said: 'We went to see Frank Kearny.'

'Did you?'

'See him? No.'

'There's not much chance of finding him there during the day,' she said carelessly, 'but he's there every night.'

'So we were told.' Guild took cigarettes from his pocket and held them out to her. 'Where do you think we could find him now?'

The girl shook her red head as she took a cigarette. 'You can search me. He used to live in Sea Cliff, but I don't know where he moved to.' She leaned forward as Guild held his lighter to her cigarette. 'Won't whatever you want to see him about wait till night?' she asked when her cigarette was burning.

Guild offered his cigarette to the District Attorney, who shook his head and murmured: 'No, thanks.'

The dark man put a cigarette between his lips and set fire to it before he answered the girl's question. Then he said: 'We wanted to find out what he knows about Columbia Forrest.'

Elsa Fremont said evenly: 'I don't think Frank knew her at all.'

'Yes, he did, at least as Laura Porter.'

Her surprise seemed genuine. She leaned towards Guild. 'Say that again.'

'Columbia Forrest,' Guild said in a deliberately monotonous voice, 'had an apartment on Leavenworth Street where she was known as Laura Porter and Frank Kearny knew her.'

The girl, frowning, said earnestly: 'If you didn't seem to know what you're talking about I wouldn't believe it.'

'But you do believe it?'

She hesitated, finally said: 'Well, knowing Frank, I'll say it's possible.'

'You didn't know about the Leavenworth Street place?'

She shook her head, meeting his gaze with candid eyes. 'I didn't.'

'Did you know she'd ever gone as Laura Porter?'

'No.'

'Ever hear of Laura Porter?'

'No.'

Guild drew smoke in and breathed it out. 'I think I believe you,' he said in a casual tone. 'But your brother must have known about it.'

She frowned at the cigarette in her hand, at the foot she was not sitting on, and then at Guild's dark face. 'You don't have to believe me,' she said slowly, 'but I honestly don't think he did.'

Guild smiled politely. 'I can believe you and still think you're wrong.' he said.

'I wish,' she said naively, 'you'd believe me and think I'm right.'

Guild moved his cigarette in a vague gesture. 'What does your brother do, Miss Fremont?' he asked. 'For a living, I mean?'

'He's managing a couple of fighters now,' she said, 'only one of them isn't. The other's Sammy Deep.'

Guild nodded. 'The Chinese bantam.'

'Yes. Charley thinks he's got a champ in him.'

'He's a good boy. Who's the other?'

'A stumble-bum named Terry Moore. If you go to fights much you're sure to've seen him knocked out.'

Boyer spoke for the first time since he had declined a cigarette. 'Miss Fremont, where were you born?'

'Right here in San Francisco, up on Pacific Avenue.'

Boyer seemed disappointed. He asked: 'And your brother?'

'Here in San Francisco too.'

Disappointment deepened in the District Attorney's young face and there was little hopefulness in his voice asking: 'Was your mother also an actress, an entertainer?'

The girl shook her head with emphasis. 'She was a schoolteacher. Why?'

Boyer's explanation was given more directly to Guild. 'I was thinking of Wynant's marriage in Paris.'

The dark man nodded. 'Fremont's too old. He's only ten or twelve years younger than Wynant.' He smiled guilelessly. 'Want another idea to play with? Fremont and the dead girl have the same initials—C. F.'

Elsa Fremont laughed. 'More than that,' she said, 'they had the same birthdays—May twenty-seventh—though of course Charley is older.'

Guild smiled carelessly at this information while the District Attorney's eyes took on a troubled stare.

The dark man looked at his watch. 'Did your brother say how long he was going to stay in Hell Bend?' he asked.

'No.'

Guild spoke to Boyer. 'Why don't you call up and see if he's there. If he is, ask him to wait for us. If he's left, we'll wait here for him.'

The District Attorney rose from his chair, but before he could speak the girl was asking anxiously: 'Is there anything special you want to see Charley about? Anything I could tell you?'

'You said you didn't know,' Guild said. 'It's the Laura Porter angle we want to find out about.'

'Oh.' Some of her anxiety went away.

'Your brother knows Frank Kearny, doesn't he?' Guild asked.

'Oh, yes. That's how I happened to go to work there.'

'Is there a phone here we can use?'

'Certainly.' She jumped up and, saying, 'Back here,' opened a door into an adjoining room. When the District Attorney had passed through she shut the door behind him and returned to her place on the sofa beside Guild. 'Have you learned anything else?' she asked, 'anything besides about her being known as Laura Porter and having the apartment?'

'Some odds and ends,' he said, 'but it's too early to say what they'll add up to when they're sorted. I didn't ask you whether Kearny and Wynant know each other, did I?'

She shook her head from side to side. 'If they do I don't know it. I don't. I'm telling you the truth, Mr Guild.'

'All right, but Wynant was seen going into the Manchu.'

'I know, but—' She finished the sentence with a jerk of her shoulders. She moved closer to Guild on the sofa. 'You don't think Charley has done anything he oughtn't've done, do you?'

Guild's face was placid. 'I won't lie to you,' he said. 'I think everybody connected with the job has done things they oughtn't've done.'

She made an impatient grimace. 'I believe you're just trying to make things confusing, to make work for yourself,' she said, 'so you'll be looking like you're doing something even if you can't find Wynant. Why don't you find him?' Her voice was rising. 'That's all you've got to do. Why don't you find him instead of trying to make trouble for everybody else? He's the only one that did anything. He killed her and tried to kill Charly and he's the one you want—not Charley, not me, not Frank. Wynant's the one you want.'

Guild laughed indulgently. 'You make it sound simple as hell,' he told her. 'I wish you were right.'

Her indignation faded. She put a hand on his hand. Her eyes held a frightened gleam. 'There isn't anything else, is there?' she asked, 'something we don't know about?'

Guild put his other hand over to pat the back of hers. 'There is,' he assured her pleasantly. 'There's a lot none of us knows and what we do know don't make sense.'

'Then—'

The District Attorney opened the door and stood in the doorway. He was pale and he was sweating. 'Fremont isn't up there,' he said blankly. 'He didn't go up there.'

Elsa Fremont said, 'Jesus Christ!' under her breath.

8

Night was settling between the mountains when Guild and Boyer arrived at Hell Bend. The District Attorney drove into the village, saying: 'We'll go to Ray's. We can come back to Wynant's later if you want to.'

'All right,' Guild said, 'unless Fremont might be there.'

'He won't if he came up to see the body. She's at Schumach's funeral parlor.'

'Inquest tomorrow?'

'Yes, unless there's some reason for putting it off.'

'There's none that I know of,' Guild said. He looked sidewise at Boyer. 'You'll see that as little as possible comes out at the inquest?'

'Oh, yes!'

They were in Hell Bend now, running between irregularly spaced cottages towards lights that glittered up along the railroad, but before they reached the railroad they turned off to the right and stopped before a small square house where softer lights burned behind yellow blinds.

Callaghan, the raw-boned blond Deputy Sheriff, opened the door for them. He said, 'Hello, Bruce,' to the District Attorney and nodded politely if without warmth at Guild.

They went indoors, into an inexpensively furnished room where three men sat at a table playing stud poker and a huge German sheep dog lay attentive in a corner. Boyer spoke to the three men and introduced Guild while the Deputy Sheriff sat down at the table and picked up his cards.

One of the men—thin, bent, old, white-haired, white-mustached—was Callaghan's father. Another—stocky, broad-browed over wide-spaced clear eyes, sunburned almost dark as Guild—was Ross Lane. The third—small, pale, painfully neat—was Schumach, the undertaker.

Boyer turned from the introductions to Callaghan. 'You're sure Fremont didn't show up?'

The Deputy Sheriff replied without looking up from his cards. 'He didn't show up at Wynant's place. King's been there all day. And he didn't show up at Ben's to—to see her. Where else'd he go if he came up here?' He pushed a chip out on the table. 'I'll crack it.' He had two kings in his hand.

Schumach pushed a chip out and said: 'No, sir, he didn't show up to look at the *carpus delicti*.'

Lane dropped his cards face-down on the table. The elder Callaghan put in a chip and picked up the rest of the deck.

His son said, 'Three cards,' and then to Boyer: 'You can phone King if you want.' He moved his head to indicate the telephone by the door.

Boyer looked questioningly at Guild, who said: 'Might as well.'

Guild addressed a question to Lane while the other three men at the table were making their bets and Boyer was using the telephone. 'You're the man who saw Wynant going into the Manchu?'

'Yes.' Lane's voice was a quiet bass.

'Was anybody with him?'

Lane said, 'No,' with certainty, then hesitated thoughtfully and added: 'unless they went in ahead of him. I don't think so, but it's possible. He was just going in when I saw him and it could've happened that he'd stopped to shut his car-door or take his key out or something and whoever was with him had gone on ahead.'

'Did you see enough of him to make sure it was him?'

'I couldn't go wrong on that, even if I did see only his back. My place being next to his, I guess I've seen a lot more of him than most people around here and then, tall and skinny, with those, high shoulders and that funny walk, you couldn't miss him. Besides, his car was there.'

'Had he cut his whiskers off, or was he still wearing them?'

Lane opened his eyes wide and laughed. 'By God, I don't know,' he said. 'I heard he shaved them, but I never thought of that. You've got me there. His back was to me and I wouldn't've seen them unless they happened to be sticking out sideways or I got a slanting look at him. I don't remember seeing them, yet I might've and thought nothing of it. If I'd seen his face without them it's a cinch I'd've noticed, but—You've got me there, brother.'

'Know him pretty well?'

Lane picked up the cards the younger Callaghan dealt him and smiled. 'Well, I don't guess anybody could say they know him pretty well.' He spread his cards apart to look at them.

'Did you know the Forrest girl pretty well?'

The Deputy Sheroff's face began to redden. He said somewhat sharply to the undertaker: 'Can you do it?'

The undertaker rapped the table with his knuckles to say he could not.

Lane had a pair of sixes and a pair of fours. He said, 'I'll do it,' pushed out a chip

'Tong gunman?'

'I don't know. I know him pretty well, but I don't know that. You know how they are.'

'I don't know,' Guild said.

A quarrel had started in the other end of the room. Two men were standing cursing each other over a table. Kearny screwed himself around in his chair to stare at them for a moment. Then, grumbling, 'Where do these bums think they are?' he got up and went over to them.

Elsa Fremont stared moodily at her glass. Guild watched Kearny go to the table where the two men were cursing, quiet them, and sit down with them.

The woman who had talked about the skin tightening on her forehead was now saying in the same tone: 'Character actress—that's the old stall. She's just exactly the same kind of character actress I was. She's doing bits—when she can get them.'

Elsa Fremont, still staring at her glass, whispered: 'I'm scared.'

'Of what?' Guild asked as if only moderately interested.

'Of Wynant, of what he might—' She raised her eyes, dark and harried. 'Has he done anything to Charley, Mr Guild?'

'I don't know.'

She put a tight fist on the table and cried angrily: 'Why don't you do something? Why don't you find Wynant? Why don't you find Charley? Haven't you got any blood, any heart, any guts? Can't you do anything but sit there like a—' She broke off with a sob. Anger went out of her face and the fingers that had been clenched opened in appeal. 'I—I'm sorry. I didn't mean—But, oh, Mr Guild, I'm so—' She put her head down and bit her lower lip.

Guild, impassive, said: 'That's all right.'

A man rose drunkenly from a nearby table and came up behind Elsa's chair. He put a fat hand on her shoulder and said: 'There, there, darling.' He said to Guild: 'You cannot annoy this little girl in this way. You cannot. You ought to be ashamed of yourself, a man of your complexion.' He leaned forward sharply, peering into Guild's face. 'By Jesus, I believe you're a mulatto. I really do.'

Elsa, squirming from under the fat drunken hand, flung a 'Let me alone' up at the man. Guild said nothing. The fat man looked uncertainly from one to the other of them until a hardly less drunken man, mumbling unintelligible apologies, came and led him away.

Elsa looked humbly at the dark man. 'I'm going to tell Frank I'm going,' she said in a small tired voice. 'Will you take me home?'

'Sure.'

They rose and moved towards the door. Kearny was standing by the elevator.

'I don't feel like working tonight, Frank,' the girl told him. 'I'm going to knock off.'

'Oke,' he said. 'Give yourself a hot drink and some aspirin.' He held his hand out to Guild. 'Glad I met you. Drop in any time. Anything I can ever do for you, let me know. You going to take the kid home? Swell! Be good.'

9

Elsa Fremont was a dusky figure beside Guild in a taxicab riding west up Nob Hill. Her eyes glittered in a splash of light from a steet-lamp. She drew breath in and asked: 'You think Charley's run away, don't you?'

'It's likely,' Guild said, 'but maybe he'll be home when we get there.'

'I hope so, but—I'm afraid.'

He looked obliquely at her. 'You've said that before. Mean you're afraid something's happened to him or will happen to you?'

She shivered. 'I don't know. I'm just afraid.' She put a hand in his, asking plaintively: 'Aren't you ever going to catch Wynant?'

'Your hand's cold,' he said.

She pulled her hand away. Her voice was not loud: intensity made it shrill. 'Aren't you ever human?' she demanded. 'Are you always like this? Or is it a pose?' She drew herself far back in a corner of the taxicab. 'Are you a god-damned corpse?'

'I don't know,' the dark man said. He seemed mildly puzzled. 'I don't know what you mean.'

She did not speak again, but sulked in her corner until they reached her house. Guild sat at ease and smoked until the taxicab stopped. Then he got out saying: 'I'll stop long enough to see if he's home.'

The girl crossed the sidewalk and unlocked the door while he was paying the chauffeur. She had gone indoors leaving the door open when he mounted the front steps. He followed her in. She had turned on ground-floor lights and was calling upstairs: 'Charley!' There was no answer.

She uttered an impatient exclamation and ran upstairs. When she came down again she moved wearily. 'He's not in,' she said. 'He hasn't come.'

Guild nodded without apparent disappointment. 'I'll give you a ring when I wake up,' he said, stepping back towards the street-door, 'or if I get any news of him.'

She said quickly: 'Don't go yet, please, unless you have to. I don't— I wish you'd stay a little while.'

He said, 'Sure,' and they went into the living-room.

When she had taken off her coat she left him for a few minutes, going into the kitchen, returning with Scotch whisky, ice, lemons, glasses, and a siphon of water. They sat on the sofa with drinks in their hands.

Presently, looking inquisitively at him, she said: 'I really meant what I said in the cab. Aren't you actually human? Isn't there any way anybody can get to you, get to the real inside you? I think you're the most—' she frowned, selecting words '— most untouchable, unreal, person I've ever known. Trying to—to really come in contact with you is just like trying to hold a handful of smoke.'

Guild, who had listened attentively, now nodded. 'I think I know what you're trying to say. It's an advantage when I'm working.'

'I didn't ask you that,' she protested, moving the glass in her hand impatiently. 'I asked you if that's the way you really are or if you just do it.'

He smiled and shook his head noncommittally.

'That isn't a smile,' she said. 'It's painted on.' She leaned to him swiftly and kissed him, holding her mouth to his mouth for an appreciable time. When she took her mouth from his her narrow green eyes examined his face carefully. She made a moue. 'You're not even a corpse—you're a ghost.'

Guild said pleasantly, 'I'm working,' and drank from his glass.

Her face flushed. 'Do you think I'm trying to make you?' she asked hotly.

He laughed at her. 'I'd like it if you were, but I didn't mean it that way.'

'You wouldn't like it,' she said. 'You'd be scared.'

'Uh-uh,' he explained blandly. 'I'm working. It'd make you easier for me to handle.'

Nothing in her face responded to his bantering. She said, with patient earnestness: 'If you'd only listen to me and believe me when I tell you I don't know any more what it's all about than you do, if that much. You're just wasting your time when you ought to be finding Wynant. I don't know anything. Charley doesn't. We'd both tell you if we did. We've both already told you all we know. Why can't you believe me when I tell you that?'

'Sorry,' Guild said lightly. 'It don't make sense.' He looked at his watch. 'It's after five. I'd better run along.'

She put a hand out to detain him, but instead of speaking she stared thoughtfully at her dangling wrist-scarf and worked her lips together.

Guild lit another cigarette and waited with no appearance of impatience.

Presently she shrugged her bare shoulders and said: 'It doesn't make any difference.' She turned her head to look uneasily behind her. 'But will you—will you do something for me before you go? Go through the house and see that everything is all right. I'm—I'm nervous, upset.'

'Sure,' he said readily, and then, suggestively: 'If you've got anything to tell me, the sooner the better for both of us.'

'No, no, there's nothing,' she said. 'I've told you everything.'

'All right. Have you got a flashlight?'

She nodded and brought him one from the next room.

When Guild returned to the living-room Elsa Fremont was standing where he had left her. She looked at his face and anxiety went out of her eyes. 'It was silly of me,' she said, 'but I do thank you.'

He put the flashlight on the table and felt for his cigarettes. 'Why'd you ask me to look?'

She smiled in embarrassment and murmured: 'It was a silly notion.'

'Why'd you bring me home with you?' he asked.

She stared at him with eyes in which fear was awakening. 'Wh-what do you mean? Is there—?'

He nodded.

'What is it?' she cried. 'What did you find?'

He said: 'I found something wrong down in the cellar.'

Her hand went to her mouth.

'Your brother,' he said.

She screamed: 'What?'

'Dead.'

The hand over her mouth muffled her voice: 'K-killed?'

He nodded. 'Suicide, from the looks of it. The gun could be the one the girl was killed with. The—' He broke off and caught her arm as she tried to run past him towards the door. 'Wait. There's plenty of time for you to look at him. I want to talk to you.'

She stood motionless staring at him with open blank eyes.

He said: 'And I want you to talk to me.'

She did not show she had heard him.

He said: 'Your brother did kill Columbia Forrest, didn't he?'

Her eyes held their blank stare. Her lips barely moved. 'You fool, you fool,' she muttered in a tired flat voice.

He was still holding her arm. He ran the tip of his tongue over his lips and asked in a low persuasive tone: 'How do you know he didn't?'

She began to tremble. 'He couldn't've,' she cried. Life had come back to her voice and face now. 'He couldn't've.'

'Why?'

She jerked her arm out of his hand and thrust her face up towards his. 'He couldn't've, you idiot. He wasn't there. You can find out where he was easily enough. You'd've found out long before this if you'd had any brains. He was at a meeting of the Boxing Commission that afternoon, seeing about a permit or something for Sammy. They'll tell you that. They'll have a record of it.'

The dark man did not seem surprised. His blue eyes were meditative under brows drawn a little together. 'He didn't kill her, but he committed suicide,' he said slowly and with an air of listening to himself say it. 'That don't make sense too.'

H. Rider
Haggard
MR. MEESON'S WILL

Melville
Davisson Post
MASTER OF MYSTERIES
THE COMPLETE UNCLE ABNER COLLECTION

Jack
London
THE ASSASSINATION
BUREAU LTD.

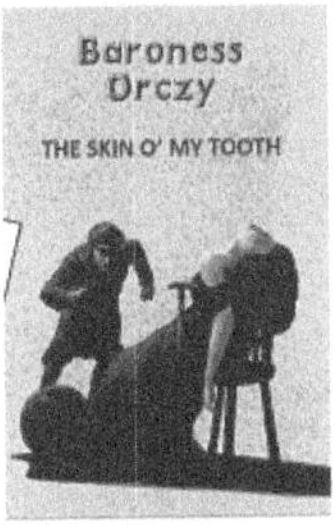
Baroness
Orczy
THE SKIN O' MY TOOTH

Earl Derr
Biggers
SEVEN KEYS TO BALDPATE

Horace
Walpole
THE CASTLE OF OTRANTO

Sexton
Blake
THE SEXTON BLAKE
COLLECTION
VOLUME 1

Francis
Beeding
THE HOUSE OF
DR. EDWARDES

A. E. W.
Mason
AT THE VILLA ROSE

Fergus
Hume
THE MILLIONAIRE
MYSTERY

Donald
Henderson
A VOICE LIKE VELVET

Richard
Hallas
YOU PLAY THE BLACK AND
THE RED COMES UP